'What the devil are you doing?' Eyre demanded. 'You're not going to shoot him, not in cold blood!'

'Of course not,' said Lathrop. 'I am simply giving the chap a chance to leave my property, and my employ, as smartly as he likes. 'Boy!' he called again. 'Stop that singing and chanting now, and be off with you! That's it! Make yourself scarce!'

'Sir!' called Yanluga. 'Please ask Captain Henry to tie up the dogs first.'

'You just be off,' said Lathrop. 'Captain Henry will take care of the hounds when he pleases.'

'Sir, if I run, sir, the dogs will chase me.'

'As well they might. Now, let's have a look at those sandy-white heels of yours. And make it quick! I've lost enough sleep tonight as it is!'

'You can't do this,' said Eyre. 'Mr Lindsay, listen to me. Those dogs will tear him to pieces before he can get halfway across the garden.'

Lathrop continued to squint along his musket-barrel. 'There are several things you don't understand, Mr Walker; and one of those things is the meaning of justice. What you are seeing now is justice. The wronged employer gives the ungrateful servant the opportunity to leave his property as expeditiously as possible. You won't find one magistrate who won't congratulate me for my fairness and my magnanimity.'

GRAHAM MASTERTON

CORROBOREE

SPHERE BOOKS

A *Sphere* Book

First published in Great Britain by W. H. Allen & Co.
First published in paperback by Sphere Books Ltd 1991
This edition first published by Sphere Books 1996

Copyright © 1984 by Graham Masterton

The right of Graham Masterton to be identified as author of
this work has been asserted by him in accordance with the
Copyright, Designs and Patents Act 1988.

Printed in England by Clays Ltd, St Ives plc

ISBN 0 7474 0487 9

Sphere Books Ltd
A Division of
Macdonald & Co (Publishers)
Brettenham House
Lancaster Place
London WC2E 7EN

For Wiescka,
and for Roland, Daniel
and Luke,
with love

Prologue

More than anything else, said Netty, her mother would like a musical box for Christmas: one of those musical boxes with six or seven different and interchangeable cylinders, so that she could play 'Silent Night' and 'The Wonderful Polka' and 'Sweet Heart's Delight'; and think of all the days gone by, happy and sad, and how God had blessed her so, and punished her, too.

Eyre listened with amusement, smoking his cigar, his eyes bright; and at last he said. 'Very well, if that's what you want to give her, I'll ask Mr Granger,' and he reached out to lay his hand on the parting of his daughter's shining hair, as gently as a blessing. His only daughter, and although he didn't yet know it, his only child.

Outside, in the garden, the sun shone in brilliant skeins, like the straw in Rumpelstiltskin which had been spun into gold; and the birds whooped and laughed, and one of the grooms called 'Wayandah! Wayandah!' as he tried to lead Eyre's favourite stallion back into the stables. And across the lawns, watered and fed so that they looked unnaturally green in this dusty December landscape, Charlotte moved this way and that in her clotted-cream-coloured dress, bobbing now and again to pick a flower, stopping occasionally to scold the gardening-boy; Charlotte with her

7

perfect bonnet and her perfect ribbons and her perfect parasol; a picture of perfection wherever she went, and whatever she did.

Only Eyre understood what pain and loss her perfection so perfectly concealed Only Eyre heard her sobbing at night, a thin, inconsolable whining; or knew what she was thinking about on those evenings when the sun was gradually burning itself out behind the branches of the stringy-bark trees, and she stared out across the river valley; silent, her face severe.

He said to Netty, 'She'd like some perfume, too, if I can get Mr McLaren to send some up.'

'Oh, *do*,' enthused Netty. 'And some lace, too, if there's any to be had. I could make a collar for that green velvet dress—the one she wore at Governor McConnell's birthday party.'

'Netty,' smiled Eyre, 'I sometimes think you were sent by the angels.' Netty took his hand, and pressed it against her cheek. 'Dear father,' she said. 'I hope I can be everything to you: friend, and son, and daughter, all three.'

Eyre drew her towards him, and kissed her twice, once on each cheek. 'You always look so much like your mother,' he smiled. 'There was one night, long ago . . . well, you look just like her, the way she did on that night.'

Netty said nothing. She knew that he was flattering her, for her mother was still a remarkably beautiful woman. But she also understood that he was thinking back to the time before her mother was sad, those few brief months before the loss of her son, Netty's brother, whom Netty had never known. His absence from their family, even after twenty years, was like an empty bedroom, or a photograph-frame with no picture in it. Every year, on his birthday, her mother would light candles for him. Every year, she would buy him a small Christmas gift, and lay it beside the others, in case he came back. A necktie, or a diary. Once, she had bought him a harmonica.

Eyre smoked for a while, and then said, 'There always used to be snow at Christmas, when I was a boy.'

Netty smiled, and shook her head. 'I can't imagine it. I've tried. I've looked at pictures. But I just can't imagine it.'

'Well,' he said, 'it isn't easy to describe. It isn't so much the whiteness, or the coldness, it's the *sound* of it. The whole world suddenly becomes muffled. Everything somehow seems to be more private. They say Eskimos are great natural philosophers, you know. Perhaps that's because the snow makes you turn in on yourself. Think more.'

'The desert must do that, too,' said Netty.

Eyre looked at her and his eyes were peculiarly remote. 'The desert?' he asked her. He was still smiling, but his smile had nothing at all to do with his eyes.

'Yes,' she said, uncertainly. 'It must be very silent out there.'

'No,' he told her. Then, after another long pause: 'No. The desert isn't silent at all. The desert is . . . Babel, a whole Babel of voices. All speaking at the same time. Never quiet. Thousands of them: the voices of the past and the voices of the future.'

'I don't understand what you mean. What voices?'

Eyre was about to say something more, but suddenly he stopped himself, and smiled instead, and stroked Netty's hair. 'A figure of speech,' he explained; but Netty wouldn't be put off.

'What do they say?' she asked him, intently.

'What does who say?'

'The voices. The ones in the desert.'

'They don't say anthing,' Eyre told her. 'Now, come on, let's forget all about it, and call your mother in for tea.'

'But they must say *something*,' Netty insisted. 'Otherwise you wouldn't have called them voices.'

Eyre twisted his side-whiskers thoughtfully. They were greying now, and made him look less saturnine than when he was young; although his eyebrows were still dark and swept-up; and his cheeks were still hollow. Charlotte had once teased him that he looked like the night-devil; but

9

that was before they had lost their son. She would never tease him like that now.

Eyre said, 'The voices tell stories. Everything that happened in the past, how the mountains were made, why the lakes are all dry, how the blue heron brought in the tide, how the no-drink bear lost his tail. And they tell what will happen in the future, too. Which years are going to be dry, which years are going to be happy. Who will die, who will lose his way. Who will honour his promises, and who will not.'

He was silent for a moment, and then he added, in a dead-sounding voice, 'Who will regret what he has done.'

Netty sat on the floor looking up at him. 'Do they really say things like that? Can you really hear them?'

'You hear whatever is inside your own head,' said Eyre. 'That is why the desert is never quiet.'

A whole hour seemed to pass between them in what could only have been a few seconds. Charlotte came in from the garden, and kissed them both, Eyre and Netty, and Eyre said, 'How's Yalagonga? Do you think he's going to make a good gardener?'

Charlotte put down her basket of flowers, and unlaced the ribbons of her bonnet. 'He's confident, I'll give him that! He wanted to clear all the wattle from the back fence and cut down my favourite apple tree. But, I think he's going to do. I'd rather have a boy who's going to be strict with the garden, than one who lets it grow wild. Do you remember Jackie? He wouldn't cut a single weed, in case it offended the spirits.'

'Shall we have some tea?' asked Eyre, in the manner of someone who has been asking the same question day after day for nearly twenty years.

'I think I deserve it,' replied Charlotte. 'In fact, I think I may have some of the coconut biscuits, too.'

Eyre nodded to Netty, who got up from the floor and went over to the large carved limestone fireplace, and rang the bell-cord.

10

'I suppose you two have been discussing politics again,' said Charlotte.

Eyre smiled. 'Actually, we've been trying to decide what to buy you for Christmas.'

'Well, that's easy enough. It doesn't need a discussion. I want a new hut for treating the children, more linseed oil, and as much tincture of catechu as you can get.'

'Don't be so practical,' said Eyre. 'I'm talking about perfume, and lace.'

'What on earth is the use of perfume and lace, out here at Moorundie? I'd rather have medicines.'

'Charlotte . . .' Eyre began, but then he sat back, and tried to keep on smiling as if he had only been teasing her about the perfume, and the lace. He knew that the children were her main preoccupation, with their sores and their runny noses and their shivering-fits. He knew why, too. And he knew that whatever he gave her for Christmas, it would never do anything to make up for the loss of their boy-child.

He could see it now, as clearly as if it had happened last night, instead of twenty years ago. The open window, the curtain blowing in the warm night wind. The empty crib, still warm and indented from the baby's sleeping body; still smelling of mother's milk and freshly-washed hair. And he could remember the pain, too: the pain that was so much greater than he had expected. More than a sense of loss; more than a sense of sacrifice, and duty. It had been like having his arm twisted and torn out of its socket by the roots. An actual physical tearing-away.

The black trackers had spent hours scouring the garden. 'Three,' they had said. 'Two men, one woman, all barefoot, blackfellow.' They had tried to follow the footprints into the bush, but the kidnappers had been too wily. They had backtracked, run through streams and brushed their trail with wattle-branches. The black trackers had come back four hours later glistening with sweat, and admitted that whoever had taken the boy had been an exceptionally skilful hunter; or a ghost.

11

Fly-posters offering rewards had been displayed all around Moorundie for weeks. But the boy seemed to have disappeared without a trace; melted into the setting sun. Eyre had offered £500 and a free pardon for his return. But there had been nothing, not a word; although the ironic part about it had been that Eyre had actually known where his son was; or at least who it was that had taken him. Yet he had been unable to speak, for fear of condemning himself, and for fear of destroying both his marriage and his career.

For somebody that night had left the main gates of the house unlocked. And somebody had carelessly (or thoughtfully) propped up a ladder by the child's bedroom window. And somebody had left the window unlatched, so that all an intruder had to do was ease up the sash, and climb straight into the room.

The blackfellows must have been ten miles to Woocalla before anybody had noticed that the boy was gone. And Eyre had known, as he had stood at the end of the crib, breathing in the very last vestiges of baby-smell, that any attempt to take the boy away from them would be suicidal, perhaps worse. An Aborigine uprising had always been on the cards. Any attempt to arrest blackfellows *en masse*, or take reprisals against them, would be madness.

Times had changed since he had first arrived in Australia. Your blackfellow nowadays was either a great deal more skilled and co-operative, or else a great deal more vicious.

When the last of the scouts and the trackers had reported no sign of the baby, Eyre had been obliged to say, 'That's it. Don't search any more. Whoever took him means to keep him.'

But of course life had never been the same since then; and Eyre had always felt that Charlotte was accusing him of carelessness, or cold-heartedness, or both. They wanted the baby because it was yours, she had insisted, over and over again. They wanted the baby because you're famous, and because you always show them that you understand

12

them. Perhaps they kidnapped him as a compliment. What a compliment, to lose your own flesh and blood. They probably worship him, as if he were the son of God.

'*Charlotte!*' Eyre had snapped at her, but the hurt had already been inflicted; and even through years of friendliness and sweetness and shared kisses, it was never undone. When they had lost their son, they had lost their first fresh love, and whatever came afterwards was a compromise, an attempt at living together with as little pain as possible.

Charlotte said, 'Can you call Molly, and ask her to arrange these flowers for me? I think I'm going to take a bath.'

'You're not tired, are you?' Eyre asked her. 'I mean, not too tired?'

'For tonight's dinner? Hmh! I think I'll be able to manage it.'

'Wear the white,' Eyre told her.

'The white?'

'I just want you to.'

'I don't know,' said Charlotte. Her eyes were so wide, her hair was so blonde; but somehow behind all that beauty there was nothing at all. Looking into Charlotte was like looking behind a magic-lantern screen; all you could see was the same picture you had seen on the front of the screen, in reverse.

Eyre touched Netty's shoulder. 'I think I'll take a bath, too. It's been so damned hot today.'

Charlotte stood up, with a rustle of skirts. But at that moment, there was shouting from outside, in the garden. Whoops, and cries, and someone saying, 'Biranga! They brought Biranga!'

Eyre was out of his chair immediately. He pulled aside the lace curtains and hurried out into the hot sunshine, followed by Netty. Charlotte called, 'Netty! Your bonnet!' but Netty took no notice.

Eyre strode across the lawns. His shadow followed him like the scissor-man in *Struwwelpeter*. A party of seven or

13

eight blackfellows had come to the front gate of his house, and were standing there, calling and clapping. He saw one of his principal helpers, Wawayran, and shouted out, 'Wawayran! What's going on?'

'They brought him in, sir! They brought in Biranga!'

Eyre pushed the Aborigines aside, and looked down at the ground. Lying in the dust, on a crumpled blanket that had obviously been used to carry him for several miles, was the blood-caked body of a young man. He was naked, except for a twisted string around his waist, and his chest and shoulders were patterned with decorative scars. His face was white with pipe-clay, although part of it had flaked off, and some of it was crusted with blood. It looked as if the man had been savagely beaten around the head and shoulders, and then speared in the stomach.

'Who killed this man?' asked Eyre.

'I did, sir,' said one of the Aborigines, quietly. He was a tall, stooped fellow, dressed in European clothes, a well-patched white shirt and drooping khaki trousers. 'I was looking after the sheep for Mr Mullett, sir, and I saw him by the fence. I knew he was Biranga, sir, because he was so white, sir, just like you said, just like a ghost.'

Eyre knelt down beside the body and lifted its limp, disjointed wrist.

'What was he doing by the fence?'

The Aborigine shook his head. 'Just standing, sir; just staring.'

'Was he alone?'

'There were five, six more, sir; but they ran off. I think towards Nunjikompita.'

Eyre was silent for a long time. Then he said to Wawayran, 'Fetch me a rag, soaked in water.'

'Yes, sir.'

Eyre stood up, and turned, and frowned against the sunlight. Charlotte was waiting on the verandah, one hand slightly raised as if she were about to call out to him. Netty was a step or two behind her. They could have been posing

14

for a daguerreotype of *Two Ladies At Moorundie, 1861*. One more faded colonial record.

Charlotte called, in a high-pitched voice, 'Is it Biranga?' 'I think so,' Eyre replied.

There was a short pause, and then Charlotte said, 'Is he quite dead?' 'Yes,' Eyre told her.

'Ten pounds bounty, sir,' said the Aborigine who had killed him.

'You speared him,' Eyre remarked. It was almost an accusation.

'Only to make sure, sir. First of all I hit him with my club.'

'Well, so I see.'

'He said nothing, sir. But I couldn't trust him. He didn't even put up his hand to save himself.'

Eyre thoughtfully put his hand over his mouth, and looked down at Biranga's battered body. Biranga had been a fugitive from the South Australian police for nearly six years now, ever since the trouble over at Broughton, when two Aborigines had been shot by white farmers as a vigilante punishment for rape and murder. Four days later the farmers had been speared to death themselves by Biranga and several other tribesmen, including Jacky Monday and a boy called Dencil.

Eyre had himself put up the offer of £10 for Biranga's capture, dead or alive. Eyre was fair and considerate when it came to dealing with the tribesmen of the Murray River district; but also firm. Some of the blackfellows called him 'Take-No-Nonsense' after one of his own favourite phrases.

Biranga, however, had successfully eluded Eyre and his constables, until today. He had been seen scores of times, although the majority of sightings had been very questionable, since a shilling was paid for each report, and most of the Aborigines around Moorundie would have sworn blind that they had seen a real live Bunyip for a penny, and a herd of Bunyips for twopence. Biranga had also been blamed for almost every unexplained theft or act of

15

vandalism for over four years. Eyre's black trackers would make a desultory search in the bush whenever something went missing, and then come back to say, 'Biranga took it. That's what we heard.' If Biranga had really been as industrious a larcenist as the Moorundie blackfellows tried to suggest, then he would have been walking around the bush with beehives, rifles, sheets of corrugated iron, and scores of blankets.

Some of the blackfellows had said that Biranga was a ghost, because of his unusually pale skin. Captain Billington had suggested that he might be an albino. Wawayran had declared that he was a real phantom. But everybody agreed that he had to be caught. It was unsettling for all of the civilised Aborigines who lived on the missions, or as servants in European homes, if a wild black tribesman was running free, doing whatever he pleased, and cocking a snook at the white authorities.

Governor McConnell had written to Eyre and added dryly, 'I expect you to be able to report within a few weeks that you have been able to apprehend the native they call the Ghost of Emu Downs, the fellow Biranga.'

The Ghost of Emu Downs, thought Eyre, as he looked down at Biranga's broken body. Some ghost. Wawayran came up with a wet rag, and Eyre took it, and knelt down again, and began carefully to wipe away the pipe-clay that encrusted the dead Biranga's forehead and cheeks.

The face that appeared through the smeary clay was startlingly calm, as if the man had died peacefully and without fear, in spite of his terrible injuries.

It was also an unusually cultured-looking face, almost European, although the forehead and the cheeks were decorated with welts and scars, marks which Eyre recognised as those of a warrior of the Wirangu. Eyre hesitated for a moment, and then peeled back one of the man's eyelids with his thumb. The irises were brown; although not that reddish-brown which distinguished the eyes of so many Aborigines. Carefully, Eyre pushed the eyelid back.

He was not squeamish about touching dead men: he had touched so many, and some he had embraced.

He suddenly became aware that Charlotte was standing close behind him, looking down at the body.

'Charlotte,' he said, 'this is not a place for you.' But there was very little hint of admonition in his voice. He knew that she had to look; that she would not be satisfied until she did.

Charlotte said quietly, 'He could almost be a white man.'

'Just pale, my dear. Some of them are. Sometimes it's caused by disease. Poor food, that kind of thing. I've seen some Aborigines who looked like snowmen.'

'Snowmen,' Charlotte whispered.

Eyre stood up. 'Come away now,' he said. 'There's nothing to be done. I'll have to make a report to the governor; and perhaps a note to Captain Billington, too.'

Charlotte stayed where she was, the warm wind blowing the hem of her cream-coloured dress into curls. 'Do you think—?' she began. But then she stopped herself, because she had asked the same question already in her mind, and so many times before, and the answer had always been the same: that she would never know. The desert does something to a child. It makes a child its own; as do the strange people who walk the desert asking neither for food nor for water; except what they themselves can discover from the ground.

Eyre had explained that to Charlotte time and time again, in different ways, perhaps to prepare her for this very moment.

She turned and looked at him, and there were so many anguished questions in her eyes that he had to look away—at the lawns, the kangaroos in the distance—at anything that would relieve him from the pain which she was using like a goad—forcing him to face up again and again to the most terrible secret of his whole life.

'It's not possible,' he said. Then he reached out his hand, and said, 'Come on. Come away. There's no profit to be had from staying here.'

17

'I always thought—' she blurted; and then she took a breath, and controlled herself, saying in a wavery voice, 'I always thought that he might have survived somehow, and been taken care of. I mean—why else would they have taken him? Except for money perhaps, and they never asked for that. I always imagined that he might have grown up amongst them; and lived a happy life, for all that had happened. Even Aborigines can be happy, can't they, Eyre? You know them better than I do. The men, I mean. They *can* be happy, can't they?'

'Yes,' said Eyre.

He took her sleeve, but she twisted away from him, and looked down again at the body lying in the lawn.

'He looks so contented,' she said. 'They killed him, and yet he looks so peaceful. As if he were at home, at last.'

Eyre frowned towards the Aborigine who had brought Biranga in; and thought of what he had said. *'He didn't even put up his hand to save himself. He was just standing, sir; just staring.'*

He said to Wawayran, 'Make sure this fellow gets buried; soon as you like.'

'Yes, sir.' Then, 'Please, sir?'

'What is it?'

'Well, sir, the burial, sir. Christian or Wirangu, sir?'

'This man's a Wirangu, isn't he?'

Wawayran didn't answer at first, but stared at Eyre in a peculiar way.

'He's a Wirangu?' Eyre repeated, sharply.

'Yes, sir.'

'Well, then, give him a Wirangu burial.'

'Yes, sir.'

Charlotte had already returned to the house. Eyre stood on the lawn for a moment, undecided about what he should do next. Before he could turn away, though, one of the black boys came towards him with his hand held out, and said, 'Mr Walker, sir, this was found in Biranga's bag.'

Eyre peered at it, and then picked it up. It was a fragment of stone, carved and painted with patterns.

'This is nothing unusual,' he said. 'It is only a spirit-stone.'

'But what it says, sir.'

'What do you mean?'

The boy pointed to the patterns and the pictures. 'The stone says, this is the mana stone which will be carried by the one spirit who comes back from the world beyond the setting sun; and by this stone you will know that it is truly him.'

Eyre turned the stone over and over in his hand.

'Yes,' he said, at last. 'I saw something like this before, once upon a time.'

'Well, sir, if Biranga was carrying the stone, do you think that was the spirit who come back from the world beyond the setting sun?'

Eyre looked at the boy, and then laid a hand on his shoulder.

'Do you believe in spirits coming back from the land beyond the setting sun?'

The boy hesitated, and then said,'No sir.'

'No, sir,' Eyre repeated. Then, 'Neither do I.'

And the time will come when a dead spirit visits the earth from the place beyond the setting sun, so that he may see again how beautiful it was.

Many will be frightened by the spirit's white face; but he will be befriended by a simple boy, who will guide him through the world.

In return for this kindness, the spirit will try to teach the boy the magical ways of those who have passed into the sunset.

However, he will forget that the boy is only mortal, and in trying to teach the boy how to fly like a spirit, he will cause the boy to drop from the mountain called Wongyarra, and die.

And the spirit in his grief and remorse will seek out the cleverest of all clever-men, and will give him the magical knowledge of the dead; so that the clever-man may pass the knowledge on to every tribe; and to every tribesman.

And in this way the grief of the spirit will be assuaged; and the tribes of Australia will be invincible in their magical knowledge against men and devils and anyone who wishes them harm.

And this will be the beginning of an age that is greater and more heroic than the Dreaming.

— Nyungar myth, first recorded by J. Morgan in Perth, 1833, from an account by the Aboriginal Galliput

One

There was an extraordinary commotion at the Lindsay house when he arrived there on his bicycle. Mrs McMurtry the cook was standing on the front lawn screaming shrilly; while upstairs the sash-windows were banged open and then banged shut again; and angry voices came first from the west bedroom and then from the east; and footsteps cantered up and down stairs; and doors slammed in deafening salvoes. Yanluga the Aborigine groom scampered out of the front porch with his hair in a fright crying, 'Not me, sir! No, sir! Not me, sir!' and rushed through the wattle bushes which bordered the garden, like a panicky kangaroo with greyhounds snapping at his tail.

Eyre propped his bicycle against a hawthorn tree and approached the house cautiously. Mrs McMurtry had stopped screaming now and had flung up her apron over her face, letting out an occasional anguished '*moooo*', as if she were a shorthorn which urgently needed milking. The front door of the house remained ajar, and inside Eyre could just see the bright reflection from the waxed cedar flooring, and the elegant curve of the white-painted banisters. Somewhere upstairs, a gale of a voice bellowed, 'You'll do what I tell you, my lady! You'll do whatever I demand!'

Then a door banged; and another.

Eyre walked a little way up the garden path; then took off his Manila straw hat and held it over his chest, partly out of respect and partly as an unconscious gesture of self-protection. He was dressed in his Saturday afternoon best: a white cotton suit, with a sky-blue waistcoat with shiny brass buttons, from the tailoring shop next to Waterloo House. His high starched collar was embellished with a blue silk necktie which had taken him nearly twenty minutes to arrange.

'Is anything up?' he asked Mrs McMurtry.

Mrs McMurtry let out a throat-wrenching sob. Then she flapped down her apron, and her face was as hot and wretched as a bursting pudding.

'The mutton-and-turnip pie!' she exclaimed.

Eyre glanced, perplexed, towards the house. 'The mutton-and-turnip pie?' he repeated.

'*Moooo*!' sobbed Mrs McMurtry. Eyre came over and laid his arm around her shoulders, trying to be comforting. Her candy-striped kitchen-dress was drenched in perspiration, and her scrawny fair ringlets were stuck to the sides of her neck. In midsummer, cooking a family luncheon over a wood-burning stove was just as gruelling as stoking the boilers of a Port Lincoln coaster.

'That's not Mr Lindsay I hear?' asked Eyre.

Mrs McMurtry snuffled, and sobbed, and nodded frantically.

'But surely Mr Lindsay wasn't due home until Friday week!'

'Well, *mooo*, he's back now, aint he; came back this morning in the blackest of humours; too hot, says he, and nothing to show for a month's dealings in Sydney but expenses; and he kicks the boy for not grooming the horses as good as he wanted; and he kicks the dog for sleeping in the pantry while he was gone; and then he shouts at Mrs Lindsay for letting Miss Charlotte dress herself up like a fancy-woman, *mooo*, and for walking out without his say-so, with only the boy for chaperone; and then he sees that

22

it's mutton-and-turnip pie, and what he says is, *mooo*, what he says is, "I hates the very *sight* of mutton-and-turnip pie, so help me.' that's what he says, and he tosses it clean out of the kitchen window and upside-down it lands plonk in the veronica.'

Eyre took his hand away from Mrs McMurtry's sweaty shoulders and wiped it unobtrusively on his jacket. He looked towards the house again and bit his lip. This was extremely bad news. He had wanted to tell Lathrop Lindsay about his freshly flowered affection for Charlotte in his own particular way. Mr Lindsay was unpredictable, irascible, and no lover of 'sterlings', those who had newly arrived from England, or what he called 'the burrowing class', by which he meant clerks and salesmen and junior managers. Mr Lindsay had a special dislike of Eyre, and not just because Eyre was a 'sterling', or because he worked as a clerk for the South Australian Company down at the port. He disliked Eyre's manner, he disliked Eyre's smartly cut clothes, and he very much disliked Eyre's bicycle. It was probably fair to say that he disliked Eyre even more than he disliked mutton-and-turnip pie, and for that reason Eyre had wanted to prepare the ground for his announcement with ingenuity and care. He had already run two or three useful errands for Mrs Lindsay; and advised her where to find a reliable gardener, one who could conjure up English primroses as well as acacia. And back at his rooms on Hindley Street he had stored up five bottles of Lathrop Lindsay's favourite 1824 port-wine, which he had obtained in barter from the bo'sun of the *Illyria* in exchange for two nights' use of his bed, and an introduction to a benign and enormously fat Dutch girl called Mercuria.

Now all this expense and inconvenience had gallingly gone to waste; and Eyre cursed his rotten luck.

'I never saw Mr Lindsay in such a bate,' protested Mrs McMurtry.

One of the upstairs windows was lifted again. Mrs

Lindsay leaned out, white and fraught, with her primrose hair-ribbon halfway down the side of her head.

'Mr Walker!' she called, breathily. 'You'll have to make yourself scarce! My husband has come back, and I'm afraid that he's terribly angry at Charlotte for having stepped out with you. Please—you must go at once!'

At that moment, another window opened up, on the other side of the house. It was Lathrop Lindsay himself, crimson with indignation.

'What's all this calling-out?' he demanded. 'Phyllis!' Then he caught sight of Eyre standing in the garden with his hat over his heart and he roared incontinently, 'You! Mr Walker! You stay there! I want to have a word with you!'

His window banged down again. Mrs Lindsay waved to Eyre in mute despair, and then she closed her window, too. Eyre took two or three steps in retreat, towards the garden gate, but then stopped, and decided to stand his ground. If he were to flee, and pedal off on his bicycle, he would never have the chance to walk out with Charlotte again. He had to face up to Mr Lindsay; one way or another. Not only face up to him, but win him over.

My God, he thought. How am I going to convince a snorting bull like Lathrop Lindsay that I could make him a suitable son-in-law? He cleared his throat, and wiped sweat away from his upper lip with the back of his sleeve. Mrs McMurtry had stopped *mooo*-ing now, and was staring at him with her hands on her hips with a mixture of suspicion and pity.

'He'll eat you up alive,' Mrs McMurtry told him. 'The last fellow Charlotte walked out with, Billy Bonham, he was a new chum like you; and Mr Lindsay cracked three of his ribs with a walking-cane, so help me. And he was a lot better connected than what *you* are.'

Eyre gave her a quick, dismissive scowl. She hesitated, huffed, and then flounced off back to the house, swinging a cuff at Yanluga as he re-appeared through the shrubbery.

'Sterlings and Abbos,' she grumbled. 'Bad luck to the lot of 'em!'

Yanluga came cautiously up towards Eyre, biting his lips in apprehension. He was only fifteen but he had a natural way with horses, a way of calming them and whispering to them. Charlotte said that she had once seen him whistle to a kangaroo on the south lawn; and freeze the animal where it was, head raised, and then walk right up to it, and speak to it gently, although she hadn't been able to hear what he had said. He was very black, Yanluga, a wonderful inky black, with bushy hair and a face that defied you not to smile at him. Eyre's mother would have called him 'sonsy'.

Only Lathrop Lindsay found Yanluga irritating; but then Lathrop found the whole world irritating; and not only because of his inflamed piles. Lathrop had been dispatched to Australia by the Southwark Trading Company as a polite but very firm way of telling him that his books were not in order; and ever since then he had fought a ceaseless and irascible crusade to re-establish his self-esteem, both social and moral. Lathrop spoke a great deal of God, and Mary Magdalene, and also of Surrey, which he missed desperately; but more usually of the natural superiority of those who were neither clerks, nor black.

Yanluga said, gently, 'I'm sorry, Mr Walker, sir.'

'Sorry?' asked Eyre. 'What for?'

'Mr Lindsay asked me, did I take you and Miss Charlotte out for rides, sir, and I said yes. And then he asked me, did we have a chaperone, sir, and I said no.'

Eyre ruffled Yanluga's wiry hair. 'Don't you worry yourself,' he said, trying to be reassuring. 'It's better that you told the truth, in any case.'

'Sir, one of my cousins knows Steel Bullet the Mabarn Man.'

'Is that so? I didn't think that anybody knew Steel Bullet—not to speak to; I thought he hunted on his own; and never let anybody find out where he was.'

'I tell you the truth, sir. One of my cousins knows Steel

Bullet, sir, and maybe if you paid enough money, Steel Bullet would come in the night and kill Mr Lindsay for you, sir.'

Steel Bullet the Mabarn Man was a legend in South-Western Australia; and whalers had already brought tales of his horrifying behaviour as far east as Adelaide. He was an Aboriginal called Alex Birbarn, and he was said to possess the magical powers of a Mabarn Man—including the ability to fly hundreds of miles at night, and to change himself into anything he wished, such as a rock, or an anthill. So far he was credited with the murders of seventy people, and he was notorious for following kangaroo hunts, and making off with the kangaroo skin or sometimes the whole kangaroo before the exhausted hunters realised they had a thief in their midst.

Eyre said, 'I don't want to kill Mr Lindsay, Yanluga. I just want to persuade him to be reasonable.'

'Mr Lindsay never reasonable, sir. Never.' He shook his head violently.

'Well, yes, I know that, but what can I do?'

'Call the Mabarn Man, sir. Steel Bullet will chop him up into very small pieces for you, sir. Please, sir. Everybody would be very happy to see you marry Miss Charlotte, sir. Especially Miss Charlotte, sir.'

Eyre looked at Yanluga carefully. 'Miss Charlotte told you that?'

'Yes, sir.'

'You're not making it up?'

'Honour of Joseph, honour of Jesus, honour of God who always sees us.'

'Hm,' said Eyre. He pushed a finger and thumb into his tight waistcoat pocket, and took out sixpence, which he held up for a moment, so that Yanluga could see the sunlight wink on it; and which he then tossed up into the air, and smartly caught.

'You can do something for me, young Yanluga. You can go tell Miss Charlotte that I absolutely adore her; you know what adore means? Well, never mind, just say it. And you can tell her to meet me at ten o'clock tonight by the back fence, and not to worry about Old Face-Fungus.'

'Face-Fun-Gus?' Yanluga frowned. He was one of the better-educated Nyungars, but he found it difficult to follow what Eyre was saying when he spoke in his broadest Derbyshire accent.

Eyre slapped him on the back. 'Never mind about that,' he said, impatiently. 'Just make sure that Charlotte's outside the back gate at ten. Tell her to dress warmly: it can get devilish cold at that time of night. But I'll bring a blanket and a bottle of wine. Come on now, cut along, here's Mr Lindsay.'

Lathrop Lindsay was bustling down the front steps of the house, clutching a black-lacquered cane in both hands, his knuckles spotted with white. 'Now look here,' he called, and then he waved his stick at Yanluga, and cried, 'Be off with you! You idle black bastard!'

He steamed up to Eyre with all the boisterous energy of a small tug boat, his pale eyes bulging, his mouth tight. He wore tight white cotton trousers and a scarlet embroidered waistcoat, and a red necktie. His bald head was beaded with sweat.

'Now then, Mr Lindsay,' said Eyre, backing away a little, and lifting his hands to show that he surrendered.

'Now then yourself, you blackguard,' puffed Lathrop. 'You and your beguiling ways. You and your yessir nossir. And what happens the moment I'm away? Take advantage, don't you? Yessir. That's what you're interested in, isn't it, courting my daughter; nothing to do with shipping or business, nossir. And to think I believed you honest. To think I said to Mrs Lindsay, not a day before I went away, there's a trustworthy chap, albeit a new chum, and still white as milk. Yessir.'

'Mr Lindsay, please, I think there's been a frightful misunderstanding,' Eyre protested. Then, more persuasively, he said, 'Please.'

'Well, then?' Lathrop demanded. 'Did you go walking out with Charlotte or didn't you?'

'Yes, sir.'

'And did you take a chaperone with you?'

'No sir.'

'And what, pray, do you think that does for my daughter's reputation? Bad enough, by Heaven, that she walks out with one of the burrowing class. Bad enough, by God. But to walk out unattended, when anything might happen. *Anything*; and you know what *anything* means. Anything means shady goings-on, at least in the common mind, at least in the vulgar imagination, that's what anything means.'

'Mr Lindsay—' Eyre began.

'Mr Lindsay nothing,' Lathrop interrupted him. 'You'll be off at once, or I'll have the dogs on you. And you'll not be back, nossir. If I catch you once around this property; just once; if I catch you sniffing around my daughter; well you whelp I'll have you arrested by God and locked up, yessir, and beaten, too; whipped.'

'Eyre stood his ground. 'Mr Lindsay,' he said, 'I love your daughter. I love her with all my heart. And, what's more, I believe that she loves me in return.'

Lathrop stared at Eyre like a madman. His hairy nostrils widened, and his whole body seemed to quake uncontrollably.

'Mr Lindsay—' Eyre cautioned him. But Lathrop grew redder and redder, and his eyes popped, and with peculiarly stiff movements he raised his cane in his right hand, and began to advance on Eyre with dragging, paralytic steps; as if his entire nervous system had been congested by sheer rage.

'You dare to speak to me of love,' he boiled. 'You dare to come to my house on a bicycle and speak to me of love. By God, you young cur, I'll take the skin off your back.'

'Mr Lindsay, please, you're not yourself,' Eyre told him, retreating towards the garden gate. 'This is not you, Mr Lindsay. Not the calm and ordered Mr Lindsay, of Waikerie Lodge.'

He backed quickly out of the garden gate, and closed it.

The two of them faced each other over the low white-painted palings; Eyre trying every possible expression of appeasement in his facial repertoire; Lathrop Lindsay gradually coming to the point of spontaneous combustion.

'Mr Lindsay, I don't know what to say,' said Eyre. 'I imagined that I was a friend of the family. You gave me to *believe* that I was. I apologise if I mistook your charm and your courtesy for friendship. Perhaps you were just being nice to me for the sake of politeness. Please; it's all my fault and I apologise. Can't we start afresh?'

Lathrop threw open the garden gate and began to stalk after Eyre along the dusty sidewalk.

'You, sir, are trying my temper to the very utmost,' he trembled. 'And if you are not astride that contraption of yours, that ridiculous pedalling-machine, and gone; if you are not gone by the time I reach you with this cane, then, God help you, I will have that skin of yours; and I will stretch out that skin of yours on my fence.'

Eyre reached the hawthorn-tree and retrieved his bicycle. 'You can consider me gone already,' he said, tilting his nose up haughtily. 'If I'm not welcome, then I'll leave you. But a sadder man, let me tell you. And a disillusioned one, too. I used to respect you, Mr Lindsay, as a man of great social grace. I used to believe that you could charm the birds out of the trees.'

'By God,' Lathrop threatened him; but at that moment there was a dull dusty flopping sound on the sidewalk next to him; and then another. He looked around in surprise, and saw that two currawong birds had fallen unconscious out of the hawthorn-tree, one after the other, and were lying in the dirt with their legs in the air.

It was a common enough sight at this time of year, when the birds gorged themselves on dozens of fermented hawthorn berries and fell out of the trees in a drunken stupor. But the apt timing of their appearance led Lathrop and Eyre to stare at each other in utter surprise. Eyre couldn't help himself: he burst out laughing.

'I told you, Mr Lindsay! And it looks as if you can still do it!'

Lathrop let out an unearthly growling noise, and rushed towards Eyre with his cane lifted. Eyre pushed his bicycle four or five quick paces, then mounted the saddle and pedalled off along the street as rapidly as he could.

'I'll thrash you, you blackguard!' Lathrop screamed after him. 'You stay away from Charlotte, do you hear me! You burrower!'

Eyre raised his hat in mocking salute, and pedalled off between the rows of houses and hawthorn trees. Three Aborigine children in mission-school dresses stopped and stared at him as he balanced his way past them. He was whistling defiantly, a new popular song that had just found its way to Adelaide from London, 'Country Ribbons', and he sang the first verse of it as he turned right at the end of the road and bumped his way downhill on the dry ridgy track that led towards the centre of town.

In her hair were country ribbons,
Tied in bows of pink and white;
In her hair were country ribbons
In her eyes a gentle light.'

But he stopped singing long before he reached the corner of Hindley Street; and as he approached his lodging-house he dismounted from his bicycle and walked the rest of the way. The truth was that he had grown far fonder of Charlotte than he had actually meant to. There was something so unusual and provocative about her; something that stirred him in the night, when he was curled up under his blanket and trying to sleep. Charlotte Lindsay was special, and Eyre was afraid that what he had said to Lathrop was painfully true: he loved her. In fact, he loved her so much that he almost wished that he didn't.

His landlady's husband, Dogger McConnell, was sitting in his red-painted rocking-chair on the porch, smoking his pipe. Dogger had once been a dingo-hunter, out beyond Broken Hill, and he reckoned that in his life he had killed thousands of them. 'Bloody thousands.' His face was as creased as a creek-bed, and his conversation was unremittingly laconic. He could tell tales of the outback that, in his own words, would 'shrivel your nuts', but he rarely did. He preferred instead to smoke his pipe in satisfied silence on the porch and watch the comings and goings along Hindley Street, and take a prurient interest in the activities of his wife's eleven lodgers, who were all male, and all clerks, and all desperate for female company, always.

'Back early, Mr Walker,' he remarked

'Yes. The young lady's father was home. Rather unexpectedly, I'm afraid; and not in the best of sorts.'

'Hm, I've heard tell of that Lathrop Lindsay. Old Douglas Moffitt used to do odd-jobs for him, painting and suchlike. Not an easy man, from what Douglas used to say.'

'No, certainly not,' said Eyre. He wheeled his bicycle into the cool dusty shadows under the verandah. He only left it there so that the leather saddle wouldn't get too hot in the afternoon sun, not because he was frightened that anyone might steal it. Apart from the severe punishments which met any kind of pilfering, hardly anybody in Adelaide apart from Eyre knew how to ride a bicycle, and even when they had seen him do it, many of the blackfellows still believed that it was impossible, or at the very least, magic. The children called him Not-Fall-Over.

Eyre came back out and sat on the steps.

'You're glum, chum,' said Dogger. He puffed his pipe and frayed fragments of smoke blew across the sunny street.

'Well,' said Eyre, 'you'd be glum if you were in love.'

'With her?' Dogger cackled, gesturing behind him with his thumb. 'You've got to be bloody joking.'

'I don't know why you're so hard on her,' said Eyre. 'She's a fine woman. She's always good to me, anyway.'

Dogger took his well-gnawed pipestem out of his mouth and leaned toward Eyre with a wink. 'She's good to me too, chum. Always has been and always will be. But as

31

for love. Well, no, love's in your head. You can't love any more, when you grow older, you don't have the brain for it. And the things I've seen, out at Broken Hill. Different values, you see, out beyond the black stump. And, to tell you the truth, you don't have the steam for it. Do you know what I mean? And she's had eleven children, Mrs McConnell. Eleven; nine still living, seven normal, two potty. Left her as capacious as the Gulf of St Vincent, without being indelicate.'

'Indelicate?' said Eyre, mildly amazed.

They sat together on the verandah for a while in silence. The sun began to nibble at the branches of the gum trees on the other side of the street and the dusty lanes and gardens began to glow with the amber light which Eyre could never quite get used to, even after a year in Australia; as though everything around them, houses, trees, and sun-dusted hills, had become theatrically holy.

Dogger said, 'There's a jug of beer in the kitchen, bring some out. Maybe I'll tell you about the time that poor old Gordon Smith had to cut his horse's throat, just for something to drink. And listen chum, I'd forget that girl of yours, I would, if I were you.'

Eyre turned to him, and looked for a moment into that brown, crumpled-handkerchief face, and then turned away again. 'Yes,' he said, 'I suppose I ought to.'

Two

But he couldn't, of course. He had the same obstinacy in him as his father; the same determination to have what he wanted in the face of every discouragement possible. And he very much wanted Charlotte.

That was why, at a quarter to ten that evening, he was crouched among the wattle bushes at the rear of Waikerie Lodge, whistling tonelessly from time to time so that if Charlotte had managed to venture out into the garden, she would be able to hear him over the sweatshop clamour of insects and night parrots.

He had brought a plaid blanket with him, as well as a bottle of sweet Madeira wine, which was Charlotte's favourite; and a handkerchief with a few of Mrs McConnell's apple turnovers tied up in it, in case they felt peckish.

He was probably being wildly over-optimistic. Lathrop would more than likely have kept Charlotte confined to her room, in disgrace. Lathrop was the kind of father who would allow his daughter every indulgence, except the freedom to choose her own lovers. Not that he was particularly unusual. Eyre had already discovered that most of the upper-quality families in Adelaide were stiff and virtuous, and kept a very short rein on their daughters, regardless of how plain they were.

Eyre felt tense and lustful at the same time; and his starched collar cut into his neck. He wished very much that he hadn't drunk quite so many glasses of Dogger's home-made beer; for if Charlotte didn't appear soon, he was going to be obliged to hide behind the stringy-bark gums which screened the end of the Lindsay's garden, and relieve himself.

He whistled again, low and flat. Still there was no reply.

The moon was not yet up, although the sky was a pale luminous purple, the colour of parakeelya flowers. Lathrop Lindsay's grand white-painted mansion had taken on the appearance of a house made of sugar, with gingerbread shingles and frosted verandahs. Like most of the statelier homes in Adelaide, it had been shipped from England piece by piece, pillars and newels and architraves all numbered and ready for reconstruction among the gums and wattles of the Lindsays' private estates.

The Lindsays lived to the north-west of Adelaide, in common with almost all of the richer and better-connected settlers; eschewing the streets and squares and parks that had been laid out for them by Adelaide's Surveyor-General, Colonel William Light, only five years ago. Last year, soon after Eyre had arrived, Adelaide had been declared Australia's first municipality, and land prices in the centre of town had soared, up to £10,000 a section, but the heart of Light's city was still neglected. Those brave souls who ventured for a walk into Victoria Square, the small park halfway along King William Street, were still quite liable to become frighteningly lost, and have to spend the night under the shelter of fallen gum-trees.

Lathrop had several times thrust his thumbs aggressively into his waistcoat, and told Eyre, 'Planners don't make cities; people do. And the manner of man who has chosen to make South Australia his home, free and self-determined, is going to build his house where he wishes. We're not convicts, by God; nor refugees political or religious; nor anybody's minion, neither.'

Eyre took out his silver pocket-watch and sprung open the case so that he could check the time. Ten o'clock and half-a-minute; and still no sign of Charlotte. He shivered, partly with cold and partly because he was bursting to empty his bladder. But supposing he went for a piss and missed Charlotte altogether? Or supposing she came out, all perfume and beauty, and caught him at it? He swore to God that he would never drink beer again.

He whistled again, and listened. A parrot creaked and chattered, and fluttered in the branches off to his left. One of the windows in the Lindsay house dimmed, and then the window next to it brightened, as if someone were

34

carrying an oil-lamp from room to room. A window was closed, and then four or five shutters. It sounded as if the family were preparing to go to bed.

Eyre thought of the afternoon when he and Charlotte had walked in the abandoned Botanic Gardens, among the wild and scraggly bushes, down by the Company's bridge. A flock of sulphur-crested cockatoos had suddenly risen from the river-banks like a shower of snow, and circled around them, fluttering and crying, and then gradually settled again. And while Yanluga had sat placidly at the reins of the carriage, smoking his small clay pipe, Eyre had drawn Charlotte close to him, and kissed first her cheek, and then her forehead, and then her lips, until she had lifted her fingers gently and touched his mouth, to make him stop, because he was disturbing her so.

A dog barked three or four times, over by the mill. Then there was silence again, for endless minutes; except for the insects, and the night-birds, and the whispering of the trees.

Eyre decided that Charlotte wasn't coming; and that it was time to give up this amorous vigil as nothing but self-inflicted torture, both physical and mental. He collected up his blanket and his bottle of wine and his parcel of cakes, and retreated from his hide-out by the Lindsay's back gate at a slow backstepping crouch, until he was well beyond the stringy-bark gums. He paused for a clattering pee; and he was just buttoning himself up again when Yanluga appeared out of nowhere, the whites of his eyes as bright as a beast's, and his teeth shining in a disembodied grin.

Eyre let out a whoop of fright.

'Mr Walker, sir,' said Yanluga, clutching his sleeve.

'Yanluga! You scared me out of my skin.'

Yanluga couldn't help giggling. 'You were making *kumpa* on the dry tree-bark. Anybody could hear, for miles and miles.'

'Only if they had ears like a blackfellow; or a dingo. Where's Miss Charlotte?'

'Miss Charlotte had to go to her room, sir. Mr Face Fun-Gus say so.'

'Damn it,' said Eyre. 'I thought as much. Damn. Can you give me another message for me?'

'You shouldn't worry, sir,' said Yanluga. 'Miss Charlotte said, wait for just a little while, and she can escape from her room. Then she will come to the garden to see you. *Ngaiyeri* Face Fun-Gus is very tired from travelling; and from *ngraldi*, from anger.'

'*Ngraldi*,' Eyre repeated. 'I think that describes it perfectly. Will she be long?'

'One minute, two minutes. But wait here.'

Eyre laid down his blanket and his wine, and then reached out and took Yanluga's hand, and squeezed it. 'Teach me another word,' he said. 'The blackfellow for "friend." '

Yanluga kept on smiling, but he was silent for a very long time.

'What's the matter?' asked Eyre.

'No white sir ask me that before,' said Yanluga.

'Well, there's always a first time.'

Yanluga squeezed Eyre's hand in return. 'Friend is *ngaitye*, in my tongue, sir,' he said.

'*Ngaitye*,' Eyre pronounced; and then he said, 'That's you.'

Yanluga hesitated, and then he bowed his head, and said, 'I go find Miss Charlotte, Mr Walker, sir.'

'Good,' Eyre told him. 'And next time, don't come jumping out at me like a ghostly golliwog.'

Yanluga laughed, and raised both hands like a demon's claws. 'You be careful of Koobooboodgery, sir, the night spirit.'

'You be careful of yowcheroochee, the box on the ears,' Eyre retorted; and smiled to himself as Yanluga rustled quickly off into the golden wattles again and disappeared towards the house.

Eyre felt much more cheerful now, and spread out the blanket on top of the crisp, curled-up bark from the

36

surrounding gum-trees. He hummed to himself the chorus from 'Country Ribbons'.

'In her hair were country ribbons, tied in bows of pink and white . . .' and uncorked the bottle of Madeira and took a mouthful straight from the neck to warm himself up.

Over his right shoulder, the moon had risen over the distant undulating peaks of the Mount Lofty Range, and Mount Lofty itself, the mountain the Aborigines called Yureidla. The dogs over at the new flour mill began to yip and howl again; but probably because there were dingoes around, hunting for Mr Cairns's poultry.

He thought of the morning he had first seen Charlotte, seven months ago, when her father had brought her down to the wharf to watch the unloading of pumping machinery from England. It had been a bright, busy day, with a fresh wind blowing across the mouth of the harbour; and Eyre had been supervising the loading of a ripe-smelling cargo of raw wool, bound for Yorkshire, with the stub of a pencil stuck behind one ear, and his scruffiest britches on.

His fellow clerk Christopher Willis had nudged him, and said, 'What do you think of that, then, Eyre, for a prize ornament?'

Eyre had raised one hand to shield his eyes from the sun; and had stared at Charlotte in complete fascination. She was small, white-skinned, and angelically pretty, with blonde curls straying out from the brim of her high straw bonnet. At first she had appeared almost too doll-like to be true, especially the way in which she was standing so demurely beside her father in her pink fringed shawl; but when she turned and looked towards Eyre he saw that she had a mouth that was pouty and self-willed and a little petulant; the mouth of a spoiled little rich girl who needed taming as well as courting. The sort of girl who could benefit from being put over a chap's knee, and spanked.

'Well, well,' Eyre had remarked, and grinned across the wharf at her and winked.

'That's not for you, Master Walker,' Christopher had

chided him. 'That's Lathrop Lindsay's only and unsullied daughter; and he's keeping her in virginal isolation until royalty comes to Adelaide, or at the very least a duke; or an eligible governor, not like poor old George Gawler.'

'She scarcely looks real, does she?' Eyre had murmured. 'And by all the stars, look, she's smiling at me.'

'Scowling, more like, if she takes after papa,' Christopher had told him. 'Lathrop Lindsay's temper is one of the hazards that they warn settlers about, before they embark from Portsmouth; that, and the heat, and the death-adders, and the tubercular fever.'

'No, no, she's definitely smiling at me,' Eyre had insisted, and had ostentatiously doffed his hat, and bowed.

'Who's that impudent ruffian?' he had heard Lathrop demanding, in a voice like a blaring trumpet. 'You! Yes, *you*, you scoundrel! Be off with you before I have you thrashed!'

Eyre hadn't seen Charlotte for several weeks after that; although he had bicycled out several times to Waikerie Lodge, where the Lindsays lived, and sat on the wrought-iron seat across the road in the hope of catching a glimpse of her, occasionally smoking one of his brandy-flavoured cheroots, or eating an apple.

That was why it had been such a stroke of good fortune when Lathrop's senior manager, a morose man called Snipps, had visited the offices of the South Australian Company where Eyre was working, and had asked if Mr Lindsay could be expeditiously assisted with a cargo of wheat, which was lying at the dockside without a merchantman to take it. Eyre had immediately arranged for a Bristol ship which was already half-loaded with wool to be unloaded again, and for Mr Lindsay's cargo to be taken in preference; and at a preferential rate. The irate sheep-owner whose wool it was hadn't discovered that his cargo was still in the warehouse at Port Adelaide until the ship was already halfway across the Great Australian Bight; but

Eyre had been able to mollify him with the promise of the very next ship, and a case of good whisky.

Most important for Eyre, however, had been an invitation two weeks later to a garden-party at Waikerie Lodge, in gratitude for his assistance. There, on the green sunlit lawns, where peacocks clustered, he had been introduced formally to Lathrop; and to Mrs Lindsay, and at last to Charlotte. He and Charlotte had said nothing very much as Lathrop had brought them together; but there had been an exchange of looks between them, his challenging, hers provocative; and Eyre had known at once that they could be lovers.

Later, munching one of Mrs McMurtry's teacakes, Eyre had spoken for a while to Lathrop of shipping costs; and how those who knew friendly clerks in the South Australian Company could save themselves considerable amounts of money, especially if the bills of lading showed that cargoes weren't quite as weighty as one might have imagined them to be. And Lathrop (who hadn't once recognised Eyre as the 'impudent ruffian' from the wharf) gave him a sober and watery-eyed look that meant business.

From then on, Eyre had been a regular visitor at Waikerie Lodge, either on business or on social calls; and he and Charlotte had been drawn together like two dark solar bodies, feeling the tug of each other's sexual gravity and being unable and unwilling to resist it.

Eyre looked at his watch again. On the inside of the lid was engraved a crucifix, and the words 'Time flies, death urges, knells call, heaven invites, hell threatens,' and then 'Henry L. Walker, 1811'. The watch was the only gift that his father had given him when he had decided to emigrate to Australia; and he both treasured it and resented it; but it told the time with perfect accuracy, and now it was eleven minutes past ten.

He heard a low call. Yanluga, skirting around the garden. Then he heard the back gate creak open, and the swishing of skirts on the grass. Before he knew it, Charlotte was there, in her shawl and her blue ruffled dress, pale-faced and smelling of lily-of-the-valley. Her blonde curls shone in the moonlight, and her eyes glistened with emotion. Eyre held out his arms to her, and she came to him, in a last quick rustle of silk; and then they were holding each other close, closer than ever before.

'Oh, Eyre,' she said. 'I'm so sorry about what happened. If only I had known that father was coming back so soon.'

He kissed her forehead, and then her eyes, and then her lips. 'Shush now; it wasn't your fault. If anybody's to blame, it's me, for upsetting your family so.'

'Hold me tight,' she begged him. 'I'm so frightened that father won't allow us to see each other again.'

'He can't do that.'

Charlotte shook her head. 'He can; and if he's really angry, he will.'

'Yanluga says he suffers from *ngraldi*.'

'*Ngraldi*?' asked Charlotte. She rested her face against his lapels, and held him tight around the waist, as if she were afraid that he might suddenly become lighter than air, and bob up into the night sky like a gas balloon. Eyre stroked the parting of her hair, and grunted with amusement.

'What's *ngraldi*?' she asked.

'Rage. I just like the sound of it. There's your father, getting into a *ngraldi* again.'

'But you've upset him terribly. He couldn't talk about anything else at dinner, except how you'd besmirched my reputation.'

Eyre kissed her again; right on her pouting mouth. 'Don't you worry about your father. He'll calm down, I'm sure of it; especially when he remembers how much money I'm saving him every month on shipping costs.'

'I don't know. He had a partner once, Thomas Weir, and even though he lost thousands of pounds, he refused to take Thomas Weir back, once they'd argued. He's so set in his ways; and he always believes he's so *right*.'

Eyre said, 'Sit down. I've brought a blanket. And some

Madeira wine, too, if you can manage to drink it out of the bottle. I couldn't work out a way of carrying glasses on my bicycle.'

Charlotte spread her skirt and sat down on the rug under the stringy-bark gums. She looked like a fantasy, in the unreal light of that cold and uncompromising moon; and the gums around her shone an unearthly blue-white, as if they were frightened spirits of the night, the slaves of Koobooboodgery.

Eyre flipped up his coat-tails and sat down close to her, taking her hands between his.

'It's so good to see you,' he said. 'This afternoon, I began to be worried that I might never set eyes on you again.'

Charlotte said, 'Dear Eyre. But it isn't going to be easy. Father doesn't go away again until just before Christmas, when he usually travels to Melbourne.'

'Surely he won't stay angry for as long as that.'

'Eyre, he wants me to marry into the aristocracy.'

'Of course he does. Every father in Adelaide wants to see his daughter married to a man who's wealthy, or famous, or well-bred; or all three. But the truth is that there aren't very many of those to be had. Some of those fathers will have to accept the fact that if their daughters are going to be married at all, they will have to put up with clerks for husbands, or farmers, or dingo-hunters, if they're not too quick off the mark.'

'Father said he would gladly see you hung,' Charlotte told him. She kissed him again, and he felt the softness of her cheek, and the disturbing lasciviousness of her lips. She was a girl of such contrasts: of such pretty mannerisms but such provoking sensuality; of bright and brittle intelligence but stunning directness; polite but candid; teasing but thoughtful; flirtatious but brimming with deeply felt emotions. Sometimes she was a woman who had not yet outgrown the coquettishness of girlhood; at other times she was an innocent girl whose life was slowly nudging out into the heady stream of sexual maturity, like a boat on the Torrens River. She was trembling on the cusp of

41

nineteen; and tonight she was probably more desirable than she would ever be again; sugar-candy and butterflies and claws. She knew how captivating she was; and yet she had not yet learned to use her attraction cruelly, or cynically, simply for the pleasure of seeing some poor beau dance on a string.

Eyre kissed her in return; much more forcefully, much more urgently. Their tongues wriggled together, until Eyre's tongue-tip penetrated Charlotte's slightly opened teeth, and probed inside her mouth, tasting the sweetness of it.

They parted for a few moments. Charlotte lay back on the blanket and stared up at him, without saying anything. Her mouth was still moist with their shared saliva, and she made no attempt to wipe it away.

Eyre said, 'Yanluga told me something today. I don't know how true it was; whether he was just trying to be nice to me.'

'Yanluga thinks the world of you. You're the only white man who has ever treated him with any respect. Men like my father don't think anything of the blackfellows; they don't even believe that they're human. Father's always striking Yanluga with his riding-crop. Once he made him pick up a coin that he had dropped, and then stepped on his fingers, just to hear him howl. He says they're like babies, the blackfellows, it's good for them to howl.'

Eyre was silent for a moment. Then he said, 'Yanluga told me you'd quite care to marry me, if you could.'

Charlotte slowly smiled.

'Is it true?' Eyre asked her.

She nodded. 'But he wasn't supposed to tell you. I shall whip him myself when I get back to the house.'

Eyre said, 'I want to marry you, too. And if that sounds like a proposal, well, I suppose it is. I very much like the sound of "Mrs Charlotte Walker." '

Charlotte said, 'Father won't allow it, you know. He won't even let you come near the house.'

'Can't your mother intervene?'

'She's tried. Poor dear mother. She was trying all evening to persuade father what a wonderful upright person you were; but he wasn't listening. He doesn't *want* to listen. He never thinks of my happiness, that's why. All he can think about is being the father-in-law to some English baron; or some famous explorer; or something that will give him glory.'

Eyre looked down at her, and stroked her cheek, and then her neck. 'What can we do, then?' he whispered.

'We could wait until I'm twenty-one; although he can make it difficult for me even then, because of my inheritance. Or you could go off and do some magnificent deed, and be knighted for it.'

'What magnificent deed could a clerk do?' asked Eyre. 'Fill in three thousand bills of lading in a week? Write up a record number of ledgers? And even if I *could* think of something magnificent to do, how are we to manage in the meantime, with a love that can't even be admitted in daylight?'

Charlotte reached up and held the hand that was stroking her cheek. She kissed his fingers, and then she said, 'We can manage. We must manage. But you mustn't be shocked.'

'Shocked?' he asked her.

She put her fingertip up to her pursed lips. 'Sssh,' she said; and then she reached down and unlaced the ribbon that held the bodice of her pale blue dress.

Eyre said, 'Charlotte?' but she shushed him again, and slowly drew out the criss-cross ribbon until her bodice was open to the waist. Then, eyes dreamily half-closed, she took his hand and slid it underneath the white silk lining until it was cupping her warm bare breast.

She whispered, 'You mustn't be shocked, or then I will shock myself. I love you, Eyre; I want you to touch me. I want you to love me just as much in return. Sometimes I tease you but I want you. I have dreams about you, dreams about kissing you; dreams that make me wake up feeling hot, and confused.'

Slowly, fascinated, he caressed her nipple between finger and thumb until he could feel it crinkle tight. Charlotte let her head drop back on to the blanket, her eyes completely closed now, her breath coming quick and harsh from between her parted lips.

'We must *make-believe* that we are married, if my father won't allow us,' she told him, in the same urgent, sleepy voice. 'If he discovers us, he will probably kill you, and he will most certainly whip me. But we don't mind the danger, do we, my darling lover? The risk is what makes us both so excited!'

Eyre was so aroused now that his britches could hardly contain him. He knelt over Charlotte, and drew the bodice of her dress wide apart, so that both her breasts were exposed to the moonlight. They were high young breasts, very white, well-rounded, and the nipples were as wide and pink as rose-petals stuck to a rainy window.

A night-parrot shrieked startlingly above them; and Eyre lifted his head for a moment in alarm. But then he realised that everything was quiet, and that they were still alone, and he bowed over her breasts, kissing them in quick, complicated patterns, teasing at her nipples with his teeth, pressing the soft flesh against his face.

'Eyre, I must be asleep; I must be dreaming,' sighed Charlotte, twisting and rustling beneath him, one arm raised so that he could see the pattern of blue veins on her thin white wrist, a single string of pearls around her neck. And all the time there was that needful sibilant whisper of silk, as she rubbed one thigh against the other.

'You've been sent to me ... from heaven,' he murmured, as he kissed her. 'And I *will* make you my wife . . . I promise it . . . one day.'

He reached downwards, and raised the frilly hems of her dress. At that moment, she opened her eyes and stared at him, and said in a high voice, 'I'm not at all sure what one does.' But Eyre leaned forward again, and brushed his lips against hers, and said, 'I'll show you.'

'But do you really *want* to?' she asked.

44

He smiled. 'Of all the people in all the world, upside down or right way up, I want to show *you* more than anybody.'

He paused, and then added, 'In fact, you're the *only* person I want to show.'

His hand caressed her silk-hosed knee, and then her thigh. Bloomers had not yet reached Australia as a universal fashion, and beneath her silk dress and her silk hooped underskirt, Charlotte wore nothing at all. Eyre's hand on her bare hip made her shudder, and when at last he ran his fingers around the curves of her bottom, and touched lightly the slipperiness between her legs, she cried out; a strange suppressed little cry like a shriek.

'You're safe,' Eyre comforted her. 'You're quite safe, and you're very beautiful.'

Wide-eyed, she lay back, and allowed him to touch her further; but she was tense now, and less sure of herself. She thought she heard a door banging over by the house, and she half-lifted her head, but Eyre gently pushed her back again, and said, 'It's nothing. You're safe. Just close your eyes and enjoy yourself.'

She flutteringly closed her eyes for a few seconds. She felt Eyre's fingers stroking her, and the sensation was so intense that she bit her lip. Then she could feel him peeling her sticky lips apart. His fingers were so tender! And then he slid one slowly right inside her; and she felt as if she were a geyser that was beginning to come to the boil, as if heat and bubbles were rising inside her and that they would have to come bursting out. The danger and the excitement and the lewdness of having a man's finger, Eyre's finger, right up inside her, right under her skirts! And she held his wrist tight between her silk-sheathed thighs, gripping him there, wanting to keep him there for ever, wanting him deeper, wanting him so much that it almost gave her backache.

'Eyre,' she garbled, and she could hardly understand her own voice. 'Eyre, please, whatever it is, show me, please.'

He knelt astride her. She heard him unbuckling his belt, and his britches buttons being pulled apart with a soft sound like an opening seed-pod. Then he took her hand, her small white uncertain hand, and brought it downwards; urged it downwards; and laid in it a hot thick sceptre of flesh. So hard, so demanding, so impossibly big. And she stared up at him for reassurance, and comfort; but all she saw in his eyes then was an inexplicably glazed look, as if he were somehow suddenly possessed; as if instead of being Eyre he were *all* men, at the moment of taking a woman.

Eyre said, 'Now.' His throat was constricted, and he was shaking. Charlotte clutched him tighter, and tighter still, as if by clutching him so tight she could make him burst, and bring to a finish this strange and suddenly frightening act of passion; and exorcise the devils that had arisen in both of them, tongues and forks and fire, to stoke up their lust.

Eyre shifted his weight forwards, kneeling on the back of her dress, trapping her, and forcing her thighs apart, indecently wide. She released her hold on him, and desperately clutched at the blanket, and at the fragments of loose bark on the ground; and she thrashed her head from side to side in perplexity and fear and mounting desire. What was happening to her? She felt as if she were actually alight. She was going mad! Was this what it was like to go mad? She was burning! But she was chilled, too, sharply: she could feel the chill between her wide-apart thighs, exciting and terrifying at the same time. And Eyre was pushing against her, pushing and pushing, and urging himself into her. Not that! It was far too big! It would kill her, it would split her apart! It was like a huge crimson truncheon!

And then Eyre had fiercely grasped both of her shoulders, and tugged her towards him; so that the enormous crimson truncheon was forced right up between her legs; and she shrieked and shrieked at the top of her voice, scattering parrots and jacks and galahs all through the trees in a furious explosion of wings and feathers.

Three

A window banged; and then a door. Then they heard somebody shouting in dialect. '*Naodaup*? What's the matter? *Unkee*. A woman. *Tyintin*. Stay there.' And then something about searching in the trees—'*Tuyulawarrin!*'

Eyre was already on his feet, swiftly buttoning up his britches. Charlotte banged at her upraised dress with her fists, as if it were a disobedient puppy that refused to lie down. She was panting, and whimpering, embarrassed at her own panic, and furious at Eyre for allowing her to humiliate herself. 'You shouldn't have done!' she kept flustering. 'Eyre, you *shouldn't*!'

Eyre tightened his belt, and then knelt down beside her again. He felt shaky and breathless, and so irritable at having been interrupted right at the very instant of possessing her that his teeth were on edge, as if he had been biting lemons.

Charlotte held on to his sleeve. 'I told you I didn't know what was supposed to happen,' she persisted. 'You shouldn't have done it, Eyre! It hurt so much!'

'You were frightened, that's all,' said Eyre, taking her wrists and trying to coax her on to her feet. 'It doesn't usually hurt, not like that. Usually, it's the most marvellous thing you can imagine. But you're right. I shouldn't have led you on. Not here; and not tonight.'

'I just didn't *know*,' Charlotte told him; and now she started to weep.

Eyre heard dogs barking, over by the stable-block. 'Come on, now,' he said. 'Your father's let the hounds out. We don't want to be caught here. Is there any way you can get back to your bedroom without him seeing you?'

Charlotte sniffed, and blew her nose on her little lace handkerchief. 'I think so. Once I get back through the garden gate, I can go along the ha-ha until I reach the kitchen. Then I can go up the back stairs.'

'Well you'd better hurry in that case,' said Eyre. 'It sounds as if he's brought out the whole pack. And if they can catch a red kangaroo, they can certainly catch us.'

'Eyre,' said Charlotte, lifting her face, wet with tears, to kiss him. 'Eyre, I'm sorry. You must think me so ridiculous.'

He kissed her, and then held her head close to his cheek, his fingers buried in her curls. 'It's my fault. I love you now and I always will. Now, please, you'd better go.'

The hounds were being led around the side of the house now, yipping and snapping. Eyre took Charlotte's arm and guided her swiftly to the garden gate; where he kissed her one last time before letting her go. She hurried off along by the stringy-bark gums at the end of the lawns, her blue ruffled dress shining pale in the moonlight, a fleeing ghost in a garden of ghostly trees.

Just before she could reach the ha-ha at the far side of the garden, however, and disappear from view; flashing lanterns appeared at the side of the house, and Eyre saw Lathrop's two Aborigine dog-handlers, Utyana and Captain Henry, struggling across the south-east patio with six greyhounds each. The dogs were straining at their leads until their eyes bulged, their claws scratching and skittering at the stone pathways.

'Koola! Koola!' Captain Henry shouted to his dogs, and they snarled and gnashed and writhed against their leads in a froth of hunting-lust. 'Koola' was Aborigine for kangaroo, and these dogs had been trained for two years to chase after kangaroos and bring them down as quickly

48

and as bloodily as possible. The dogs had to be strong and vicious because the kangaroos were strong and vicious; even the youngest kangaroo could run for miles before the hunt caught up with them, and a fully grown buck could fling a greyhound into the air and break its back. Kangaroos were unnervingly intelligent, too. Last season a big red had caught Lathrop's favourite hound Rocket with its front paws and held it under water at the Nguru waterhole until it had drowned.

Eyre shouted, 'Charlotte! Hurry!' and Charlotte at last reached the shelter of the ha-ha and began to run towards the house with her skirts raised. But the dog-handlers had already seen her, and must have thought she was an intruder, or even (knowing how superstitious they were) a Koobooboodgery. And now Lathrop himself appeared, in his flapping nightshirt, carrying a lantern in one hand and a musket in the other.

Captain Henry must have asked for permission to let the dogs loose; for Lathrop nodded, and in the next instant six of the greyhounds were streaking across the moonlit grass in sudden silence; pale shadows so quick that Eyre found it difficult to follow them.

He wrenched open the garden gate, and shouted at Lathrop, 'It's Charlotte! Call them off, Mr Lindsay! It's Charlotte!'

Lathrop stared at him from twenty yards away in complete amazement. 'Walker?' he demanded, lifting up his lantern. 'What the blue devil are you doing here?'

'It's Charlotte!' Eyre screamed at him.

'What?' Lathrop turned, frowned towards the ha-ha, frowned back at Eyre; and then said, 'Charlotte? What's Charlotte?'

'There! For the love of God, call those dogs off!'

It was then that they heard Charlotte scream, and the growling and snapping of the dogs.

Lathrop suddenly understood what was happening, and roared at Captain Henry, 'Call them off, man! Call them off! They'll kill her!'

Captain Henry held his hands on top of his head in complete misery. 'Can't do it, sir. Won't come now, sir. Not until they bring the *pipi*, sir.'

Eyre felt cold. He knew what *pipi* meant—entrails. Without thinking of anything at all, he began to run across the lawn towards the ha-ha, his vision a jumble of grass, gum-trees, flashes of moonlight. He could hear himself panting as he ran as if somebody else were running close beside him.

He reached the brink of the ha-ha, his shoes skidding on the dry grass. Charlotte had stopped screaming now; and was desperately trying to scramble up the side of the slope, one hand pressed to her face to keep the greyhounds from tearing at her nose and eyes. All six dogs were leaping and snapping and hurling themselves at her like suicidal acrobats. Two of them clung on to her petticoats to drag her down, while the others bit at her arms and her ankles and her bare shoulders.

Eyre roared at the top of his voice, and bounded down the ha-ha and right into the tussle of dogs, shouting, 'Off! You damned creatures! Get off! Damn you!'

He kicked one dog hard in the ribs, and it screamed like a child. Another went for his trousers, but he seized its hind leg and threw it end-over-end, howling, into a patch of bottlebrushes. But two more dogs launched themselves at his calves, and one of them bit right through into the muscle with an audible crunch of flesh, and the other scrabbled with sharpened claws at his ankles, ripping off skin in ribbons. Eyre shouted out loud, and yet another dog threw itself at his elbow, gripping the bone with relentless jaws and refusing to let go, even when he twisted its ear right around.

He dropped to the grass; first to his knees, then as the dogs went for him again, on to his back. He was too frightened even to cry out; and angry, too, in an extraordinary way.

Captain Henry reached the ha-ha, and managed to beat off two of the hounds with a stick; at least for long enough for Charlotte to be pulled, crying and bloody, to the safety of the dog-handler's side. But now the rest of the dogs hurled themselves at Eyre with redoubled fury, and one of them bit him right in the cheek, only an inch below his right eye, while two more of them ripped at his arms and his legs.

He thought, Jesus Christ, I'm dead. I'm already dead. These dogs are going to kill me. And his whole world was crowded with snapping and biting and flying saliva and flailing claws.

Quite suddenly, however, he felt the dogs stiffen, and lift their heads. One of them stepped back from him, and then the others followed, and in a moment all six of them changed from snarling beasts into elegant canine statues, standing in the light of the moon quite motionless, noses slightly lifted, as if they had inhaled some rare and indefinable essence that was undetectable by humans but which could instantly turn greyhounds into figures of limestone.

Lathrop said abruptly, 'Utyana. Tie the rest of those dogs up and bring Mr Walker up here. Captain Henry, do you hold your ground.'

'Yes, sir, Mr Lindsay.'

Digging his heels into the grass, Eyre managed to push himself a little way up the side of the ha-ha on his back. He was shocked and trembling and he felt as if his skin had been curried all over with a wire brush. Utyana hurried over and lifted him the rest of the way out of the ditch; and then he lay back on the grass, sniffing and shaking, and up above him the sky was impossibly rich with stars.

Utyana knelt beside him, taking off his wide felt hat so that he was wearing only a red headscarf over his scalp. He was big-nosed and ugly, and his breath smelled of sour fruit, but he smiled at Eyre and touched his forehead very gently.

'How's . . . Miss Charlotte?' asked Eyre.

'Yes, sir,' nodded Utyana.

'Going to be all right, no thanks to you,' remarked the

51

vinegar voice of Lathrop Lindsay, from somewhere out of sight.

'And me?' Eyre whispered. 'I'm not going to die, am I?'

'Yes, sir,' nodded Utyana.

'Only English the blighter ever learned,' said Lathrop. 'Understands it, doesn't speak it'.

Eyre reached down and felt his chest. His waistcoat was badly torn, and his lapels were hanging in shreds. Then suddenly he felt his stomach, and to his utmost horror he could feel something wet and stringy. He lifted it up in his hand, and raised his head a little way, and there between his fingers was a bloody mess of tatters, with something pulpy right in the middle of it all.

He let his head drop back on the grass. 'Oh my God,' he said, out loud. A feeling of nausea surged up in him, and his mouth flooded with blood and bile.

Lathrop came into view, on the right-hand side, and peered down at him. 'What's the matter with you?' Lathrop asked him, shortly.

Eyre took three or four quick breaths. 'I'm going to die, aren't I? Those dogs have ripped my guts out.'

Lathrop stared at him, and then down at his stomach. 'That, you mean?' he asked, poking at the stringy mess with his finger.

Eyre said nothing, but nodded rapidly. He was sure that he could already feel the coldness of death seeping into his legs; soon it would overtake him altogether.

'That's the lining of your jacket,' Lathrop told him. 'Got torn, that's all; and that bit there's your pocket, with your pocket-handkerchey. Ripped your guts out my Aunt Fanny. Wish they damn well had, the damage you've done.'

Eyre took another, longer breath, and then looked at Lathrop and attempted a friendly chuckle. It came out like a ghastly, irrational honk; and he was glad that Lathrop didn't hear it, and turned away.

It was then that Eyre realised how hushed the garden was; even the night-parrots were silent; and the insects had hesitated as if rain were expected, or an unfelt earth tremor had shaken the deeper levels of the surrounding hills.

Eyre said to Utyana, 'What's going on? Help me sit up.'

'Yes, sir.' Utyana smiled, and continued to stroke his forehead.

'For God's sake!' Eyre demanded. 'I want to sit up!'

Utyana at last realised what he wanted, and gripped him under the armpits with his thin black muscly hands, and helped him to sit. Eyre looked around, and the tableau that he saw in front of him was so strange that at first he couldn't believe that it was real.

The greyhounds were still poised in the ha-ha; with Captain Henry standing a little way back; and Lathrop commanding the scene with one hand firmly planted on his hip, his musket angled over his shoulder, and the evening breeze billowing his nightshirt around his thick white ankles. But it was Yanluga who caught Eyre's attention. He was sitting cross-legged on the far edge of the ha-ha, his back very straight, and he was whispering, a peculiar hollow whisper that gave Eyre a prickly feeling all the way down his back, the way some particularly plaintive music can.

Yanluga was charming the greyhounds as if they were children. They stood hypnotised, their ears and their tails depressed, their white eyes wide, watching him as if they couldn't bear to let him out of their sight for a single instant. Eyre didn't recognise the words that Yanluga was using; they didn't even sound like Wirangu. But the effect they had on the greyhounds was undeniable; they stood pale and still like dogs from the Bayeux Tapestry; and the moon which had now moved out from behind the stringy-bark gums gave the garden a look of enchantment. Yanluga would have called it a *mirang*, a place where magic is practised.

Lathrop took two or three steps back, so that he was standing next to Eyre.

'Remarkable, isn't it?' he said, without taking his eyes

off Yanluga. 'You'd be quite amazed at what some of these blackfellows can do. Sensitive to nature, that's what it is; only a step away from being animals themselves, and there's the proof of it. What civilised man could speak to a pack of greyhounds, so that they'd listen?'

Eyre said thickly, 'It seems that he saved my life.'

'Well, you're probably right,' replied Lathrop. 'After all, those are rare hounds, more than £50 apiece they cost me, and I'd have been loathe to shoot them, especially for the sake of a chap who's already trespassed twice in one day both on my property and on my patience; and abused my hospitality to the point of theft. You realise that if I speak to Captain Tennant, I could have you locked up; hanged, even. It wouldn't do you any harm at all, hanging. It might improve your manners.'

Eyre said, 'I am conscious, sir, that I owe you an apology. But I hardly think that being in love with Charlotte can be construed as a capital crime.'

'Abduction is a capital crime, sir.'

'There was no question of abduction, sir. Charlotte came to meet me of her own free will.'

Lathrop slowly turned his head to look at Eyre with small and shiny eyes.

'If I was the kind of father who was unaware of his daughter's extreme wilfulness; and was not quite accustomed to tantrums and foot-stamping and deliberate disobedience, especially during discussions about which young men are suitable companions for a girl of her quality and which young men are not; then I would be quite minded to whip you. But as it is, I *am* aware, and I *am* accustomed, and consequently I shan't.'

Eyre climbed slowly and painfully to his feet, with Utyana staying close by in case he needed help. He wiped his bloody mouth with the back of his bloody hand.

'I think I should go now,' he said. 'I'd like to wash out these bites before they go septic, and bandage myself up.'

Lathrop stared at him with a tight, forced smile. 'Of course you would, of course you would. Bandage yourself up, that's right. But there's one small aspect of this evening's amusements which still concerns me.'

Captain Henry called over, 'Can I leash the dogs now, sir? Seems as if they're growing restless.'

'In a moment,' Lathrop told him; then turned back to Eyre. 'What I'd like to know is, how was tonight's tryst arranged? That's what I'd like to know. And why is young Yanluga here? He was the one who drove you around with my own daughter in my own carriage while I was off in Sydney, wasn't he? Could it have been *he* who helped you to meet my daughter in the woods, in the dark, under the most improper of circumstances?'

Eyre glanced across the ha-ha. Yanluga had raised his arms now, and was chanting to the dogs, a long, repetitive chant. But there was no doubt that the hounds were beginning to twitch now, and lick their lips, and paw at the grass.

Lathrop said, 'I haven't punished him, you know; and until I discovered him here tonight I wasn't intending to. I like to think that I'm a forgiving employer, on occasions, as well as a stern one. But what he did tonight was really unforgivable.'

'He saved my life,' Eyre repeated.

'Ah,' said Lathrop. 'But had you not been here; had Yanluga not arranged a sweetheart's meeting for you; then there would have been no need for him to save your life, now would there? So, who do we have to blame for all of tonight's distress? Why, Yanluga.'

Eyre said, 'Leave him be. Please, for Charlotte's sake. For pity's sake.'

Lathrop peered at Eyre maliciously, as if he were trying to make out where he was in a particularly obnoxious fog. 'Let me tell you something, sir. I am an exemplary husband, a benevolent father, and a trustworthy businessman. But, I am not a monkey. I have never been a monkey and I never will be a monkey, and you won't make me one, I promise you.'

With that, he lifted his musket from his shoulder; and,

still smiling at Eyre, cocked it. Then he swung around, and aimed it directly at Yanluga.

'Boy!' he called.

Yanluga didn't look up at first; couldn't, because he was trying to keep the hounds calm. But then he glanced up quickly once; and then again and squinted at Lathrop in uncertainty and fear.

'What the devil are you doing?' Eyre demanded. 'You're not going to shoot him, not in cold blood!'

'Of course not,' said Lathrop. 'I am simply giving the chap a chance to leave my property, and my employ, as smartly as he likes. Boy!' he called again. 'Stop that singing and chanting now, and be off with you! That's it! Make yourself scarce!'

'Sir! called Yanluga. 'Please ask Captain Henry to tie up the dogs first.'

'You just be off,' said Lathrop. 'Captain Henry will take care of the hounds when he pleases.'

'Sir, if I run, sir, the dogs will chase me.'

'As well they might. Now, let's have a look at those sandy-white heels of yours. And make it quick! I've lost enough sleep tonight as it is!'

'You can't do this,' said Eyre. 'Mr Lindsay, listen to me. Those dogs will tear him to pieces before he can get halfway across the garden.'

Lathrop continued to squint along his musket-barrel. 'There are several things you don't understand, Mr Walker; and one of those things is the meaning of justice. What you are seeing now is justice. The wronged employer gives the ungrateful servant the opportunity to leave his property as expeditiously as possible. You won't find one magistrate who won't congratulate me for my fairness and my magnanimity.'

'You windy old fraud!' Eyre shouted at him. 'That's a boy's life you're talking about! Now, put down your gun, tie up those dogs, and let him be.'

Lathrop turned back to Eyre with his face already darkening with anger. He poked the muzzle of the musket at him, and said, in a shaking voice, 'You, Mr Walker—*you*, Mr Walker—you by God have crossed me just once too often. And let me remind you that I could blow your brains out where you stand, and still be well within the law; because you're a trespasser, sir; an illegal interloper; and a known eccentric.'

'Don't you dare to wave that gun at me,' Eyre told him; but at that very instant, on the other side of the ha-ha, Yanluga twisted around and jumped to his feet, and with his head down began to run towards the distant shelter of the gum-trees.

'Ha! Ha!' shouted Lathrop. 'You see! You see what I mean! Doesn't that show you! Isn't that it! The guilty ones always take to their heels! Captain Henry—the dogs, Captain Henry!'

'Yes, sir, Mr Lindsay,' acknowledged Captain Henry, and whistled through the gap in his front teeth, a weird, loud, rising whistle that gave Eyre the irrational sensation that something was flying through the air towards him, like a boomerang. The greyhounds barked, and pranced, and Captain Henry called, '*Koola! Koola! Taiyin! Koola!*'

'No!' shouted Eyre; but Lathrop lifted his musket and discharged it in the air. There was a flat, ear-slapping bang; and a flash; and a sharp smell of gunpowder. Lathrop reappeared through the swirl of smoke with a look in his eyes that was so piggish and menacing the Eyre couldn't find the words to curse him. Instead, he turned to look across the lawns to see if Yanluga had managed to outrun the dogs.

Yanluga had almost reached the gum-trees; but the dogs had gone rushing off after him as soon as Captain Henry had given the word, and now they were only two or three yards behind him, swift as Yanluga's own shadow. Eyre breathed to Lathrop, 'By God, Mr Lindsay,' and hobbled down the side of the ha-ha, and then up the other slope, making his way as quickly as he could manage to the end of the garden. Under the trees, where the bone-white moonlight couldn't penetrate, it was difficult to see what was happening; but for a moment Yanluga's running silhouette was outlined against the pale bark of a large gum, followed hotly by the bobbing heads of the dogs.

'*Koola! Hi! Hi!*' whistled Captain Henry, off to Eyre's left.

Yanluga reached the trees. Eyre could hear his bare feet sprinting across the dry, crackling bark. Then, instantly afterwards, the rush of the dogs. With a high-pitched shout of effort, Yanluga leaped up and grasped an over-hanging branch; first with one hand, dangling for a moment, and then with the other. Two of the greyhounds jumped up at his feet, but he kicked them away, and then tried to swing his legs up so that he could work his way even higher into the tree, suspended underneath the branch like an opossum.

'Yanluga!' Eyre shouted, through swollen lips. 'Yanluga, hold on!'

'Now then, Mr Walker, sir,' called Lathrop, from the far side of the ha-ha. 'Don't give me any trouble.'

Eyre turned around, staggering on his lacerated leg. 'Trouble?' he yelled, almost screeching.

Yanluga was grimly silent, struggling to edge his way further up the blistery bark of the tree, while the dogs sprang and hurtled just beneath him. He had almost reached an elbow in the branch, where he would be able to perch well out of the reach of the greyhounds' jaws. Eyre had limped within ten yards now, and bent down painfully to pick up a dry fallen bough, to beat the dogs away. 'Yanluga!' he called again. 'Hold tight, Yanluga!'

The dogs spun around and around in a yapping frenzy; jumping up at Yanluga like vicious grey fish in a turbulent sea. One of them tore at the back of his shirt, and Yanluga beat at its snout with his hand. But that was all the other dogs needed. One of them sprang up and seized Yanluga's wrist in its jaws; and even though Yanluga shouted and thrashed, the dog hung on to him, its body twirling and swinging in the air, its sharp teeth deeply embedded in his flesh. Another jumped up, and then another, ripping at Yanluga's arm and shoulders. Yanluga held on for one more agonising second, and then dropped heavily to the ground with a cry more of hopeless resignation than of fear.

Eyre came limping forward, swishing his stick fiercely from side to side; but he was already too late. The dog which had first caught Yanluga was worrying and tearing at his wrist, and at last tore the boy's hand right away from his arm, in a grisly web of tendons, and snarled and tossed it. Another dog ripped at Yanluga's thighs, so that the flesh came away from the bone with a terrible noise like tearing linen; and it was then that Yanluga started to scream—a high, warbling scream.

'Off! Jesus! Get off, you devils!' Eyre shouted at the greyhounds, and struck out at them with his stick. But they had caught the smell of fresh blood now, *koola* or Aborigine; and a few glancing blows on the back weren't going to be enough to drive them away.

'Off! Get off! Get off!' Eyre roared at them; and one of them turned for a moment, so that Eyre could catch it a smart blow at the side of the head, and knock it aside. Savagely, it went for Eyre's arm; but Eyre struck it on the shoulder, and then the spine, and yelping it staggered and collapsed in front of him. Shuddering with anger, inflamed with pain, and with Yanluga's agonised screams tearing inside his mind like a fast-growing thorn-bush, Eyre hoisted the bough vertically upright, hesitated, and then brought it down in a piledriving blow right on top of the dog's skull. With a crack, the dog's eyes were squirted out of their sockets, and its head was smashed into fur, bone, blood, and a grey cream of brains.

The ferocity of the remaining five dogs was unabated. Eyre saw Yanluga lift the bloody stump of his wrist in a last attempt to beat them away; but they had already torn open his shirt, and tugged the muscles away from his ribs, and now one of them was stepping backwards, snarling and shaking its head, trying to free itself from a garland of yellow-purplish intestines. Another had torn off most of his scalp, and half of his ear; while a third was chewing and tugging at the rags of his penis.

'*Ngura!*' Captain Henry commanded, from a little way across the lawns. '*Hi, hi, hi! Ngura!*'

The hounds were satisfied now. Bloody-snouted, trailing liver and muscles and intestines behind them, they bounded across to Captain Henry and laid their prizes at his feet. He patted each of them; and then commanded again, '*Ngura!* Back to your shelter!'

Eyre stood still for a moment or two, and then let his stick fall to the grass. He knelt down beside Yanluga; and quite magically Yanluga was still conscious, still alive, and staring at him out of bright red haemorrhaged eyes. His stomach gaped open, and his insides had been draped out for yards across the garden, so that he looked as if he had exploded. But he was still gasping a few last breaths; and his lips still moved.

'*Koppi unga,*' he whispered.

Eyre said, 'What is it? Tell me, what do you want?'

'*Koppi unga,*' Yanluga repeated. His eyes were like those of a demon.

'I don't understand you,' Eyre told him, miserably.

'Ah . . .' said Yanluga. He was silent for nearly a minute, but Eyre could hear him breathing, and hear the sticky sound of his lungs expanding and contracting. 'Water . . .' he said.

Utyana was now standing close by, and when Eyre turned around, he silently handed him a leather bottle full of warm water. Eyre shook a few drops on to his fingers, and touched Yanluga's lips with them. Yanluga said, with great difficulty, 'You are my *ngaitye*, my friend. You must not let them bury me here. This is important to me, sir. Do not let them bury me here, or take me to the hospital and cut me up. Please, sir. I shall never join my ancestors from the dreamtime . . .'

He coughed, a huge spout of blood. Then he said, 'Please sir, find the clever-man they called Yonguldye, he will bury me . . . Please. If I can call you friend.'

Eyre said huskily. 'I will find the man they call Yonguldye. I promise you. Do you know where he is? In Adelaide?'

Yanluga stared at him glassily.

'I have to know where to find him,' Eyre repeated. 'Please, Yanluga. Is Yonguldye in Adelaide?'

Yanluga coughed again, and then again. Lathrop had walked up to them now, and was standing watching over them with his gun crooked under his arm. 'Chap's gone, I should say,' he remarked.

Eyre said, 'Yanluga, please. You have to tell me.'

Yanluga's face was grey now, like a grate of burned-out ashes. A large shining bubble of blood formed on his lips, and then burst. The smell of blood and bile and faeces was almost more than Eyre could stomach. It was the terrible odour of real death; and Eyre closed his eyes and prayed and prayed that God would take Yanluga out of his pain.

Yanluga whispered, 'Yonguldye is northwards, sometimes; sometimes west; Yonguldye is The Darkness; that is his name.'

Lathrop said, 'Chap's raving. Think I ought to put him out of his misery?'

Yanluga tried to lift his head. His last words were, '. . . *kalyan . . . ungune . . .*' and then the blood poured from the side of his mouth like upturned treacle, and he died.

Eyre stayed on his knees for a long time. Lathrop watched him, whistling 'D'ye Ken John Peel' over and over again, tunelessly. At last Eyre turned to him, and said, 'You've killed a man. You understand that I'm going to have to report you.'

Lathrop shook his head. 'I don't think so, Mr Walker. Chap was mine, you see. My servant. My responsibility. Welfare, board and lodging; discipline too. Chap disobeyed me. You know it for yourself, for you were a party to it. Hence, chap gets punished.'

'You call this punishment?' Eyre demanded, spreading his hands to indicate the gruesome remains which were twisted across the lawns.

'I call it justice,' Lathrop retorted. 'And if I were such a stickler for punishment as you believe me to be, I'd have you reported for killing my dog. Lucky for you it was a slow one, long in the tooth. But that dog was worth £30 of any man's money; and you've killed it; no reason; no provocation. Whereas this chap, why, only paid him £3.2s. 6d the year; worth a damned sight less than the dog.'

Eyre stood in the moonlight, shaking. He was too shocked and too painfully injured to argue with Lathrop now about the value of a man's life. He knew, too, that Lathrop would be given no trouble by the law. At a time when Englishmen were still liable to be hung for stealing a hat, blackfellows had no rights to life whatsoever. It was only two years ago that twenty-eight Aborigines had been murdered at Myall Creek; and the defence put up at the trial of the settlers who had killed them had been that 'we were not aware that in killing blacks we were violating the law, as it has been so frequently done before'. Seven settlers had been hung; but the Myall Creek trial had done nothing to change the general view of Adelaide's colonists that blackfellows were little more than indigenous vermin, filthy and primitive.

Eyre said, 'I'll pay you for the dog, if you can accept recompense by the instalment. They don't pay me very much down at the South Australian Company.'

'Don't let me see hide nor hair of you again; that'll be recompense enough,' said Lathrop.

'One thing more,' said Eyre. 'I'd like to take this boy's body with me. If your servants could find a box for him, I'll come by with a cart in the morning.'

Lathrop stared at him. 'What's your game?' he wanted to know. 'You can't take that body; that belongs to me. What do you think you're going to do with it? Sell it to the hospital? Or show it to the magistrate, more like.'

'He asked me—just before he died—for a proper Aborigine burial.'

'A what?'

'A ritual burial, according to his own beliefs.'

'That's barbaric nonsense,' Lathrop protested. 'He'll have a Christian burial and like it.'

'But he wasn't a Christian,' Eyre insisted. 'And if you don't bury him according to his own beliefs, then his soul won't ever be able to rest. Can't you understand that?'

Lathrop eyed Eyre for a moment, and then pugnaciously bulged out his jowls, like a sand goanna. 'Captain Henry,' he said, quite quietly.

'Yes, sir, Mr Lindsay.'

'Mr Lindsay, please listen to me,' Eyre urged him.

'I have listened enough,' Lathrop retorted. 'Now clear off my property before I have the dogs let out again. Captain Henry, do you take out the pony-trap and take this gentleman back to his diggings, wherever they may be. Utyana!'

'Yes, sir.'

'Clear this rubbish off the lawn before it attracts the dingoes. You understand me? Sweep up.'

'Yes, sir.'

Captain Henry helped Eyre to limp over to the stables. Eyre stood against the stable gate with his eyes closed, his legs and his arms throbbing and swollen, while Captain Henry harnessed up one of Mr Lindsay's small bays, and wheeled out the trap.

'Captain Henry,' said Eyre, without opening his eyes.

'Mr Walker?' asked Captain Henry, softly, anxious that Lathrop should not overhear him.

'Captain Henry, tell me what *kalyan ungune* means.'

'*Kalyan ungune lewin*, sir. It means "goodbye".'

Four

Mrs McConnell had already girded herself to retire to bed when Captain Henry brought Eyre back to his apartments on Hindley Street. She came out on to the front verandah in curling-papers and a voluminous dressing-gown of flowered cotton, her lantern raised high, like a lighted thicket of moths and flying insects; and a long pastry-pin swinging from a string around her wrist, in case it was blackfellows, or burglars, or drunken diggers.

High above the roof of the house, the Southern Cross hung suspended, its two brightest stars, Alpha and Beta Crucis, winking like the heliographs of distant civilisations.

Mrs McConnell said, 'God in his clouds, what's happened?' and came down the steps to the pony-trap with her pastry-pin rattling against the banisters. Captain Henry climbed down from the trap and held the horse, while Mrs McConnell lifted her lantern over Eyre's bruised and bloodied face.

'What's happened to you?' demanded Mrs McConnell. 'Who did this? You, blackface, who did this? And no demurring.'

Eyre said awkwardly, 'It's all right, Mrs McConnell. I was involved in an accident, of sorts. Fell off my bicycle.'

'Fell off your bicycle into a passing tribe of cannibals, more like it,' said Mrs McConnell. 'Look at you, you're bitten all over. Those are *bites*!'

Eyre attempted to stand up and greet Mrs McConnell with bravado. He almost managed it; but his legs closed up like cheap penknives and he sat down very hard again on the pony-trap's horsehair seat; and couldn't manage anything more than a puffy, lopsided smile.

'Tie up that pony, blackface, and help me to carry the poor gentleman inside,' Mrs McConnell told Captain Henry. Captain Henry did as he was told, and then between the two of them they managed to drag Eyre up the wooden steps, across the verandah, and into the hallway, where they laid him down on the brocade-covered sofa on which it was Mrs McConnell's pleasure (believing herself to be quality) to keep all her visitors waiting, even her friends from the Sewing Circle.

'You look regularly chewed,' said Mrs McConnell. 'It's a wonder you're still with us. Who did this, blackface? Who's the folk responsible?'

'Not my position to say, madam,' said Captain Henry, uncomfortably.

Mrs McConnell brandished her pastry-pin at him, and Captain Henry squinted at it in alarm.

'How about a crack on the skull?' Mrs McConnell asked him. 'And believe you me, when you're cracked with *this*, you know it. Not like your clubs or your bangarangs.'

'Please, madam, all I can say is that I work for Mr Lindsay, madam; and that this gentleman was hurt by Mr Lindsay's greyhounds.'

'Lathrop Lindsay? That bullfrog? Well, then, be off with you and tell Mr Lindsay from Mrs McConnell that he had better not take Hindley Street for a year or so; unless he fancies a crack on the skull with Chumley here.'

Captain Henry gratefully retreated from the hallway; and out into the street, and turned the pony-trap around, and whipped up the pony with a high cry of 'whup! whup!' Mrs McConnell closed the door and came across to Eyre with a sweep of her dressing-gown, her forehead solicitously ribbed like a sand-dune.

'We're going to have to clean up these bites at once,' said Mrs McConnell. 'I remember a friend of Dogger's, Mr Loomis, he was bitten by dogs and died of the lockjaw in less than a week. Can you manage to climb the stairs?'

Eyre nodded; and with Mrs McConnell helping him, he managed to climb one stair at a time up to his room. He knew better than to ask if Dogger might not lend a hand. Dogger was invariably unconscious at this time of the evening, after three jugs of home-made beer. His snores were already reverberating across the landing, like a man giving poor imitations of a prowling lion. Mrs McConnell said, 'Off with your trousers, Mr Walker; and I'll fetch a basin.'

Eyre hesitated, but Mrs McConnell said, 'I've seen a few men in my day, Mr Walker; and I'm beyond embarrassment. There used to be a telescope at Brighthelmstone beach, you know, which the young girls used in order to spy on their young beaux bathing in the sea; and many a girl was saved from a disappointing marriage by being afforded a view in advance; although my aunt used to say that they were nothing more than so many whelks.'

With that strange non sequitur, she bustled off, all curling-papers and flowery skirts, to fetch the jug and the basin, and the Keatings Salve, which she always swore was so effective that it 'could heal a severed leg'.

Eyre lay back on his narrow iron-framed bed, still trembling with shock. The bite in his leg hurt the most; a penetrating ache that felt as if the metal teeth of a kangaroo-snare had been embedded in his thigh. His right eye had almost closed up, and when he touched his cheek, he could feel a crust of dried blood on it. He supposed that he ought to undress himself, ready for Mrs McConnell's nursing, but somehow he felt too sensitive, as if he wasn't going to be able to bear the sensation of moving his sleeves over his skin.

'Oh, God,' he whispered. Then, even more softly, 'Oh, Charlotte.'

He looked around him; and his room, through half-focused eyes, had the blurriness of a room in a dream. It was plain enough, wallpapered with brown-and-white flowers, with a cheap varnished bureau; and a bedside table that had once belonged on the SS *Titania*, complete with brass handles and tobacco-pipe burns; and a carved mahogany wardrobe that looked as if it had been the only entry in a competition for upright coffins. Beside him, enhancing the blurriness with a halo of light, stood an oil-lamp with an engraved glass globe, and beneath it, his small brass carriage-clock, and the two oval-framed daguerreotypes of his mother and his father; the first long dead and the second far away.

Eyre looked at the picture of his mother and for the first time in two years his eyes filled with tears. He felt suddenly alone, and hurt, and further away from Derbyshire than he could ever remember. He couldn't even assuage his grief by laying flowers on his mother's grave. But he could think of the rain, and the green silent hills of Baslow and Bakewell; and he could still remember those days as a boy when he had sat watching a distant rainbow, and his mother had gently touched his shoulder, and said, 'God's paintbox, Eyre, that's what it is.'

And now he lay here shivering, thinking of Charlotte, erotic but innocent, tempting but afraid; and of his mother, calm but dead. He thought of time, and how quickly it had passed and taken his mother's life away and how his small brass carriage-clock was measuring his own life away, second by second, month by month, unceasingly.

His father had been the vicar of St Crispin's, in Baslow. Thin-faced, with drawn-in cheeks, and old-fashioned sidewhiskers, and a row of black silk-faced buttons in front that must have taken him ten minutes each morning to fasten. The Reverend Leonard Walker, dry and determined, the one and only messenger of God. Conscientious, grave, a believer in angels and Holy Grails; and also in the life everlasting, at least for those who were saved. And he, of course, was the only agency through which the people of Baslow could achieve salvation.

He would take Eyre for walks: miles across the Dales, in rain or sleet or misty sunshine. But the walks were not for enjoyment or for exercise; they were visits to the poor; to dribbling grannies or Mongol children; or to vermin-ridden cottages where filthy women suckled filthier children, and where fathers mounted their daughters, night after night, with the energy born of desperation, regardless of what the Bible might say; or of how many idiot children they might conceive. And the Reverend Leonard Walker would rest his dry, thin-fingered hands on their lousy heads, and bless them; and accept their gifts of salt pork and lardy-cakes; but leave them in no doubt whatsoever when he said goodbye tht he would expect them in church that Sunday, to save their miserable souls.

Eyre had been brought up in the gloom of the vicarage and the light of God. He had sat at his desk on hot summer afternoons, dressed in thick woollen socks and buttoned-up jackets, watching the days pass him by through closed windows, his nail-bitten hands resting on his open copy of *Pilgrim's Progress*. 'Then I saw that there was a way to hell, even from the gates of heaven.' And the pendulum-clock on the wall had measured his childish weariness hour by hour; until it was time for supper; and prayers; and bed.

By the time he was ten, Eyre had felt that life was nothing but tedious duty, of silent meals with grace to begin them and grace to end them, and of books with no pictures.

He had been quiet, friendless, and withdrawn. His only toys had been a whipping-top and a wooden Noah's Ark. On the few occasions when his father allowed him out to 'disport himself', as he put it, Eyre had walked down the muddy lane to talk to the neighbouring farmer's collie-dog, which stood chained and miserable by the fence. Eyre used to have daydreams about setting the dog free, and running away with it to sea. He had never seen the sea; but old Mr Woolley had been apprenticed to an East Indiaman, and had told Eyre with great earnestness that the sea was 'like glass, and like moving mountains, and sometimes like hell and damnation all put together'.

Eyre's mother had been a gentle quiet-spoken Derbyshire girl of no particular beauty. But although she had been completely overwhelmed by his father's strictness, she had graced Eyre's childhood with a warmth that had at least made it tolerable. He remembered the softness of his mother's cheek, the soapy-scenty smell of her neck, the sharpness of her starched aprons. One day, when Eyre was twelve, she had walked all the way to Bakewell market in the rain, and a week later she had died of pneumonia. So white! and not like his mother at all. And after that, life at the vicarage, already strict, had become an endless penance of catechism and parochial duties, to say nothing of the undercooked tripe and slippery onions with which Eyre had regularly been served by his father's housemaid, the turkey-necked Mrs Negus.

When he was twenty, Eyre had been sent by his father to Chesterfield, to study divinity under Dr Croker. But there, two people had changed his life forever. The first had been his landlady's daughter, a flirtatious and friendly young girl called Elaine, who had teased him and winked at him, and at last (the day after his twenty-first birthday) had taken his virginity from him, in his own rumpled bed, all giggles and perspiration, on a stormy afternoon when the thunder had rolled around and around Chesterfield's twisted spire, and the rain had clattered in the gutters outside his bedroom window. Eyre had delighted in her plump white pink-nippled breasts, sugar-mice he had called them; and in her chubby thighs, and the moist blonde hair between her legs; and most of all in the conspiratorial way she had whispered in his ear, her breath like the wind from a church-organ bellows, 'I'm glad you're a bit of a devil, Eyrey, as well as an angel.' Eyre had thought of his catechism, and of *Pilgrim's Progress*, but then he had smiled less than shyly and kissed her, and decided that God really could be bountiful, after all. And that His gifts could embrace more than fishes, and loaves of wheatmeal bread, and more than divine inspiration, too.

Then there had been John Hardesty, a fellow student, curly and serious; who had given up his theology studies after two terms to go to Australia, to raise sheep. John had been the son of a wealthy Derbyshire sheep farmer, and had been enthused for years with the idea of making his own fortune in a strange land. His father had stood against him, and insisted that at least one member of his family should be given to God, but at last John had decided that he would have to go. He had begged Eyre to emigrate with him. In South Australia they were all free men, and from what he had heard, they were making thousands. Thousands! And not a word of religion; thank God.

Eyre had been tempted. But whenever he had returned to the vicarage at Baslow, he had been unable to summon up the courage to tell his father that he was leaving. Four years had passed; four years of unhappiness and silent suppers; until the time had come for Eyre to be ordained. It was then that he had simply told his father, 'I'm leaving for Australia. I'm sorry. I think I'll probably go tomorrow.'

His father had stared at him. 'You're due to be ordained in three weeks.'

'Yes,' Eyre had told him. Then, quite gently, 'Nonetheless, I'm going.'

There had been a moment of unexpressed emotion; a moment which Eyre would remember for the whole of his life. His father had stared at him with such anger that Eyre almost believed that supernatural forks of lightning would flicker from his eyes; and thunder blare out of his mouth. But then he had reached across the table and laid his hand on top of Eyre's hand, and said, 'I shall pray for you. And I shall ask of you only one thing: that you always remember that I love you.'

In that one moment, Eyre began to understand for the first time the spirit of Christian tolerance; and also to see how lovingly, as well as how severely, his father had brought him up.

He and his father had taken a last walk together on Big Moor, the evening before Eyre was due to leave. The clouds had been dark and soft and a stirring wind had blown through the grass from the south-west. There had been rain in the air, and the moistness of the atmosphere made distant noises sound clearer: the barking of dogs, the jingling of bridles.

Eyre's father had stood a little way off, his face to the wind. 'Don't go believing what people tell you,' he had said. 'But never say you can't to anybody. What you want to be done, through the power of God, can be done. What needs to be done, will be done.'

The next morning, with all of his bags packed, Eyre had held his father very tight. His father had seemed so bony and smelled of Latakia snuff. Patting Eyre's back, his father had said, 'Don't cry; for we shall never see each other again.'

Five

Eyre had sailed seven weeks later from Portsmouth, bound for Port Adelaide on the merchant-vessel *Asthoroth*. On a drizzling day in early September he had left behind him an England over which Queen Victoria had reigned for only a year; in which Charles Dickens had just launched a periodical called *Master Humphrey's Clock*; in which Gordon of Khartoum was a five-year-old boy living at Woolwich; and from which transportation to Australia for life was still a common punishment for stealing cheese, or sheep, or linen.

As the *Asthoroth* had sailed past Whale Island on a slackish wind, Eyre had seen at close quarters the hulk of the *York*, moored to a dismal row of other hulks. It was on these rotting hulls of old sailing-ships that convicts were held before they could be embarked at Spithead for Australia, and they were a particular Purgatory of their own. Eyre had watched the *York* in awe as the *Asthoroth* had slid silently by: the hulk had no masts or sails now, and her superstructure had been replaced by a crazy collection of wooden cabins, complete with smoking chimneys, ladders, balconies, walkways, and washing-lines. The stench of ordure and grease as they passed downwind made Eyre's stomach tighten with nausea and dread.

He had heard about the hulks; about the vicious whippings and the diet of rotten food; and how many sick and elderly convicts died in their bunks, still within sight of England.

The *York*'s sinister bulk had impressed him deeply. No sound had come from its decks and cabins, no singing; only the steady muffled throb of a drum. He had stood by the *Asthoroth*'s after-rail as she bent at last to the breeze beyond Southsea, watching the convicts' tattered washing as it idly flapped on the lines, and the fishy-smelling smoke of their midday meal, as it tumbled away to the east like vanishing hopes. Eyre had thought of the words of Jeremy Bentham's imaginary judge, as he sentenced a thief to transportation, 'I sentence you, but to what I know not; perhaps to storm and shipwreck; perhaps to infectious disorders; perhaps to famine; perhaps to be massacred by savages; perhaps to be devoured by wild beasts. Away—take your chance; perish or prosper; suffer or enjoy. I rid myself of the sight of you.'

He had turned away at last to find one of the *Asthoroth*'s crew watching him, a red-headed Hampshire man with striped pants and earrings, and eyes as sharp as whalebone needles.

'You hear that drum?' he had remarked, in an oddly challenging voice. 'They're flogging a man, and that drum marks the time. Fifty lashes, by the count so far.'

'Well, God have mercy on him,' Eyre had replied.

The red-headed sailor had snorted mucus from his nose, and wiped it on his arm. 'Don't you go feeling sorry for them wretches,' he had said. 'You'll have trouble enough looking out for yourself, once we reach Australee.'

'I was thinking how they're treated as refuse; as men without souls,' Eyre had said.

'Yes,' the red-headed sailor had agreed. 'For once sentenced, that's what they be.'

It had taken the *Asthoroth* eight-and-a-half months to

reach Port Adelaide, in the last week of June 1839. During the voyage Eyre had become a stone thinner and his dark hair had become streaked by the sun. He had also become more confident, more sure of himself, although he had still been uncertain what he would do to make his fortune once he reached Australia.

He had rounded the Cape of Good Hope on a spanking bright day, and seen Table Mountain with her grey-and-white crown of clouds. He had crossed the Indian ocean under a sun that was as hot as a blacksmith's hammer. He had eaten fresh pineapples in Colombo, in Ceylon, on a night when the rain thundered down among the leaves; and had his fortune told in Singapore, in the hush of a Buddhist temple, with incense drifting across the courtyards like ghosts. The fortune-teller had warned him, 'Beware of your own fortitude. Beware of your own faith. Your own determination is your greatest weakness. Beware, too, of the sun; for the sun will be your most implacable enemy, and you will learn to curse it.'

He had seen parakeets and leaping dolphins and the sleek fins of cruising sharks. He had awoken one morning off Tandjung Puting, in Borneo, to find the ocean as still and steamy as a laundry, with no wind, and no sound but the cries of invisible fishermen in the fog. And he had sighted Australia at last, *Australia Felix*, as Major Thomas Mitchell had named it, 'Happy Australia'; a long low coastline with a cream of surf, and clusters of dark green trees.

'Don't be tricked by what you see on the coast,' the red-headed sailor had told him sharply, as the *Asthoroth* had tacked across the green seas of the Great Australian Bight on her last leg to Port Adelaide. 'Beyond that there coastline is nothing but desert; at least, as far as anybody's gone, and lived to tell about it. Some say the land has a great freshwater ocean, right in the middle of it, for many rivers run that way, inland. But I wouldn't trust my chances to find it. Not me, sir. Some's even gone off into the desert with boats. Boats, if you please! And they've found the boats later on the sand-dunes, crewed by skellingtons.'

Eyre had listened, and eaten a pomegranate, and said nothing. The red-headed sailor had seemed to have a down on Australia, in any case; and had complained ever since they had left Portsmouth that Australia was the Lord's joke.

'Why, what can you make of a land where winter is summer, and summer is winter; a land in which there are birds with wings but don't fly; and animals with heads like rabbits which bounce instead of walking; and evergreen trees which are no use at all for building, but are always crowded with birds—birds that sit still all day and laugh. Laugh! They can drive you clean mad with their laughing.'

He had often spoken, too, of the blackfellows. 'A less Godly race of human animals there never was; bare-bum naked most of them, women too; but they paint their faces and smear themselves with ashes and grease, so you wouldn't take a fancy to any of them. They think that rocks and trees and pools of water all have souls of their own; that *places* have souls, and a sadder lot you could never meet. They sleep at night with wild dogs for blankets, when it's cold, but don't ever suppose that they're friendly. Most of them will spear you through, just like that, like a pork-chop if you give them the chance.'

The red-headed sailor had sniffed loudly, and said, 'If you ask me, Australia was the land which the Lord used for practice, before He created the rest of the Earth; and so learned by His mistakes. Not a land to love, Australia.'

They had sailed into Port Adelaide on a cool, still, overcast afternoon. The port itself was a collection of long wharves and tall warehouses, and a few untidy stores and office-buildings. The water had been lapping up to the silty edge of the shore, cluttered with nodding beer-bottles and discarded spars and empty broken baskets. In the far distance, off to the east, barely visible through the cloud, Eyre had been able to make out the greenish-blue peaks of the Mount Lofty range, dark with grass after the winter rains.

The red-headed sailor had watched Eyre from the quarter-deck as he disembarked; and grinned; and spat noisily into the water. Eyre had hesitated, and looked back at him; but then he had turned his face away, towards the land he would now have to call his own.

He had written to his college friend John Hardesty the Christmas before last, telling him that he was considering coming out to Australia, but of course he had left England well before any reply could have reached him, if John had replied at all. But he had an address at Angaston, and tomorrow he would hire a carter to take him out there.

He had been looking for a baggage-porter to carry his trunks for him, and to advise him where he might spend the night, when he had caught sight of his first Aborigines; two of them, standing by the unloaded luggage; and he had stopped where he was, jostled by disembarking passengers and messenger-boys and busy men in tall hats and bright waistcoats, and he had openly stared.

There had been a tall bearded man, quite upright and handsome, except that his face was smeared with grease and wilga, a thick red ochre. The man had been wearing a European jacket, but he had fastened it around himself like a cloak, and tucked up the superfluous sleeves. He had worn a loin-cloth, fastened with bone pins, and a band of stringy fur around his head. In one hand he had held a long spear. His other hand had rested on the shoulders of a young girl; small, broad-faced, and shaggy-haired, but surprisingly handsome. She had been wearing a rough cloth cloak tied up in the same way as the man's jacket, with an untrimmed hem; but to Eyre's disturbance, nothing else. One breast had been bared like a glossy black aubergine, and her curly pubic hair had been visible to all who crowded the wharf.

'Carry your trunks, sir?' a bald old man had demanded.

'Yes. Yes, please,' Eyre had replied, distracted.

The bald man had loaded Eyre's baggage on to a small

two-wheeled cart, drawn by a moth-eaten donkey, and had bidden Eyre to climb up on to the seat. But as they had trundled away from the *Asthoroth*, Eyre had been unable to take his eyes off the two Aborigines, standing in such a striking pose, attenuated black figures against the pearl-grey water of the harbour, half-wild, mysterious, magic, sexual; like no people that Eyre had ever seen before.

'First time?' the old man had asked. He had boasted scarcely any teeth at all and his bald head had been as brown and wrinkled as a pickled walnut.

Eyre had nodded. The cart had bounced and rattled out of the port; and south-eastwards towards the settlement of Adelaide itself. The rough muddy road was lined with scrubby bushes; and off to the right Eyre could see rows of sand-dunes, and hear the waters of the Gulf of St Vincent slurring against the beach.

'Got a place to kip, squire?' the old man had asked.

'No,' Eyre had told him. It had begun to drizzle; a thin, fine, rain from the mountains.

'Well then,' the old man had decided. 'It's Mrs Dedham's for you. Every boy's mother, Mrs Dedham. Solid cooking, clean sheets, and Bible-reading afore bedtime.'

They had driven through the low-lying outskirts of Adelaide, the donkey slipping from time to time on the boggy road, and the rain growing steadier and heavier; until the old man took a sugar-sack, which he had ingeniously rolled up into a kind of huge beret, and tugged it on to his head. Eyre had watched the rain drip from the brim of his hat, and shivered.

They had rolled slowly past sheds, mud-huts with calico roofs and calico-covered windows and even an upturned jolly-boat, with windows cut into its sides, and a tin chimney. But then at last they had reached the wide, muddy streets of the city centre, where there were rows of plain, flat-fronted houses, and shops, and courtyards; all interspersed with groves of gum-trees and acacias; and quite handsomely laid out. Although it was a wet afternoon, Eyre had been impressed by the number of people in the streets, and the scores of bullock-carts and carriages. He had expected the people to be roughly-dressed, but apart from a group of bearded men in tied-up trousers who were probably prospectors, most of the passers-by were smartly turned-out in tail-coats and top-hats. The women looked a little old-fashioned in their bonnets and shawls, but what they lacked in modishness they made up for in the self-assured way they promenaded along the wooden sidewalks, mistresses of a new and confident country.

Eyre had seen more Aborigines, most of them dressed in *bukas*, or native capes, but a few of them in European clothes, although one girl had been wearing an English skirt with her head and one arm through the waist, and the other arm protruding from the open placket.

Mrs Dedham had owned a fine large house at the east end of Rundle Street, built like its neighbours out of limestone, brick, and pisé. She had come bustling out to greet Eyre as if he were her prodigal son; even hugged him against her huge starched bosom; and offered him steak-and-kidney pudding at once. In the kitchen, as he had eaten with determined unhungriness, she had told him how she had come to Australia from Yorkshire with her dear husband Stanley, and how Stanley had started a sheep-farm at Teatree Gully, only to be taken at the peak of his success by 'shrinking of the mesenteric glands', an ailment that would later be diagnosed as peritonitis. Mrs Dedham had sold off the farm and bought herself what she like to call 'a gentleman's hotel'; three good meals a day, no visiting women, no whistling, and a communal Sunday lunch after church.

That night, in his unfamiliar bed, with an unfamiliar light shining across the ceiling, Eyre had lain awake and thought of his father. Outside in the street he had heard laughter, and a woman calling, 'Fancy yourself, then, do you?' Then more laughter.

The following day, he had paid Mrs Dedham's

handyman four shillings to drive him out to Hope Valley, to find John Hardesty. It had still been raining as they had followed the narrow rutted track between dripping gums and wet sparkling spinifex grass; until at last they had arrived at the sheep farm, and the rain had begun to ease off.

The farm's owner had been a stocky man in a wide leather hat, his face mottled by drink and weather. He had said very little, but taken Eyre to the back of the house, and shown him the wooden-paled enclosure where John Hardesty had been buried, over two years ago.

Eyre had stood by the grave for five or ten minutes, then returned to the farmhouse. 'Had he been ill?' he had asked.

The farmer had shrugged. 'You could say that.'

Eyre had replaced his hat. The farmer had stared at him for a while, and then said, 'Did away with himself. Hung himself with wire in his own barn. Nobody knows why.'

'I see,' Eyre had said; and then, 'Thank you for showing me.'

He had decided to stay on at Mrs Dedham's; and so that he could pay her rent of 2s 0½d the week, he had found himself a job in the tea department of M. & S. Marks' Grocery Stores, on Hindley Street, scooping out fragrant Formosas and Assams, and also brewing up tea in barrels, since some customers still preferred to buy their tea the old-fashioned way, ready infused, for warming up at home. Just after the New Year, however, he had met Christopher Willis at a party given by Marks' for all of their suppliers; and Christopher had arranged for him to take up a clerical post with the South Australian Company, for 1s 3d more per week. 'And far more future, old man, than tea.'

His first sweetheart in Adelaide had been a saucy young Wiltshire girl called Clara, daughter of one of the aides to the Governor and Commissioner, Colonel George Gawler. Clara was green-eyed and chubbily pretty and Eyre had courted her with the frustrated enthusiasm that only a single man living at Mrs Dedham's could have mustered. He had bought his bicycle solely to impress her, even though it had cost him two weeks' wages; and he had taken her for a wobbling ride on the handlebars from one end of King William Street to the other, with Clara shrieking and kicking her ankles.

On his return to Mrs Dedham's that evening, he had found a note waiting for him, to the effect that Clara's father had complained that Eyre had made 'an unforgivable public exhibition of his daughter's virtue'. Mrs Dedham herself had told him the following morning, over veal pudding, that she considered it best if he sought alternative accommodation.

'I don't expect my gentlemen to be bishops,' she said, bulging out her neck, and lacing her fingers tightly together under her bosoms. 'But I don't expect them to be hooligans, or peculiars, either.'

That was how he had found himself staying with Mrs McConnell, on Hindley Street; and from the beginning Mrs McConnell had taken a special shine to him, and pampered him so much that in three weeks he had put on all the weight he had lost on the voyage from Portsmouth. She cooked marvellous pies, with glazed and decorated crusts, and washed his shirts and starched them until they creaked. All he had to do in return was call her 'Mother', and accompany her once or twice a month to the Methodist chapel by Adelaide barracks. She did so like to go to chapel in company; and Dogger wouldn't go for anything. Dogger said that he had carried on quite enough conversations with the Lord in the outback; and that if he went to chapel, the Lord would only say, 'Christ, Dogger, not you again.'

'You have to understand that a fellow needed God, in the outback,' Dogger had frequently explained. 'You didn't have anybody else, after all. The kowaris didn't talk to you; the dingoes didn't talk to you; and the damned skinks and shinglebacks, they'd either puff themselves up or yawn at you something terrible.'

Eyre had nodded sagely, although it was not until later

that he had learned that kowaris were desert rats, which preyed ferociously on insects and lizards and smaller rodents; and that skinks and shinglebacks were both prehistoric-looking species of lizard.

Mrs McConnell came back with the jug and the basin and the pale green jar of Keatings Salve.

'You've not undressed,' she said.

Eyre started to unbutton his shirt. 'I felt too sore,' he confessed. 'And a little too tired, too.'

'The salve will soon make you feel better.'

She tugged off his clothes in a businesslike way, until he lay naked on the bed. Then she carefully washed out his bites, and sponged the rest of his body, his chest, his back; and laid a cool wet cloth on his forehead. 'You sometimes remind me of my son Geoffrey,' she said.

'Yes,' Eyre acknowledged. She had told him that several times before.

'Geoffrey always used to say that life was like a sugar-basin.'

'Yes,' Eyre agreed.

Mrs McConnell washed the dark crucifix of hair on his chest, so that it was stuck to his skin in whorls. Quite matter-of-factly, she held his penis, and rolled back the foreskin, and washed that, too. He looked at her through puffy, half-closed eyes, and he was sure that for a second he saw something in her expression that was more than matronly; but then she smiled, and clapped her hands, and said, 'You must have a clean nightshirt. I'll bring you one of Geoffrey's.'

He lay on the bed waiting for her. He smelled of camomile and vanilla and tincture of zinc, which seemed to be the principal ingredients of Keating's Salve. He found himself thinking of Geoffrey. Poor Geoffrey who had said that life was like a sugar-basin, because every taste of it was so sweet. Geoffrey had gone riding, a keen and straightforward young boy of eighteen; so far as Eyre could gather; and been bitten in the ankle by a death-adder, the snake the Aborigines called *tityowe*. Mrs McConnell had stayed in her back parlour with the drapes drawn for nearly three months, until Dogger had at last come home from Broken Hill, and persuaded her to start living her own life again.

That night, Eyre dreamed of Yanluga, sobbing, crying for help. He dreamed of Charlotte, too, gliding across the lawns of Waikerie Lodge as if she were on oiled wheels, instead of feet. He dreamed that Mrs McConnell came into his room naked, but with the black body of an Aborigine woman, and that she knelt astride his face and buried him between her thighs.

He woke up at dawn; when the sky was a thin, cold colour; and he was shivering. He climbed stiff-legged out of bed in his ankle-length nightshirt and went shuffling to the window, and leaned against the frame. Hindley Street was deserted. The only signs of life were the lighted window of Keith's Fancy Bakery across the street, and a single Aborigine boy sitting close to the bakery steps wrapped up in his *buka*, a puppy crouching between his bare feet.

Eyre began to feel that something momentous was about to happen, and that his life had already changed beyond recall. He sat down on the side of the bed, frowning, still shivering, not understanding why he felt this way. And the morning breeze which lifted the dust in the street also rattled the casement like a secret message from one prisoner to another, 'it's time to be free.'

Six

Mrs McConnell brought him a breakfast of oat cakes, ham, and soft-boiled eggs, with honey from old Mr Jellop's apiary. She parked her big bottom on the bed and watched him eat; smiling and nodding in encouragement each time he forked a piece of ham into his mouth, or bit into an oat cake.

'You're going to have to rest for a few days, get your strength back,' she said.

'Mrs McConnell, I'm a little bruised, but that's all. I really want to go and get my bicycle back, before some blackfellow steals it, or Lathrop Lindsay finds it and smashes it to bits.'

'You're not thinking of going out there today?'

'As soon as I've finished my breakfast, as a matter of fact. And then I'm going to cycle over and see Christopher.'

'But you're still invalid! I can't allow it! Supposing you came over queer?'

'Mrs McConnell, I can't tell you how much I appreciate your nursing. You've been more than kind. But I'm really quite well.'

'*Well*? Do you call that *well*? Your eye looks like a—like a squashed cycad fruit.'

At that moment, Dogger appeared in the doorway, his hair sticking wildly up in the air, his face in a condition of chronic disassembly, his striped nightshirt as crumpled as if he had been tossed into a wool-baler.

'Constance,' he said. 'Don't mollycoddle the boy. He's not your boy. And besides, my brains won't stand arguing.'

'Just because you've drunk yourself silly, don't go picking at me.' Mrs McConnell retorted. 'I've had boys, I know what's best for them. And what's best for this boy is a day or two in bed.'

Eyre took hold of her hand. 'Mrs McConnell, I'll come to a compromise. If you let me go out this morning, I'll make a point of coming back to bed this evening early; and you can dress the bites for me, too, if you please.'

Dogger sniffed, and ran his hand through his hair, making it look even wilder. 'There you are, you see,' he remarked, to an invisible referee who was standing next to the wardrobe. 'The voice of sanity prevails. Thank God for that. Now, where's my breakfast?'

Mrs McConnell patted Eyre's mouth with his napkin, kissed him on the forehead, and stood up. 'I'll make it for you now,' she told Dogger, still smiling at Eyre. 'The fish, I'll be bound.'

Dogger gave a twisted, exaggerated grimace. After an evening of heavy drinking, the only breakfast which he could physically stomach was salted sea-perch, with red pepper; and a large glass of buttermilk. About an hour after that, he would be ready for another jug of home-made beer.

Eyre walked up to Waikerie Lodge. The morning was bright and dusty. The twin plagues of Adelaide were dust in the summer and mud in the winter; apart from the flies, and the fog, and the occasional outbreak of typhus, or 'mesenteric fever'. The dust rose up with the wind and whistled softly through the sugar-gums like hurrying ghosts, and everything it touched it turned to white; so that after it had died away the countryside looked as if it had been blanched, and aged, as if by some terrible experience.

His bicycle was exactly where he had left it, propped up against a bush, untouched except for a splash of parrot guano on the saddle. He walked cautiously up to the back gate of Lindsay's house, and looked across the lawns, but apart from a few scuff-marks on the grass, there was no trace of last night's horror. There was no trace of Charlotte, either, although he skirted through the bushes so that he could see up to her bedroom window. The family had probably gone to church. If so, Eyre hoped without

cynicism that they would pray for Yanluga. They had
certainly done nothing else to assure that their servant's
spirit would rejoin his dreamtime ancestors.

Captain Henry came out on to the patio, wearing a red
string headband and a shabby frock-coat, and leading half-
a-dozen of Mr Lindsay's greyhounds. He was probably
doing nothing more than taking them out for a walk, but
Eyre decided that retreat was more sensible than suicide,
and crept away from the perimeter of Waikerie Lodge, and
retrieved his bicycle, and pedalled off to visit Christopher
Willis.

A little way off, though, he stopped, and looked back
towards Waikerie Lodge. All he could see through the
surrounding trees was the edge of its brown shingled roof,
and the white columns that flanked its grandiose porch. It
was like an impregnable castle in a Grimm's fairy tale;
ruled over by a king who had set impossible standards for
his daughter, the Princess Charlotte. She would probably
die an old maid, imprisoned by her father's ambition,
particularly since South Australia's economy, buoyant at
first, had gradually begun to collapse; so that week by
week, the likelihood of a visit from an eligible English
baronet was becoming increasingly remote.

Down at the South Australian Company, Eyre had
already seen three major merchant banks withdraw their
money from Adelaide; and more letters of withdrawal
were expected by the end of the year. The returns had not
been high enough, or quick enough, and the general
feeling in the City of London, which in the early days had
been adventurous and optimistic, was that Australia, on
the whole, was 'a damned odd duck'.

These days, the only English quality that Adelaide saw
were the exiled sons of shabby Sussex landowners; or
botanical eccentrics whose trunks were crammed with
magnifying-glasses, and tweeds. Nobody suitable for a girl
like Charlotte.

Eyre cycled off towards the racecourse. It was warm
now, and the wind had dropped, although high creamy

clouds had mounted in the east, and there was a chance of thunder. The mid-morning light had become curiously metallic; as though the landscape had been cured in spirits of silver, and the spokes of Eyre's bicycle wheels flashed brightly along the pathway towards the racecourse. He usually sang as he cycled. This morning he was silent. A distant church-bell clanged from the centre of the city; and he allowed himself to whisper a verse from the 62nd Psalm, one of his father's favourites.

'How long will you assail a man, that you may murder him, all of you, like a leaning wall, like a tottering fence? Men of low degree are only vanity, and men of rank are a lie; in the balances they go up; and they are together lighter than breath.'

Eyre repeated, with relish, 'a tottering fence', and tried to swerve so that he ran over a Holy Cross frog that was squatting on the track, but missed it.

Christopher Willis was packing his horse-panniers to go out fishing when Eyre arrived on his bicycle, and he didn't look particularly pleased to see him. Nonetheless, he put down his nets, and said, 'Hullo, Eyre; you look as if you've been boxing with kangaroos.' Then, as Eyre parked his bicycle, he peered at him more attentively, and said, 'And the kangaroos won, by the look of it. Are you all right?'

Eyre said, 'I'm recovering, thank you. My dear Mrs McConnell is taking care of me better than I have any right to expect.'

'Ah,' said Christopher. 'Your dear Mrs McConnell. I always suspected that she wanted to adopt you. In fact, I rather believe that she thinks you're Geoffrey—Geoffrey, is it?—returned from the grave.'

He sniggered. That was the type of joke he always enjoyed. He had the appearance of a very disjointed public schoolboy, and the humour to match. He was big-nosed, with wide-apart eyes, and he always seemed to be growing out of his clothes, even though he was twenty-five. He parted his hair severely in the middle, and sometimes stuck it down with bay rum, or violet essence, especially when he was going to meet a young lady, which he did with unexpected regularity. They were never young ladies of the very best breeding, but they were invariably willing, and giggly, and of course they always wanted him to marry them, at once, which he wouldn't.

Eyre grudgingly admired Christopher's lack of sensitivity. He didn't very often feel like courting a girl himself, and when he did, it was invariably a painful and caustically romantic experience. How could you love a girl at all without wanting to love her for ever? He still thought of Clara with regret, the girl for whom he had first bought his bicycle.

He sat down on one of the frayed basketwork chairs on Christopher's untidy verandah. 'If you want to know the truth, I was attacked by Lathrop Lindsay's dogs. Worse than that, they set on Yanluga, too, his Aborigine groom, and killed him.'

Christopher took off his wide straw hat. 'Well, now,' he said. 'That *is* bad luck. Killed him, hey? My dear chap. Won't you have a glass of something? Old Thomas came past yesterday with four bottles of brandy.'

'Thank you,' said Eyre.

Christopher looked at him closely, as if he were testing his eyesight, and then said, 'You *are* all right? That's a frightful bite on your phizzog. If I were you, I'd sue the bugger.'

'I can't do that. I was trespassing. In law, he had every right.'

'Hm,' said Christopher. 'He's a bugger, nonetheless. Didn't I tell you that Charlotte wasn't for you? You can't beat a bugger; not when it comes to a bugger's one and only daughter; and he's a bugger all right, his lordship Lathrop Lindsay. Everybody says so.'

'Who's everybody?'

'Well, *I* say so. Who else do you need?'

Eyre couldn't help smiling. 'Go and get me that brandy,' he admonished Christopher.

They sat and drank for a while in silence, secure in their

companionship. A few hundred yards to their right, a dull chestnut yearling was being cantered and turned, in training for the winter season. The rider lifted his crop in salute to Christopher, and shouted, 'halloo', and then galloped off towards the billowing white tents which formed the major part of the racecourse.

'Sam Gorringe,' Christopher remarked. 'Terrible rider. Rotten horse, too. Just in case you were ever tempted to back him.'

Eyre sipped his brandy; and let it burn its way slowly over his tongue, and down his throat.

'My father disapproved of gambling,' he said. 'A short-cut to hell, that's what he called it.'

'Oh, well, yes.' said Christopher.

There was another silence, less relaxed this time. Then Eyre said, 'I've decided to bury him.'

'Bury him? Who? Lathrop Lindsay?'

'No, you lummox. Yanluga.'

'Yanluga? Isn't that Lindsay's responsibility?'

'Lindsay is going to give him a Christian burial.'

'Well?' asked Christopher, swilling his brandy around and around in his glass.

'Well, he wasn't a Christian, was he?' Eyre retorted.

'He was a heathen,' Christopher declared.

'Heathen? How can you say that? You've lived here longer than I have. You know how religious the blackfellows are. They have all kinds of religious rites; especially when it comes to burial. Don't they break the body's bones, and then burn it? And don't they sometimes have dances, and processions on the river? The poor chap should at least be given the ceremony that his beliefs demand, don't you think? Or perhaps you don't.'

Christopher balanced his glass on the warped verandah table. 'Well,' he said, 'I must say that you're really getting yourself in rather deep. Especially for the son of an Anglican vicar.'

'What my father believes is nothing to do with it. My

87

father hasn't met any Aborigines; he doesn't know how magical they are.'

'They're *superstitious*, I'll give you that. Do you know that boy from Moomindie mission? The one who came up here to mend my fences? He was supposed to have been converted to Christianity, *and* cricket, but he wouldn't stay here after dark because of the Yowie. The Yowie! Can you imagine it? A completely mythical monster, and the poor lad went beetling back to the mission as soon as the sun went down, as if all the devils in hell were after him.'

Eyre looked at Christopher sharply. 'But of course,' he said, 'there *are* devils.'

Christopher frowned, and then pouted. 'You can actually be rather tiresome at times, Eyre, did you know that?'

'Is it tiresome to want to give Yanluga the burial he begged me for?'

'Not entirely. Although it might be a bit too saintly.'

'I'm not a saint, Christopher,' Eyre smiled at him. 'I never will be, either. But the boy liked me, and respected me, and I liked and respected him. And I think that's reason enough.'

'If you say so. But how will you go about it?'

'I need to find an Aborigine chief called Yonguldye. Apparently he knows what to do.'

'Hm,' said Christopher. He stood up, and pushed his hands into the pockets of his baggy white trousers, and walked to the end of the verandah, where he stood looking out over the windy racecourse with his lank hair flapping across his forehead.

'I suppose it's no use telling you that you're really wasting your time?' he asked Eyre. 'In fact, more than that, you're doing yourself a positive disfavour. A chap like Lathrop Lindsay can make or break you. And it doesn't do one's reputation much good to be associated with blackfellows. They're a miserable lot, on the whole.'

Eyre said, 'I think I'd be miserable, too, if I was treated worse than vermin, and dispossessed of my hunting grounds, and shot for the sport of it. And I care very little for Lathrop Lindsay, thank you. What man can set dogs on to a boy, in the sure knowledge that they will tear him to pieces? My only regret is that it was my rash affection for Charlotte which led him to die; and for that reason I feel as responsible towards him as if he were my own brother.'

Christopher turned around, and folded his arms over his grubby yellow waistcoat. 'I was right, y'know,' he said. 'You're *far* too saintly; and it will be the death of you.'

'Perhaps,' Eyre replied, conscious that he was being melodramatic.

'Well, then,' said Christopher, 'what's to be done? Have you heard at all from Charlotte?'

'Nothing.'

'Do you think that you will?'

'I don't know,' said Eyre. 'It depends whether or not she still feels any passion for me; and whether or not her father has managed to prevent her from geting in touch.'

'Is she yours?' Christopher asked, bluntly.

Eyre glanced up. 'I suppose so, in a manner of speaking.'

'What? You've been fiddling, and that's all?'

'Christopher, don't be so damned indelicate.'

'Indelicate? I thought we always shared our confidençes; and our conquests. Didn't I tell you absolutely everything about Anne-Marie? My God, apart from me, and a captain at Adelaide barracks, you're the only person on the entire continent who knows that Anne-Marie has a mole right next to her left nipple.'

Eyre lifted his empty glass. 'What about some more brandy?'

Christopher went to fetch the bottle. 'I hope you're not *really* in love with this Charlotte girl,' he said.

'And what if I am?'

'You'll have *pain*, my dear fellow, that's what, and nothing else. From what you tell me, Lathrop Lindsay would rather see you cremated alive than have you court his daughter. Perhaps the very best thing you can do is tell me everything about her, and then try to put her out of your mind; and that goes for that Aborigine fellow, too. Exorcise your feelings of romantic lust; and your guilt, as well; and start tomorrow morning with a clean slate, determined to do nothing more complicated with pretty girls than take ungentlemanly advantage of them; and nothing more with blackfellows than kick them very hard in the arse, whenever the feeling takes you.'

Eyre swallowed more brandy; then wiped his mouth with the back of his hand. 'I can't,' he said, shaking his head, and Christopher saw then that he meant it.

'Well,' he said, 'damn it. I knew you couldn't. Damn it.'

'Why do you say "damn it"?'

'I say "damn it" because from the very moment I first met you I knew you were one of these chaps who has to do something *noble* in life. I knew you'd never be satisfied with fun, not for its own sake. No, you're the kind of chap who has to have a cause, and I do believe now that you may have found it. You're going to go off searching for this Aborigine chief and that's probably the last we'll ever hear of you.'

'I'm not afraid of the Aborigines,' said Eyre.

'You ought to be. Captain Sturt was.'

'That was ten years ago.'

'Well—let me tell you—Captain Sturt will be at Colonel Gawler's house on Thursday evening, for the Spring Celebratory Ball.'

'I didn't know that Captain Sturt was even in Adelaide.'

'He came in on Friday, on the *Albany*. He's staying with the Bromleys. A quiet, private visit, supposedly; but he's too much of a showman to let it stay quiet and private for very long. And I do think, since he's here, that you ought to meet him. *He'll* tell you what scoundrels the blackfellows can be.'

Eyre said, 'I'm not sure that I want to hear such a thing.'

'Nonetheless, don't tell me you're going to go looking for this chief of yours completely unprepared; and without asking South Australia's greatest living explorer what you might hope to find. It's an opportunity, let's be honest.'

'I haven't got a ticket.'

'Aha. There I can help you. Daisy Frockford has six, and two to spare.'

'I suppose you're going to ask Captain Sturt to dissuade me from seeking Yonguldye out altogether.'

Christopher finished his second glass of brandy. 'I'll try, believe me,' he said, frankly. 'But, even if he won't; or even if he *will* and you still decide that you want to go off on your wild Aborigine chase; then at least you'll have some idea of what dangers you may be up against.'

Eyre said, 'Christopher, I do believe you're a true friend.'

'I am, God help me.'

'In fact,' said Eyre, 'if I do make up my mind to go and look for Yonguldye, I'd very much like you to come with me.'

Christopher hesitated. Then he said, 'Oh, no. Not I. You won't ever catch *me* looking for Aborigine chiefs; not a hope of it.' And then, when Eyre kept on smiling, 'Listen, Eyre, I'm going to do my level best to make sure that *you* don't go; let alone me.'

Seven

Eyre had a busy week down at the port. Two vessels had docked from England, with ploughs and shovels and timber; and there were five separate consignments of wheat to be loaded. It rained heavily, too, the last heavy rains of the winter, and the offices he shared with Christopher and four other clerks were dark and humid and thick with tobacco-smoke. On Wednesday morning, he stood on the wharf in his oily rain-cape, waiting for the fat wife of a newly appointed government official to be rowed ashore in a jolly-boat, rotund and placid under her umbrella, a red plaid shawl around her shoulders, and he wished very much that he was away from here, and out in the bush, where the problems of life were uncomplicated, and the only threats to life and sanity were the sun, and the snakes, and the lack of water.

Perhaps Christopher had been right about him all the time. Perhaps his life *was* committed to some noble and historic adventure. After all, there must have been some saintly determination inside his father, to make him such a dedicated priest. And saintly determination could well be hereditary.

Yet he felt that it was no more than a sense of ordinary justice that had outraged about what had happened to Yanluga; a plain conviction that no matter how wealthy or influential Lathrop Lindsay might be, he had no right to deny Yanluga the burial ceremony that all Aborigines considered essential, not only to protect the living from his spirit's anger, but to avenge his death, and to ensure that he returned by way of the sky to the spiritual centre of his tribal life.

Like most white men, Eyre knew practically nothing about the blackfellows; and until now, he had felt no particular need to. The only blackfellows he had ever spoken to were dressed-up servants like Yanluga and Captain Henry; or those dissolute families who had become dependent on the Europeans for food and whisky, and lived in sorry brushwood shelters on the outskirts of the municipality, miserably exiled from their own nomadic way of life, and even more miserably attached to the *amerjig*, the white man.

Even the tamest of Aborigines talked very little of their magic, and their rituals, since to divulge their songs and their secret places to the white men was to disenchant them, and lose them forever. Yanluga had often spoken to Eyre about a place he called *Yeppa mure*, the dust hole, where he had spoken with his ancestors from the dream-time; but he had never told Eyre where it was, nor invited him to see it, for all of their mutual respect.

The fat wife of the newly appointed government official arrived at the wharf. Eyre helped her disembark, and the jolly-boat swayed dangerously.

'Well,' she piped, as she clambered heavily on to the wharf. 'I was told that the climate of Adelaide was amenable. I might just as well be back in Manchester.'

Eyre drew back his rain-cape and offered her his arm. 'Indeed, ma'am, you might,' he told her, although she missed the meaningful sharpness in his voice. She was too busy shaking the rain from her heavy ruffles.

'Such a voyage,' she said. 'If I was unwell once, I was unwell a hundred thousand times.'

'I'm frightfully sorry to hear it,' said Eyre.

The woman abruptly stopped, and clutched at Eyre's arm. 'Are you one of those lonely Australian bachelors?' she asked him. 'You won't mind my asking.'

'I am a bachelor, ma'am.'

'Well, in that case, before I leave the dock you must write down your name for me. I have a sister back at Audenshaw who has been trying to find a husband for nigh on eighteen years, without success; and you would certainly suit her nicely, even if you are a little tender.'

'You're very complimentary, ma'am.'

'It has been said,' the woman bustled; pleased with herself.

A black carriage drew up, slick with rain, and the woman's husband alighted, thin and whiskery and looking tired. He accepted her kisses as if he were being rhythmically slapped in the face with a soaking-wet duster. Eyre raised his hat, and said, 'Good morning, sir. Good morning, ma'am. Welcome to Adelaide, ma'am.'

The government official gave Eyre a tight, twisted smile, and handed him a shilling.

'Come along, dear,' he told his wife. 'You don't want to catch your death.'

Eyre was just about to go back to his office when somebody else caught his sleeve. He turned quickly and to his complete surprise it was Charlotte, in a hooded cloak, her eyes wide, the front curls of her hair stuck against her forehead with rainwater.

'Eyre,' she appealed, clinging on to his cape.

'Charlotte! My God! I thought I'd never see you again.'

'Eyre, oh Eyre! Oh look! Your poor dear face.' She hesitantly touched the triangular scar under his eye. 'You don't know how desperate I've been to see you. And it was all my fault. Why did I scream so, when you were all that I wanted? Oh, your face. Does it hurt still?'

Eyre took hold of her wrist, and hurried her across the slippery planking of the wharf; until they were sheltering under a lean-to roof where kegs of nails and ship's caulking were usually stored. There was a pungent smell of tar, and hempen rope.

'Charlotte,' said Eyre, and held her close to him, and kissed her. He felt absurdly breathless, as if he had just been running; and confused, too, so that none of his words seemed to come out straight. 'Charlotte, my God. I thought that was the end of us.'

She took a breath, and patted the lapels of his cape with her fingertips, quickly, fussily, like something she had to do for luck.

'Father's furious. I won't be able to see you again; not for ages; if at all. He says you're a devil. Oh, please don't be angry. He says you're a devil and that he should have set the dogs on you, as well as poor Yanluga.'

'Yes,' said Eyre. 'Poor Yanluga.'

'Oh, please, Eyre. He was only an Aborigine.'

Eyre looked at her for a long time, while the rain dripped along the rim of the lean-to roof in sparkling droplets, one after the other, each droplet a tiny winking life of its own.

Out in the harbour, a sailing-ship silently glided through the rain, with wet sails, a ghost on a ghostly voyage.

Eyre said, 'Yanluga was a boy; a human being. Your father deliberately had him killed.'

Charlotte looked at him oddly, and then shuddered, as if she had wet herself a little.

'I love you,' said Eyre. 'Despite everything that's happened.'

Charlotte turned away; but he loved her profile just as much. Those long, curled lashes; and those high, well-rounded cheeks, like two young clouds. She said distractedly, 'I love you, too; although I have resisted it. I think I was probably very shallow until you showed me that I could be deeper, and more thoughtful, and you still make me ashamed of some of the things I say. I suppose the trouble is that girls are not brought up to be thoughtful, or even to be considerate, especially not in Australia. We have to think of the marriages that will advance us best; of lords and viscounts, and men with money. All my friends do. Some of them say that they don't even mind if their husband is ugly, as long as he is titled, and rich.'

She looked back at Eyre, and there were tears shining in her eyes, more droplets, more sparkles.

'I screamed because you frightened me. Well, I think I frightened myself even more. I thought you were going to—*damage* me. I know now that you couldn't have done. I talked to Mrs McMurtry, the cook. She said that the first time was always difficult. And I didn't really know what to expect. It was, you know, the very first time.'

She paused again, and now the tears slid freely down her cheeks. 'I don't know what to say, Eyre. I feel so unhappy. I was so wrong; so stupid. And I have to tell you why. So please forgive me. And please believe that I'm trying to love you, very hard. And poor Yanluga. I feel so sorry for poor Yanluga.'

Eyre held her close. He could feel the warmth of her tears against his shirt. 'Well,' he said, a little tightly. 'I expect that Yanluga will appreciate your sorrow, wherever he is.'

'Oh, Eyre, don't blame me. Please.'

'I blame myself.'

They stood for almost five minutes under the lean-to,

while the rain fell across Kangaroo Island in slow, persistent draperies.

Eyre said, 'Do you know what your father has done with Yanluga's body?'

'Buried it, of course. Out at the back, where the mulga grows. He buried his horse there, too, do you remember Kookaburra? Dear Kookaburra. It shows how sorry he felt.'

'It also shows that he thought of Yanluga as somewhat less than a human being.'

Charlotte reached up on tiptoe and kissed his lips. 'You mustn't be bitter, my love. I do believe that father means well. It's just that he sees life so differently from you and me.'

'Yes,' said Eyre. He held her very close. He could have held her all day, feeling the softness of her breasts against him, and breathing in her perfume. He twisted one of her damp curls of hair around his finger, and then kissed her forehead.

'Shall I see you again?' he asked her.

'Whenever I can get away; but we may have to go to Angaston for a week or so; and father's started to drop hints that he might be taking me to Melbourne.'

'I shall wait for you. You know that, don't you?'

'Oh, Eyre,' said Charlotte.

At that moment, Robert Pope, one of Eyre's assistants, appeared on the wharf with a large umbrella. 'Eyre? Sorry to interrupt you, old man, but Mr Duffy wants to know when you can arrange to ship that wool of his. He's in the office now.'

Eyre squeezed Charlotte's arm, and kissed her once more, on the lips. 'I shall have to go,' he told her. 'But remember that I love you.'

'Please say you forgive me,' Charlotte begged him.

'There's nothing to forgive.'

Eyre followed Robert back to the office. The rain blew in his face as he turned the corner on to the wharf. Charlotte remained under the lean-to for a while, until an unshaven matelot in an oilskin hat stopped and stared at her, and hitched up his trousers, and said, 'What ho, my darlin'.'

Eight

Mrs McConnell knocked excitedly on the door of Eyre's bedroom to tell him that their hired carriage had arrived outside. He knew, he had seen it, but he dutifully said, 'Oh! Excellent!' Mrs McConnell also announced that Christopher was downstairs in the front parlour, drinking small beer with Dogger, although he knew that, too. He had heard Christopher's giggling through his red-patterned carpet, and guessed that Dogger was relating his favourite story of the Nyungar Aborigines at New Norcia. These proud and independent tribesmen had been given trousers and sandals by the missionaries there, and told to cover their shamefulness; only to return the following week with their trousers on their heads, and their sandals ostentatiously buckled around their penises.

Eyre had just finished tying his black silk cravat, and he pivoted around on his heel for Mrs McConnell to admire him. He was dressed in a magnificently cut black tailcoat, and double-breasted waistcoat, with satin-trimmed britches and black-kid slippers. Severe, but correct, and very handsome. His collar was extravagantly high, which he understood to be the latest fashion in England; but it did require him to keep his head rather loftily raised, and Dogger had described it as a Patent Double-Chin Cutter-Offer.

'Lord have mercy,' said Mrs McConnell. 'You could be the King of South Australia.'

'Well, Mrs McConnell, if only I were. The things I wouldn't put right.'

'You're not still worrying yourself about the blackfellow? You'd be best off forgetting about that.'

Eyre picked up his cane and his gloves. 'I can't, Mrs McConnell. I would that I could.'

'But you're such a gay fellow, Mr Walker. Why should you let such a grave affair distress you?'

Eyre took her hand, and affectionately pressed it, and kissed her cheek. 'A man can only be gay when his conscience is at ease, my dear. I saw Yanluga die, and it was my fault that Mr Lindsay set his dogs on him. Therefore, the task with which Yanluga charged me is a most serious responsibility. He must be buried according to the dignity of his own beliefs, and not laid to rest in some pet's graveyard, with foreign words spoken over him by a man who had nothing but contempt for the sanctity of his life.'

Mrs McConnell looked a little flustered. 'Well,' she exclaimed, 'I can only say that your father must have been a rare preacher.'

Eyre said nothing. He tried to look happy, but it wasn't especially easy. The truth was that every night since Sunday, he had been having grotesque nightmares about Yanluga's death, and about frightening Aboriginal rituals in which he had been somehow compelled to take part. He had heard weird ululating voices, and seen black flickering silhouettes, and hooked devices that tumbled over and over in the air, whistling as they went. And every morning he had woken up with his nightshirt tangled and sweaty, and the vision of Yanluga's ripped-open entrails vivid in front of his eyes.

To dress up for this ball tonight was a marvellous relief; quite apart from the fact that he wanted to meet Captain Sturt. He led Mrs McConnell down the stairs, and into the front parlour. Christopher was waiting for him there in a bright peacock-blue coat and yellow britches, his hair frizzed up with curling-tongs; and Dogger was just pouring out two more small beers. Mrs McConnell said happily, 'Doesn't Mr Willis look the very picture?'

'Smartest I've ever seen you,' Eyre grinned, and shook Christopher's hand. 'Not sure about the hair, though. You look as if you've been struck by lightning.'

'I'm glad you've come down to rescue me.' Christopher replied. 'Any more of Mr McConnell's small beer and I do believe I wouldn't have been able to stand up tonight; let alone dance.'

Dogger stood up, sniffed dryly and lifted his glass. 'Since I myself have no dancing to do, I'll venture a toast. To the young Queen who promises to be good; and to Britannia herself who needs no bulwarks; and to the man who said that black's not so black, nor white so very white.'

Mrs McConnell, unusually indulgent, poured a glass of beer both for herself and for Eyre, and with all the self-conscious solemnity of the English during moments of extreme patriotism, they drank. Eyre thought that the small beer tasted exactly like the thinned-down varnish with which the verger at St Crispin's used to refurbish the pews, but he smiled at Dogger nonetheless, and said, 'Excellent.'

'Now,' put in Christopher, rubbing his hands, 'we must be on our way to collect Daisy Frockford. And you'll be delighted to hear, my dear Eyre, that May Cameron will be accompanying us, too.'

The muscles in Eyre's cheeks tightened a little. 'Why should I be delighted to hear that?'

'Why? My dear fellow, you must have heard that May's engagement to Peter Harris was broken off, after Peter lost all that money at the races. And apparently she's desperately anxious to be seen walking out with somebody else, just to spite him. And when I say *desperately* anxious, well, please excuse my implications, Mrs McConnell. May Cameron's a healthy girl.'

Mrs McConnell furrowed up her forehead, this time in disapproval. 'Remember this is a Methodist home, Mr Willis.'

'I apologise,' said Christopher, bowing his fluffed-up head. 'We do live in practical times, however. Not all appetites can be satisfied with hymn-books.'

Dogger cackled. 'That reminds me of another story they told me at Mallala; how they found some of the Aborigine women taking Bibles back to their camp in their dilly-bags, and stripping off the leather bindings for a tasty chew. They even boiled the glue off the spines, and drank it like soup.'

'Now then, you're right, Christopher, we really must go,' said Eyre; who was afraid that Dogger's beer had already made Christopher too pompous and Dogger himself too reminiscent. He took Mrs McConnell's hand, in its fine crochet mitten, and kissed her neat little cuticles. Then he took Christopher's arm and led him out on to the verandah. The carriage was waiting under the lamplight; a hired phaeton from Meredith's, rather dilapidated, and leaning askew on its worn-out suspension, but brought up to a high polish nonetheless, and harnessed up with two quite respectable-looking bays. The coachman was a stout, broad-shouldered fellow with a high hat and a face like a Mile End prizefighter, with scarred eyebrows and a twisted nose. He climbed down as Eyre and Christopher came out of the house, and put down the step for them, so that they mount up and take their places on the dusty green upholstery.

'You know where to go first, don't you?' Christopher asked him.

'Flinders Street, sir, no need to remind me,' the coachman told him, with undisguised aggression. He climbed back up on to his box, and snapped his whip, and the phaeton began to lurch off with an eccentric up-and-down motion which caused Eyre and Christopher to look at each other and laugh in amusement.

'You may walk if you wish, gents,' the coachman told them.

'I wouldn't dream of it,' Christopher replied. 'This

carriage has all the safety and comfort of a vehicle which travels on land; and yet all the general hilarity of a boat.'

'Well, sir, in that case, you've nothing to complain of,' replied the coachman, in a voice as hoarse as a parrot.

'Nothing but your manners,' Christopher told him.

'My manners, sir?' The coachman shifted himself around in his seat and stared at Christopher with eyes as black as waistcoat-buttons. 'Well, sir, you'll have to forgive me for being one of the blunter sort. But then bluntness was never on the catalogue of criminal offences, was it, sir?'

'Your employer may have different views,' said Eyre, who was beginning to find this fellow irritating. 'Now trot along, and let's have less of this chatter. We've come out this evening for amusement, and we don't want any sourness, especially from you.'

The coachman looked as if he might have a less than courteous reply to that remark; but he closed his mouth tight, like a doctor's portmanteau, and shifted around on his seat again, and stung the horses' ears with the tip of his whip. 'Hee up, you shamblers.'

'I hope you haven't made a mistake, hiring this coach,' Eyre said to Christopher, under his breath, as they wallowed towards the end of Hindley Street. He inclined his head towards the coachman. 'He may very well be perfectly respectable, but he looks like a legitimate to me.'

'Nonsense,' said Christopher, running his hand through his fuzzed-up hair. But then he leaned across and said, 'He does seem a trifle uncouth, though, for a coachman.'

'Legitimate' was the generally accepted euphemism for 'ex-convict'. There were comparatively few in Adelaide, which had been founded as a free settlement; but a few score of pardoned men had sailed here from Sydney to seek their fortune in farming and prospecting and keeping sheep, and most of all to try to escape the social stigma of having been 'sent out'.

Eyre said, 'I suppose it's all right. The firm where you hired the coach was respectable enough, wasn't it?'

'Of course it was; although this isn't one of their usual carriages. Everything else was taken for the ball.'

Eyre raised an eyebrow at Christopher, and sat back on the seat in a conscious attempt to appear relaxed; although he wasn't.

'Well, this is all nonsense,' Christopher repeated. 'You're just trying to put the wind up me.'

Eyre looked around. They were now in a particularly deserted part of Pulteney Street, by an area of waste ground; and the only inhabited houses that he could see were a group of small workers' cottages behind a high picket fence, and the lamps were lit in only one of them. There was a tippling-house called the Cockatoo a hundred yards further along the street; and three or four men were sitting out on the verandah with bottles of rum, singing and laughing. But apart from these, and apart from the ghostly pale gum-trees which rustled in the evening wind, they appeared to be all alone.

The coachman eased out his reins, and said, 'Ho, now,' to his horses, and gradually the lop-sided carriage began to slow down, almost to walking-pace.

'What's going on?' Christopher asked him. 'What have we slowed down for?'

The coachman didn't turn around; but said something in a hoarse mutter, like 'traces slipped', or 'braces tripped', or 'brakes is stripped'. Eyre said loudly, 'What?' but at that moment the coachman applied the phaeton's brake and the whole assembly jingled to an awkward halt.

Eyre heard running feet, and at once said to Christopher, 'Out, and make a dash for it!' But the coachman just as quickly swung himself down from his box, and hurried back to their door, wrestling the handle open and banging down the step. He jumped up into the carriage, and Eyre saw that there was a heavy hardwood truncheon in his hand, which he brandished under Christopher's nose. 'Legitimate indeed!' he snapped, roughly. 'I'll break your nose for you; see how *you* care for it!'

Three more men appeared, as promptly as Jack-in-the-boxes, a trio of hardened old ruffians in baggy sailcloth britches and woollen hats. One of them hoisted himself up on to the opposite side of the carriage, and grinned up at Eyre with a face like a withered red pepper. Eyre raised his arm defensively and said, 'Get away!' but the man simply grinned and swung up a shining machete, and said, 'I'll geld you first, mate.' Another man, limping, went around to hold the horses' bridles, sniffing as he went.

'It's your money and your timepieces, that's all, sirs,' said the coachman. 'And it's your promise of silence, too; for we have too many loyal friends for you to think of grassing on us. Go to the military, and say one single word, sirs, and our friends will have your gizzards slit within the hour. A friendly warning, sirs, that's all; for what you're losing tonight is nothing as painful as your life.'

Eyre looked at Christopher, and said, 'I think, under the circumstances, we'd be better off doing what he says, don't you?'

Red-pepper-face grinned even more broadly, and spat, and said, 'You're cool enough, aren't you, mate?'

Eyre unfastened his watch-chain, and held up the watch that his father had given him. 'That's only because the Lord is with me,' he said. 'And because you'll most certainly get your punishment in Heaven, even if they fail to catch you in Adelaide.'

The coachman snatched the swinging watch, and stuffed it into his pocket. 'Don't preach, sir,' he advised. 'I'm not partial to being preached at, especially when I'm hoisting.'

Christopher handed over his purse. 'I hope you're damn well satisfied,' he told the coachman. 'I worked a month of late hours for that.'

'Oh, *well* satisfied, sir,' said the coachman. Then he turned to his fellow thieves, and whistled, and said, 'Come on, now, we're set.'

Just then, however, Eyre heard another whistling; softer and lower. It sounded as if something were flying towards them through the air, like a fast and predatory hawk. And then the coachman was suddenly knocked in the side of the head by a whirling piece of wood, and shouted, '*Ah!*'—just that—and somersaulted right over the side of the phaeton and fell heavily on to the dust.

Red-pepper-face stepped back in surprise, but then there was another whistle, sharper this time, and a long stone-tipped spear flashed right throught his throat, in one side and out of the other. He looked up at Eyre in outrage, his eyes crimson with shock; and then he raised his hands and clung on to the shaft which protruded from either side of his neck, and opened his mouth in an enormous bloody yawn.

A second spear hit the bodywork of the coach, so violently that the phaeton rocked on its worn-out springs. The limping man who had been holding the horses began to shuffle-*kick*-shuffle-*kick* back across the street, in the direction of the Cockatoo tippling-house; but a third spear struck him squarely in the back, and he dropped flat on his face.

The last of the thieves ran off so fast that a kangaroo couldn't have caught him, his sailcloth trousers flapping in panic.

There was a moment of utmost tension. Eyre slowly raised his head, and peered into the darkness of the waste ground. The insects were still singing, and the moths still pattered around the carriage-lamp. Over at the Cockatoo, one of the men had fallen dead-drunk off his chair, and the others were bawling at him to *wake up, Jack, you idle sod*, and hooting with laughter.

Down on the roadway, the coachman stirred and moaned. 'Christ Almighty.'

'What happened?' Christopher asked, floury-faced.

'I'm not sure,' said Eyre. 'Wait.'

They stayed where they were, with Christopher gripping Eyre's wrist, listening and sweating. Then, unexpectedly close, a skeleton appeared out of the darkness; or what looked like a skeleton. When it came nearer, Eyre saw that it was a blackfellow, his ribs and his bones outlined on his grease-smeared body in chalky white. He was naked except for a headband of kangaroo fur and feathers, and he carried two spears and a spear-thrower.

One by one, silently, like remembered shadows from a prehistoric past, other Aborigines appeared, until there were seven in all, standing around the carriage naked and painted. Eyre could smell them on the wind; that distinctive fatty pungent odour, mingled with the fragrance of woodsmoke.

One of them, the tallest, leaned over and picked up the fighting boomerang which he had used to knock down the coachman.

Eyre stood up in the coach, holding on to the door for support. 'You came to our rescue,' he said, his voice off-key. 'We thank you for that.' He rubbed at his shoulder with his free hand and suddenly realised that he was cold.

The skeleton Aborigine came forward and stood close to the coach. He raised his fingers in a quick series of complicated signs, without saying a word. Then he solemnly reached into a small kangaroo-skin pouch which hung around his neck, and took out a piece of stone. He handed it to Eyre, bowed his head slightly, and then retreated into the darkness. The other Aborigines followed him; until within a few moments they were all gone.

'Well, now,' said Christopher, sounding shaken. 'What the devil was all *that* about? I'd like to know?'

Eyre sat down, and examined the fragment of stone. It was a piece of granite, sharpened and pointed, with curling decorations carved on it, and red ochre rubbed into the indentations.

'It looks like a token,' he said. 'Some sort of a sign.'

'But what's it all *about*, Eyre? For goodness' sake! And what are we going to do about these chaps? Dead as dodos, those chaps in the street, I should say. And the coachman looks rather more than out of sorts.'

Eyre dropped the stone into his pocket, and climbed down from the phaeton. The coachman was sitting up now, dusty and dazed; a huge red lump rising on the side of his forehead.

'Christ Almighty,' he cursed; and spat dust and saliva.

Eyre knelt down beside him, and retrieved his watch and Christopher's purse. 'You're fortunate you weren't killed,' he said. 'Your villainous friends were, though, two of them.'

The coachman squinted through unfocused eyes at the bodies of red-pepper face and the limping man lying in the road. His high hat had been knocked off by the boomerang, and Eyre could see now by the light of the coachlamp that his head was shaved, a lumpy skull covered with bone-white bristles. It gave him a brutish, half-human appearance; but at the same time there was something remarkably vulnerable about him; like a retarded child.

'Christ Almighty,' he spat again.

'You realise I'm going to have to call the police,' said Eyre.

Grunting, the coachman managed to heave himself up on to his feet, and lean unsteadily against the phaeton's rear wheel. He dragged a rag out of his pocket, and wiped his face. 'Well, then, sir,' he said, 'that, I suppose, is your privilege. But I should like to know what happened here. Was it *you* who knocked me down? And what are these spears?'

Red-pepper-face was lying legs-apart on his back, his dead hands still clutching the shaft of the spear which had skewered his neck. His eyes were wide open; and he looked as if he were just about to explain what had happened to him.

'It seems we have friends, this gentleman and I,' said Eyre.

'Blackfellows, sir?'

Eyre nodded. He was quite as confused and disoriented as the coachman must have been; but he thrust his hands into his pockets and did his best to walk confidently around the side of the coach as if he had expected this sudden rescue all along.

'I wish they had done for me too,' the coachman said, glumly. 'By God I do.'

Eyre looked at him questioningly.

'Well, sir,' the coachman said, 'they'll hang me this time, and no mistake; or worse.'

'What could be worse than hanging?' asked Eyre.

'You don't know the penal settlements, sir, if you don't know what's worse than hanging.'

Eyre said, curiously, 'What's your name, fellow?'

'Arthur Mortlock, sir.'

'Well, Arthur Mortlock, tell me why you tried to rob us tonight, if you're so much afraid of the penal settlements.'

Mortlock looked down at red-pepper-face, and his black dry blood in the dust. 'That man's Duncan Croucher, sir; and he and me was together for seven years at Macquarie Harbour. We're ticket-of-leave men, both of us; and we was supposed to stay within sight of Sydney; but there was no work for us there. So we absconded and came to Adelaide, I suppose to find ourselves a respectable living. They always told us that Adelaide was just the place for respectability, sir. The kind of town where a man isn't looked down on for being a Crown pensioner, sir; nor ostracised.'

'That doesn't explain why you tried to rob us.'

Mortlock dabbed gingerly at the lump on his forehead. 'No, sir. But I expect you understand. We tried to start up a carriage business between us, on account of Croucher was a cabbie, back in London; and I was a drayman for Bass. But the times aren't good, sir, and tonight was the first bit of legitimate business we'd had for a fortnight.'

Christopher, irritable and frightened, said, 'Come on, Eyre. We're frightfully late. Let's call the police and have this chap locked up where he belongs. Daisy and May will be quite frothing by now; and the Ball will have started.'

Eyre said, 'Just a moment, Christopher. I want to hear from Mr Mortlock what it is that is worse than hanging.'

Mortlock raised his eyes; and they were black and bright and a little mad. Not the madness of rage or felony; but the madness of fear. The madness that dogs' eyes show, when their owners whip them; and which drives their owners to whip them even harder.

'I was sent out for losing my temper at the brewery, sir, and beating my foreman; but one fine day I lost my temper again and beat my guard; and for that they sent me to Macquarie Harbour. There they flogged me four times in all; two hundred and seventy lashes altogether; but one day I lost my temper yet again and beat a fellow prisoner; and that was when they locked me into solitary confinement, for a year, Christmas to Christmas, with my face covered all the time in a helmet of rough grey felt, sir, with holes pierced for the eyes. And when they let me out of there, and eventually gave me my ticket-of-leave, I was still inclined to lose my temper, and act rash, as I have this evening. But the effect of that confinement, sir, was such that I would rather cut my own throat than go through it for one more hour. You have no idea, sir.'

Eyre put his hand across his mouth. Both Christopher and Mortlock watched him; Christopher with nervousness and badly disguised impatience, and Mortlock with dreadful fascination.

After a moment, Eyre asked, 'Do you think you can still manage to drive the carriage?'

'I don't understand, sir.'

'Come,' said Eyre. 'Let's drag these two bodies into the bushes, and leave them lie. We didn't murder them ourselves, after all; and they still have Aborigine spears in them. Let's leave Major O'Halloran's constables to think that they were slain by wandering tribesmen.'

Christopher burst out, 'This is preposterous! You're not going to let this fellow go free?'

'I was thinking of it,' said Eyre.

'But for goodness' sake, the fellow tried to rob us; he would have killed us himself if he'd half a mind to.'

'I don't suppose you've heard about the spirit of Christian forgiveness,' Eyre retorted.

'Well, of course I have. But I've also heard the commandment which says you shall not steal; and I should think that also includes *attempted* robbery, wouldn't you?'

Eyre said, 'For now, Christopher, I'm not going to argue with you. Mr Mortlock, help us pull these bodies into the bushes. Then let us get on our way exactly as if nothing had happened; and we can discuss the morals of it later. Let me tell you one thing, though, Mr Mortlock.'

Arthur Mortlock looked at Eyre disbelievingly, and nodded his head.

'From now,' said Eyre, 'from this very moment, in fact, you must live your life as if you were aspiring to be one of the angels. For if you do not, I will make quite sure that a letter is held in safekeeping which will condemn you at once. Do I make myself clear?'

Mortlock stood up straight. 'You're asking a lot of me, sir.'

'Of course. But I'm also *giving* you a lot. Your continued freedom; possibly your life.'

'I know that, sir.'

'Well, then, let's be quick. One of those boozy fellows at the Cockatoo is going to look across here soon and wonder what we're up to.'

Mortlock retrieved his high hat, and brushed it. 'Yes, sir, and God bless you, sir.'

It took them only a few minutes to drag the limping man and red-pepper-face into the thorn bushes. It was a grisly business; and they had to kick dust over the bloodstains on the road. But then they climbed up into the carriage again, and were driving lopsidedly off towards Daisy Frockford's house.

As they passed the Cockatoo, the men outside were swinging their bottles of rum in time to a filthy old song from the slums of London.

If you ever want to charver wiv a leper,
Make sure you chooses one wiv biggish tits.

On account of when you charver wiv a leper,
Yer avridge leper usually falls to bits.'

From the carriage, Eyre could see in the men's faces a
desperate happy brightness; a terrible oblivious joy; and
he was disturbingly reminded of a young blind farm-
worker he had once seen on the road to Baslow, who was
laughing in desperation because his daughter could see a
rainbow.

Christopher was sulking. Even when they drew up
outside the smart imported-wood house on Flinders Street
where the Frockfords lived; with its sparkling lamps beside
the door, and its two dark spires of Araucaria pines in the
exact centre of each front lawn; he would do nothing more
than pull a face and say to Eyre, as Mortlock pulled down
the step for them, 'You're making a serious mistake, Eyre.
A *very* serious mistake. You mark my words.'

Nine

The driveway outside Colonel Gawler's residence on North
Terrace was impossibly cluttered with carriages when they
arrived; and as they jostled in through the gates, Eyre
could detect a certain lowering of Mortlock's head into his
shoulders, which suggested to Eyre a well-suppressed
urge in Mortlock to lay about him with his whip, and flick
off a few hats and ostrich feathers, and clear a way.

The lawns were lit with sparkling lanterns, which swung
prettily in the evening wind, and even the colonel's tame
kangaroos had been dressed up with white silk bows
around their necks. Two footmen in green frogged coats
stood by the door; one of them as tall as a Tasmanian pine,

the other almost a dwarf; and between them, awkwardly, they helped the ladies to alight from their barouches. Each lady as she stepped down glanced quickly around her like an alarmed emu, in case she should see a gown in the same design as hers, or (worse) a gown in the same particular shade of silk. Fine fabrics from London and Paris were in short supply in Adelaide this season, and there were only two dressmakers in King William Street capable of sewing a really fashionable gown; so for the past four or five weeks, fear and secrecy had been intense in the parlours and dressing-rooms of Rundle and Grenfell Streets.

Daisy Frockford, who now sat beside Christopher fanning herself furiously and uttering little yelps of impatience and disapproval, was dressed in a gown of vivid emerald-green, with white leaf patterns of pearls and diamante all around the hem. She wore a head-dress that looked to Eyre like an overgrown garden-gate, with creepers hanging from it; and it had the effect of making her fat little face seem even fatter, and even littler, like a vexatious baby.

May Cameron, Eyre's companion, was quieter, almost melancholy. She was wearing pale pink moiré silk, with seed-pearls sewn on to it in the pattern of butterflies. She was dark-haired, with a profile that reminded Eyre of engravings he had seen of the young Queen Victoria: just a little too plump to be beautiful. Her breasts were quite enormous, and lay side by side in her lace-trimmed décolletage with the gelatinous contentment of two vanilla puddings. Now and then she sighed, and attempted the smallest of small sad smiles, and Eyre supposed she was thinking of the wastrel Peter Harris.

Wedged in close to Daisy Frockford was an aunt of Daisy's who had been introduced to Eyre and Christopher as Mrs Palgrave; a talkative woman with a perfectly oval face and false teeth that clattered whenever she spoke, which was often.

At last, by jamming his dilapidated phaeton in between

111

two highly varnished landaus occupied by some of the wealthier local aristocracy; a manoeuvre which caused one of their coachmen to glare hotly at all of them, and scowl, 'Bustard,'; Arthur Mortlock brought them up to the entrance, and the two footmen opened their door for them and assisted them down. Mrs Palgrave caught her foot in her hem, and performed the most extraordinary little dance, but the dwarf footman managed to catch her around the waist, and hold her upright while she disentangled herself.

'I declare the silliest thing that ever happened,' Mrs Palgrave flapped. 'I shall have that seamstress in court see if I don't. Could have tumbled head-over-heels and broken my neck and then what.'

Eyre walked around to the front of the phaeton and spoke to Arthur Mortlock. Arthur Mortlock took off his high hat and looked down at him with unreadable eyes.

'I'd like you to be here when the Ball finishes, to take us home,' said Eyre. 'That's unless you want to make a run for it.'

'I'm done with running, sir,' said Mortlock.

'You realise that when the militia find your two companions, they may start making enquiries after you; and if they discover that you're a ticket-of-leave man, they'll take you directly back to Norfolk Island.'

'I repeat, sir, I'm done with running. All I ask is that you vouch for me, sir, if it comes to trouble. I suppose that's an impertinence to ask, after this evening's bit of business; but I've made you a promise, sir, that I'll stay on the straight and narrow, and that's all I can say.'

Mrs Palgrave said, 'Pushing and shoving, no wonder I tripped. Look at them all, like monkeys in the menagerie see if they aren't, supposed to be high-and-mighty and pushing away rude as you like.'

Eyre looked up at Arthur Mortlock and gave him a small nod of encouragement. 'Very well,' he said. 'Let's see if you really have been converted on the road to Damascus.'

Mortlock drove the phaeton away to the rear of the

stables, where the horses would be fed, and the coachmen would share a pipe or two of tobacco and play cards until it was time for carriages. Eyre and Christopher guided May and Daisy into the wide parquet-floored hallway, with its crystal chandelier and its idealistic paintings of Mount Lofty and the valley of the Torrens River; and there they were met by Colonel Gawler's head footman, all wig and catarrh, who took their invitations and hoarsely announced their arrival to the disinterested throng in the reception room.

There was music from a small orchestra which had been formed the previous year by Captain Wintergreen, a retired bandmaster from the New South Wales Corps: quadrilles played like cavalry charges, and waltzes so emphatic that it was obviously going to be easier to march to them than dance to them. At the far end of the room, with a distracted smile, Colonel Gawler himself was standing in his full regalia as Governor and Commissioner, his chest shining like a cutlery canteen with tiers of decorations, trying to make intelligent responses to a tall woman with an exceptionally meaty nose, whom Eyre recognised as Mrs Hillier, one of Adelaide's few schoolmarms. Captain Bromley was there, too, with his corn-coloured hair and his stutter; and the Farmer sisters, in a bright shade of blue; and the Reverend T.Q. Stow, with his hands clasped adamantly behind his back and his face squeezed up like a closed umbrella. Mrs Maria Gawler, the Governor's wife, was wearing an unbecoming brown dress, and fluttering her hands about like little birds.

The noise was tremendous. Not only the whomp-ti-bomping of the orchestra, but the screeching and laughing of the ladies, and the overblown boasting of the gentlemen: a strange relentless roar of competitive sound, as Adelaide's socialites did their absolute utmost to outcry, outpose, outshout, and out-amuse each other. Already the reception room was suffocatingly hot, and the ladies' fans were whirring everywhere, giving the impression that the

113

house was crowded with birds which couldn't quite manage to raise themselves into the air.

'What a din I declare, never heard the like,' complained Mrs Palgrave. 'Toss them nuts and apples I would, see if they scramble for them. Monkeys in the menagerie.'

'Is Sturt here yet?' Eyre asked Christopher, as they piloted their lady companions into the middle of the room. May nodded her head at one or two friends whom she hadn't seen since her engagement had been broken off. Daisy, who couldn't see anyone she knew, fanned herself even more violently.

Christopher lifted his head and looked around. 'Can't see him. But he'll be here, all right. Loves the admiration. We might have to wait until the end of the evening before we can talk to him, though.'

Daisy said, 'I'd adore a glass of punch.'

'Then you shall certainly have one,' said Christopher.

'And you, May, would you care for a glass?' Eyre asked her.

She nodded. 'But I'd prefer to drink it outside, if we may. The noise and the heat in here is making me feel dizzy already.'

They beckoned over a perspiring waiter, who handed them glasses of scarlet punch, rum and grenadine and pineapple-juice, and while Mrs Palgrave perched herself on a small gold-painted chair, and talked to Mrs Warburton about tattooing, and how there wasn't an ounce of civilized behaviour from Para Scarp to Port Adelaide, Christopher and Daisy went off to find somebody who might give Daisy a compliment, and Eyre took May out of the open French windows and on to the verandah.

May sat on a garden-chair, while Eyre leaned against the wooden balustrade. Beyond them, in the lantern-lit gardens, the kangaroos slowly hopped, like large animated £-signs; and the night parrots did their best to compete with the screeching ladies indoors.

The governor's new house was white-painted, and comparatively elegant, although only the east wing had

114

been fully completed. The original house had been built for Colonel Gawler's predecessor, Captain John Hindmarsh, out of mud and laths; but because he had employed sailors and ship's carpenters to put it up, they had forgotten to give him a fireplace, or a chimney. This house was more in keeping with the status of governor and commissioner of South Australia, and Eyre quite coveted it. Sitting on the balustrade with his drink, he felt successful and confident already; and he thought that May wasn't too bad a companion, either, even if she was a little solemn.

'You must learn to smile again,' he told her, lifting his glass.

'I do try,' she said.

'Were you so very upset about your engagement?'

She nodded. 'I loved Peter enough to want him for my husband. But after he lost all that money, father forbade it. Most of the money had been lent to him by my uncle; some by my mother. He said he was going to invest in a mining company, and that we should all be paid back a hundred times over.'

'And instead, he put it on horses?'

'I don't know why,' she said. There was a sparkle of tears in her eyes. 'I suppose he wanted to impress me, and win my father over.'

'Fathers can be a problem,' said Eyre. 'Especially fathers who worship their daughters, and want only the very best for them.'

May sipped her punch, and glanced up at Eyre, and tried to smile. Eyre didn't know if it was the effect of the heat, or the noise, or the music, but he suddenly began to think that he might have taken quite a fancy to May. There was something about her cupid's-bow lips, something tempting because they looked so sweet, and naive. And he found himself admiring her breasts, and imagining what they must look like when they were uncupped from her gown. And he thought of her body, too, white-skinned and chubby, with fleshy hips and thighs between which a man could happily suffocate. A virgin, too. Well brought up and well protected; and sentimental to a fault.

'May,' he said, 'you and I must dance. We must endeavour to be happy together, even though we are both feeling sad. Just for tonight, we must forget what might have happened, and try to think of what *could* happen.'

May sipped a little more of her drink, and twiddled the stem of her glass around. 'Daisy said that you're a vicar's son.'

'Well, Daisy's quite right.'

'She said that you're very religious, when the mood takes you; or so Christopher told her.'

'Religious? Well, I believe in God, and the sacrament of Holy Communion, if that's what she meant.'

'Well, I don't know. She said that you could be rather *dogged*, at times. I hope you don't mind my saying that.'

Eyre stood up, and walked around the verandah. 'Dogged? I suppose I *can* be rather dogged when I feel seriously about something. But I don't count that altogether wrong, do you? Doggedness in the defence of what is right, and what is just, and in the upholding of Christian principles—well, you can hardly call that a vice.'

'Daisy said something about an Aborigine boy; how you wanted to give him an Aborigine funeral.'

Eyre nodded slowly. 'I do. That's one of the reasons I've come here tonight.'

'But Aborigines are *savages*.'

'You may think so. Most people do, and I suppose that they can be forgiven for it. The government does nothing to help us understand them. But it seems to me that the Aborigines are one of the most magical and religious of peoples on the face of the earth. Just because they live in innocence and nakedness, that doesn't mean that they're savages. Adam and Eve lived in innocence and nakedness; and far from being savages, *they* were the most divine of all human beings ever; nearer to God than anybody today could imagine. It could very well be that Aborigines are the results of God's attempt to start again: to create for a

116

second time a perfectly innocent society. If that is so, and it *could* be so, then I believe that it is our duty to protect the Aborigines and to prevent them from losing their innocence. Perhaps the Garden of Eden now lies here, in the unexplored centre of Australia. Perhaps the significance of this strange country is divine, as well as geographical. Whatever it is, I believe that we should be cautious, and respectful, and that we should be very wary of imposing our own way of life on the blackfellows. We, after all, are the descendants of Adam and Eve: we are the sinful children of sinners. The Aborigines know no sin; and to that extent we should envy them. To that extent, they are our superiors.'

May stared at him. It was quite plain that she could hardly believe what he had said.

Eyre stopped pacing, and reached out his hand towards her. 'Don't let's talk of such serious matters tonight; why don't you dance with me? They're playing *Le Pantalon*.'

'I—ah—I think I'd rather not,' said May, considerably flustered. 'Really.'

'Because of what I said about Aborigines?'

'Well—how can you possibly suggest that an Aborigine could be your own superior? Or mine?' She was flushed, and she didn't know what to do with her glass of punch.

'May—what I said—it's only a theory. But Australia is such an extraordinary country that you can't close up your mind to *any* possibility. Why does it exist at all, this peculiar continent with foxes that fly but birds that won't? We know hardly anything of it, especially the interior; the very centre of it; how can we make any assumptions at all? It's a work of God; there's no doubt of that at all. But what a work!'

May said, 'Please, don't talk like that. It upsets me.'

'Why? Because it could be true?'

'It makes me feel . . . uncomfortable, that's all.'

Eyre knelt down beside her, on one knee. 'In that case, forgive me. I brought you here to enjoy yourself, not to feel uncomfortable. I know that I might sound rather odd,

117

but the truth is that I adore Australia and all of its mysteries; and I truly believe that there's a meaning behind it being here; and a reason for its existence.'

May was just about to answer him, when they were interrupted by a spattering of applause from the garden. Eyre turned around in surprise, and saw a tall man in side-whiskers walking towards him across the lawn, clapping his hands as he came. The man had an intelligent, amused face; and eyes that were bright with self-confidence and pleasure. Nobody could have called him handsome. But his plainness was commanding in its own particular way; and as Eyre stood up to greet him, he knew at once that here was a man both to trust and to like.

'You must accept my apologies for eavesdropping on you,' the man said, warmly. 'But you are the first person I have heard for many a long month who has dared to question the very being of this continent; and to acknowledge what it has to offer us now as well as what it may surrender in the future.'

The man stepped up on to the verandah, bowed deeply to May and kissed her hand, and then shook hands with Eyre. His handshake was very firm and strong, and Eyre noticed that there was a white scar across the base of his thumb, and another scar across his forehead.

'Charles Sturt,' the man announced himself. 'I believe I was supposed to be guest of honour here tonight; but I'm afraid that my nerve rather failed me.'

'I'm honoured to know you, sir,' said Eyre. 'My name is Eyre Walker, and this young lady is Miss May Cameron.'

Sturt took May's hand again, and kissed it; allowing himself a closer inspection of her creamy-white cleavage. 'Charmed,' he said, richly.

Sturt dragged over a chair, and sat himself down on it, uninvited. 'I'm supposed to be the most social of creatures; but believe me that's only a façade. I enjoy applause, and general admiration. Don't we all? But the thought of spending the entire evening recounting my expeditions to endless numbers of open-mouthed ladies and their sceptical husbands . . . well, it's been almost enough to give me a headache.'

'You surprise me, sir,' said Eyre.

'Well, I often surprise myself,' Sturt replied. He reached into his pocket, and took out a silver cigar-case, and opened it. 'But I consider that to be one of the essentials of a worthwhile life; to keep on surprising everybody, including oneself.'

He said, 'You won't mind if I smoke?' and lit up a small cigar. 'I have a particular weakness for the indigenous tobacco. One of the tastes I acquired on the Murrumbidgee.'

Inside the reception room, another fierce quadrille had struck up; and the floor was drummed by dancing feet.

'I must say that I think your theory about Australia has some merit,' remarked Sturt, leaning back in his chair, and blowing out strong-smelling smoke. 'Whatever seems to hold good in the northern hemisphere seems to be quite reversed here; and I have wondered many times whether there is any divine logic behind such a reversal. The very essence of this land is its upside-downness, if I might call it that; and to discover its secrets one must first of all invert every interpretive facility that one possesses.'

'I read about your expedition of 1829,' Eyre told him. 'I was much impressed.'

Sturt's exploration of the Murrumbidgee and Murray Rivers was already legendary. He had set out from Sydney with a 27 foot whaleboat carried on horse-drawn drays; and in this and in another boat which they had hewn out a giant forest tree, he and his companions had rowed for six weeks along the Murrumbidgee and Murray Rivers, until they had reached the coast of the Indian Ocean, thirty minutes south of Adelaide at Lake Alexandrina. When they had arrived there, however, there had been no ship to meet them, and with their supplies dwindling, they had been obliged to row all the way back to where they had started from, over 800 miles, upstream.

Sturt had gone temporarily blind during the last days of

the expedition, and some of his companions had collapsed in delirium. But all had survived; and when Sturt returned to Sydney with his stories of the spectacular cliffs and idyllic lakes that they had seen, and the sweeping floods on the Murray, and the 'vast concourse' of Aborigines who had followed them, clamouring and shouting and shaking their spears he had immediately been fêted as a hero, and a great explorer.

His eyes were better now; although Eyre noticed that they still had a slightly stony look about them. His enthusiasm for exploration, though, was as fervent as ever.

'I long now to open up the interior,' he said, smoking in quick little puffs. 'If there is an inland sea there, I want to sail on it before I die. If there is a Garden of Eden there, as you suggest, then I wish to walk in it, close to God. It is one of the last great mysteries of the globe; a secret that only the Aborigines know; and perhaps even they have never succeeded in penetrating to the very core of the continent.'

Eyre said, 'It was about Aborigines that I wished to speak to you.'

'Well, I'm not sure that I'm your man,' said Sturt; still affable, but suddenly and noticeably less interested. 'Your Aborigine is a sad and particular creature, and there are many who know him better than I.'

'But you encountered so many of them when you were exploring the Murrumbidgee and the Murray. You said so in your reports.'

'I read them, too,' ventured May. 'They sounded an extraordinarily warlike people to say the least.'

Sturt coughed, and brushed ash from his trousers. 'They were threatening, and raucous, the first time we saw them. They lined up on the banks of the river, and up on the cliffs, and chanted war-songs at us; and for a time I must admit that we were very alarmed. They were shining with grease, and they had painted themselves like skeletons and ghosts. Their women appeared to have capsised a

120

whole bucket of whitewash over their heads. But, in the end, they did little more than stamp at us, and shout, and then retreat. They didn't hurt us; not once; and when at last we did manage to make some kind of contact with them, and talk to them by signs and gestures, we found that they were a very unfortunate people indeed. Rich in superstition and myth, no doubt of that. But scratching a living from food that would horrify you, if I were to tell you of it, and wandering from place to place with a restlessness that totally precludes the development of any kind of civilisation. They were riddled with syphilitic diseases, even the very youngest of them; in fact some of the sufferers were so young that I can only pray that they were born in that diseased condition. I agree with you, Mr Walker, that the Garden of Eden may indeed be found in the centre of this continent; but I must say that I doubt very strongly whether the Aboriginals are the truly innocent people whom God intended to dwell there.'

May, who had been listening to this with some discomfort, took Eyre's arm and said, 'Shall we dance now? I really would rather dance.'

Eyre said, 'Of course. But please let me first ask Captain Sturt if he knows how a particular Aborigine might be found.'

'I beg your pardon?' asked Sturt. 'A *particular* Aborigine?'

'That is what I wanted to ask you. I have to find a chief, a Wirangu I think, whose name is Yonguldye, The Darkness.'

'Now then,' said Sturt, 'that may present some problems. The blackfellow will stay in each location for only a limited time, according to the season, and according to what magical and traditional obligations have brought him there. In September, for example, many of the Wirangu will be seen at Woocalla Rock; where they will hold a corroboree to mark the victory of Joolunga over the Lizard-Man, long ago in the time they call the dreaming.

Then, they will be gone. All you will find of them will be their ashes and the bones of the animals they have eaten.'

Eyre said, 'It may seem curious to you, Captain Sturt; even a little desperate, perhaps, but I recently made a promise to a dying Aborigine boy that I would ensure his burial according to Aborigine custom. He told me before he died that I should look for the one they called The Darkness.'

'Eyre,' said May, tugging at his arm again, 'can't you speak of this later? They're playing 'Dufftown Ladies.'

But Eyre held back for a moment, and waited for Sturt to answer him. After a while, Sturt looked up with a mixed expression on his face; as if only Eyre himself could resolve how Sturt was going to feel about him.

'Why should a young man like yourself feel obligated to a blackfellow?'

'I made a promise, sir, that's all. And I have to confess that, in a way, I was responsible for his dying.'

'Has he been buried already?'

'So I understand; but according to the Christian service.'

'But are you not a Christian yourself?'

'My father was a vicar, sir, in Derbyshire.'

Sturt sucked at his cigar, so that the tip of it brightened like a red-hot cinder. 'There is more to this, don't you think, than simply a promise of burial to one unfortunate black boy?'

Eyre stared at Sturt carefully. 'There may well be,' although he didn't fully understand what Sturt was implying.

Sturt nodded. 'I had with me two or three young men like you when I rowed down the Murray. You, Mr Walker, have the calling. You know that, don't you?'

'The calling, sir?'

Sturt raised an arm, and swept it around to suggest the far and unseen horizons of Australia. 'You have the calling of the great and terrible interior. You may be a new chum; you may be fresh to Australia; but you are not a coast-squatter, like so many; afraid even to contemplate the

Ghastly Blank that lies to the north of us. Ah, you have the vocation my boy! I can sense it! All you have to determine now is whether you have the strength.'

Eyre said nothing. Sturt had touched too many silent strings inside his mind; and for the first time played for him the inaudible but irresistible music of real ambition. He began to see that his promise to Yanluga may have been far more significant than a simple commitment to one dying boy; it may have been a promise to himself, and to his future life, and to the unknown continent of Australia.

His life of girls and bicycles seemed suddenly frivolous; and without any purpose or satisfaction. But even when he had been cycling, and flirting, and drinking home-made beer with Dogger McConnell, something must have been happening within him; some deep and vibrant change. Why had he felt so responsible to Yanluga? Why had he agreed to let Arthur Mortlock go free? Perhaps he had sensed in them, as Captain Sturt had sensed in him, that they were true children of the Australian continent, and that it was they and their descendants who would reveal at last the frightening and mystagogic significance of *Terra Australis Incognita*.

At that moment, Mr Brough stepped out on to the terrace, and cried, 'Why *there* you are, Captain Sturt! We've been a-hunting for you everywhere! Do come inside, the ladies are all agog to meet you.'

Sturt took a last suck at his cigar, and then tossed it glowing into the acacia bushes. 'Very well,' he agreed, trying not to sound too resigned about it. Then he took May's hand, and kissed it again, and shook hands with Eyre, and said, 'We must discuss this some more. Where do you think I might find you?'

'I work at the port, sir, for the South Australian Company.'

'Well, that's capital, for I shall be down at the wharf tomorrow morning. If you can persuade the company to allow you a few minutes' spare time; there are one or two matters we could discuss. And I might be able to assist you in locating your mysterious Mr Darkness.'

Sturt went inside, to be greeted by spontaneous applause, and a quick burst from the orchestra of *For He's A Jolly Good Fellow*, immediately followed by *The Rose of Quebec*, which Eyre supposed to be an obscure acknowledgement of Sturt's military service in Canada, just before Waterloo.

'Now then,' he said to May, 'perhaps we can dance. I'm sorry to have spent so much time talking about exploration, and Aborigines.'

'Well, it was a pleasure to meet Captain Sturt,' said May. But then she squeezed Eyre's hand, and added, 'The only trouble is that men like you and he, well, you perplex me.'

Eyre ushered her in through the open French doors. The room was hot and crowded and even noisier than before, with a new and shriller chorus of voices now as the men drank too much punch and the women tried to attract the attention of Captain Sturt.

'You mustn't let such things worry you,' Eyre told May. 'Men like Captain Sturt and I, we perplex ourselves.'

Ten

Inexplicably, Christopher appeared to be bitterly put out that Eyre had already been speaking to Sturt, and that Sturt had done nothing to dissuade Eyre from going in search of Chief Yonguldye. To show his annoyance, he stamped his feet furiously as he danced a quadrille with Daisy, and glared at Eyre with such wrath that a dear old lady in a pearl head-dress rapped Eyre's elbow with her fan, and said, 'I do believe that gentleman is trying to attract your attention, young man. Do you think he might be in pain?'

After the quadrille, however, as Christopher came stalking over to argue with him some more, Eyre immediately swept May out on to the floor to dance a long, slow, clockwork waltz, around and around, with Christopher's indignant face appearing with bright-red regularity on the third beat of every tenth bar.

Eyre found May quite provocative; and his britches tightened as they danced. But provocative as she was, her conversation was nothing but a shopping-basket of confusions, worries, second-hand notions, and unrelated facts about nothing of any importance. With his imagination already widening to encompass the 'calling' which Captain Sturt had spoken about; with his mind's-eye repeating for him again and again the sweep of the arm with which Sturt had outlined the furthest reaches of the Ghastly Blank; Eyre found it difficult to follow what May was saying, and even more difficult to come up with any sensible replies.

'Everybody knows that Aborigines are little more than dirty children,' said May, as Christopher's face swung past her shoulder, followed by the glittering chandelier, and a footman carrying punch, and a white-faced young man with fiery red hair.

'I'm sorry?' said Eyre.

'They steal, and they lie, and they're no use at all to man or beast.'

'What? Who do?'

'Oh, *Eyre*,' protested May, 'you're being absolutely impossible.'

Eyre kissed her on the forehead, just at the moment that Mrs Palgrave was peering at them both like a custodial bandicoot. 'Forgive me: let's go and find something to eat.'

Christopher caught up with them in the dining-room, where the long walnut table had been laid out with terraces of food.

'Eyre, you're being quite impossible.'

'I know. May has just told me that.'

'But to talk to Captain Sturt like that; really. What on earth did he think?'

'He didn't think I was insane, or anything of that nature, if that's what you imagine.'

'But you're going through with this ridiculous idea?'

Eyre picked a chicken vol-au-vent from the very top of a mountain of vol-au-vents, and bit into it. 'Of course I am. Especially now that Captain Sturt seems to think that I could have all the makings of an explorer.'

'That's nonsense. He was only being polite.'

'I don't think so,' said Eyre, shaking his head.

'Well, even if he wasn't, what would you explore?'

Eyre stared at him. 'What do you *think* I would explore? Australia, of course! There are countless thousands of square miles of quite uncharted territory out there. For all we know, there may be a vast inland sea. Or a huge tropical forest. Or an undiscovered range of mountains.'

They walked along the whole length of the table. There were smoked hams, tureens of white cockatoo soup, wild ducks stuffed with beef and apricots, chickens, Goolwa cockles, roasted emu thighs, and lamb cutlets with crisp golden fat on beds of wild celery and spinach. There were boiled crabs, glistening oysters, and freshly-opened lampreys, as well as silvery smoked sea-perch, baked snapper, and steaming tureens of green-turtle broth. Eyre picked here and there; and forked up tidbits for May and Daisy; while Christopher hovered around him and sulked.

'I really can't understand why you're so upset,' said Eyre, with his mouth full.

'You're making a fool of yourself, that's why. Chasing off after Aborigines.'

'I've invited you to come with me. Then we can *both* make fools of ourselves.'

Christopher said nothing, but forked himself up a slice of emu meat, which was coarse and lean and rather like mutton; and chewed it with concentrated aggression.

Eyre said, 'I haven't really worked out what I'm going to do yet. Tomorrow, after I've spoken to Captain Sturt again, perhaps I shall know more clearly. But I shall go in search of Yonguldye; and, as I go, I shall chart whatever countryside I come across, and make maps.'

Christopher swallowed his meat, and looked away.

Eyre touched his back. 'You could come with me, you know. It would be quite an adventure; and, who knows, we might come back from it as heroes. Look at Captain Sturt.'

Christopher shrugged, and still didn't answer.

'I *have* to go,' said Eyre. 'I owe it not only to Yanluga, but to myself, too.'

'If you must,' retorted Christopher.

Eyre hesitated, and then took Christopher aside, where they could be overheard only by a large bronze bust of Matthew Flinders, the man who had discovered the site of Adelaide in 1801. 'Something is upsetting you,' said Eyre. 'I think you should explain to me just what it is.'

Christopher looked at him, watery-eyed. 'It is not an easy matter to explain without your misunderstanding it altogether.'

'Can you try?'

Christopher shrugged. 'The fact of the matter is that I have formed a considerable affection for you. Not a physical affection—please don't think that it is anything to do with matters of that nature. But, I suppose I must say that I love you.'

Eyre held his friend's hand. 'That's nothing to be ashamed of. I love you, too, with all my heart.'

'Not quite as I do, my dear chap. I love you—' and here he swallowed as if he were still trying to force down his mouthful of emu flesh, '—romantically.'

Eyre couldn't find any words to answer him; but he kept hold of his hand, and gripped it firmly, to show that he was neither disgusted nor repelled.

After a moment or two, Christopher said, 'This has only happened to me once before in my life, at college, and I

127

never imagined for a single instant that it would ever happen again. But during the year in which I have known you, I have become as attached to you as a young girl might have done. That is why the thought of your leaving on this incredible expedition to find Yonguldye fills me with such dread. There have been many explorers, Eyre; and very few of them have been as lucky and as successful as Captain Sturt. There may be an inland sea. There may be a wonderful forest. But those who have tried to penetrate the interior and survived have come back with stories of nothing but treeless desert, and of unimaginable heat, and death.'

Eyre licked his lips, to moisten them. The dining-room suddenly felt dry, and stuffy, like a brick oven. 'I have already said that you could come with me. Your feelings about me give me no cause whatsoever to change my mind.'

Christopher said, 'No. I am afraid that such ventures are not for me. If I were to go, I would die just as surely as you would survive. I am not a hero, Eyre, for all of my bombast, and for all of my womanising. You said to me once that you envied me and my ability to court girls without becoming over-attached to them. Well, now you know why.'

Eyre insisted, 'You *must* come with me; because you will never persuade me not to go.'

'No,' said Christopher.

'But we will be properly equipped. Captain Sturt will give us all the advice we need. We will take plenty of water with us, and at least two other companions; and an Aboriginal guide. How can we fail? And if we *do* fail, then all we have to do is to turn back.'

'Do you think that those poor souls whose bones lie out on the sand-dunes didn't believe the same thing? You know how hot it can be here in the summer: further north the heat becomes more and more intense. No, Eyre, it is a land of death, and when you speak about this expedition I can feel death itself on my shoulder.'

May came over, her white breasts bouncing, and said brightly, 'You two *do* look serious. For myself, I think this ball has quite recovered my spirits. And that dear Lance Baxter has asked me to dance with him, twice!'

'A cataclysm,' complained Mrs Palgrave, whose hair had begun to slip sideways. 'The way they fell upon the food like orang-utangs. All eating with their fingers, greasy lamb cutlets and all, even soup it wouldn't surprise me. Civilisation all gone to pot.'

Daisy pouted, 'Eyre, you haven't danced with me at *all* yet. I do believe that you're becoming miserable, and mean.'

'Very well, then, we shall dance,' Eyre agreed. He gave Christopher's hand one last reassuring press, and then he tugged on his white evening gloves so that he and Daisy could gavotte.

Daisy was a peculiarly cater-footed dancer, and Eyre kept finding himself in corners of the dance floor where he hadn't intended to be; but she chattered about all the latest scandal in Adelaide; Mimsy Giles had been sent by her parents to Perth for kissing one of the gardeners; and the Stewart family were in a terrible furore over Mr Stewart's affair with Doris King; and Eyre found the gavotte unusually instructive, even if it wasn't particularly accurate.

Christopher watched them morosely from the corner of the room, but Eyre determined to himself that nobody was going to be sad on his account, for any reason; and he made up his mind that he would persuade Christopher to come with him on his expedition to find Yonguldye, whatever happened.

It was odd, to find himself loved by a man, especially a man he knew so well. But he thought of his father's favourite proverb, from the Bible: 'Hatred stirs up strife, But love covers all transgressions.'

The gavotte was almost finished when Eyre noticed a familiar face on the far side of the room. Big, and boiled-looking, the face of Lathrop Lindsay. He twirled Daisy around, so extravagantly that she almost lost her balance; searching quickly from left to right for a sign of Charlotte. At first he couldn't see her there, and he began to think that Lathrop might have come to the Spring Ball with nobody but his wife, and left Charlotte at home at Waikerie Lodge.

When the music came to a scraping, irregular finish, however, and he escorted Daisy back to the custody of Mrs Palgrave, Christopher came over and said, tersely, 'Lathrop Lindsay's here.'

'Yes,' Eyre acknowledged. 'I've seen him.'

'Charlotte's here too.'

'I didn't see her.'

'She's taking some supper. But, Eyre—'

Eyre looked at Christopher sharply; but Christopher simply raised his hands in surrender. He wasn't going to interfere in Eyre's affections for Charlotte, no matter how tempted he might be. Nor was he going to allow this evening's admission of his unnatural love for Eyre destroy their friendship. Perhaps it would, in time. Perhaps it would strengthen it. It would certainly alter it irrevocably. But just for this evening, Christopher knew that it was better to leave well enough alone.

Eyre walked into the dining-room, looking around for Charlotte. He didn't recognise her at first, because she was wearing a white lace mantilla over her loose, fair curls. But then she turned, and he saw that remarkable profile, and those long eyelashes; and that half-dreamy innocent-sinful look of hers that had attracted him right from the very first moment he had caught sight of her on the wharf. She was helping herself to fillets of smoked fish, with whipped mayonnaise; and he said not loudly, but clearly 'Charlotte!'

She turned at once but so did the tall young man standing beside her, a square-faced fellow with the pale golden tan of a natural-born Australian. He was one of those vigorous, healthy, confident young colonists whom later arrivals skeptically called 'cornstalks', because of the upright way in which they walked about.

'Eyre!' said Charlotte, blushing. 'I didn't imagine that you would be here!'

Eyre defiantly looked across at Charlotte's escort, and kissed Charlotte on both cheeks. 'I came to see Captain Sturt,' he said. 'Christopher arranged it.'

Charlotte drew the young Australian boy forward, and in a flustered voice, announced, 'Eyre, this is Humphrey Clacy. Humphrey, this is Mr Eyre Walker. Humphrey is a friend of the family, Eyre; son of a Sydney family with whom father does business.'

'How do you do?' Eyre asked Clacy.

Humphrey Clacy said, uncertainly, 'Well, thanks.'

'Can we talk?' Eyre asked Charlotte. 'Your father's busy for the moment, trying to make himself known to Captain Sturt. Perhaps we could go out on the terrace.'

'Eyre, really, I don't think I can,' said Charlotte, hesitantly.

'Charlotte, we must talk; even if it's only for a moment or two.'

Charlotte took his hand. 'Eyre, please. It's all so difficult.'

'I'm only asking for two or three minutes, Charlotte. But I must tell you what I plan to do.'

'Eyre, you must understand. Father was so adamant that you and I should never see each other again. I've—I've grown resigned to it. Well, I've *tried* to grow resigned to it. You don't want me to go through any more pain, do you? You don't want me to suffer any more than I have already? Please, Eyre, I do love you; I'm terribly fond of you; but if we can never be together, what is the point of torturing ourselves so? Believe me, my dear, I'm thinking of you, too.'

Eyre breathed crossly, 'Charlotte, for goodness' sake. All I want to do is talk to you for five minutes.'

'Eyre, I'm sorry.'

Humphrey Clacy laid his arm around Charlotte's shoulders, and said in a strong 'flash' accent, 'I think you'd better leave the lydy alone, Mr Walker.'

Eyre stared at him in exaggerated surprise. 'He speaks!' he cried.

'Eyre, please, don't make one of your scenes,' begged Charlotte. 'We can talk later perhaps; or tomorrow. But, please, try to think of the pain that I've been feeling. It must be as sharp as your own. Please, let it be; and leave us.'

'Come on, Mr Walker,' Humphrey Clacy urged him; his cheeks suddenly firing up. The other guests were beginning to turn around now, and whisper to each other, and over in the far corner somebody dropped a plateful of potato salad on to the carpet.

'He speaks again!' Eyre shouted, angrily. 'Ladies and gentlemen, this indigenous animal has the power of communication!'

Charlotte hissed, 'Eyre, *please*! I must do what my father says. Eyre, please don't make me cry.'

'Ah, but that's the trouble,' said Eyre. 'I never make *anyone* cry. Not real tears, anyway. You can only cry for those you love, and those you respect; and neither you nor your father ever respected me, my love, for all of your sentimental words.'

'Eyre, of course I respect you.'

'You don't, Charlotte! You don't! Not for one moment! And I will never believe that you do until your father does; for you will never stand against him. A clerk, at the port? A newly-arrived burrower? You don't respect me in the least. All you cared for was my nonchalance, and my bicycle, and most of all the fact that I irritated your father.'

Humphrey Clacy took hold of Eyre's shoulder, and twisted his jacket. 'Mr Walker,' he said, in a tone which he obviously believed was very menacing, 'if you don't leave here immediately, and allow Miss Lindsay to finish her supper in peace, then I regret very much that I shall be obliged to hit you.'

Eyre looked this way and that, in furious mock-astonishment. 'I declare that it's miraculous! Why, I knew they could dig; and I knew that they could drink; and I knew that they could spit. But nobody told me that they could come along to parties, and make real conversation, even if it *is* offensive to listen to.'

There was sudden laughter. Eyre realised that he might be drunk. He was certainly very angry. The orchestra struck up with a polonaise, erratic and harsh. There was more laughter. And then Lathrop Lindsay appeared through the throng in the doorway of the dining-room, his face volcanic.

'Colonel Gawler, sir!' he called.

Somebody said, 'Fetch the Governor.'

Lathrop stepped forward like an elderly fighting-cock. He was dressed in full formal evening wear, with a wide pink cummerbund. He beckoned Charlotte to stand aside, and then he addressed himself directly to Eyre, his forehead shiny with perspiration, his lower lip protruding with stubborn rage.

'I tried to get him to leave, sir,' ventured Humphrey Clacy. 'He wouldn't hear of it.'

'That,' boiled Lathrop, 'is because he is chronically deaf. Deaf to advice, deaf to warnings and entreaties of all kinds, and above all deaf to the moral guidance of his betters, of whom there are very many.'

'I was simply asking to speak to Charlotte,' said Eyre.

'Well, you may not speak to Charlotte,' Lathrop retorted. 'You may neither speak to her nor see her. She has no desire to have any further to do with you. She finds you unspeakably offensive; as do I. I have called for Colonel Gawler, as I know that you will make trouble if any of us attempt to eject you forcibly; but you will probably understand that it would be far more satisfactory for you to leave quietly, and to leave at once, of your own volition.'

'I have a ticket and I shall stay,' Eyre declared. 'And let me say that if Charlotte does not wish to speak to me, then she can quite easily say so herself. She is an intelligent and spirited girl who has no need of a frothing father to speak for her; nor the company of a barely literate wheat-farmer with all the social graces of a duck-billed platypus.'

This was too much for Humphrey Clacy, who had already become over-excited by the appearance of Lathrop, and by the amusement of those who were standing around listening, and by the prospect of seeing Eyre ejected from the Ball by Colonel Gawler's footmen. He struck Eyre quite suddenly in the right ear, without warning, a sharp painful knock that sent Eyre staggering two or three steps sideways.

Eyre turned, stunned, not even sure what had happened. But then he saw Humphrey with his fists raised in the classic pose of a prizefighter, his blue eyes staring, his mouth pugnaciously pursed, and the frustration of everything that had happened to him in the past week burst out, with spectacular consequences.

He pushed Humphrey Clacy smartly in the chest; and Humphrey Clacy fell heavily backwards, the back of his legs striking the dining-table, so that he overbalanced. For one split-second everybody believed that he could save himself. But then he toppled with a tremendous crash of plates and silverware, right into a display of fresh fruit and shellfish and savoury jellies, bringing down rumbling pineapples and avalanches of ice and then a whole fragile castle of glass dishes filled with compôte of pears and charlotte russe. Some of the women screamed. Charlotte herself gave a cry like a wounded dove. Many of the drunker men gasped helplessly with laughter; and one of them, still laughing, offered Humphrey Clacy a hand up, only to let him slip back again, knocking over a tall arrangement of crab's-claws and plums and stuffed poussins.

'You are a walking disaster!' Lathrop roared at Eyre. 'You have brought down on me nothing but embarrass-ment and tragedy!'

'You're wrong!' Eyre shouted back at him. 'I have brought down on you *this*, as well!'

So saying, he lifted up from the table a huge cut-glass

dish of apple trifle, and promptly upturned it over Lathrop's head. Custard and apples splattered all over Lathrop's face and shoulders; and he stood for a moment like an unfinished clay statue, his eyes blinking out through the creamy sliding dessert in utter disbelief at what had happened.

Unsteadily, like a man on a tightrope, Eyre made his way across the food-strewn floor, and then crossed the reception-room at a pace that was almost a canter. He ran out through the french windows on to the verandah, and then down the stone steps into the garden. The first cries of 'Where is he? Where is the fellow?' were beginning to rise up from the house as he jogged around the corner of the stables, and found the carriages assembled there, and the coachmen drinking ginger-beer and playing cards.

Arthur Mortlock stood up immediately. 'Anything amiss, sir?' he asked, picking up his high hat.

'Nothing for you to worry yourself about,' Eyre panted. 'But I think it would be wiser if I were to leave directly. Take me back to my lodgings fast as you can; then come back and collect the rest of my party later.'

Arthur unhooked the feedbags from the horses' noses, and patted them.

'Trust it's nothing serious, sir,' he remarked, as he climbed up on to the box.

Men in evening dress were running this way and that across the lawns, some of them shouting, some of them laughing hysterically. There were cries from inside the house, and the off-key trumpeting of a French horn from the orchestra. One man had saddled up his grey mare, and was riding her backwards and forwards across the garden, trampling the acacia, frightening the kangaroos, and setting up a whooping and mewling among the peacocks.

As Arthur Mortlock's lopsided phaeton rolled noisily out of the gates, and turned back towards Hindley Street, Eyre heard the head footman shouting hoarsely. 'Stop him if you can! But be careful! He's violent!'

Eleven

Charles Sturt said, 'On an expedition, you know, you have to learn to control your emotions. You have to take the greatest triumphs and the greatest disasters with equal equanimity. There is no more terrible sight than to come across explorers whose fear has overtaken their judgement; to find their huddled bodies not five miles away from supplies, and food, because they eventually lost confidence in their ability to survive.'

He paused, and looked out towards the grey glittering waters of the Gulf of St Vincent. 'I will never forget when we arrived at last at Lake Alexandrina, the lake which I named for our young queen-to-be. It was separated from the Indian Ocean by nothing more than a few sand-bars; and the plan had been to carry our boats over the sand-bars to be loaded on to a ship. We could have sailed back to Sydney in complete comfort! But there was no ship there, and our food and water were almost exhausted. Now, the angry and emotional thing to do would have been to curse our luck, and wait for a ship to arrive. But, had we done that, we would most certainly have died. No: we had to resolve ourselves calmly to row back again, all the way up the Murray, and all the way up the Murrumbidgee.'

He watched Eyre closely; and his voice was so quiet that Eyre could scarcely hear it above the wind.

'We rowed,' Sturt said, 'from dawn until dusk, for six weeks, with a single mid-day break of one hour only. We had scarcely anything to eat, and we were too exhausted even to talk to each other. Our hands were blistered until they bled and then the raw flesh became blistered in its turn. Often we fell asleep while still rowing, and dreamed while we rowed. When we got back to Sydney, we were starving wrecks; and, as you know, I myself went blind for several months, through deficiency of diet. But we remained calm, and we never once railed at God, or at our terrible fortune, and all of us are still alive today.'

They walked a little further down the sand-dune, until they reached the shore. It was a grey, warm, overcast morning, a little after eleven o'clock, and they were strolling southwards on the beach at Port Adelaide. Eyre had arranged for Robert Pope to take care of his bills of lading while he talked with Captain Sturt; and fortunately the head wharfinger, Thomas Taylor, had been called up to Angaston for two days, to discuss the shipment of wool.

Eyre had half-expected that Sturt would not come, especially after the débâcle in the dining-room at last night's ball. What he hadn't known, however, at least until Sturt had told him, was that Sturt disliked Lathrop Lindsay more than almost any other man in South Australia; and that he and Lathrop had fallen out years ago, shortly after Sir Ralph Darling had appointed Sturt as Military Secretary of New South Wales. Sturt had counted the apple-trifle incident as one of the great amusements of the year, and had personally begged Colonel Gawler not to take the matter any further.

'Do you know what they're saying about you this morning?' Charles Sturt had said to Eyre, the very first moment he had walked into Eyre's office this morning. 'They're saying, "Beware of Eyre. He is definitely not a man to be trifled with. Especially apple-trifled with." '

Eyre said, as they walked on the beach, 'I'm disgusted with myself.'

'Well,' said Sturt, 'it *was* rather incontinent of you. But, it shows spirit.'

'I wish I'd never seen the girl. The trouble is, I still adore her.'

Sturt smiled at him. 'I'm sure that she still adores you. But she's very young, remember. She's bound to be influenced by what her father tells her. Give her a chance.'

Eyre went down on his haunches, his coat-tails trailing on the sand, and selectively picked up shells. 'I don't think it's up to *me* to give *her* a chance. I can't get near her. And after last night, I should think that Lathrop Lindsay would quite happily see me beheaded.'

'You need to become a hero,' said Sturt.

Eyre gathered up a handful of cockles, and stood up, and tossed them one by one into the breakers of the sea. 'Clerks,' he said, grunting with the effort of throwing, 'do not become heroes.'

'Come now! Last night you were full of heroism.'

'That was last night. Today, I have a serious headache.'

'Well, I hope you haven't lost your heroism permanently, because I have decided to put up a considerable sum of my own money to finance your expedition to find Yonguldye, and also to map the interior due north of Adelaide, and beyond; which is where you are most likely to find him.'

Eyre stared at him. 'You really believe that I *can* find him?'

Sturt nodded. 'There are several Aboriginals from the Murray River area who frequently help us with tracking, and letter-carrying, and even with escorting prisoners. The best of these is Joolonga; whom I met on my first expedition; and he will go along with you and help you to find the man you seek. He is an interpreter, too, and that should assist you in your search.'

'But will that be the sum of the expedition? Just Joolonga and I?'

'Of course not. You should take with you at least two reliable friends; and two more Aborigine bearers. You may take more, if you wish; but personally I believe it unnecessary, and of course it will add to the expense.'

Eyre tossed away the last of his shells, and then walked along the beach, close to the line where the surf sizzled, his shoes leaving water-filled tracks in the sand. Sturt followed, a few yards further off, climbing up and down the dunes as he went, holding his hat to prevent it from being blown away.

Eyre said, 'Supposing I find Yonguldye straight away,

within ten miles of Adelaide? What kind of an expedition will that be?'

'There has to be some give-and-take,' said Sturt. 'If I am to finance an exploration; then there must be some results.'

'What sort of results?'

'You spoke yourself of an inland sea, or a Garden of Eden. Perhaps Yonguldye knows how these may be reached, and will guide you there. Alternatively, he may be able to help you locate a good cattle-herding route to the north. To be able to drive cattle directly from Adelaide to the north coast of Australia would be of tremendous financial advantage. Then again, Yonguldye may know where there are opals to be found.'

'Opals?'

Sturt took off his hat, tired of keeping it clamped on his head with one hand. 'Several Aboriginals have spoken of secret opal diggings, rich beyond all imagination. Now think what you could be if you were to find one of those.'

Eyre turned around, and stopped where he was. Sturt stopped too. Eyre said, 'All I wanted to do to begin with was find Yonguldye, and bring him back here to Adelaide so that he could bury Yanluga. But now it seems as if I'm also supposed to go looking for seas, and gardens, and cattle-trails, and opals.'

Sturt came sliding awkwardly down the side of the sand-dune. Above him, a flight of black swans flew through the morning wind, crying that sad, silvery cry. He stood close to Eyre, and said, 'Australia is not a land for the selfish, Mr Walker. You have your own obligations to fulfil, I understand that. But when I spoke to you yesterday evening about the calling, I was talking about the greater good; the good of all Australians; and you have that calling, and all of the responsibilities that go with it.'

'Well,' said Eyre, feeling evasive and unsure of himself. 'I'm not sure that I do.'

He had dreamed those dreams again last night; in the first heavy sleep of drink; and he had heard those blurred, slow, extraordinary voices, speaking to him in tongues that he was unable to understand. Voices that spoke of *yonguldye*, the darkness, and *tityowe*, the death adder. And there were other noises: the hissing of sand in the wind, and the whirring of boomerangs, and that distinctive whip-like sound of a spear launched from a *woomera*. He had woken, at the very moment that Mrs McConnell's clock had struck three, and he had walked in his nightshirt to the window and seen that same Aborigine boy sitting across the street, with his scruffy wild dog lying at his feet, while the moon shone through the branches of the gum-trees like a prurient face. He had remembered then the stone that the Aborigine had given to him when their carriage had been ambushed, and he had gone to his wardrobe and searched in his jacket until he had found it.

He had heard of *tjuranga*, the sacred stones of the Aborigines, which were supposed to contain the spirits of ancient dreamtime people or animals. Perhaps this was one. Whatever it was, it must have some kind of mystical significance, something to do with Yanluga. Eyre had held it up to the moonlight, and traced the carved patterns on it with his fingertips. He had almost been able to convince himself that he felt a magnetic tug between the stone and the moon itself; as if the stone were an alien mineral, from somewhere unimaginably distant, carved and decorated according to protocols that were not of this earth.

It frightened him, although he didn't know why. But it also re-affirmed his determination to seek religious justice for Yanluga; and to discover as much as he could about the primaeval secrets of Australia.

Today, on the beach with Captain Sturt, he was no less determined to find Yonguldye and to embark on whatever exploration the search would demand. But he had become suspicious of Sturt himself: not only of Sturt's sudden and copious friendliness, and his immediate readiness to put up the money to send Eyre northwards, but of his repeated explanations that it was necessary for the expedition to be quickly profitable.

Sturt said, 'Whenever capital is invested, for whatever

purpose, there must always be some return. You appreciate that, don't you?'

'I'm not sure that the value of burying one black fellow according to his religious beliefs could be totted up in a balance-book,' replied Eyre, although he did his best not to sound sarcastic.

'Well, of course not,' said Sturt. 'But we're actually hoping for a little more than that; as I've been trying to tell you. I mean—I haven't misjudged you, have I? You *are* the exploring type? I thought I saw so much vision in you last night. So much imagination. It takes imagination, you know, to be a good explorer. What could lie beyond the next range of mountains? Where could that river run? That wasn't just liquor, was it, that sense of imagination? I mean—you won't think that I'm being offensive, or personal. But today you seem to be more—well, how can I put it?—*closed-up*, as it were. Inward, in your attitudes.'

Eyre said, 'I'm not lacking in gratitude, Captain Sturt. Please don't think that.'

'I don't, Mr Walker, not for a moment. But I do want you to understand that it wouldn't be possible for me to finance a venture like this solely for the purpose of finding one Aborigine chief, and bringing him back to Adelaide. There must be benefits for everyone, not just Yanluga; and let us not forget that Yanluga is already dead.'

Eyre thrust his hands into the pockets of his britches, and walked on a little further. He couldn't think why Sturt's proposition disturbed him so much. After all, he was a white man; and he worked for a commercial company which depended on South Australia flourishing, and on the exploitation of whatever riches and facilities the land had to offer. Yet he knew from what Yanluga had told him that the Aborigines had already been dispossessed of many of their magic places, and that scores of sacred caves and creeks had been lost to them for ever. And what the white man did not yet understand—if he ever would— was that the Aborigines depended on being able to visit these places in order to remind themselves of their complicated and mystical past. None of their stories and songs were written down; none of their magic was recorded in books. The places themselves were the culture; the rocks and the creeks were invested with all the knowledge that the Aborigines needed in order to live and die according to what they believed. Once the places were gone, the culture was gone, irrevocably. To deny the Aborigines access to them was like burning down cathedrals.

Eyre watched a Dutch whaler sailing slowly around the point on its way to the waters of the South Indian Basin, its triangular sails shining in the morning sun. He said, 'Perhaps I'm just being eccentric. Mr Lindsay is always accusing me of eccentricity. It's just that I feel that whatever we find in Australia we ought to protect as well as exploit. Scores of Aborigines have died of the measles, because they were infected by British settlers. Some tribes have died out altogether. Who will ever know now what they believed, and why they lived the way they did? Each time we destroy something here, we destroy one more secret. I'm simply afraid that if I find opals, or gold, or even a passable cattle-trail—well, this Garden of Eden will very quickly go the way of all Gardens of Eden. Trampled underfoot.'

Sturt dragged a large red handkerchief out of his sleeve, and loudly blew his nose. When he had folded the handkerchief back up again, and tucked it out of sight, he said, 'You're quite right. Or at least Mr Lindsay's quite right. You *are* eccentric. In fact, you're eccentric enough to be a really great explorer.'

Eyre picked up more shells; and began to skip them over the surf.

Sturt said, 'Let me put it this way, Mr Walker. I have lived among your Aboriginal at very close quarters; and believe me there is no more wretched specimen of humanity. He survives on insects and frogs and all kinds of repulsive creatures; nourishment to which a civilised man could never turn, even in his direst need.'

'Alexander Pearce excepted,' commented Eyre, skipping another shell.

Sturt ignored that sharp remark. Alexander Pearce had been a Macquarie Harbour convict, a one-time pie-seller from Hobart, who had twice escaped from prison, and twice survived by eating his companions.

Sturt went on, 'Every Aboriginal I have come across who has encountered the white man has benefited from the experience. True, many of them have unfortunately caught diseases not endemic in Australia; but Doctor Clarke tells me that they will eventually form a satisfactory resistance to most of the commoner sicknesses. And a few hundred deaths, no matter how regrettable those deaths may be, is a small price to pay for the advantages of Christianity, and clothing, and a good wholesome diet. I must tell you, Mr Walker, that it has long been my dream to teach and train the Aboriginals, to make them into happy servants. Many of them are already useful as constables, and guides, and houseboys. And when they are properly housed, and taught the elements of agriculture and the keeping of sheep and cattle, they will at last be able to develop for themselves the rudiments of civilisation. Do you want to see them forever outcast from normal society? Do you want to see them live in hardship and poverty and shameful nakedness, ignorant and filthy, ridden with venereal diseases, for generation after generation? Do you call that protecting them? They are backward children, Mr Walker; and as such their condition begs every paternal care that we can offer them.'

Eyre said, 'Does that mean we have to overrun their land, and dig out of it everything and anything valuable? Does that mean we have to desecrate their sacred places?'

Sturt laid his hand on Eyre's shoulder, and smiled at him rather too closely, so that Eyre could see the hairs growing out of his nostrils.

'To use the natural gifts that the land of Australia holds within her bosom, to give succour and support to her natural inhabitants; that is scarcely destructive. Of what use to an Aborigine are opals? Or copper? Or gold, even? Far better that we should take the gold, and the opals, and whatever other minerals might be discovered, and sell them where they are most wanted, and in return give the Aborigines food, and education, and proper clothing, and Goulard's extract, and Holy Bibles. Come, Mr Walker; you are the son of a minister. What do you think *he* would have said? Your father?'

Eyre let his remaining shells fall to the beach, one by one. 'I suppose he would have agreed with you,' he said, quietly.

'Of course,' said Sturt. 'Of course he would. A Christian minister.'

'But I still don't believe that it's necessary to destroy the Aborigine beliefs, and their sacred grounds.'

Sturt smiled again, and shook his head. 'Omelettes can't be made without breaking eggs, Mr Walker. I know how strongly you respect the native superstitions. That, after all, is your motivation for seeking out this one chief Yonguldye. But sacredness is relative. And the sacred Christian nature of this one great mission, to explore and develop South Australia well, that simply *must* take precedence over the erratic beliefs of a few score of unschooled savages. I very much regret all those sacred places and magical artefacts which must have been lost; but I suppose one could express the same sort of regret about the Dissolution of the Monasteries. And in those historic days, we were dealing with the same God, weren't we, and not with peculiar creatures like the Bunyip and the Yowie, and the Kangaroo-Men. No, Mr Walker, much as we would prefer to preserve these places, we cannot; and if the Aborigines forget their gods because of it, well, they will have forgotten nothing more holy than the boogie-man.'

It was gradually becoming clear to Eyre why Captain Sturt had picked him so quickly, and with such certainty. If Sturt was going to mount an expedition to explore the territory north of Adelaide, and look for cattle-trails and natural riches (and he had obviously been considering such an expedition for quite a long time) then who better to lead it for him that a man with inspiration, unusual vision, and an uncommon sympathy for the Aborigines? Sturt must have decided that an expedition could be smaller, cheaper, and that it would have a far greater chance of survival, if only the Aborigines could be persuaded to give it every possible assistance along the way.

It occurred to Eyre that Captain Sturt didn't even like him very much. In fact the longer he spoke to him, the more sure of it he became. But like him or not, Sturt wanted him, and quite badly.

Eyre said, 'I'm interested to know why you don't want to lead this particular exploration yourself.'

Sturt laid a hand on his chest. 'My health, I'm afraid. I'm still not quite the man I was. Eyesight's poor; lungs still clog up a bit. My wife's not keen, either. And, besides, I feel confident that you would carry it out far more successfully than I.'

Eyre nodded, slowly. He really had no more questions. Not for Captain Sturt, anyway. There was one question, however, which he had to ask of himself; and that was whether he was prepared to search for Yonguldye on an expedition which was intended to bring about the eventual extinction of everything that the Aborigines held to be holy; of their gods, and their totems, and their hunting-grounds; in fact of their existence.

If he went, and if he were successful, Yanluga's spirit could at last be guided to its resting-place in the sky; but it was possible that his discoveries would hasten the white colonisation of South Australia by months, if not years, especially if he were to find opals, or gold. If he didn't go, then the Aborigine's lands might remain unexplored for decades, but Yanluga would have to remain where he was, buried like an animal next to Lathrop Lindsay's favourite horse, his soul unsettled for ever. And there was no guarantee that Sturt himself might not decide to undertake the expedition; or any one of half-a-dozen explorers, some of them far more inconsiderate towards Aborigines than Sturt.

To Eyre, the responsibility of making up his mind was like a physical pain, and he stood for almost five minutes on the shoreline, his fingertips pressed to his temples, staring out to sea. Sturt, however, seemed to be prepared to wait for him, and sat on a broken wooden bucket nearby, quite calm, and smoked a cigar.

Destiny, thought Eyre. The terrible *jug-a-nath* of destiny. One day he had been responsible for nothing and nobody more than himself, and for keeping the wheels of his bicycle well-greased with emu fat. Then he had fallen for Charlotte, and become acquainted with Yanluga. Now Yanluga was dead, and Eyre had become responsible not just for him, but for every Aboriginal in South Australia. He knew it: he sensed it. What had Christopher called him? 'One of these chaps who has to do something *noble*.' Why had he been unable to let Yanluga lie? Was it because he still loved Charlotte; and carrying out this expedition gave him one last tenuous connection with her? Or was it truly a Christian sense of duty? The need to do something noble?

He thought of his father, on the night when he had told him that he was going to emigrate; and that he was not going to take holy orders. 'I am extremely sad,' his father had admitted, 'but I have to say that I respect what you believe All I require of you is that you in your turn, always respect the beliefs of others.'

Had the words of an English country vicar, spoken over supper two years ago to his disobedient son, now become the *leitmotiv* for the gradual dismemberment of an entire primaeval civilisation? Perhaps they had. Perhaps that was the real devastating power of God's holy word, from halfway around the world.

Because what could Eyre believe? In Christ crucified, and the holy testaments? Or in Kinnie-Ger, the cat beast; and Yara Ma, who could swallow a human being whole, and suck up a creek so that a whole village would die of drought? And much of what Captain Sturt had said was true. The blackfellows in the bush were filthy, and under-nourished, and appallingly ignorant. Could it be that Yanluga's death had set in motion an historic series of events that would at last bring them health, and content-ment, and the spiritual satisfaction of knowing that they were the children both of Her Majesty the Queen, and of God?

Eyre turned his back on the sea, and walked across to Captain Sturt with his hands still pressed, a little melodra-matically, to his temples. He was conscious of the melo-drama, but Sturt was, too; and Sturt played his part by smoking his cigar with equanimity and saying nothing.

It was then that Eyre caught a glimpse of a movement among the distant sand-dunes. He slowly lowered his hands, and looked more carefully. At first there was nothing; but then he saw a thin stick, like a reed, or a wand, moving rhythmically behind the curves of the dunes. It began to rise higher and higher, and at last it revealed itself to be a long spear, being carried up the far side of the dune by an Aborigine warrior, fully decorated with ochre and feathers.

The Aborigine stood on the skyline for no more than a quarter of a minute, but it was plain to Eyre that he had meant to be seen; and that his presence there was not accidental. He made some kind of distant hand-signal, and then he disappeared from sight.

Captain Sturt turned around on his bucket just too late to see what Eyre had been looking at.

'Are you all right?' he asked. He glanced back once towards the dunes and then he tossed his cigar-butt into the surf. 'Perhaps we'd better be getting back.'

'Yes,' said Eyre. An extraordinary feeling passed over him, as if he were going to pass out. He blinked at Sturt and for a moment he couldn't think who he was; or what either of them were doing here.

They began to walk back towards the port. A sudden shower started to fall, but at the same time the sun came out, and the gulf was bridged by a three-quarter rainbow, intensely vivid against the graphite-coloured sky. Then a second rainbow appeared, but fainter.

'An omen, perhaps,' smiled Sturt.

Eyre turned his high coat-collar up against the spattering rain. He was wearing a new silk necktie, maroon, and he didn't want to get it wet.

'Perhaps,' he said. 'In any case, I accept your offer.'

Sturt looked at him, as if he were expecting him to say more. But when Eyre remained silent, he said, 'Very well. That's excellent.' Then, 'Good. I'm very pleased about that.'

They walked as far as the wharf, which was silvered with wet. They shook hands, and Sturt said, 'I want to have a talk to Colonel Gawler; then I'll be in touch with you again.'

Eyre said, 'You knew what I was going to decide, didn't you?'

'My dear fellow,' smiled Sturt. 'I never had any doubt of it.'

'You know what consequences this expedition may have? On Australia, I mean; and the Aborigines?'

Sturt kept on smiling, but the expression in his eyes was quite serious. 'The interior of this continent is quite uncharted,' he said. 'That means that the explorations of one man can have extraordinary effects on the lives of thousands. I myself discovered the second greatest river network in the entire world, after the Amazon. What you may discover on this expedition could be equally momentous. The great inland sea, perhaps; which could be wider than the Caspian. The greatest forest beyond the continent of Africa. You will be making history, Mr Walker; you will be finding rivers and mountains and deserts that no white man has ever found before.'

He paused, and then in quite a different voice, he said, 'You will be finding something else equally important—and I speak now from my own experience. You will be finding yourself.'

Twelve

After the offices of the South Australian Company had been locked up that evening, he bicycled home to Hindley Street. The day's showers had cleared the air; and it was one of those bright marmalade-coloured Adelaide evenings, with the fragrance of acacia in the air. His bicycle left criss-crossing tracks on the muddy streets.

He felt quiet, and rather depressed. He had explained to Christopher what Captain Sturt had said to him during their walk on the beach; and told him that he had decided to look for Yonguldye and whatever geographical or geological features Captain Sturt might be interested in. He hadn't told him about the appearance of the lone Aborigine warrior, but then he felt for the time being that he would prefer to keep it to himself. He didn't yet understand the visitation himself, and he didn't want to share it until he did.

He felt like Macbeth must have felt, after seeing Banquo's ghost.

As he turned into Hindley Street, three or four ragamuffin Aborigine children began to run after him, shouting 'No-Fall-Over! No-Fall-over!' and 'Come -To-Jesus!' which were the very first words that Aborigine children were taught at missionary school. The street was scattered with bright blue puddles, like mirrors, and the children skipped barefoot into the mirrors and smashed them into splashes.

Dogger McConnell was sitting on the verandah under a wet canvas tent, which he wore as if it were a particularly badly designed evening cloak. He raised a jug of beer, and called, 'Good evening, mate! Come and have a drink!'

Eyre dismounted and put away his bicycle. 'Why are you sitting out here?' he asked Dogger. 'You could have caught pneumonia, in all that rain.'

Dogger jerked his head towards the front door. 'We had a bit of a horse-and-cow, me and the estimable missus. I was told never again to darken the parlour. Well, it was my fault. She's a saint, really. A saint who's married an objectionable old devil. Want a drink? It's the first jug of the new batch; better than last time. Last one made you fart, didn't you find? All day on the dunny playing *Oh God Our Help In Ages Past* and never a shit to show for it.'

'I think I'll wait until the brew's matured a little, thank you,' said Eyre. 'Besides, I have some sensible thinking to do.'

'Ah,' said Dogger. 'Thinking. That's something I haven't done for a while. Well, never mind. There's plenty of beer here, once you've finished. Need your liquid, in this climate. Worse in the outback, of course, out beyond the black stump. Saw a fellow sitting under his mule once, waiting for it to piss, he was so thirsty. Saw another fellow squeezing shinglebacks in between his bare hands, just to get their juice.'

Eyre touched Dogger's shoulder. 'Perhaps I'll come out and talk to you later. Leave some for me.'

Mrs McConnell was in the kitchen, her sleeves rolled up, flouring a board so that she could roll out her pastry. There was a good strong aroma of mutton and carrots curling out of the big black pot on the front of the range; and a steamed pudding was clattering away at the back.

'A blackfellow called by,' said Mrs McConnell. She nodded towards the stained pine dresser. 'There's a letter for you there.'

Eyre took down the pale blue envelope and tore it open. He knew at once that it was from Charlotte. The writing was firm and clear, with loops like rows of croquet-hoops.

Eyre read it through quickly; then drew across one of Mrs McConnell's bentwood chairs, and sat down to read it again.

My darling Eyre, (Charlotte had written) after everything that occurred at the Spring Ball, I think that I owe you both an apology and an explanation. What I said to you on the wharf, my dear, that I would always love you, that was quite true, and remains true. Every moment that I am without you, you are dearer to my heart, and I miss you most dreadfully.

The day after poor Yanluga died, however, my father confided in me that he was seriously ill. He had suffered a seizure of the heart whilst in Sydney, and that was the reason why he came home before he was expected. His doctors have told him that he must take great care, otherwise his next seizure might prove fatal.

Of course, he is a volatile man, and it is difficult for him to keep his temper, but I know that he loves me in spite of everything and that he is trying in his own way to do his best for me. He is so sure that his time is short that he is anxious to put his family and his business affairs into order, and that I should be happily and appropriately settled.

To begin with, he had nothing against you personally, dear Eyre. It was just that he wanted to make sure that his only daughter should be secure and contented and well cared-for; and he did not believe that a mere clerk could do that for me. Of course, events since then have unhappily led to a personal argument between you, but father is not an unforgiving man, and the time may come when you will again be on speaking-terms with him.

In the meanwhile, please understand that I must do everything I can to keep my father rested and calm, and not to provoke him. It is my sacred duty as a daughter, I know you will realise that. That is why I spoke to you the way that I did at the Ball.

May I please beg of you not to disclose to anyone anything concerning my father's health, since his business interests would suffer badly if it were suspected that he were unwell. Please remember my darling that *whatever happens* I shall always love you and think of you, no matter how many years go by.

Your adoring Charlotte.

Eyre folded up the letter and tucked it into his pocket. Mrs McConnell said, 'Not bad news, is it?'

'Well,' said Eyre, 'good and bad.'

'Somebody's died and left you a fortune?

'Hm, I wish they had.' He stood up, and walked around to the range, lifting up the pot lids to see what was cooking. 'Is supper going to be very long?'

'You've time to change.'

Mrs McConnell wiped her hands on her apron, and reached across to touch Eyre's arm. 'It's that girl, isn't it, Miss Charlotte?'

Eyre nodded.

'I thought it was. I recognised the blackfellow who brought the letter. One of Mr Lindsay's boys. She hasn't written to say that she doesn't love you any more?'

'No,' said Eyre, and for some unaccountable reason he felt a lump in his throat as big as a crab-apple. 'She still loves me; but we may not be able to see each other for quite a long time.'

He paused, and then he said, 'We may not be able to see each other ever. Mr Lindsay is determined to marry her off to somebody wealthy.'

Mrs McConnell heard that downsloping, near-to-tears catch in his voice, and came around the kitchen table and held him, without any ceremony or affectation, and kissed him like a mother.

'You don't *always* have to be brave, you know,' she told him. Her eyes were pale blue, like a washed-out spring sky, with tiny pupils. 'It isn't necessary; not for women, nor for men, neither. I know how much you like her. She's a very pretty girl. Not much in her head, perhaps, except for fun and flattery, but what girl has. Well, I never had much more, when I was younger, and there were times when Dogger piped his eye over me, I can tell you, although you're on your honour not to tell him now. Why do you think I put up with him; what with his beer and his snoring; and he can't eat anything without making a crunching noise, not even porridge.'

Eyre looked down at Mrs McConnell and suddenly laughed. He kissed her on the nose, and then on both cheeks, and hugged her.

'You're a rare lady, Mrs McConnell. You've cheered me up.'

'Are you sure? Because you can cry if you feel the need.'

Eyre shook his head, and kissed her again. 'I don't think so. I'll go upstairs and get changed for supper.'

They sat around the dining-room table, under the slightly smoking oil-lamp, and ate mutton stew and suet dumplings and fresh greens cooked crunchy and bright. Dogger drank two pots of beer and told a long story about the Aborigines at Swan River; and how they had developed an insatiable enthusiasm for linen handkerchiefs, and broken into white men's huts and cottages searching for nothing else, not guns, not flour, but linen handkerchiefs.

'I suppose with hooters as big as theirs, linen handkerchiefs were quite a comfort,' Dogger ended up, obliquely.

While Mrs McConnell washed up the dishes, Dogger and Eyre played a game of draughts out on the verandah.

Dogger said, 'You're quiet tonight, mate. Something preying on your mind?'

Eyre crowned one of his draughts, and then shook his head. 'Nothing serious. But I may be going away for a while.'

'Away? Where?'

'Exploring. Well—partly exploring and partly looking for someone.'

'Not in the outback?'

'Yes.'

'But, Christ Almighty, you don't know the first thing about exploring! Do you have any idea at all what it's *like* out there? How hot it can be? How *dry*? You can walk for weeks and never see water. Who's going with you?'

'One or two friends. Christopher Willis, I hope.'

'You're not serious. Christopher Willis, that wilting plant? He wouldn't stay alive for three days in the outback.'

Eyre said, 'We're taking Aborigine guides along with us.' He felt quite hurt and embarrassed that Dogger should think so little of their chances. 'The main guide will be a blackfellow called Joolonga, if you've ever heard of him.'

'Joolonga? Joolonga Billy or Joolonga Jacky-Jack?'

Eyre shrugged. 'He's a constable, apparently.'

'That's Joolonga Billy, then. Lucky for you, I suppose. He's experienced enough. I met him a couple of times out at Eurinilla Creek. He used to teach some of the new chums how to track, how to tell one kind of footprint from another. He did it the same way they teach Aborigine children: making tracks for them to follow and then hiding behind a rock, to see if they could find him. He could make counterfeit tracks, could Joolonga Billy: snake-tracks with his kangaroo-hide whip, and dingo tracks with his knuckles. But he always said there was only one way to make counterfeit camel-tracks, and that was to use a bare baby's bottom.'

'Well,' said Eyre, 'it seems as if we'll be properly taken care of.'

Dogger looked down at the draughts board. Above his head, hanging from the rafters, the oil-lamp was thick with insects and moths, and their shadows flickered across the squares of the board like the shadows in Eyre's dreams.

'How far are you going?' asked Dogger, trying hard not to sound interested.

'I don't know. I have to find an Aborigine chief called Yonguldye. As far as I understand it, he could be absolutely anywhere north of Adelaide. Depending on whether I find him or not, and depending on what he tells me, if he tells me anything, I could go no further than fifty miles away. On the other hand, I may go hundreds of miles away—as far as the northern coast.'

Dogger moved one of his draughts. 'You'll die, you know,' he told Eyre, matter-of-factly.

He looked up at Eyre and there was such an expression of care and certainty on his face that Eyre didn't know what to say to him.

154

After a while, though, Eyre said, 'It was Captain Sturt who suggested we might get as far as the north. In fact, he's going to put up the money for the whole expedition.'

'Captain Sturt,' said Dogger.

'That's right, Captain Sturt. He came down to the port to talk to me this morning. He firmly believes that the centre of Australia is covered by an inland sea; as large as the Caspian, he said. All we have to do is reach its southernmost shore, and then we can sail for most of the way.'

'Sail,' said Dogger.

'You don't have to sound so sceptical,' Eyre retorted. 'There may not be an actual sea. There may be a forest, instead. But if there are trees there, we'll soon be able to find water, and fruit to eat; and only God can guess what manner of creatures might inhabit it.'

'Bunyips, I wouldn't be surprised,' said Dogger, pouring himself some more beer.

There was a long and difficult silence between them. Then Dogger wiped his mouth with the back of his hand, and said, 'There has to be a first time for everybody, I suppose. But you just make sure that your first time isn't your last. When you're out in that mallee scrub, with the wind blowing willy-willys all around you; and your horses scared to death; and you haven't had a drink of water for four days; you just remember what Dogger McConnell told you. There isn't any sea in the middle of Australia, and there isn't any forest. There's sand out there, that's what there is, because I've been there; or at least as far as anyone has; and all I've ever seen is sand, and scrub, and more sand; and sometimes I've seen skeletons, of dogs, and mutton-birds, and men.'

Eyre finished his beer. It was lukewarm, and flat. 'I'll remember what you said,' he told Dogger. Then, 'Seriously, I'll remember.'

Dogger grunted. 'Who's winning this damned game?' he wanted to know.

'I am,' said Eyre.

'Well, you damned well shouldn't be. You can't have everything.'

Eyre looked at Dogger with a smile. 'You're jealous,' he said.

'Jealous? What in hell do you mean?'

'You're jealous about my going on this expedition. That's what it is.'

'Why should I be jealous?' Dogger asked him, caustically. 'I've had enough of sand and rats and flies and murderous blackfellows to last me a lifetime.'

'I still think you're jealous.'

'Play the damned game,' Dogger growled.

Eyre crowned another of his draughts, and then said, 'You'd come, wouldn't you, if you were asked?'

Dogger was silent for a very long time. His head was bowed over the board but Eyre knew that he wasn't concentrating on the game. His face was completely concealed by the dark semi-circular shadow of his hat; but his hands were illuminated by the lamplight, hands with callouses and scars and broad, horny nails, and fine hairs that had been gilded by the sun.

Dogger sniffed, and then said, 'I can remember one morning I was camping up in the Flinders Range. I was lost, as a matter of fact, although I never admitted it to anybody. I woke up in the middle of the morning, round about nine or ten o'clock, and the sky was blue, deep blue; and up against it the mountains rose up like a fortress. Red they were, you've never seen such red. The Aborigines say that a giant emu used to live there, and that when it was slaughtered, its blood splashed all over the rocks. Actually, it's red ochre; the stuff they call *wilga*. They come from hundreds of miles to collect it, just to rub all over themselves; but that's the Aborigines for you.'

He picked up his beer-glass; realised it was empty; and set it down again.

'I woke up,' he said, 'and there was a blackfellow staring at me; with emu feathers in his headband, and *wilga* all over his face, silent he was, staring at me.'

Dogger lifted his head, so that the lamplight delineated the triangle of his nose.

'He could have killed me, you know, while I was sleeping. He could have killed me when I woke up. He was fully armed, with a spear and a boomerang and a kind of a club made out of animal bone, or a human bone, who knows. But instead he made a sign with his hand, three fingers down, one finger raised, and that means "who are you?" I knew that, so I said, "Dogger McConnell." '

'Well?' asked Eyre. 'What did he do?'

Dogger shrugged. 'He blinked at me, and then he made the sign again, "who are you?" as if he couldn't believe what I'd told him. So I said, "Dogger McConnell" and, damn me, do you know what he did?'

'Tell me,' Eyre insisted.

'He laughed, that's what he did. That damned impudent blackfellow, his face all covered in mud and ochre and God knows what else, stark naked, you certainly couldn't have taken him home to meet your mother. But he laughed and laughed; I thought he was going to be sick. And then he pointed at me, and said 'Dogger McConnell', clear as a bell, and laughed even more. And then, when he'd finished laughing, he rubbed his eyes, and walked off, and that was the last I ever saw of him.'

Eyre said, 'Dogger.'

Dogger gave a sharp sniff, and cleared his throat. 'Come on, now, Eyre. You know what I'm trying to tell you.'

There was another long silence between them. All around the house, the cicadas sang; and the moon that had haunted Eyre the previous night rose again behind the gums.

Dogger said, 'Once you've been there, once you've seen it, the colours, the trees, the smell of eucalyptus oil; once the Aborigines have laughed at you, and taken you for just a friend, well—'

He grasped Eyre's hand, tightly, quite unexpectedly. 'I'd do anything to come with you,' he said. 'Anything at all.'

157

Eyre said, 'I'll have to see. It depends on how much money Captain Sturt is able to raise.'

'But you'll consider it?'

Eyre looked down at the draughts board. Then he looked back up at Dogger. 'Play the damned game,' he told him.

Thirteen

Eyre was almost asleep that night when there was a rapping at his bedroom door. He opened his eyes, and lay still for a moment, unsure if the rapping had been real, or a dream. But then it came again: softly, almost furtively.

He threw back the quilt and walked across to the door. He leaned his head towards the door, and said, 'Who is it?'

Mrs McConnell whispered, 'It's me. Dogger's asleep.'

Eyre opened up the door. Mrs McConnell was standing on the landing in her capacious linen nightdress, with a frilly mob-cap covering her hair, a lamp in one hand, and a big white mug of steaming-hot meat stock held up in her other hand like the Holy Grail.

'I thought you might want a drink before you went to bed,' she told him.

'Oh. Well, thank you.'

He held out his hand for the mug but she kept it just out of his reach. 'I wanted to have a little talk to you, too,' she said.

'Can't it wait until the morning? I must say I'm rather tired.'

'It won't take long, I promise.'

'Well, er—come in,' said Eyre, and opened his bedroom door wider.

Mrs McConnell bustled past him; after all the bedroom did belong to her; and set the mug of meat stock down on top of the bureau. Then she said, 'Close the door,' and when Eyre hesitated, 'It's quite all right. I can do what I like in my own house. I don't need anybody else in Hindley Street to tell me what morals are.'

Eyre stood there in his nightshirt, raking his fingers through his scratchy hair. He wished that he were wearing britches; or his new nightshirt at least; but this one was old and worn-out, with a hole on one side through which two weeks ago he had accidentally pushed his great toe. It didn't make any difference that Mrs McConnell always washed and ironed it for him: he felt shabby and ill-at-ease.

Mrs McConnell sat herself down on the end of the bed, and patted the quilt imperiously as an instruction to Eyre that he should sit beside her.

'Dogger was talking to me tonight,' she said. 'It seems that you're going off on some kind of an expedition.'

'Yes,' said Eyre. 'It looks as if I am.'

'Don't you think it was your duty to tell me first, before Dogger?'

'I don't really see why. It isn't definite yet; and when it is, you'll be the first to know. It was just one of those things that comes out in conversation.'

'Dogger says that you promised to take him along.'

Eyre shook his head. 'That's not true. I'm sorry, but it isn't. He asked me to consider taking him, but I don't even know yet how much money is going to be put up; or how many people I'll be able to take.'

'Dogger says that you're going to go north.'

'That's right. We'll be looking for minerals, and cattle-tracks, and whatever else we can find. Captain Sturt believes that we may be able to reach the inland sea.'

Mrs McConnell looked at him with motherly solicitude. The lamplight behind her head gave her mob-cap the appearance of a home-made halo; and lit up the stray wisps of hair that curled out from underneath it. The Madonna of the Boarding-House. She touched Eyre's hand and for some reason he shivered, not because she repelled him in any way, but because he suddenly remembered his mother; in fact, more than remembered her, felt her, smelled her, sensed her; all around him, like a warm and actual ghost.

Yet he knew it was only memory. His mother lay under her grey granite gravestone in St Crispin's churchyard; rained-on, snowed-on, lit by rainbows; gone forever. And thinking of that, he admitted to himself for the first time something that he had never been able to admit to himself before, that he would never return to England; ever.

Mrs McConnell said, 'Would you think me foolish if I asked you not to go?'

He frowned at her. 'Is there any particular reason?'

'If I were to give you one, would it make any difference?' Mrs McConnell asked him. Her hand still touching his.

Eyre shrugged. 'I don't know. I don't really think so.'

'Are you going because of her?'

'You mean Charlotte? Well, partly; but not really.'

'I lost my son, you know,' said Mrs McConnell. She lowered her head, so that Eyre found himself looking at the top of her mob-cap. There was a tiny silk bow in the middle, like a butterfly.

Eyre said, 'Do you still miss him so badly?'

'I haven't missed him so much since you've been here.'

There was a curious silence between them. No wind rattled at the window, no dogs barked, no moths tapped at the lampshade. It was so silent that they could hear each other breathing, and Eyre was suddenly embarrassed by a little gurgle in his stomach.

Mrs McConnell looked up again. Her face was glistening with tears. 'I'm a ridiculous woman,' she said, 'but I've grown to think of you as my second son, and that's why I don't want you to go. I beg you.'

'I'll come back,' Eyre told her. 'I promise you.'

'No,' she said. 'Either you'll die, which is what I'm really afraid of; or else you'll be acclaimed as a hero. And if you're acclaimed as a hero, you won't want to live here any more, not at Mrs McConnell's boarding-house. No, it'll be King William Street for you, or North Terrace. Eyre, think of what you're doing. You have a home here, and you always will.'

Eyre didn't know what to say. He tried to smile at her, and he laid his hand on her shoulder, but she wouldn't be comforted. The tears basted her cheeks, and her mouth was puckered miserably, and she trembled all over as if she were chilled.

He held her close to him. He felt slightly absurd and extremely uncomfortable, but she clung on to him tightly, quivering from time to time, and there was nothing he could do to break free. He found himself looking over her shoulder at the mug of meat stock on the bureau, with its wisp of steam like an advertisement for Twining's tea; and at his own face in the mirror where he kept his hair-brushes. A serious, thinnish young man, with well-trimmed side-whiskers, and anxious eyes. His nose was a little too narrow, he always thought; and his mouth too melancholy, especially for somebody who liked to laugh as much as he did. But he thought he looked eminently suitable for Charlotte. Handsome, particular, intelligent. Pity about the nightshirt with the toe-hole in it.

Mrs McConnell shivered. 'I'm cold,' she said. 'I don't know why. I feel as if the whole world is freezing.

'Would you like to wrap my quilt around you?' asked Eyre.

She lifted her head and looked at him. Her face was full of questions. 'Could I lie with you in your bed for a little while? Could you hold me, and warm me up?'

Eyre smiled and then immediately stopped smiling. 'Well,' he said. 'Well.' Then, 'It's not quite—well.'

'Hold me,' Mrs McConnell pleaded.

With some difficulty, Eyre manoeuvered himself backwards, and lifted up the quilt, and pushed his legs beneath it. Mrs McConnell climbed in beside him, so that they were both sitting upright side by side in the rigid little brass bed. Eyre cleared his throat, and then awkwardly lifted his right arm, like a chicken-wing, and put it around Mrs McConnell's plump back. She kissed his cheek; and then smeared away her tears with her fingers, and said, 'You don't know how much you mean to me; I promise you that. You don't have the slightest idea.'

'Well,' said Eyre, 'nobody could have wished for a better landlady. Or, indeed, for better care.'

'Is that all?' asked Mrs McConnell.

'Oh, well, no—of course not. Affection as well as care. And sympathy, too. And consideration. And, well—'

'Yes?' asked Mrs McConnell, her eyes moist and bright, like newly opened cockles.

'Well, love,' he admitted.

There was a pause. She beamed at him beatifically. Then she patted the quilt, and said, 'Let's lie down. Hold me. Keep me warm.'

There was a prolonged bout of jostling and struggling, and at last they managed to position themselves face to face on the bed. Mrs McConnell, with sudden joviality, kissed Eyre on the nose.

Eyre said, 'What about the light?'

'Do you mind the light?' asked Mrs McConnell.

'Not particularly.'

'Well, then, let's leave it.'

'All right,' said Eyre.

They continued to lie side by side for several minutes. The meat stock on the bureau grew slowly cooler and steam no longer rose from the rim of the mug. Far away, out in the darkness, a night parrot cackled; and the wind began to rise again and lift the dust along the street, with a soft sifting noise that Eyre had sometimes mistaken for rain. Mrs McConnell said, 'I'm feeling warmer now, thank goodness.'

Eyre tried to reposition himself more comfortably, and found that his penis was suddenly resting against Mrs

McConnell's thigh. He gave her the thinnest of smiles, and tried his best to think of something else. He thought about Arthur Mortlock, and Lathrop Lindsay. He thought about his father, and *Pilgrim's Progress*, and even the words of John Selden. 'Pleasures are all alike simply considered in themselves. He that takes pleasure to hear sermons enjoys himself as much as he that hears plays.'

But all the time his penis wilfully unfolded itself, and rose, and then stiffened so hard that it was pressing against Mrs McConnell's bulging stomach through the material of her nightdress.

Eyre was sweating. He stared at Mrs McConnell at very close quarters and Mrs McConnell stared at him. Then suddenly he felt her fingers around him; and slowly she began to caress him, up and down.

He said nothing. To begin with, he didn't want to; and then later, he didn't need to. She rubbed him and rubbed him and he closed his eyes. There was a strong smell of meat stock in the room, and Mrs McConnell was panting lightly, under her breath.

Suddenly the room seemed to tighten, like the shrinking pupil of an owl's eye, and then Eyre anointed Mrs McConnell's hand, in three warm spurts.

'Ssh,' she said, kissing him again. She didn't seem to be at all embarrassed. Instead, what she had done for him was as kindly and as matter-of-fact as bathing a cut, or easing a headache with a cold compress.

After a while, though, Eyre said, 'We can't really stay like this all night, can we?'

Mrs McConnell smiled. 'In your own house, you can do whatever you wish.'

'But Dogger—'

'Don't you go worrying about Dogger. I've had no attention from Dogger these past five years. Dogger can sleep off that skinful of drink and mind his own business.'

At last, however, she climbed out of bed, and brushed down her nightdress, and went to collect her lamp.

'Your drink's gone cold,' she told him.

'Well,' he said. 'Never mind. I can always have some water if I'm thirsty in the night.'

'You'll think about staying?' she asked.

'I can't make you any promises.'

'I don't want to lose you, you know. Not like that.'

Eyre didn't say anything. There was nothing he could think of to say. How could you bluntly hurt the feelings of a woman who was prepared to treat you like her own son; nurse you and coddle you; and even relieve you sexually? He knew with a kind of detached amazement that if he had wanted to mount her, and fornicate with her, she probably would have let him. In fact she probably would have done anything at all. That was the measure of her emotional need.

She leaned over the bed and kissed his forehead. 'You sleep well now, and I'll see you at breakfast.'

'Goodnight, Mrs McConnell.'

She brushed back his hair with the tips of her fingers. 'When we're alone together, you can call me Constance.'

'Thank you.'

There was a lengthy pause, while she stood beside him with her upraised lamp. 'Goodnight, Constance,' he told her; and she kissed him again, and left, closing the door behind her as quietly as if it were a nursery, where her baby was sleeping; and hesitating just for a moment on the landing outside in case he should call for anything.

He lay awake for hours, thinking of what had happened; and when he did sleep, in the cold silent time before dawn, he dreamed of his mother laying out alphabet blocks for him, one after the other, and he dreaded what they might eventually spell out.

Fourteen

On Saturday morning, he received an unexpected visit from Captain Sturt and a man called Pickens, whose face was as yellow as custard, and who introduced himself as Captain Sturt's accountant. They sat in Mrs McConnell's front parlour, drinking Mrs McConnell's sherry-wine, and they told Eyre expansively that they had been able to raise from the Adelaide business community subscriptions amounting to £1,103 and some shillings, which would be more than adequate to finance a six-week expedition to the north, in search of precious minerals, passable stock-routes, and God favourable, the legendary inland sea. Or forest, Captain Sturt qualified himself. Or, indeed, swamp.

'Or desert,' remarked Dogger, who was sitting in the corner, refusing to mind his own business.

Captain Sturt turned around in his chair. 'My dear fellow, I know that you have an extensive knowledge of the country as far north as the Flinders Range, and Broken Hill; but when you go even further north, it becomes quite evident that all the rivers and natural drainage systems are flowing not towards the sea but in the opposite direction, towards the very heart of Australia. Where does all this water go? The very simplest mind can deduce that there must be an inland ocean.'

'Or forest,' said Dogger.

'Or swamp,' agreed Captain Sturt.

Dogger opened his small penknife-blade with his teeth, and began to cut at the hardened dottle in his pipe. 'All I can say, sir, is this: that there may well have been an ocean there once, just as there were lakes and creeks and rivers all over the outback. But these days it's fierce out there, sir; as hot as a furnace; and I never saw water survive for long in a furnace. That sun can make a man's blood boil dry; and I will lay you money that it can make an ocean boil dry, too, just as easy.'

Captain Sturt let out a peculiarly feminine laugh, and turned to Eyre and Pickens with amusement. 'He's quite a character, your Mr McConnell. Quite a character. Salt of the earth.'

Eyre glanced at Dogger in embarrassment, but Dogger was studiously cleaning out his pipe and ignoring Captain Sturt's patronising banter as if it were nothing more than the clacking of parrots.

Captain Sturt leaned forward and said to Eyre, 'You will take Joolonga and two more Aborigines, a carrier called Midgegooroo and a boy called Weeip. Then I suggest you take two companions of your own choosing; for although I know one or two fellows who are sturdy and helpful and ready to take part in whatever adventures might befall them, I believe from my own experience that your choice of travelling-companions must be your own. They must be men that you trust, and like, and with whom you feel easy. There will be exhausting days ahead of you; sometimes dangerous days; and to have with you men whom you dislike is to court disaster.'

Eyre said, 'I have one or two ideas for travelling-companions. It may depend on whether I can persuade them to come with me.'

'Well, don't take them if they require too much persuading, or you will find that, when times become difficult, which they assuredly will, they will blame you for every hardship and privation they have to endure. I truly believe that the qualities you have to look for are loyalty, and stamina, and a degree of personal courage. No man is experienced in exploring this territory, for no man has ever been there before. So what you need to look for are friends, rather than veterans.'

With that, he gave an odd jerk of his neck.

Eyre said, 'I beg your pardon?'

Captain Sturt smiled at him, and then jerked his neck again. Eyre suddenly realised that he was jerking his neck towards Dogger.

'You mean I shouldn't take Mr McConnell with me?' he asked Sturt, in a loud voice.

Captain Sturt frowned, and flushed. 'Nothing of the kind. I didn't mean that at all. I simply meant that you should consider your travelling companions with unusual care.'

'Is there any quality which Mr McConnell particularly lacks, which renders him unsuitable?' Eyre asked him.

Pickens said, in a nasal tone, 'I'm not sure that Captain Sturt was trying to suggest that Mr McConnell is in any way unsuitable. I believe that he was simply suggesting that one ought to consider how one's companions are going to behave in extreme circumstances.'

Eyre stood up, and walked around behind Pickens, so that the yellow-faced accountant was obliged to twist uncomfortably around in his chair in order to see him.

'I appreciate that Captain Sturt and several other businessmen in Adelaide have been generous enough to finance me, and to give me guidance,' he said, in almost schoolmasterly tones. 'However, the idea of looking for Yonguldye was mine, and remains my obligation; and it is *my* life that will be at risk. I have already told Captain Sturt that I will do my best to locate whatever minerals may be to hand; and that I will also attempt to find a reasonable track for driving stock. But that is as far as I will go in return for money. I expect to be able to choose whoever goes with me, for whatever reasons I wish, and which route I take, and when the expedition has gone far enough.'

Captain Sturt clapped his hands. 'Bravo!' he shouted.

Eyre looked across at him in surprise.

'I say "bravo!" because I know what kind of a fellow you really are,' Sturt enthused, standing up, and looking around him as if he were well pleased with himself. 'You are a young man of vision, and fortitude; and you will not give up until you have discovered everything which you set out to discover. I trust you, Mr Eyre Walker! By God, I trust you! You will be back here in Adelaide inside of eight weeks, with news that you have found opals, and copper, and even gold; and that you have sighted in the distance the glittering shores of the inland sea, even if you haven't actually sailed on it!'

He came over and clapped Eyre enthusiastically on the back, and then Pickens; but when he went towards Dogger, his hand lifted in gladsome welcome, Dogger glared at him with such a grotesque expression of contempt that he was obliged to skip and swivel and pretend that he had only stepped towards the corner of the room to adjust his necktie in the mirror.

'Well, now!' Sturt enthused. 'You must come to lunch on Monday, Mr Walker; and tell me what plans you have devised. We will go over the latest maps, and discuss the very best course of action. If you can, I would like you to tell me who you have chosen to go with you; so that I may talk to them too.'

'Very well,' said Eyre. He glanced towards Dogger, who was now carefully packing the bowl of his pipe with home-grown tobacco. 'Where are you staying?'

'On Grenfell Street, with the Wilsons. Come at half-past eleven, sharp. Mrs Wilson is a capital cook; you'll enjoy it.'

'Yes,' said Eyre. 'Mrs McConnell is a capital cook, too.'

'And more besides,' said Dogger, obliquely.

Captain Sturt and Pickens both left, raising their hats several times too often to Mrs McConnell. Eyre stood on the verandah watching them climb into their carriage, and then went back into the house.

'Well?' asked Dogger.

'Well, what?' Eyre replied.

'Well, are you going to take me with you? You said you had one or two ideas for travelling-companions.'

Eyre sat down opposite him, and laced his fingers together. Dogger watched him expectantly; but when Eyre didn't speak, and when the clock on the chimney-shelf at last struck half past ten, Dogger put down his pipe and his penknife and sat well back in his armchair, and looked at Eyre with an expression both of forgiveness and of desperate disappointment.

'I didn't think you would,' he told him. 'Too old, I suppose. Drink too much. Don't want a sodden old dingo-hunter on a smart expedition like this; not with Captain Charles Sturt putting up the money for it, no sir. Well, I can't say that I blame you; not completely. But I would be more of an asset than a liability, and I'd never drink a drop, not me. And it could be that I would save your life.'

Eyre said, 'Don't think that I haven't considered taking you, Dogger. I have; and very deeply. There's only one thing that prevents me.'

'The beer? Come on, now, Eyre, I can easily give up the beer.'

'It's not the beer, Dogger, it's Constance.'

Dogger was outraged for a moment, and bulged out his bristly cheeks, and planted his hands on his hips, and couldn't think of a single word to express how furious he felt.

'Constance?' he burst out, at last.

Eyre nodded. 'You and I both have a responsibility to Constance. You know that, because your responsibility is far greater than mine. But if both of us were to die on this adventure, then she would have nobody to take care of her at all, and that would be more than she could bear. You left her for years and years, while you went out hunting for wild dogs; but she's used to you now, used to having you around the house. Used to your grumbling, and your drinking, and your bad temper. And, believe me, Dogger, she loves you.'

'I don't need a raw carrot like you to tell me my wife loves me.'

Eyre shrugged. 'I don't know. Perhaps you do.'

Dogger said, 'You're a damned preacher, do you know that? Too damned religious by half.'

'Well,' said Eyre, amused, 'perhaps I am.' He raised his hand as if he were bestowing a blessing on Dogger, and intoned, ' "You husbands, live with your wives in an understanding way, as with a weaker vessel. You have pursued a course of sensuality, lust, drunkenness, carousals, drinking parties, and abominable idolatries.'' The first letter of Peter.'

'Oh, bollocks,' said Dogger.

He went to the window and lifted back the flower-patterned nets so that he could look out over the dusty street. Then he said, 'I'm sorry. I didn't mean to blaspheme. It's just that I feel so useless here; shut in, do you see, like a dog in a kennel.'

Eyre watched him sympathetically but said nothing.

Dogger said, 'I just wanted to see the outback one more time. All those twisted trees, like demons and devils. All those cracked rocks, and dry creeks. And smell that smell, when the sun gets really hot, and the eucalyptus oil comes up from the trees in a vapour. And most of all, the sky. You don't know what a really blue sky is, until you've been out beyond the black stump.'

'I'm sorry,' said Eyre.

'Well,' sighed Dogger, 'I suppose I can understand your reasons.'

Constance came in, and asked them, 'Do you want some luncheon? It's mutton cutlets, and soubise sauce.'

'Want a beer before you eat?' Dogger asked Eyre.

Eyre said, 'I'd love one.' Dogger went off to pour a jug out of his latest barrel; but Constance McConnell stayed where she was, wiping her hands on her apron, looking at Eyre with that expression of warning and concern.

'Did you and Captain Sturt come to any conclusions?' she asked.

'Conclusions?'

'Have you decided to go?'

Eyre nodded. 'Yes, I have.'

'I see,' she said. 'I suppose there's no further use in appealing to you.'

'No.'

She sat down, and stared at him for a very long time. Outside in the street they could hear dogs barking and the cries of a man who would sharpen knives, and shears, and worm your cat.

'You're not taking Dogger with you, though?' asked Mrs McConnell.

'No. I'm afraid he's a little too old. We want to find water and cattle-trails and opals out there; not graves.'

'Well I suppose I can thank you for that.'

Eyre knelt down beside her chair, and held her arm. 'Constance,' he said, 'I'm going to make you one solemn promise. Whatever happens, I'll come back to you. Do you understand me? You've taken care of me. I promise in return that I'll take care of you.'

Constance McConnell lowered her head. Eyre stayed beside her for a little while, and then stood up. 'Shall we have some lunch?' he asked her.

At that moment, however, there was a sharp banging at the door-knocker. Dogger went to answer it with his jugful of beer in his hand, and it was Christopher Willis, in a baggy linen suit, and Arthur Mortlock, rather incongruously dressed as a waiter, with a red waistcoat and rows of shiny brass buttons.

'Sorry to barge in,' said Christopher, 'but do you think we could have a private word? Good morning, Mrs McConnell; fine day. Fine smell from the kitchen, too. Mutton stew?'

'Cutlets,' Mrs McConnell told him, snappily.

Arthur Mortlock took off his derby hat to reveal his prickly scalp, and grinned at Mrs McConnell with a clash of artificial teeth. 'Nothing to which I'm more partial than mutton cutlets,' he remarked. 'Especially when they've been cooked by a fair gentlewoman; near to raw; and then sprinkled with a little mustard-seed.'

Mrs McConnell blinked; unsure of what she ought to say. But Arthur bowed, and sniffed, and said, 'Please don't think that I was after inviting meself to lunch, mum. As it turns out, I don't have the time. I'm helping out a friend at the Adelaide Hotel just at the moment, waiting on table,

171

seeing as how he's short of fellows what knows the difference between a fish-fork and a kick in the nostril.'

Eyre reassuringly took Mrs McConnell's arm. 'Mr Mortlock is an acquaintance of mine, Mrs McConnell. He's quite respectable.'

'Well, then, a fine good morning to *him*', said Mrs McConnell, and bustled off back to her kitchen.

Dogger poured out beer for everybody, frowning at the jug when it was empty, and then ambled distractedly off to stoke up the kitchen range and lay the table. Christopher peered down the hallway to make sure that he was gone, and then closed the parlour door. He also went to the window, to see if there was anybody watching the house from the street outside.

'What's up?' asked Eyre.

'Arthur came to see me this morning and said that two men took rooms at the Adelaide Hotel late last night, presumably off the packet from Sydney. They told the porter they were on the lookout for ticket-of-leave men who had absconded from Botany Bay; and they gave the names Croucher, Philips, Bean, and Mortlock. Then this morning, over breakfast, they told another waiter that they had discovered already that Philips and Croucher were dead, killed and robbed by Aborigines; but that Bean and Mortlock were still at large, and that they were quite determined to run them to earth.'

Eyre said to Arthur, 'I presume Bean was the other man with you; the man who ran off.'

'Yes, sir,' said Arthur. 'I never knew his other name, sir, only Bean; and as far as I know that was the way his mother had him baptised, Bean and nothing more.'

'Have you heard from Bean since the night of the Ball?'

'No, sir. But he won't have gone far. He was never the adventurous kind. Nerves of seaweed, sir, had Bean.'

'If these men were to track Bean down, and question him, do you think you could rely on him not to tell them where you might be found?'

Arthur said, 'Hard to say, sir. But I doubt it. Bean was

never a hard case, sir, not in that sense of it. And if they threaten him with flogging, well, you can't blame a fellow for wanting to keep the flesh on his back, can you?'

'You must leave, then,' said Eyre.

Christopher fanned himself with his hat. 'It's a little more difficult than that, Eyre old chap. Apparently these fellows have got the roads watched, and they've been talking to all the Aborigine constables to make sure that nobody slips out of Adelaide through the bush. I was down at the port this morning, too—in fact, that's where Arthur came to find me—and all sea-captains and fishermen and boat owners have been told to keep a weather-eye open for men who want to leave Adelaide by sea in anything of a hurry. They've been offering rewards, too: bottles of rum for information; gold sovereigns for capture.'

'Well,' said Eyre, looking at Arthur warily. 'It seems as if they've made up their minds that they're going to run you down.'

'So it would seem, sir,' Arthur agreed.

'Of course, we have another little problem,' said Christopher. 'It's an offence to harbour a wanted criminal, and that means that both you and I are equally liable to be arrested and charged. And if this Bean decides to describe what happened on the night when Philips and Croucher were killed, why, we might very well find ourselves charged with aiding and abetting murder, too, and conspiracy, and obstructing justice.'

Eyre said, 'Come on, now, Christopher, we've done nothing criminal.'

'Oh, haven't we just? If you'd had the sense that night to call the police; or at least let Arthur run off, then we would have been quite all right. But here we are, almost as guilty of absconding from Botany Bay as he is.'

'Arthur will have to hide,' Eyre decided.

'Hide? But where?'

'There must be somewhere at the racecourse.'

'There's a hut there, which they use to keep the scythes

173

and the shovels in; but he won't be able to stay there for longer than two or three nights. There's a race meeting on Wednesday afternoon.'

'That may be as long as we need,' said Eyre.

Christopher frowned. 'I'm not sure that I follow you.'

'It's very simple,' said Eyre. 'In three days, we shall be able to assemble everything we need for my expedition. Food, water, horses; we shan't need to take anything particularly fancy. Joolonga is arriving in Adelaide tomorrow, and the other Aborigines are already here.'

'I hope you're not suggesting what I *think* you're suggesting,' said Christopher, in a pale voice.

'It seems to me the very best way of killing two birds with one stone,' said Eyre. 'I need two companions to come with me on this expedition. I was already thinking of you, Christopher, if I could persuade you; and of Robert Pope. But I am prepared to substitute Arthur here for Robert. After all, Arthur seems to have been something of an expert when it comes to surviving under harsh conditions. We could dress him up, and perhaps give him a large hat and a pair of spectacles to wear, and we could say that he was a cousin of mine from England. Then all three of us could ride out of Adelaide without any trouble or hindrance whatsoever. No bounty-hunters are going to question the departure of a geographical expedition financed by Captain Sturt, of all people.'

Christopher looked at Arthur closely, quite unconvinced. 'A cousin of yours from England?'

'Perhaps we can find him a wig,' Eyre suggested.

'Well, that's all very well,' Christopher protested, 'but what about me? I don't even want to go on this expedition. I was very much hoping that *you* wouldn't go.'

'Under the circumstances, I would think it wiser if you changed your mind,' said Eyre. 'Especially since *I* am intending to go, whatever happens; and no matter what anyone says to deter me.'

'You're inordinately stubborn, you know,' Christopher complained.

'Perhaps.'

'No *perhaps* about it. When it comes to stubbornness, I'd set you up against two mules and a kangaroo any day of the week.'

Arthur cleared his throat. 'Is it all right if I say something, sir?'

'Of course,' said Eyre.

'Well, sir, the thing is that there's no need for either of you gentlemen to feel in any way obligated to me, sir. I never did nothing for you but try to rob you of what was yours; and that's hardly a worthy recommendation for anyone. If I was to give myself up right away to these two gentlemen what seems to be searching for me, then there wouldn't be any need for either of you to get yourselves tangled up in it; and that would be the end of the matter.'

'Except that they could take you back to Norfolk Island and flog you so hard that they would probably kill you,' Eyre put in.

'I took my own risk, sir, when I jumped the boat for Adelaide. I always knew the consequences, should I be caught.'

Eyre was silent for a minute or two. Christopher sat crossing and uncrossing his legs; and staring at Eyre with such concentration that if it had been possible for him to persuade Eyre by thought-transference that Arthur should give himself up, then he certainly would have succeeded.

Eyre, at last, said, 'I'm not a judge, Arthur. I don't enforce the laws which sentence men to years of transportation for stealing hats, and sheep, and loaves of bread. Nor do I give the orders for men to be flogged, or kept in solitary confinement. It seems to me that you have served out your sentence, and yet the very fact that you have to remain here in Australia means that, in a way, you are serving your sentence still. You broke the conditions of your ticket-of-leave, I suppose, and you did attempt to rob us. But it is not for me to demand that you give yourself up; nor even to expect it; and if you wish to come along on this expedition, then you are welcome.'

Christopher covered his face with his hands. 'I *knew* it,' he said. 'I sensed it, the very moment you mentioned the idea of it. I hate camping; and I hate riding horses; and I hate discomfort of all kinds. And yet here I am, condemned to join an expedition into the very harshest country known to man. Eyre Walker, I wish I'd never set eyes on you.'

'No, you don't,' Eyre smiled at him.

'No,' said Christopher. 'The trouble is, I don't.'

Arthur said, 'If that's a genuine offer, sir, then I feel it in my water to take it, if that's agreeable.'

'You realise that I may be condemning you to a worse fate than any you might meet at Macquarie Harbour.'

Arthur sat up straight. 'I'd rather die ten times in the company of gentlemen, sir, than just once by myself, with a cloth bag over my head, in deep disgrace.'

'Well, wouldn't we all?' said Christopher. 'Or, I don't know. Perhaps we wouldn't.'

Just then, Mrs McConnell came in and announced that luncheon was almost ready.

'I don't suppose you'd find it in your heart to root around for a spare cutlet, would you mum?' Arthur spoke up.

Mrs McConnell glared at him; and then at Eyre. Eyre twinkled his eyes at her, and gave her the most winning smile he could manage. And a little nod of his head, as if to say, go on, just for me, give the man a cutlet.

Mrs McConnell hesitated. Then she turned and called down the hallway, 'Dogger! Lay the table for two more, please! Yes, soup spoons, too!'

Fifteen

On Monday, Eyre and Christopher ate lunch with Captain
Sturt at the Wilson's house on Grenfell Street. Mrs Wilson
was a plain, flustering woman who baked raised pies that
could have been exhibited in a museum, and perhaps
should have been: perfect to look at, but tasting of nothing
very much at all, except shortening, possibly, and potatoes
boiled without any salt. The dining-room was heavily
curtained and painted in brown, and on the sideboard
there was a huge sorry-looking salmon in a glass case.

Every time Captain Sturt said anything witty, Mrs
Wilson would let out a sound like a stepped-on mouse; a
quick, suppressed squeak; and then giggle. Captain Sturt
obviously found her responses almost intolerable, for
every time she squeaked he closed his eyes for a moment,
and gripped his fork as if he could cheerfully jab her with
it.

Christopher glanced across the table at Eyre with some
unease. But Eyre was determined that the expedition
should go ahead as he and Captain Sturt had agreed, and
as quickly as possible.

Sturt, in fact, had been most industrious since he had
last spoken to Eyre. He had already talked to Mr Town-
send of the South Australian Company and arranged for
Eyre to take whatever leave of absence might be required;
and now he knew that Christopher was to accompany
Eyre, he would make the same arrangement for him.

He had bought half-a-dozen horses; complete with
saddles and saddle-packs; and leather bottles for the
carrying of water. He had also arranged for the delivery
of jerked meat, dried fruit, flour, salt, rice, and tea. These
would be carried on a mule, although he hadn't yet been
able to find a satisfactory mule.

The single item of provisions which he plainly considered to be the most valuable, however, was a leather-

bound copy of his own *Expeditions*. This he laid reverently on the table in front of Eyre, and opened the cover to show him the inscription on the title-page. 'For Mr Eyre Walker, in Trust and Confidence, that he will follow in my footsteps to the very heart of the Australian continent.'

Eyre picked up the book, and leafed through it. He was actually very moved; because for all of Sturt's pomposity, he was still the greatest explorer the Australian continent had yet seen, and he was certainly the most celebrated man in Adelaide.

He said, 'Thank you, Captain Sturt. I shall treasure this above everything.

'Not above food and water, I hope,' Sturt grinned at him. 'Although you will notice that the binding is leather, and that it may always be good for nourishment. Before they started dining on themselves, you may remember, Alexander Pearce and his companions actually devoured their kangaroo-skin jackets. Did you know that? Men can be pushed to extraordinary extremes in the outback.'

Mrs Wilson squeaked and sniggered, and Captain Sturt pulled a twisted kind of a face.

'Do you think it will be possible for us to leave on Wednesday?' asked Eyre.

Sturt forked up the last of his pie, and washed it down with a liberal mouthful of red wine. 'I don't doubt it,' he said. 'Mrs Wilson, that was a capital pie. A pie by which all other pies should have to be judged.'

Squeak, and giggle, from Mrs Wilson's end of the table.

Eyre said, 'I'm sorry my cousin couldn't be here today. He likes his pie; and, of course, he was very anxious to make your acquaintance, Captain Sturt.'

'I've never met him, I suppose?' asked Sturt. 'Did you tell me his name?'

'His name? Well, yes, I believe I did. Mr Martin Ransome, that's it. One of the Clerkenwell Ransomes.'

Sturt buttered himself a large piece of soda-bread, and nodded, although it was plain that he wasn't really interested. That was just what Eyre had been counting on: a general lack of curiosity about his soon-to-be-bespectacled cousin that would allow them to set off from Adelaide unharassed by bounty-hunters or militia.

Today, Arthur was hiding in the hut out at Adelaide racecourse, with plenty of cold mutton sandwiches and a bottle of tea, and the day after tomorrow they would be riding northwards, well away from Aborigine constables and sea-captains who would tell anything for a bottle of rum; and all the other grasses with whom Adelaide was rife. Mrs Wilson rang the bell for the pie-plates to be removed, and her freckly Irish servant-girl brought in jaunemange and baked carrot pudding.

Christopher looked at Eyre with an expression which clearly illustrated the hope that the luncheon-table would be cleaved in half by a bolt of divine lightning, and that Mrs Wilson would be burned to a manageably small cinder.

'A very agreeable meal, Mrs Wilson,' said Captain Sturt, and Eyre began to understand that it took more than twelve weeks' rowing along wild and uncharted rivers to become, and remain, a hero.

That afternoon, excused from the office, Eyre and Christopher went for a long walk in the Botanic Gardens, neglected and abandoned now; and strolled among the tangled acacia bushes and discussed the expedition. Then they went to Coppius's Hotel and sat in the high-ceilinged lounge, and ordered rum punches. A new Axminster carpet was being carried into the hotel, freshly arrived from England, and the patrons in the lounge were continually being asked to move their chairs as the carpet-fitters manhandled it in.

Eyre and Christopher were standing next to the window, waiting for the carpet to be shouldered over their table, when they saw two men by the hotel's reception desk; two dark and unfamiliar men in frock coats and stovepipe hats and side-whiskers; and there was something about them which immediately led Eyre to suspect that they were the men who were looking for Arthur Mortlock.

One of them was smoking a small cigar and reading the messages which had been left for him at the desk; the other was leaning against the wall talking to the porter.

'You see those two fellows?' Eyre asked Christopher. 'Ten to one they're our bounty-hunters.'

Christopher glanced at Eyre, and nodded. 'That's what I was thinking. They don't look at all like salesmen, or government men. Too surly for salesmen; too smartly dressed for government men. And hard, too. Look at their faces. They'd just as soon hit you in the face as say good afternoon.'

Eyre finished his drink. 'Do you want another one?' he asked Christopher, 'or shall we call it a day?'

'Too late, I think,' said Christopher.

Eyre turned around. The two dark men had begun to walk towards them, stepping over the rolled-up carpet, and circling around the table. At last they came right up to Eyre and Christopher, and stood with their hands clasped in front of them, their faces bored and arrogant, their collars clean and sharp but unfashionably low, their black silk neckties sparkling with diamond stickpins.

'You'll excuse us, gentlemen,' said one of them, in a marked 'flash' accent. 'But do we have the privilege of addressing ourselves to Mr Eyre Walker and Mr Christopher Willis?'

Eyre looked at them. The one who had spoken was thin, with a high domed forehead and a drooping moustache. He was very pale and veiny; and he gave Eyre the impression that if he were to take off his shirt, you would be able to see his heart pulsing underneath his ribcage, and his blood coursing through every vein. His companion on the other hand was thick and ruddy, with a gingery moustache and a body like beef.

Eyre said, 'What can we do for you?'

The thin man inclined his head in a bow that was patently not meant to be subservient. 'My name is Mr Chatto; this is Mr Rose. We are here on the direction of the government of New South Wales, to look for two ticket-of-leave men, one named Bean and the other named Mortlock.'

'Yes?' asked Christopher, with complete deadpan innocence.

Mr Chatto gave a thin smile, as transparent as a finger drawn through water. 'It came to our attention, Mr Walker, that you and Mr Willis were the last customers to hire Mr Mortlock's carriage; on the night of the Spring Ball at Government House; on Thursday last week.'

'Were we?' asked Eyre 'What of it?'

'We were hoping that you might have engaged Mr Mortlock in conversation,' said Mr Rose. 'Perhaps he might have told you where he lived, or where he was going.'

'Is he missing?' asked Eyre.

'He is not in immediate evidence, if we can put it that way,' said Mr Chatto. He cracked his knuckles one by one, ten distinct cracks, and looked around the hotel lounge as if he were expecting somebody; not Arthur, but somebody equally fateful. Then he turned back to Eyre and Christopher, and looked at them wanly, as if he didn't believe anything that either of them had told him, not for a moment.

'Would you recognise Mr Mortlock if you saw him again?' he asked, expressionlessly.

'Who?' Eyre frowned.

'Mr Mortlock,' Mr Chatto repeated, patiently. 'The coachman who took you to the Spring Ball.'

Eyre turned to Christopher in exaggerated bafflement.

'Mr Mortlock?' he said. 'Was that his name?'

'This gentleman seems to think so,' said Christopher.

'Come now, Mr Willis, you must recognise the name,' said Mr Chatto. 'It was you who went to Meredith's for the phaeton; and you who Meredith's sent around to Mr Mortlock, because all of their own fleet of carriages were out on hire.'

'Well, well, was that his name?' asked Christopher. 'Mortlock, hey? I could have sworn it was Keys, or Morton, or Locket, or something to do with padlocks. But Mortlock. Well, well.'

'He took you to the Ball, didn't he?' asked Mr Rose.

'Of course.'

'And then he took you home?'

'Well, naturally.'

'And in all that time, he didn't say anything at all that struck you as untoward?'

Eyre clamped his hand over his mouth as if he were thinking very deeply. Then suddenly he snapped his fingers, and said, 'There was one thing.'

Mr Chatto took out a notepad, and an indelible pencil, and licked the pencil with a tongue that was already a bright shade of laundry-purple.

'He said he was thinking of taking up the piano-accordion.'

Mr Chatto's pencil remained poised over the notepad; trembling very slightly, like the motion of a crane-fly on a late-summer porch.

He said, flatly, 'I don't think, Mr Walker, that you fully realise the gravity of our investigations; nor the weight of the authority we carry. We have been given special approval to hunt down these men by the Governor and Commissioner of South Australia himself.'

Eyre peered over the edge of his notepad. 'You haven't written down "piano-accordion",' he said, in a helpful tone.

Mr Rose put in, 'Our authority, sir, also extends to bringing to book those who may have given the fugitives succour and shelter.'

Eyre turned to Christopher, and said, 'The quality of the clientele here seems to have sunk rather low lately, wouldn't you say? I think a quiet drink at home is called for; among more civilised company.'

Mr Chatto put away his notepad and his pencil, and fastened up the buttons of his coat. 'I want you to know, Mr Walker,' he said, in a particularly drear voice, 'that your answers to my questions were not at all satisfactory, and that I regard you as under suspicion of knowing the whereabouts of Mortlock and Bean.'

'You may regard me however you like, that is your privilege,' said Eyre. 'But I had better remind you that I have influential friends; Captain Charles Sturt among them; and that if you attempt to harass me in any way at all, then he shall get to hear about it, and take whatever action he considers fit.'

Mr Chatto said, 'Even Captain Sturt is not above the law, Mr Walker. Look—this is my address—at the Torrens Hotel. Leave a message for me there if it should occur to you to change your mind about Mortlock.'

Eyre took the scrap of paper on which Mr Chatto had written the address, 75 King William Street. He crumpled it up between the palms of his hands, and tossed it on to the floor. Mr Chatto stared at him with eyes of a curiously neutral amber, in which his tiny black pupils were suspended like insects. He made no attempt to pick the paper up. Instead, he tugged at each of his cuffs; cracked at all of his knuckles; and then inclined his head to Eyre and Christopher, and said, 'Very well. I think you have made yourselves perfectly clear. Whatever it is that you know, I am to receive no help from you, whatsoever.'

Eyre smiled, and inclined his head in return, to indicate that no, he certainly *wouldn't* receive any help from them, whatsoever.

Mr Chatto and Mr Rose walked off, leaving Eyre and Christopher alone together.

'Well,' said Christopher, 'I think I could happily do with that second drink you offered me; particularly now that the air seems to have cleared itself a little. You know something, I never could abide the idea of hunting men for money. It's just not human.'

Eyre was silent. The truth was that he had found Mr Chatto and Mr Rose quite unsettling. If they were searching for Mortlock and Bean with the authority and the co-operation of Colonel Gawler, then it was entirely possible that they would find him: and then both Eyre and Christopher would be deeply implicated in aiding and abetting the escape of a wanted man. That could mean prison, or worse: particularly since these days Eyre was awkwardly short of good character-witnesses. Captain Sturt might speak up for him, but there was no guarantee of it. Eyre felt that Captain Sturt, despite his proven bravery and despite his urbanity, was something of an opportunist. The sort of friend, as Christopher had once put it, who could always be relied on to be absent in a crisis.

'I think we'd be better advised to warn Arthur Mortlock to lie exceedingly low,' Eyre replied. 'Why don't you go out to the racecourse and make sure that he's all right? Then come back to the McConnell's; and we'll see if we can't think of some way of hiding him more securely, at least until Wednesday.'

Christopher was not altogether enthusiastic about driving his waggonette all the way to the racecourse, but in the end he agreed that it would be safer. Eyre climbed on to his bicycle and pedalled his way slowly back to Hindley Street, pursued as usual by a happy little knot of dancing Aborigine children. It was a bright, sun-flecked afternoon; and kookaburras laughed madly at him as he rode over the company's bridge, and through the avenues of stringy-bark gums on the other side.

It was just as he was bouncing uncomfortably over a series of dry sunhardened ruts in the road that he caught sight of the Aborigine warrior again; standing black and tall and still as a heron by the side of a tumble-down squatter's shed. He should have been seen by everyone who passed him by, yet he was so completely motionless, and his colour was so close to the indigo colour of the afternoon shadows, that hardly anybody seemed to see him at all. The only reason that Eyre had seen him was because the Aborigine had obviously *wanted* him to.

Eyre stopped his bicycle by the side of the road, only a few yards away from the silent blackfellow and well within range of his spear. The blackfellow's hair was thickly greased and decorated with kangaroo bones, emu feathers, and dangling crab claws. His eyes were emphasised by wide circles of white painted around them, and there were *ngora*, or decorative scars, all over his chest. He wore a loincloth, in which were hung a bone axe, and a hardwood club, and a large steel knife. He watched Eyre carefully; neither inviting him nearer nor indicating that he should go away. There was something almost magical about him.

'You're following me,' Eyre called at him. 'Why?'

The blackfellow said nothing, but made some complicated hand-signs which Eyre found it impossible to follow. He shook his head, and said, more loudly, 'Is it because of Yanluga?'

A passing bush-farmer turned around in surprise to see who it was that Eyre was addressing himself to, and at first saw no one. It was only when he stopped and looked again that he made out the silhouette of the Aborigine, and then he turned back to look at Eyre, and shake his head.

'Thought you were talking to yourself, mate. No offence but.'

Eyre stayed where he was for two or three minutes, until the passing of a bullock-cart obliged him to move. By the time he had cycled around to the side of the road again, the Aborigine was gone; or at least he appeared to have gone. He was in that state of invisibility which the Aborigines usually entered when they were hunting. He may or may not have still been there. Either way, Eyre found it impossible to see him.

Eyre thoughtfully bicycled back to Hindley Street. There was no doubt in his mind now that the Aborigines expected something of him; that his seeking-out of Yong-uldye was more than just an unpremeditated act of respect for a murdered boy. Eyre almost had the feeling that he was acting out a destiny which the Aborigines had already charted for him, centuries ago, as one of their dreamtime legends. *'A boy will die at the hands of a man with white skin . . . and the man with white skin will seek out Yonguldye the*

185

*Darkness in order that he may be forgiven . . . and that the boy's
soul may lie forever at rest . . .'*

Eyre reached Mrs McConnell's house and wheeled his
bicycle under the verandah. Humming to himself, he went
up the steps and opened the front door. Mrs McConnell
was waiting for him in the kitchen, and as soon as he
closed the door behind him, she called, in a peremptory
voice, 'Mr Walker!'

'Mrs McConnell?' asked Eyre.

Mrs McConnell came into the hallway, wiping flour from
her hands on to her apron. She looked hot and
disapproving.

'Mr Walker, there's a visitor for you in the parlour. He's
been there for an hour or more.'

'Not Captain Sturt?' asked Eyre, in surprise.

Mrs McConnell opened the parlour door. 'See for yourself,' she said; and there he was. Arthur Mortlock, in his
best britches and a bright red pair of suspenders. He stood
up, and bowed his head.

'Mr Mortlock?' Eyre demanded. 'What on earth are you
doing here?'

'My humble apologies, sir. Wouldn't have come for the
world, excepting as I didn't have a choice. They came out
to the racecourse looking for me, sir, with dogs. Well, I
used a ripe-dead bandicoot to lay something of a false trail
for them, sir; but they found the hut where I was hiding,
and I think that they was fair certain that it was me who
was billeted there, sir. So I didn't have no choice, sir, but
to run for the only place where I knew I could find me
some reasonable sanctuary, sir. Being this good lady's residence, as it were.'

Mrs McConnell flounced, 'Pff! I'll have you know that
I'm not at all accustomed to giving shelter to runaway
legitimates. Nor to any manner of legitimates for that
matter.'

With an unexpected display of early-Victorian theatre,
Arthur Mortlock threw himself heavily on to his knees on
the Persian-patterned carpet, and grasped the hem of Mrs

McConnell's apron in his hands, and noisily kissed it. Mrs McConnell looked almost apoplectic, and cuffed him on both sides of his prickly head; but that didn't prevent him from bowing alarmingly low, his forehead touching the carpet, his broad bottom rising so high that it revealed a patch on the back of his black britches in green cotton, with red cobbled thread.

'Mum, I abases meself,' he pleaded. 'I hurls meself willy-nilly on your tenderest mercy, knowing as how you're sure to get what you deserve in the life hereafter.'

'Incinerated, I shouldn't wonder, you rogue, if I let you stay here,' protested Mrs McConnell. 'No, the only course that I can take with you, Mr Arthur Mortlock, is to call for the authorities, and have you locked up for life.'

Sixteen

Wednesday was hot and clear, and Eyre and Christopher arrived outside Government House early, nervously accompanied by Arthur Mortlock, whose distinctive Macquarie Harbour haircut was hidden under a wide-brimmed kangaroo-skin hat, and whose eyes were distorted by a small pair of wire-rimmed spectacles. If anything, Arthur looked even more disreputable than he had before, and Christopher said that he had all the appearance of a recently released lunatic; but he couldn't easily be recognised as Arthur Mortlock, and that was all that Eyre cared about.

After half an hour of argument, Mrs McConnell had reluctantly agreed to let Arthur stay until Wednesday morning, on the strict understanding that he kept himself locked up in his room, that he didn't show his face at any of the windows, and that once he had left he never breathed a word about staying with Mrs McConnell to anybody; nor admitted that he even knew the name McConnell.

Dogger hadn't appeared to say goodbye to Eyre; and Eyre had supposed that he was brooding about the outback. He had certainly been very uncommunicative over the past few days, and had taken to leaving the house for hours at a time, and not saying where he had been. The British Tavern, probably, for a few disgruntled drinks.

Mrs McConnell at the very last moment had melted. She had kissed Eyre again and again, and held him close to her, and at last said tearfully, 'Don't forget that you promised to come back to me.'

'I won't forget.'

'And if I've ever done you any kind of harm; or injustice; then I hope you find it within yourself to forgive me.'

He had kissed her tear-wet cheek. 'You've never been anything but good to me. There's nothing to forgive.'

She had stood on the verandah and waved her handkerchief until he had ridden out of sight. His bicycle stayed under the steps. Dogger had promised to grease it from time to time, although he had said that he would be 'utterly danged' if he would try to ride it. 'I only have to *look* at the bloody thing and I lose my balance.'

Eyre and Christopher were surprised to see twenty or thirty people already gathered in the roadway outside government house, including a party of finely dressed marines, and several notable Adelaide businessmen and merchants, in tall riding-hats and white britches. There were several carriages and waggonettes there, too, in which brightly dressed local ladies sat and twirled their parasols; and an untidy collection of children and Aborigines; shouting and kicking the dust.

Ship's bunting had been hung from the picket-fence, and from the tall flagpole the Union Jack smacked laconically in the warm morning wind.

There was a spattering of applause as Eyre and Christopher and Arthur Mortlock walked up to the front of the governor's house; and somebody even shouted, 'Huzza! huzza!'

The train of pack-horses was drawn up by the steps, and there, in a self-consciously magnificent tableau, stood Captain Sturt and Colonel Gawler and Captain Sturt's accountant Mr Pickens, as well as Mr David McLaren from the South Australian Company, Mr Ragless, and Mr Peter Percy from the Mineral Rights Board, and even the Reverend T.Q. Stow, looking flushed, and sneezing spasmodically, and wiping his nose. Colonel Gawler's five children ran around and around them all, shrieking and laughing.

'Mr Walker! Mr Willis!' called Captain Sturt. He came striding forward and shook both of them firmly by the hand. 'This is a great day! An historic occasion!'

'You seem to have drummed up plenty of enthusiasm for it,' Eyre remarked. He bowed his head to Colonel Gawler, and said, 'A very good morning to you, colonel.'

Colonel Gawler gave him a testy smile in response. It was clear that he hadn't yet forgiven Eyre for the fracas at the Spring Ball last week, however much economic hope he had invested in this expedition; however much he personally disliked Lathrop Lindsay; and however much Captain Sturt had impressed on him that he should at least be cordial to Eyre and his companions.

'In a moment I will introduce you to Joolonga, and your other black servants,' bustled Captain Sturt. Then he turned to Arthur Mortlock. 'Is this your cousin, Mr Walker? How do you do, sir, Mr Ransome, isn't it, as I remember? A fine adventure for you, Mr Ransome.'

Arthur muttered something unintelligible, and cleared his throat.

'I'm afraid my cousin has been suffering from a slight cold,' put in Eyre. 'However the dry air in the desert should do him some good.'

'I've been suffering from quite the same malady,'

complained the Reverend Stow. 'It always attacks me, at this time of year. Yesterday afternoon I was obliged to lie on the ottoman and sleep for an hour. All I could manage for breakfast this morning was a little clyster. It's quite exhausting.'

'You could try me old mum's fever draft,' suggested Arthur.

The Reverend Stow frowned at Arthur in surprise. Eyre nudged Arthur with his elbow to warn him to say no more; but it was too late. The Reverend Stow and one or two people around them had already heard Arthur's fruity East End accent.

'What, pray, is your "old mum's" fever draft?' asked the reverend.

Arthur shrugged, and shuffled his feet, and stared unhappily towards Eyre, his eyes unfocused and beady behind his borrowed spectacles.

'Please,' insisted the Reverend Stow. 'I'd love to know.'

'Well, your reverence,' said Arthur. 'It's powdered niter, and potash and two teaspoons of antimony wine, all mixed up with sweet spirits of nitre, and a pint of warm water. Very efficacious. Well, specially when you clap a bread poultice on to your bonce at the same time.'

He hesitated, and licked his lips, and then said quickly, 'I mean head. Not—' he hesitated again, and the last word came out as scarcely a whisper '—bonce.'

Captain Sturt looked across at Eyre and there was an emotionless, questioning expression on his face. He suspected Eyre of something, although he wasn't quite sure what it was. Eyre looked back at him and tried to convey by telepathy that 'Mr Ransome's' presence here was a private matter, and that it wouldn't jeopardise the expedition. But there was no flicker of an answer on Sturt's face; no indication that he had either received Eyre's silent message or understood it. But he made no attempt to question Eyre about Arthur; instead, he turned away and started talking to Mr Rutgers, of the *Adelaide Dispatch*, and telling him how Australia's great inland sea was going to be discovered at last; and that, no, if the people of South Australia insisted, he wouldn't object to them calling it Lake Sturt; or even Sturt Ocean.

Eyre, Christopher, and Arthur were called over to the train of pack-horses by the young artist George French Angas, who had come down from Angaston late the previous day in order to see them off, and to make sketches for Captain Sturt and for the press. He was a humorous, lively fellow, with a small dark moustache and irrepressible hair, and he drew them quickly and accurately.

The finished drawings that he would produce, long after the expedition had left Adelaide, would show in watercolour three serious-faced men, dressed in khaki twill shirts and wide hats and riding-britches, with high leather boots. Their faces would be shadowed by their hats, but one of them would appear to be dark, and angular, and handsome in a slightly untidy way; whereas the young man standing next to him would be fair, and lanky, and standing with one hand perched on his hip in an incongruously balletic pose, as if he were waiting impatiently to leap on to the stage during the second act of Mozart's *Les petits riens*; and the third man would appear oddly blurred, as if he were doing everything he could to avoid making a clear impression on the artist, so that all one would really be able to remember about him distinctly would be the sharp reflection on his spectacles, and the pugilistic flatness of his nose. Behind these three men would be a dappled frieze of pack-horses, heavily saddled and laden; and beyond the curves of the horses' backs would be stringy-bark gums, and the sky as clear-washed as only young George Angas could paint it.

There would be other drawings and paintings, too; some of which would be used as reference for woodcuts and steel engravings which would be sent all over the world for reproduction, to the *Illustrated London News* in England, to the *Spirit of the Times* in Philadelphia, and to *L'Histoire* in France. One of the most frequently reproduced would

191

be that of the expedition's three Aborigines. The tall, broad-faced Joolonga, dressed in a cockeyed midshipman's hat, a striped cotton shirt, and knee-britches, but with bare feet. The powerful, squat Midgegooroo, his head tied around with kangaroo-fur sweatbands, dressed in the customary *buka* and less-than-traditional loincloth. And beside them, in nothing but a small leather apron, a slender boy with wild long hair, and those hypnotically prehistoric features that had first aroused Eyre's sense of destiny and timelessness when he had arrived in Australia; and this was the boy Weeip.

Joolonga came up and saluted Eyre with a raised hand. He had small, glittery eyes, and a permanent grin. His cheeks were marked with V-shaped scars, and a white band of chalky paint was smeared across his forehead. He smelled strongly of lavender cologne.

'Mr Walker, sir, I am pleased to make your acquaintanceship.'

'And I yours,' said Eyre. 'It seems that we are going to be travelling companions for quite some time.'

'Yes , sir. Well, you will find that I speak all variety of English, sir, as well as many of the various languages, Wirangu, Nyungar, Ramindjeri. Captain Sturt tells me we are to seek the one they call Yonguldye.'

'That is part of the purpose of this expedition, yes. For me personally, it's the principal part. Finding Yonguldye is of the very greatest importance to me.'

Joolonga nodded, still grinning. 'I have heard word of this importance, sir. It is concerned with the burial of the boy Yanluga. Believe me, sir, you are not the only person who believes that it is necessary for the boy Yanluga to be buried in the accepted fashion.'

There was an inflection in the Aborigine's voice that somehow gave Eyre the impression that Joolonga was more than a little sceptical of the need for Yanluga to be given the traditional tribal burial rites. Eyre said nothing about it, not then, but it led him decide to treat Joolonga with more than the usual caution. Eyre had come across

192

one or two of these 'civilised' Aborigines before, mostly when they had come down to the harbour on errands for their masters; and he had generally found them to be arrogant, especially to their own kind; and imbalanced; and very rarely trustworthy.

Once an Aborigine had been taken into a white man's home as a servant or a flunkey or even as nothing more than a fashionable curiosity; once he had eaten like a white man, dressed like a white man, and learned something of the scope of the world outside Australia; he was imprisoned for ever betwixt-and-between, like a wasp caught in a jar of jam. He would see his own tribespeople through white eyes: as filthy and ignorant and poverty-stricken—and yet he would find it impossible to be fully accepted into white society. Eventually, the effect on his character would be catastrophic. He would suffer from tempers, grinding bouts of bottomless depression, rum-drinking, and wild displays of infantile mischief. Quite often, he would try suicide.

Joolonga, however, appeared to be somewhat wilier than those tame Aborigines like the celebrated Bennelong, who had once been taken to England and presented to King George III by his patron, Governor Arthur Phillips of New South Wales, and who afterwards had always held a scented silk handkerchief over his nose whenever his tribal relatives came to call on him at government house; or like the boastful chieftain Bungaree, of the Broken Bay tribe, who had worn a naval coat resplendent with gold lace, but no shirt, and whose six wives had been given the whimsical and degrading names of Askabout, Boatman, Broomstick, Gooseberry, Onion and Pincher. Joolonga seemed just as culturally isolated, perhaps: but very much more hard-baked, and very much more knowledgeable. He grinned all day, and he wore a cock-eyed midshipman's hat, but there was nothing of Bennelong or Bungaree about him. He was not a strutting eccentric, nor a white man's mimic, and by the way he looked back at Eyre, it was plain

193

that his life was his own, and that he danced on no man's string.

He spat tobacco-juice into the dusty flowerbed. 'You understand, sir, that Yonguldye is a Mabarn Man,' he told Eyre.

'You mean a medicine-man?'

'If that is how you wish to describe it, sir, yes.'

'Do you know him well?'

Joolonga shook his head. 'I have seen him only once, sir, when the troopers had to question him, on account of a killing.'

'Oh, yes?'

Joolonga raised his hand and pointed towards the north-west. 'He had tracked down Willy Williway, sir, over three hundred miles, after Willy Williway had stabbed and murdered one of the Mindemarra Brothers.'

'He tracked a man for three hundred miles?' asked Eyre, impressed, but a little disbelieving. He had been warned by Captain Sturt about the tall tales that Aborigines could tell; and he knew from the conversations that he had had with Yanluga that even quite 'civilised' Aborigines lived partly in the real world and partly in the dreamtime.

Joolonga said, 'Yonguldye is the strongest Mabarn Man, sir, as strong as the Steel Bullet, some believe. Many say that they have seen him fly.'

'Hm,' said Christopher. 'Many say that they have seen me fly, too, but only after a bottle-and-half of rum.'

'It is easy to disbelieve, sir,' replied Joolonga. 'But the magistrate's records show that Willy Williway murdered Jack Mindemarra in Nuriootpa, and that the medicine man Yonguldye followed him all the way to the head of the gulf; where Billy Mindemarra was able to kill him. There is a way of tracking wrongdoers, sir. The Mabarn Man will wear the *Kurdaitja* shoes, especially made of emu feathers, stuck together with human blood, and with these shoes he will be able to follow his quarry for miles and miles, sometimes with his eyes closed, over deserts and mountains and scrubs; and from the wearer of the *Kurdaitja* shoes there is no escape.'

Eyre laid his hand on Christopher's shoulder. 'It seems as if Yonguldye is a man worth finding. But tell me, Joolonga, do you think that he may be likely to help us? If I ask him to perform the necessary ritual for Yanluga to find peace, do you believe that he will do it?'

'You will have to ask him, sir,' said Joolonga, not altogether respectfully.

'Well, I can't ask him until I find him, can I? Where do you think he's likely to be?'

'The last word I had of Yonguldye's people was at the sacred place near Woocalla, sir. That is where we should go first.'

'How far is Woocalla? Many days?'

'Possibly five days, sir. Not more.'

'Very well, then,' said Eyre. 'Is everything ready for us to leave?'

'We have done our best, sir.'

Eyre said, 'You may stop calling me "sir" if you wish; since we have to live and travel together. I would prefer "Mr Walker", if you must be formal, or "boss" if you do not.'

Joolonga gave Eyre a glittery, sarcastic nod, and then went to tighten all the traces on the pack-horses, and chase away a young Aborigine boy who had discovered that one of the saddlebags contained sugar, and was dipping his hand into it. There were rifles in the packs, too: three Baker's models, which Captain Sturt had shown Eyre how to load, and fire.

Eyre beckoned to Midgegooroo, who came forward and raised his hand in salute.

'Do you speak any English?' Eyre asked him.

Midgegooroo stared at him respectfully, but said nothing.

'Joolonga!' called Eyre. 'Does Midgegooroo speak any English?'

'Midgegooroo speaks no language at all, Mr Walker-sir.

Midgegooroo has no tongue. But he understands simple orders, such as "stop", "go", "wait", "eat". And he is very strong, Mr Walker-sir. He can break limestones into chalk, just in his fist. And once he held up a carriage on his back while the wheel was changed.'

From the crowd around the picket-fence, which had now increased to nearly a hundred people, there came laughter and singing. A young boy in a green velvet suit had brought along a violin, and was playing 'All Around My Hat'. The sound of this tune had an obvious effect on Arthur Mortlock, who was becoming increasingly twitchy and impatient. The words of the tune spoke of 'my true love, who is far, far away', and 'far, far away' meant nothing more and nothing less than transportation as a convict.

Captain Sturt came forward and snapped open his gold half-hunter, peering at it officiously. 'Well, Mr Walker, nine of the clock. I believe it's time for you to leave us.'

'An admirable quest, if I might say so,' said the Reverend T. Q. Stow. 'Your father is a man of the cloth, I understand, Mr Walker? Quite admirable. The Lord has inspired so much, don't you agree?'

Eyre gave the Reverend Stow a tight little nod of agreement, and then called forward the boy Weeip. Weeip was in awe of all of them, and stood with his arms crossed over his bare chest like the wings of a fledgling galah bird, his eyes wide.

'Weeip, do you know any English?' Eyre asked him, kindly.

'Few words, boss. I went to mission last dry.'

'Well, that's something,' said Christopher. 'I was beginning to think that we would have nobody to listen to for two months but the miserable Mortlock and the jesting Joolonga.'

'Tell me what words you know,' Eyre encouraged Weeip.

Weeip closed his eyes, hesitated, and then rapidly recited in that high, clacking voice that Aborigines use whenever they become excited, 'One hour father, which are dinner then? hallo my name; give us this daily-daily breath; give us this dress purses; as we four give them their dress purses; and lead us knotting ten station; but the liver is from Beef Hill; fine in the king pond; how is the glory? ever-ever our men.'

The Reverend T. Q. Stow stared at the boy in utter astonishment. Christopher had to cover his mouth with his hand, and even Eyre, for all the tension he was feeling about Sturt and Arthur Mortlock, was unable to resist a smile.

'Well,' said Eyre, 'that was very well done. Now, why don't you go to that waggonette over there and fetch me my wooden case. The shiny wood box. Those are my medical supplies; and I want to make sure that we carry them with us.'

He ruffled Weeip's wild black curly hair. It was soft, but greasy, like a goat's. Weeip scampered off to do what he was told, and Eyre turned back to Captain Sturt and Colonel Gawler, who had now come forward to make a short official sending-off speech.

'We know that this expedition was first inspired by your personal sense of duty towards a single indigenous individual,' said Colonel Gawler, then lifted both his hands for silence, and raised his voice louder, so that the chattering crowd quietened down. 'But you have a wider duty, Mr Walker, a duty which I know you will do your utmost to discharge. And that is, towards the economic and geographical development of the free colony of South Australia; establishing its place in the world; and opening up for human investigation the unknown environment in which the municipality of Adelaide is set.

'You go with our blessing. You go with our heartfelt admiration. You go, of course, with a considerable amount of our money invested in you, and all your forthcoming endeavours. But we know that you will not disappoint us. In fact, so sure do we feel that you will accomplish

197

everything which today you are setting out to achieve, that we are making you a presentation. Mrs Dunstable!'

'They're not going to present us with Mrs Dunstable, are they?' Christopher muttered in Eyre's ear. Eyre touched his finger with his lips to tell him to be quiet.

'Sorry,' said Christopher. 'Forgive me my dress purses.'

Mrs Dunstable was ushered forward by Mr Pickens. She was one of the prettiest young ladies in Adelaide, but a widow. Her husband had died during their second winter in Australia of pneumonia, and since that time she had devoted herself to charity work, and particularly to helping all the scores of women, young and old, handsome and plain, who regularly arrived from England in search of a husband and a new life. In the face of considerable local hilarity, she had converted her house on Grenfell Street into a hostel, and spent three days of each week driving eligible young Englishwomen around the neighbouring farms and sheep-stations in a bullock dray seeking to place them with a suitable husband. Her service was politely referred to as 'Cupid's Carriage', and less politely as 'Mrs Dunstable's Wholesale Harlots'.

She was dressed in black, as always, with a black bonnet and veil; but her heart-shaped face was bright and appealing, and she stepped up to Eyre with a smile that was both pretty and completely confident, as if she were minor royalty, about to bestow on Eyre an honour which he had earned in devoted service to her most gracious person.

'Mr Walker,' she said, in a bell-like voice, and handed him an empty glass bottle with a screw top.

Eyre looked at the bottle, and then at Mrs Dunstable, who blinked at him attractively, and then at Captain Sturt.

'This bottle is a measure of our confidence in you,' announced Colonel Gawler. He took the bottle out of Eyre's hands and held it up for everyone to see. 'In this bottle, you will bring home a sample of the water from the inland sea. In this bottle, you will bring back the proof that all of Captain Sturt's theories are true, and that there is a vast untapped reservoir of water, just waiting for brave and adventurous men to push northwards and exploit its riches.'

He handed the bottle back to Eyre, and said, in a quieter voice, but with well-contrived sincerity. 'I have sent many expeditions northwards from Adelaide; all have been deterred by the conditions they have encountered soon after they have started their journey. But you, I know, will *not* be deterred. You have many compelling reasons for going, and many compelling reasons for finding those things that will make South Australia wealthy and great. Opals, perhaps. Diamonds. Lead, if you can locate it; and copper. But most of all I want you to bring back water, and that is why I have presented you with this bottle. For, once this bottle is full, it shall never again be emptied, not in my lifetime, nor yours, nor the lifetimes of anyone else who is present this morning.'

Now Mrs Dunstable was handed by one of her lady-friends a folded Union Jack, sewn of segments of silk. This she gave to Captain Sturt, who presented it to Eyre with a dramatic bow.

'This has been sewn for you by the ladies of Adelaide; so that you can carry it to the centre of the continent, there to leave it as a sign to the savage that the footsteps of civilised man have penetrated so far.'

There was a slight ripple of applause, which quickly died away. Then Captain Sturt turned, raised his arm, and cried, 'The time is arrived!' and from the side lawn of the house, a brass quintet struck up, for no discernible reason, with a ragged version of 'The March of the Davidsbündler against the Philistines'.

With the help of Colonel Gawler's Aborigine stable-boys, Eyre and Christopher and Arthur Mortlock mounted their horses; and were led by Joolonga to the front gates of Government House, and slowly through the applauding crowd. The brass quintet followed them at a slow march, alarming their mule so much that he kept braying and kicking out his heels, in spite of the weight of flour and bacon which he carried on his back.

The gentlemen in the crowd raised their hats; some tossed them into the air; and the ladies fluttered their fans and spun their parasols and giggled a great deal. Somebody let off a firecracker, which popped and danced and jumped all over the dusty road, and caused several of the horses to rear up and thrash their hooves.

They were right in the middle of the assembly, bowing and nodding and lifting their hats, when a small black gig drew up on the far side of the road. A flash of sun on its highly varnished door caught Eyre's attention, and when he saw who it was he reined his horse around and lifted a single warning finger towards Arthur Mortlock. Out of the gig stepped Mr Chatto and Mr Rose, both of them dressed in clashing check country suits, and they strode quickly and purposefully straight towards the procession as if they knew already what they had to do.

Mr Rose pushed his way through the crowd until he reached Eyre's horse, and without a word he reached up and held its bridle. He was followed closely by Mr Chatto, who came close up to Eyre and stood with his arms folded and his face peaky with satisfaction. 'Never heard of Arthur Mortlock, is that it, Mr Walker? Never knew what became of him? Well, sir, we beg to disagree, Mr Rose and I. We beg to venture that Mr Arthur Mortlock has been with you these past four days or more, and that he spent last evening with you at Mrs McConnell's lodging-house on Hindley Street. And what's more, we beg to suggest that the gentleman in the spectacles on the third horse there is none other than Arthur Mortlock himself, in person, disguised as a *bona-fide* member of this expedition.'

Captain Sturt elbowed his way up to the front of the procession. The crowd's cheers had now subsided to a discontented buzz; and a woman's voice shouted out tipsily, 'for shame!' Somebody made a ribald remark about the mule, and a shudder of amusement went through the company, but then there was silence.

'What's this?' Captain Sturt demanded, facing Mr Chatto with his fists on his hips. 'This is a government expedition!

How dare you attempt to delay it? These men must make a good distance before nightfall; and distance is money. *My* money, if you must know.'

Mr Chatto removed his hat; and Mr Rose touched his brim.

'My personal apologies, Captain,' said Mr Chatto. 'But we have reason to think that the gentleman in the spectacles is an absconded ticket-of-leave man by the name of Arthur Stanley Mortlock, wanted in New South Wales for breaking the conditions of his parole, and also for offences of violence and theft which were committed while making good his escape.'

Captain Sturt was silent. He glanced up at Eyre, and then back at Arthur Mortlock. Eyre's horse stepped nervously sideways, and its bridle clinked. Mr Rose patted its nose, and said, 'Steady, old thing, steady.'

At last, Sturt turned back to Mr Chatto, and said, 'You must be mistaken, I'm afraid.'

'I don't think so, sir,' Mr Chatto insisted. 'And the worst of it is that these two genetemen here, sir, Mr Willis and Mr Walker, are both guilty of having harboured the said Arthur Mortlock, giving him shelter and succour; and of assisting him to elude custody. You can see for yourself, captain. They're about to ride off with him right at this very moment. The felony is being committed in broad daylight, in front of a hundred witnesses.'

Eyre said, as boldly as he could, 'I'd like to see what evidence you have that this man is anything other than what he claims to be; and what *I* claim him to be. He is my cousin, not long ago arrived from England, Mr Martin Ransome.'

'This is nonsense,' replied Mr Chatto, coldly. 'I will have to detain you.'

'On whose authority?' snapped Captain Sturt.

'On the written personal authority of the Governor and Commissioner, Colonel George Gawler, if you'll forgive me, captain. Do you wish to examine it? We have been given a free hand to recapture all absconders, and to detain all those who have assisted them.'

Captain Sturt stared at Mr Chatto furiously, and then stamped his foot. 'Is this true?' he demanded. He spun around, and confronted Colonel Gawler. 'Is this true, George?'

Colonel Gawler blushed, like a young girl who has just confessed to a secret and intimate misdeed. 'Of course,' he said. 'These men came to me with letters of authority from Major Sir George Gipps himself, Charles I could hardly deny them. And, of course, one had no idea that—'

'If these men are detained, the entire expedition will have to be abandoned!' shouted Sturt. 'And that, George, is out of the question. That—is—quite—*out of the question!'*

'My dear Charles—' Colonel Gawler began.

' "My dear Charles!" What do you mean, "my dear Charles!" These whelpish hirelings are attempting to ruin the most important geographical expedition in the history of Australia! With the exception of *mine*, of course. But nonetheless!'

Mr Chatto remained where he was, unmoved by all of this blustering. 'I have the authority, captain,' he repeated, in a thin voice. 'And I must insist on exercising it.'

Eyre suddenly took off his hat, and held it against his chest. 'If I might make a remark, Captain Sturt, it seems that our detention depends entirely on this gentleman's assertion that my cousin Mr Martin Ransome is in fact an absconded ticket-of-leave man. Perhaps a few questions will satisfy him that he is mistaken.'

Colonel Gawler, anxiously tugging at the braid on his ceremonial jacket, said, 'Yes; well that might be a good idea. After all, if this isn't the man you seek—'

'I have no doubt that it is, sir,' said Mr Chatto.

'All the same,' put in Sturt, 'it seems to me fair that Mr Ransome here should not be branded as an offender until Mr Chatto has established his identity. It is hardly a cordial welcome for someone so recently arrived here.'

Mr Chatto paused for a moment, and systematically

clicked his knuckles. Then he said, 'Very well, if it's proof that you want,' and walked around Eyre's horse until he was standing close to Arthur. Arthur peered down at him through his tiny pebble glasses, and all he could see was a small curved figure with a looming head and a curled-up body, like a sinister sprouting bean. His horse shifted from one foot to the other, sensing Arthur's agitation.

Mr Chatto reached up and held the horse's throatlatch; and crooned a few words to it which settled it down. 'Shoosha, shoosha.' Then he looked up at Arthur, and said, 'You and I have no need of this pretence, do we, Mr Mortlock?'

Arthur said nothing, but noisily cleared his throat, as if it were full of dried peas.

'You *are* Mr Arthur Mortlock, late of Macquarie Harbour?' asked Mr Chatto.

'No, mate, I'm not,' Arthur managed to croak.

'Then forgive me, who are you? Surely you can't really be this gentleman's cousin. This gentleman, if you will pardon me for being so blunt, is a *gentleman*. He speaks like a gentleman, and bears himself like a gentleman; wheras you sir have the sound of the East End about you; a vulgar voice; and a ruffian's demeanour. If you'll forgive me, of course.'

Eyre said, 'Captain Sturt, I must protest about this.'

Sturt glanced up at him sharply, and said, 'I don't think you have any real justification for protesting, do you, Mr Walker? It was *your* idea that Mr Ransome should be questioned, after all; and I for one am interested to see how he answers.'

Eyre replaced his hat, and sat silent and uncomfortable on his fidgeting horse, sweating with the morning heat and with the fear that all of them were now at risk of arrest and imprisonment. Their prospects had not been helped at all by the way in which Captain Sturt had embarrassed Colonel Gawler in front of a large crowd of eminent Adelaide citizens.

Mr Chatto said to Arthur, 'Which ship did you come out on?'

'The *Beaumonde*, three weeks since.'

'The *Beaumonde* sailed from Portsmouth, did she not?'

'No, friend, she didn't. She sailed from Tilbury on the four o'clock tide on 2 March; which was a Monday.'

'Her master?'

'Captain Hoskins.'

Mr Chatto hesitated, and then he asked, 'Where did you live, in London?'

'Sixty-one Sumner's Rents.'

'And explain to us how you could be a relative of Mr Walker's.'

For the first time, Arthur looked across at Eyre, although his face was white and set, like an unpainted plaster death-mask, and his eyes were swollen from wearing Mrs McConnell's spare spectacles for too long. He said, without looking down at Mr Chatto, 'It's simple enough, friend. Mr Walker's father had an adopted brother, who ran away from home when he was ten, and made his way in London as a link-boy, and then as a brewer's man.'

'And *your* trade, Mr Ransome?'

'A little of several. Stevedore, porter, wherryman. Anything to do with the water, or the docks.'

Mr Chatto didn't seem to be able to think of any more questions; at least not questions that would catch Arthur out. He turned around, and cracked the knuckles of both hands; and then he walked back towards his colleague, Mr Rose. Eyre suddenly began to think that they had got away with it after all, and that last night's slow and painful coaching, hours of facts about the *Beaumonde*, and about childhood days in Derbyshire, and about Eyre's appeal to 'Martin' to come out and join him in Australia, might all have been worthwhile.

Captain Sturt said, in a brittle tone, 'That all seems to be satisfactory, Colonel. Do you think we might now get on?'

Colonel Gawler looked at Sturt dubiously, and then at

Mr Chatto. But Mr Chatto had been whispering in the ear of Mr Rose, and Mr Rose had been whispering in the ear of Mr Chatto; and after a minute or two Mr Chatto stood up straight and tugged at his cuffs and said to Arthur in a clear voice, 'Would you have any objections to showing us your bare back, Mr Ransome? Just to make sure that you're not wearing the red shirt?'

Eyre wheeled his horse around. 'This is quite outrageous!' he shouted. 'Mr Ransome is my cousin! Captain Sturt! I won't allow him to be subjected to these indignities! He may not speak as correctly as you and I, but he is a British subject, and a loyal servant of Her Majesty, and a Christian, and he has never committed any act of any kind that could possibly justify this manner of treatment!'

But Captain Sturt knew why Mr Chatto had asked to see Arthur's back. Arthur had been at Macquarie Harbour, and there was scarcely a single convict who had been imprisoned there who would have escaped the marks of the lash. Even the most docile of prisoners would have suffered floggings for talking, or shirking work, or singing, or sodomy.

'I'm afraid I have to say that Mr Chatto is within his rights, Mr Walker,' he said. 'To examine a man's back is quite an accepted and acceptable way of establishing what you might call his legal credentials. Mr Ransome, do you think you would be so kind?'

There was nothing that Eyre could say; because in approving the inspection of Arthur's back, Captain Sturt had actually declared his belief that Eyre was telling the truth, and that Arthur really *was* his rough-cut cousin from Clerkenwell. The trouble was, when Arthur's scars were revealed for everyone to see, Sturt would be fifty times more embarrassed and wrathful than Colonel Gawler had been and Eyre and his companions could expect very little in the way of leniency. To have broken the law was one thing; to have made a public mockery of Australia's greatest explorer was quite another. Eyre backed his horse towards Christopher, and said, out of the side of his mouth, 'Do you think we might make a run for it?'

Christopher was pallid, and there was a coronet of sweat on his forehead. 'With all these packs on our horses? And all those peppery young dragoons around? They'd catch us up and cut us down before you could say "penitentiary".' He paused, and wiped away the sweat from his face with his scarf. 'Damn it, Eyre,' he said, 'I told you this business with Mortlock would get us into trouble. I damn well told you.'

Arthur slowly climbed down from his horse, and removed his hat. An expectant, gossipy hush fell over the crowd of sightseers, and many of them shuffled nearer to get a better view. Captain Sturt folded his arms and looked handsome and stern; Colonel Gawler kept making impatient faces and planting his hands on his hips and blowing out his cheeks.

Arthur hung his kangaroo-skin hat on to his saddle-pommel. To Eyre's surprise, his scalp was no longer prickly but completely bald. But with an expression of complete resignation, Arthur took off his leather satchel, and his water flask, and unbuttoned his bush-jacket and took that off, too.

Mr Chatto approached him with the gliding self-satisfaction of a white-bellied shark that can smell blood in the water. 'That's an interesting style of haircut you have, Mr Ransome. Now, where would a man get himself a haircut like that?'

Arthur stared at him with pebbly little eyes. 'Ringworm Hall, mate, that's where.' He said it so quietly that few people in the crowd could hear him, but those that did let out a chuckle, and somebody said, 'Let the gentleman be!' and 'here's for the expedition, lads!'

Arthur now turned his back on Mr Chatto, and reached around behind him to tug the tail of his shirt out of his belt. Mr Chatto cracked his knuckles in anticipation, and smiled across at Mr Rose. For his part, Mr Rose had now released the bridle of Eyre's horse, and had walked around to cover Arthur's only way of escape, should he try to run.

Without any hesitation, however, Arthur hiked up the back of his shirt as far as he could, and revealed a brown, slightly blotchy back; but certainly not a back that bore any scars from flogging.

'Is that enough for you, friend?' he said roughly. 'Are you satisfied now? Or do you want to inspect me teeth, to see if there's any junk caught between them?'

That was a provocative, almost dangerous challenge. Few Englishmen who had never served time in a penal settlement would have known that the principal item of diet there was salted beef, either seething with maggots, or cured to the consistency of old saddle-leather, and that the common name for this delicacy was 'junk'.

But now Captain Sturt stepped forward, and took Mr Chatto almost rudely by the arm.

'I think this gentleman has made his point, sir, and clearly established his innocence. Now I require you to leave him be; and let this expedition be on its way.'

Mr Chatto stared at Sturt with undisguised horror. '*Captain!*' he protested, in a high voice.

'I have seen and heard enough, thank you,' insisted Sturt. 'George, will you be kind enough to tell these fellows to be on their way?'

Colonel Gawler humphed, and wuffled, and flapped his hand at Mr Chatto to clear off. There was a burst of applause in the crowd as Arthur tucked in his shirt, and buttoned up his bush-jacket; and at last gave everyone a sweeping bow.

'I know this man to be Arthur Mortlock!' Mr Chatto kept on. 'I can produce witnesses who will identify him quite positively!'

'Be off, for goodness' sake,' said the disgruntled Colonel Gawler.

'You cannot let him go!' shrilled Mr Chatto.

There was more laughter, and cheering, and the brass quintet began to play *King William's March* in double-time, and Mr Chatto and Mr Rose both had to retreat from the dust and the jostling spectators and the rearing pack horses. Arthur climbed back into his saddle, and lifted his hat as if he were King William himself. More firecrackers went off; more hats flew into the air; and then Captain Sturt cried out to Eyre, 'God speed, Mr Walker! God speed!' and there was a general cheer, and shouts of 'God be with you!'

With a sudden rush, the expedition was off, and trotting down the wide, rutted street. Everybody followed: dragoons, children, carriages, and dogs. Eyre and Joolonga rode side by side at the front, Christopher and Arthur a few steps behind, with Midgegooroo and Weeip keeping the horses and the mule in order. The noise and the dust were tremendous; and for a moment Eyre felt as if he were lost in a blinding golden fog, with the drumming of mysterious war-parties all around him. It was that strange sense of destiny again: that uniquely Australian feeling that he was living in two different ages simultaneously, both prehistoric and modern. A gig rattled up beside him, its young driver lifting his hat and calling 'The very best to you, sir!' and then there were more cheers, and more laughter, and the dogs yipped and barked and ran between the horses' trotting hooves.

They had crossed the river, and almost reached the northern outskirts of Adelaide, and most of their enthusiastic followers had already dropped back, when Eyre saw somebody waving with a handkerchief from a sugar-gum grove off to the left of the track. A girl, dressed in saffron-yellow chiffon, with a yellow-and-white bonnet.

'Joolonga!' he called. 'I'll catch you up!'

He veered his horse away from the main party, and trotted as quickly as he could towards the grove. Christopher shouted after him, 'Where are you going?' but he ignored him. Christopher could see very well where he was going; and while he was prepared to accept Christopher's affection, he wasn't prepared to accept his jealousy.

Under the bluey-green shadow of the gums, Charlotte

was waiting for him, accompanied by Captain Henry. He brushed the dust from his clothes with his hat, and dismounted, and Captain Henry came to hold the reins.

Neither of them said a word. They held each other tightly; and then kissed, deeply and warmly, with all the urgency of a kiss which would have to be remembered for months to come. Eyre breathed in the scent of her skin, the smell of her perfume, and felt her fine tickly hairs against his cheek.

'I couldn't let you leave without seeing you,' Charlotte told him. 'I've tried so hard to be stern with you, and yet I can't be.'

'How's your father?' asked Eyre. 'Is he any better?'

'The doctor still insists that he must rest. He's taking syrup of squills every day, and mustard poultices, and he's not permitted fatty foods or fermented liquor, and of course that doesn't improve his temper. But I pray for him, Eyre. I pray for him most earnestly.'

Eyre kissed her forehead. 'In that case, so shall I, if my prayers will do any good at all. And I shall also pray that I shall soon discover everything which I am going out to find, and that I shall be back with you before the New Year.'

'Eyre,' she pleaded. 'Love me for ever. I shall always love you.'

He kissed her one last time, and then he returned to his horse and mounted up. They remained there motionless for a second or two; under the rustling trees; trying to imprint on their minds an impression which would last for all the months of separation which were to come. Then Eyre turned his horse, and trotted off through the crackly bark, and Charlotte turned back to her carriage.

Captain Henry removed his hat while Charlotte climbed up and seated herself; and when Eyre twisted around in his saddle to look back at them, he thought how much she looked like a girl who had recently been bereaved.

He caught up with Christopher and the others just as

the dragoons were wheeling their horses around and turning back.

'Bring us back a bunyip!' one of them laughed; and then they spurred their mounts and cantered back towards Adelaide with shouts and cries and more laughter.

The expedition rode on about a mile further, none of them saying very much, up through the low hilly countryside towards Pooraka. The weather had been dry for the past few days, and the mallee bushes and mulga trees were clinging with dust. Up above them, the sky was ribbed with thin stratospheric cloud, which screened a little of the sun, and gave the morning the appearance of a dull daguerreotype. Their pack-horses snorted and flicked their tails at the teeming grey flies which crawled into their nostrils and around their haunches; and their harnesses clanked and squeaked in an endless rhythm that reminded Eyre of a funeral procession.

Joolonga said, 'Advisable to stop here, Mr Walker-sir, to look over all the equipment, and tighten the girths. If we have omitted to take anything important with us, we can at least turn back now to fetch it; and if any girth is loose we can remedy that matter before there are sores.'

'Very well,' Eyre ageed, and called the expedition to a halt. They dismounted, and drank a mouthful of water each, and strolled around while Joolonga and Midgegooroo inspected their packs and their horses' bridles. A warm wind, so slight that they could scarcely feel it, flowed against their faces from the direction of the sea.

Arthur said, 'You'll excuse me, gents, if I just adjust my clothing.'

'Pardon?' asked Christopher; but without any further ado, Arthur took off his satchel again, and tugged off his bush-jacket, and then shook himself out of his shirt.

Eyre stared at him in fascination. On his back, Arthur was wearing a large square of pale pigskin, from his shoulders to his waist, and right around under his arms, tied across his chest and his stomach with bootlaces. He unfastened it, and peeled it carefully off, and rolled it up as if it were a treasure-map on a parchment.

'I made that for meself not long after I got to Adelaide,' he said, with a sniff. 'I wore it for most of the time, for all that it made me sweat like a pig. It stopped my shirts chafing my back, for one thing; and for another thing I knew that the scars from a flogging was what bounty-men always looked for first. I saw a man caught in Sydney that way, when his scars opened and he started to bleed through his shirt.'

Eyre said, 'That is quite astonishing. Show it to me.'

Arthur unrolled the pigskin again. On close inspection, it looked like nothing more than a thin sheet of bacon rind, very dried up, and not very much like human skin at all. But Mr Chatto had been looking for weals, and scars, and the notion that Arthur's back might have once belonged to a Large White had undoubtedly never occurred to him.

'A man sees what he expects to see,' Arthur remarked, sagely, and tucked the skin into his leather satchel.

He was about to pull on his shirt again, when Eyre touched his arm. 'You'll probably think me morbidly curious,' said Eyre, 'but would you show me your back as it really is?'

Arthur took of the spectacles he had been wearing and folded them up. 'Are you sure that you want to see it, Mr Walker? It's not a sight that does much for the appetite.'

'All the same. I want to know what they did to you; and I want to know what kind of a mark they made on you.'

Arthur shrugged, and said, 'If that's what you want.'

Silently, he turned around. Eyre and Christopher looked at his bare back and neither of them spoke. Eyre felt as if the air had become impossible to breathe, and the sweat ran down the sides of his face and chilled him. He had never known that human flesh could be reduced to such a livid ruin; not purposely, not deliberately, not at all. Arthur's shoulders were criss-crossed all over with shiny mauve scars, scar upon scar, until the flesh was knotted into ropes and ridges and twisted shapes like umbilical

211

cords. Further down, the flesh had been beaten away from his backbone until only a thin transparent covering of scar-tissue remained, through which his vertebrae could be seen as whitish lumps; and the fattier sides of his back had been cut up into diamond-shaped segments, red and angry and sore with sweat.

At last, Eyre whispered, 'Thank you, Arthur,' and Arthur put on his shirt again, and fastened up his jacket.

'I wasn't the worst, by no means,' said Arthur, matter-of-factly. 'Plenty of lads were killed by flogging, and some were flogged and had salt and vinegar rubbed into their backs. Some couldn't walk afterwards, and quite a few lost their manhood, if you understand me. They'd flog you for anything at all, at Macquarie Harbour, I can tell you.'

'I honestly don't know how you managed to bear it,' said Eyre. He felt deeply shocked. So shocked, in fact, that he didn't even know if he wanted to continue with this expedition. Why was he galloping off in search of a medic-ine-man to bury a dead blackfellow according to his tribal rites, when living white men were being so mercilessly punished in the name of Christianity?

'I'll tell you how I bore it,' said Arthur. 'I didn't bear it. I was just there while it was being done to me, and that was all. They tie you up to an X-frame, wrists and ankles, stripped to the waist, and then they flog you in front of the whole company, with the six-tailed cat. It's better if the cat is knotted; it bruises more but it doesn't cut. But some of the gentlemen preferred to cut you, and one or two of them were so expert they could cut you one way and then the other, so that the flesh flew off in perfect squares. I didn't bear it because no man can bear it. A flogging is beyond bearing. It is the nearest thing to hell on earth outside of the solitary. The second time they flogged me I looked down between the angle of the X-frame and saw the ants carrying off great pieces of my back. I came away that time and I had a hump like a hunchback, and it was eight weeks and a day before I could walk.'

Eyre took off his hat. He looked northwards, out towards the scrubby horizon. 'I think we'd better get on,' he said. 'If I hear any more of this, I'm going to start questioning the very basis of my life here, and the very motive behind our going.'

Both he and Christopher were silent as they remounted their horses, and set off. Arthur, however, was in good spirits, and started to sing.

'All around my hat, I will wear the green willow;
All around my hat, for a twelvemonth and a day.
And if anyone should ask me, the reason why I'm wearing it,
It's all for my true love who is far, far away.'

Seventeen

They were to follow the coastal plain between the Gulf of St Vincent and the foothills of the North Mount Lofty mountains until they reached the northernmost point of the gulf, where the Yorke Peninsula protruded into the Indian Ocean like the cocked leg of a saucy dancing-girl. They would carry on northwards across the 'thigh' of the peninsula until they reached the head of the next inlet, the Spencer Gulf; and it was here at Kurdnatta that the Indian Ocean thrust its deepest into the underbelly of the Australian continent. Beyond, to the north, lay nothing but 'The Ghastly Blank'. Unexplored, unmapped territory, into which only the bravest and foolhardiest of doggers and prospectors had ever penetrated. Those who had seen it and survived had brought back stories of mountains like the moon and deserts that never ended, of mysterious glittering lakes that could never be reached, of dragons and monsters and extraordinary insects, and green fields that could appear and disappear overnight. It was at the same time the most alluring and the most frightening land on earth: and that night, as they camped amongst the mallee scrub, their lonely fire flickering in answer to the stars, Eyre felt the stirrings of its ancient and sun-wrinkled soul.

Joolonga sat and chewed tobacco, while Midgegooroo unloaded the horses and watered them, and Weeit squatted by the fire and cooked them up a potful of pork and brown beans. Although their fare was necessarily plain and filling, Weeip was a good enough cook. He had been taught baking at the mission, he said. Cakes, pies, and 'York Shark Pudding'. He could make a passable mug of tea, too, very hot, with molasses stirred into it.

Now that they were out of Adelaide, Weeip discarded his leather apron and went naked, except for a thin string of twined hair around his stomach. Midgegooroo kept his *buka*, but dispensed with his loincloth. Only Joolonga remained dressed in his white man's uniform and cocked hat; although on several occasions he would forget to put on his britches. Eyre had seen scores of naked Aborigine men before, but never at such close quarters, and he was fascinated to see that their penises were not only circum cised but slit open all the way from the urethral opening at the end, right back to the scrotum. He asked Joolonga about it, but Joolonga was evasive, and simply said that it was 'usual'. The sub-incision caused the Aborigines to urinate in a wide spray, but obviously it had not affected their sexual capacity, for later as young Weeip slept and dreamed, and Eyre kept watch, the boy's penis rose several times in a jutting erection.

On that first night out, they talked about Mr Chatto and Mr Rose, and Yonguldye, and what might lie ahead of them. They also talked about the penal colonies at Botany Bay and Macquarie Harbour, and Arthur gave them a long and unsettling account of his life as a 'guest of the Crown'.

214

'In particular, I think of Tom Killick—a young pale fellow fresh out from England; an accountant I think, transported for life for embezzling £2 from his employers. The first night at Macquarie Harbour, the guards amused themselves by treating him as if he was a master-criminal; and pretending they were afeared of him. They locked him up for the night with eleven of the worst knaves on the whole island; men who were little better than animals. They buggered him that night, all eleven of them, and most of them more than once; and the other unnatural acts they forced him into—well, I saw acts of that nature many a time, and I regret to say at times that I was party to them. But the effect on that delicate young fellow was to turn his mind, and by daybreak he was screaming and sobbing like a woman. You would have thought they were a-killing of him; the noises he made. And in the end, they did, in their usual way, because he killed himself. I saw him do it, in the exercise yard; stand on a box with a broom, and push the handle into his back-passage; then just let himself drop. Right through his guts, that handle went, right through his stomach and liver and lungs, and lodged inside his chest. Four of us tried to get it out, but we couldn't, so in the end we just sawed off the brush and left the rest inside of him.'

They listened to these stories seriously and unhappily. When he had finished, however, Arthur lifted his cup of rum, and said, 'There should be no long faces here, gentlemen, for you have rescued at least one wretch from that kind of life; and given him an opportunity for freedom. So here's your health, and may we find the success we're after.'

'Well, I'll drink to that,' said Christopher. 'I think I'll also drink to the hope that I never get to see the inside of one of Australia's prisons. The idea of being kept in chains!'

'Ah, it's not the chains you have to worry about, Mr Willis,' said Arthur. 'It's what they do to your mind.' He tapped his forehead, and said, 'It's up here that they do

215

the damage. Inside your bonce. They make your brave man frightened, and your good man evil, and your weak man as wild as a snarling, snavelling beast. They corrupts the pure, and they spays the strong, and they makes your wisest man into a idiot. They knows their stuff, sir; but all I can say is, on reflection, that no man ever came out of those prison settlements a better man than what he went in.'

By ten o'clock that night, Arthur was asleep, wrapped up in his blankets, in his own words, 'as snug as a sossidge roll'. Eyre wondered how a man who had suffered so long and so acutely could ever sleep again, particularly since the danger of recapture was always close. He kept thinking about the 'young pale fellow' who had impaled himself, and wondered if he would have been driven to seek the same kind of terrible escape, if *he* had been imprisoned at Macquarie Harbour. He though of the scarred gristle of Arthur's back, and tried to imagine what pain Arthur must have felt.

Christopher came and sat beside him with a fresh mug of tea. 'Do you want some? Weeip's just brewed up some more.'

'Yes, I will.'

'You're not brooding,' said Christopher.

'No,' Eyre replied, shaking his head. 'I was just thinking about those penal settlements.'

'Well, yes,' said Christopher.

'Is that all you can say?' Eyre asked him.

'What do you want me to say? That they're cruel, and barbaric, and that no man should ever be allowed to inflict such pain and indignity on other men?'

'If you like.'

'It won't be any use. The law is the law; a sentence is a sentence; and if a sentence is carried out more harshly than it ought to be, well, my only reply to that is, abide by the law. Which we haven't, of course, bringing Arthur along with us, and I must say that Arthur's stories don't make me feel any happier about it.'

'There's nothing that Chatto can do now,' Eyre reassured him.

'I wouldn't lay any money on it.'

They sat in silence for a while, and the fire flickered and popped and lit their faces in kaleidoscopic orange. Up above them, the sky was rich as ink and prickled with stars. Cicadas sang, even though a cool wind was getting up; and there was a fragrant smell of woodsmoke in the air. Eyre was beginning to feel very tired now, exhausted not only by the day's travel and by this morning's send off, but by the enormity of what he was doing. He was seeking out a strange Aborigine medicine-man in an unknown land; quite apart from whatever riches he could discover; and more than that he was also beginning that longest of all journeys—the journey to discover his own soul. To understand at last what he actually *meant*—why he was here, what forces and reasons had brought him here, with these companions, on such a night—that would be the greatest discovery of all.

While they finished their tea, Joolonga came over, and said that everything was ready for their departure at sunrise. 'Today was a slow day, Mr Walker-sir. Tomorrow we must make much more distance.'

Eyre said, 'How far north have you travelled, Joolonga? What kind of country can we expect?'

Joolonga said, 'I have travelled as far as the place they call the diamond-sparrow-water, Edieowie. The country is difficult; flat land, salt water; mountains on the east side, salt marshes on the west.'

'And ahead?'

'They speak of a lake there, Mr Walker-sir. Sometimes they say that it is a magic lake, sometimes they say that there is no lake there at all, but just the memory of a lake. They call it Katitanda. But I have never been there, Mr Walker-sir.'

Eyre emptied out the dregs of his tea on to the ground. 'Well,' he said, 'if we are to find this lake, magical or not, we had better get some sleep.'

Christopher said, 'It would certainly solve some problems if there *were* a lake there. I'm not too keen on this bottled water, are you? It tastes as if it's been gently simmering in an unwashed stew-pot all afternoon.'

Joolonga took off his cocked hat. His hair was bound tightly with kangaroo-skin twine into a pigtail; and he looked to Eyre like a black-faced parody of a dandified lawyer he had once known in Baslow. What always struck him so forcibly about the Aborigines was that they did not resemble negroes in the least, in spite of their wide-spread noses and their thick lips. They were like an ugly variety of European; and Eyre always felt that they were far more intelligent and far more alert to what was going on around them than they ever allowed anyone to see.

Joolonga said, 'Midgegooroo told me that one of his brothers' families came from the west to Katitanda; but that they died there, and that Katitanda became their *wand-alwallah*, their burial-place. He does not know why, exactly. It has become a story now, a legend, and his family have retold it so many times that nobody is sure what happened. All they know is that his brother, and his brother's two wives, and four of their children, all perished. Narahdarn swept his wing over them, and that is all they will say.'

'Narahdarn?' asked Eyre.

'Narahdarn is the Bringer of Death. Many tribes have stories about him. Captain Sturt says the story is like the beginning of the white man's Bible-book.'

'Tell me,' said Eyre.

Joolonga took out of his jacket pocket a small pipe made out of a crab's-claw, and filled it up with some of the sticky tobacco which he always carried with him. He picked a glowing twig out of the fire, and laboriously lit up. He was obviously considering at length whether he wanted to tell Eyre about Narahdarn or not.

Eventually, though, when the tarry fragrance of his tobacco was mingling with the smell of mallee scrub he said, 'All of this happened in the days of Ber-rook-boorn, who was the very first man to live in Australia. He and his wife had been made by the great being Baiame; and had been permitted by Baiame to eat and drink everything that they could find, except honey from Baiame's own sacred yarran tree. But the wife of Ber-rook-boorn was tempted by the honey, and tasted it; and out of the tree with great black wings flew Narahdarn, the monster of death which Baiame had charged with guarding his honey.

'Ber-rook-boorn's wife hid in her *gunyah*, which in the northlands is what they call a *tantanoorla*, a brushwood shelter. But the harm was done. She had let out death into the world, and after that, men were no longer able to live for ever. The yarran tree was so sad that it wept, and some of my people still say today that the red gum on the trunk of the tree is the dried tears that it sometimes sheds for the dead.'

'Adam and Eve all over again,' remarked Christopher. 'That's remarkable, isn't it?'

'And the woman still gets the blame,' smiled Eyre, 'no matter what her name is; and no matter what language they tell the story in, English, Latin, or Aborigine!'

Joolonga smoked his pipe in silence, staring at the fire.

Eyre said to him, 'You don't seem particularly anxious to tell us much about the Aborigine.'

Joolonga frowned. He didn't seem to understand; or else he deliberately didn't want to.

'You don't appear to have any desire to tell us about your people,' Eyre repeated. 'Why is that?'

Joolonga took the crab's-claw pipe out of his mouth and spat into the fire.

'What white people know, they destroy. Their knowledge is more dangerous than their rifles. You see what they have done to me? What manner of a man am I? Blackfellow, or white? I can speak like white, dress like white, hold a knife and fork like white. I can think like a white man, too, which is my worst punishment of all. And everything I know, I destroy, just like white men do. They have destroyed me, and in my turn I destroy my people.'

He looked at Eyre and Christopher for a moment with a fierce, almost frightening pride. It was the wasp, making a last noisy effort to escape from the jar of jam.

'The dreamtime may be true and the dreamtime may not be true. It is not necessary for you to know about it. It is not necessary for you to hear about Narahdarn and Baiame and Priepiggie. You should close your ears to these things. And this expedition of yours to find Yonguldye . . . do you know how much you will destroy with this expedition? Thousands of years of sacred secrets. You may even destroy a people—a people who have no need of you, and who ask for nothing more than to be left to live their lives according to legend and tradition.'

Eyre stared at Joolonga for a long time over the leaping flames of the fire. Then he said, 'You're wrong. You're wrong about me in particular and about the white immigrants in general. I have set out on this expedition to do nothing more than find Yonguldye, and bring him back to Adelaide to bury the boy Yanluga. That's all. If I find the inland sea that Captain Sturt believes in; if I find opals; or copper; or gold; or a cattle-route to the north of Australia: well, I shall be lucky, and those who invested their money in this expedition shall be rewarded. But my principal aim is to see that justice is done to a single young Aborigine boy, and if by chance the expedition has other more profitable results, then I can only be doubly satisfied. This is a huge land, Joolonga. There is space in Australia for all of us, white and black. If we white people seem to be selfish, and destructive, it is only because we are struggling to survive here, just as your people have struggled to survive here for centuries. You must forgive us for that.'

Joolonga smiled. 'Of course. And shall I forgive you for my mother, who was cudgelled to death by British sailors because she refused to take off her *buka* for them? Or the friend with whom I grew up, whose name was Bundaleer, who was burned alive in his *tantanoorla*, he and his baby daughter, because a white bushman believed that he had taken his boots? Let me tell you something, Mr Walker-sir, I despise the Aborigine because he is ignorant and filthy, and scratches the ground to survive in a country which could give him so much more; I despise him because he cannot and will not fight back against the white people, and for that reason I also despise myself. I have become their flunkey, yes Mr Walker-sir, no Mr Walker-sir. I am full of hate and yet I have to remain polite, and I will always remain faithful to you, as long as you need me. But never expect me to believe that this land is a better place because of the white man coming here. The white man has a power which is more dangerous than a bush-fire, and consumes everything it touches. After a bush-fire, the burned trees begin to grow again; but after the white man has passed, nothing grows. In a hundred years time, Mr Walker-sir, there will be no blackfellows here. The man I used to be has gone already. My father's son Joolonga has joined Ngurunderi in his place in the sky. This Joolonga who sits with you now is a white man's dog.'

Eyre took off his hat and ran his hand through his hair. 'Well,' he said, 'I don't know what to say to you.'

'It is not necessary to say anything. It is destiny.'

'Joolonga—' Eyre began.

But Joolonga raised his hand to ward off whatever Eyre was going to say. 'Say nothing, please, Mr Walker-sir. You will not hear me speak this way again. You will learn nothing from me; and come no closer to me. And whatever promises you make yourself, you cannot promise anything on behalf of any other white man. What has happened has happened; what is about to happen cannot be avoided. In this land it is better not to think of anything but your own survival. My mother's spirit rests in a certain rock; it will always be there. When the wind and the sun break the rock into dust, the dust will blow across the plain. My mother will always be there, long after the men who took her life are being punished by their own God.'

Eyre was silent. He turned to Christopher, but Christopher could do nothing but shrug. Joolonga finished his pipeful of tobacco, knocking the dottle into the fire. Then he said, 'We must sleep now. we have far to go tomorrow. I will watch first. Then Midgegooroo.'

Eyre brushed his teeth with dry liquorice-flavoured dentifrice, and then wrapped himself tiredly up in his blankets. The night seemed even darker and even windier when he was lying down; and the fire crackled like a fusillade of pistol-shots.

Christopher whispered, 'Eyre? What did you make of all that? He's quite a philosophical chap, isn't he, for a blackie? Never heard one speak like that before. Didn't know they could.'

'Well, he was well-educated,' Eyre remarked.

'Somewhat bitter, though, what?'

'Wouldn't you be, if your mother had been beaten to death; and everywhere you looked your lands were being taken over by strange people from a strange country?'

Christopher propped himself up on one elbow and stared at Eyre through the darkness. 'What do you mean "strange people from a strange country"? We're English.'

'Exactly,' said Eyre. 'Now, let me get some sleep, will you?'

Christopher was silent for a while, although he didn't lie down straight away. 'Eyre,' he said.

'Mmph?'

'Eyre, I beg of you, please don't get me wrong. I know that I've been complaining rather a lot today. You know—about bringing Arthur with us, and all that trouble we had with Chatto. But I wouldn't have missed coming along with you for anything.'

'That's all right, Christopher. Now, please get some sleep.'

'Very well. But just remember how much I admire you; how much loyalty I have for you. Just remember that in the final reckoning I dearly love you.'

Eyre was almost asleep. His mind was already beginning to swim in some deep dark silent *billa*. 'Yes, Christopher,' he said, and his voice sounded in his ears as if it were echoing across thirty centuries of lonely Australian nights.

Eighteen

It was a few minutes past five in the morning when Joolonga shook Eyre's shoulder and told him that they were being followed.

The day was chilly and grey, and there was a coastal mist over the landscape, so that Eyre felt as if he had been awakened into a world of phantoms. The fire had burned out, and Weeip was clearing away the ashes to build up a fresh one. Midgegooroo, stolid and silent, was feeding the horses. Arthur, already awake, was sitting on one of their packs, carefully scraping away at his scalp with a barber's razor.

Joolonga said, 'Two, perhaps three men are riding towards us from Tandarnya.' For some reason he used the Aborigine name for Adelaide. 'They are coming quickly, in the manner of riders who wish to catch up with us.'

Eyre pushed aside his blankets, and stood up, tugging at his tousled hair. He frowned through the mist in a south-easterly direction, but all he could see was the shifting silhouette of the horses, and the grey blotchy shadows of the mallee scrub.

'How do you know?' he asked Joolonga.

Joolonga touched his ear. 'The ground tells me.'

Eyre said, 'Show me.'

Flicking up the tails of his fancy coat, Joolonga knelt on the ground, and held his ear against it. He listened for a while, and then he said, 'Yes. I hear them still. They are closer now, maybe two miles, perhaps not so far. Two men.'

Eyre crouched down beside him, and pressed his ear to the earth, too. He closed his eyes and strained to pick up the slightest drumming, the slightest vibration. But all he could hear was the shuffling of their pack horses, and the crackle of the dry twigs as Weeip lit the fire, and the sharp scratching noise of Arthur's razor.

'Nothing,' he admitted, sitting up straight.

Joolonga stood up. 'You have to listen with your mind, Mr Walker-sir. The land will speak to you if you allow it to talk inside your head.'

Just then, Christopher came over, walking stiffly. 'What's up?' he asked. 'Do you know something, I don't think I'm ever going to get used to sleeping on the ground. I feel as if I've been pummelled all over by an entire company of dancing bears.'

Eyre said, 'Joolonga says there are two men following us, not more than two miles away.'

'Mr Chatto and Mr Rose?' Christopher suggested, at once.

'I don't know, but it's likely. I can't think of anyone else who would want to come chasing after us at five o'clock in the morning, can you?'

'Maybe we left something behind,' said Christopher. 'Maybe somebody's riding after us with extra food, or clean laundry.'

Eyre said, 'You checked our stores, Joolonga. Is there anything missing—anything that Captain Sturt would want to send out after us?'

Joolonga shook his head. 'Everything is in apple-pie order, Mr Walker-sir.'

'Well, they needn't necessarily be *chasing* us, need they?' said Christopher. 'They might just be travelling in this direction on business of their own.'

'I suppose that's possible,' said Eyre. But Joolonga shook his head again.

'They are coming after us, Mr Walker-sir. They are coming too quick for ordinary travellers. There is no settlement for twenty miles, and if they were ordinary travellers, they would be riding much more slowly. These two men are riding as if they do not think they will be going too far.'

'Then it must be Chatto and Rose,' said Eyre. He stood up, too, and brushed the knees of his britches. 'I should have realised they were too persistent to let us go. After

224

all, they won't be paid their bounty, will they, nor their travelling expenses, not until they take Arthur back to Botany Bay.'

Arthur came over, towelling his head. 'You lot look like a week of wet Wednesdays,' he said, cheerfully. 'Didn't you sleep?'

'Chatto and Rose are coming after us,' said Christopher. 'At least, that's what Joolonga seems to think.'

Arthur looked from Eyre to Christopher and then back again. 'How can he tell that?' he asked. 'It's as thick out there as a bowl of prison-house porridge.'

'He can hear the hoofbeats,' Eyre explained. 'There's a slight chance that it *isn't* them; but a far greater chance that it is.'

Arthur pulled a face. 'Well, then,' he said. 'It seems as if they won't let an old government pensioner go free after all.'

'We *can't* let the buggers have him; not now,' protested Christopher.

'I don't intend that they shall,' Eyre told him. 'Joolonga, how long would it take us to saddle up and get out of here? Could we do it before they reach us?'

'No, Mr Walker-sir. Five minutes, and they will be here.'

'In that case, break out two rifles; powder and ball.'

'Now then, Mr Walker, you can't go doing a thing like that,' Arthur spoke up. 'Those two fellows have letters of authority from the Governor of New South Wales, and from Colonel Gawler. If you were to harm them at all, sir, even a scratch, they'd have you locked up and flogged and sent out to Norfolk Island, before you could say cheese.'

Eyre turned to Christopher.

'Rather risky, I'd say,' Christopher told him. 'Not that I'm afraid, mind. Just judicious.'

'Break out the rifles,' Eyre instructed Joolonga. 'Make it quick, too, will you? They'll be on us in a minute or two.'

Joolonga called to Midgegooroo, and Midgegooroo unbuckled one of the horse-packs, and drew out two Baker rifles wrapped in waterproof oil-cloth. He brought them over, as well as a satchel filled with powder and shot. Eyre silently unwrapped one of the rifles, watched with solemnity by his companions, and then crouched down on the ground to load it, the way that Captain Sturt had shown him. He wrapped a lead ball in a patch of calico, rammed in into the barrel; then put a pinch of priming powder on the pan. Once the rifle was loaded, he handed it to Christopher, and loaded the second one.

'I'm not at all sure I'm going to be able to use this,' Christopher protested.

'Well, with good luck, you won't have to,' said Eyre.

Arthur said, 'Begging your pardon, Mr Walker, I'd much rather give meself up. *You* they may flog; *me* they'd hang.'

'I refuse to allow it,' Eyre insisted. 'You've come this far; and now you're an indispensable member of this expedition. Apart from that, you've served your time, and if they send you back to the penal colony then no justice will have been done, of any kind.'

Almost at that moment, they heard hoofbeats for the first time, muffled in the mist. Then two riders appeared, both wearing large bush hats and masked by scarves. They slowed down as they came past the line of pack-horses, and then drew their horses up only ten feet away. Their horses snuffled, and blew out vapour, and scraped at the ground. The riders themselves remained silent and upright, their eyes gleaming above their masks like the eyes of predatory animals, silvery and avaricious.

Eyre stepped forward, holding his rifle in one hand, upraised. The nearer of the two riders wheeled his horse around, so that he was well off to Eyre's left side; making it far more difficult for Eyre to shoot at both of them quickly. The rider seemed to have judged, probably rightly, that Christopher would not be inclined to fire, and that Eyre was the only man he had to worry himself about.

Eyre said, 'Show yourselves. Are you robbers, or what?'

The nearer rider pulled down his scarf. Eyre's suspicions had been correct. It was Mr Chatto, his face looking even more milky and translucent than ever, like a glass jug filled with cloudy water. There were sooty circles under his eyes, which was hardly surprising. He and Mr Rose must have ridden out of Adelaide a little after midnight to catch up with them here at dawn.

'You would be doing yourself a kindness, Mr Walker, if you laid down your rifle,' he called to Eyre.

Eyre said nothing, but lifted the muzzle of his rifle a little higher.

'We want Mortlock, that's all,' Mr Chatto declared. 'If you co-operate with us, and give us no trouble we will say nothing to the authorities about your own involvement in this affair. And I believe you already know that you could well be arrested for giving aid and succour to an absconded ticket-of-leave man.'

Eyre said, 'Turn your horses around, Mr Chatto, and go back to where you came from.'

'Not without Mortlock, I regret.'

'Your regret doesn't interest me in the slightest. Either you go back to Adelaide now, and tell your paymasters that you were unable to find any trace of Mr Mortlock at all; or else I will shoot first your horses and then you.'

'That, Mr Walker, would not be wise.'

'Perhaps not. But it would be wiser than letting you live.'

'That would be murder,' said Mr Rose.

Eyre shook his head. 'Whatever you believe, Mr Chatto, disinfestation is not a punishable offence. If you happen to kill a louse, or a leech, is anyone concerned about it? Killing you two would be no more criminal than ridding the mattress of Australia of two particularly unpleasant bedbugs.'

Mr Chatto's horse began to twitch, and shake its head. It could probably sense through the grip of his thighs that he was angry. But with Eyre, Chatto remained white-faced and utterly calm; although he never took his eyes away from Eyre's face, no matter which way his horse turned itself.

'Mortlock,' called Chatto, to Arthur.

'No Mortlock here, friend,' Arthur replied.

'Well, whatever you're calling yourself, step forward.'

Arthur came around the camp fire, and stood in front of Mr Chatto, quite close, with his arms folded.

'Will you give yourself up without protestation?' Mr Chatto asked, still keeping his eyes on Eyre.

'Mr Ransome is a member of this expedition,' Eyre answered firmly before Arthur could open his mouth. 'As such, he enjoys special protections and privileges, quite apart from the sponsorship of the Government of Southern Australia.'

'His name is Arthur Stanley Mortlock and he is under arrest; to be taken back to New South Wales in chains.'

Eyre cocked the hammer of his rifle; and in the misty atmosphere of the morning, it made a loud, flat click. He raised the gun and pointed it directly at Mr Chatto's head. Mr Chatto blinked slightly, and drew himself back, as if someone were waving their hand too closely in front of his face. 'You would be well advised to put that down, you know,' he told Eyre, his voice anxious and nasal.

'You, for your part, would be well advised to go back to Adelaide and forget about anyone called Mortlock,' Eyre cautioned him.

'That's impossible, I'm afraid. I have a job to do. Mr Rose has a job to do.'

'You have a count of five to turn around and start riding away,' said Eyre, in a constricted but level tone. 'Then, I will fire at you.'

Mr Chatto said, 'Killing me won't bring you anything but grief, Mr Walker.'

'You sound as if you don't mind the idea of being killed.'

'I have friends, Mr Walker. No matter what happens to me, my friends will always make sure that I am revenged. In a way, it is nearly as good as being immortal. They will tear you to pieces, Mr Walker, I assure you, and feed you raw to the dingoes. You will be dog meat, if you kill me; I warn you now.'

Eyre said, 'One.'

Mr Chatto stayed where he was, watching Eyre with that white-lantern face of his. Joolonga said, 'Mr Arthur should go, Mr Walker-sir. No good is going to come of shooting this man.'

'Two,' said Eyre.

'For goodness's sake, Eyre, think what you're doing,' put in Christopher. 'I mean, really. The poor fellow already offered to give himself up. There's going to be the very devil to pay if we open fire on these chaps.'

'Three,' said Eyre, and then, 'You, Christopher—you were the one who said we couldn't let the buggers have him now.'

'Yes, but I didn't think it would have to go as far as actually—'

'Four,' Eyre announced, quietly.

Mr Chatto loosened his horse's rein, and then unexpectedly swung himself out of the saddle, and in two steps was close beside Arthur, with one arm around Arthur's shoulder, as if they were the very best of friends, posing to have their picture taken.

'Now then, Mr Walker,' he called. 'Don't you think it would be foolhardy of you to shoot at me with your cousin here so close? A Baker's an accurate weapon, I'll give you that, but somewhat out-of-date. I'd hate to think what the consequences might be if you were to miss.'

'Step aside, Arthur,' Eyre instructed him, tautly.

'Ah! So you admit at last that he's Arthur!' grinned Mr Chatto. 'Well, now, that makes my task a little easier. Mr Rose, will you please take this gentleman's rifle away.'

Eyre took two or three steps back, and turned; but it was too late. Mr Rose had been shifting his horse right around behind him, and was now pointing a pistol at him from out of the folds of his riding-cape.

'The other rifle, too, Mr Willis, please,' said Mr Chatto.

Christopher hesitated, and then let the Baker fall to the ground with a clatter. Mr Rose dismounted, and came across to Eyre with his pistol now openly displayed, his hand held out for Eyre's rifle. 'There's no shame to it, sir,' he smiled, trying to be consoling. 'We're professionals, and you're an amateur. We don't expect you to be any sort of a match for us; not when it comes to tracking down beasts like our chum Mortlock here.'

'I object to you calling him a beast,' Eyre replied, coldly.

'Nonetheless, a beast he is,' said Mr Chatto. 'A beast that walks on two legs, and has the rudiments of speech. A beast that sometimes has wonderful charm; to beguile such unsuspecting people as may give him shelter and assistance. But a beast who is nothing much better than any other crawling, shambling creature of the Australian forest. A beast who thieves and kills in order to survive, and who has been condemned to Hell so thoroughly that he has no qualms about thieving and killing again. For what do you have to look forward to, Mr Mortlock, but the noose, and then the countenance of Satan?'

Arthur didn't answer. For all that he had offered to give himself up, he appeared to be stunned by his recapture. Mr Chatto said to him, 'Come here then, cully,' and led him across towards Mr Rose's horse, where there were chains and steel circlets hanging from the saddle; and as he walked across the campside, Arthur stumbled and almost lost his balance, like a Finniss Street drunk.

From the other side of the blazing fire, Joolonga and Midgegooroo and Weeip watched in respectful silence as Arthur was chained up. For South Australian Aborigines, the sight of a white man being treated as badly as a black-fellow was both frightening and fascinating. Arthur remained silent, his face set solid, his eyes already looking far beyond this misty morning to the cells in which they were going to lock him up; and the bloody wooden frames on which they would flog him; and further still to the tangled and rotting vegetation of Macquarie Harbour; and the suffocating madness of solitary confinement, and death.

Last night he had told Eyre and Christopher how the prisoners used to draw straws; one to be a 'murderer' and the other to play his 'victim'. Then, in full sight of the guards, the 'murderer' would cut his willing partner's throat, so that the guards would have no choice but to take him, and hang him. 'In that fashion, two men would get blessed relief for the effort of killing one,' Arthur had explained. 'And the rest of us would make book on who picked the straws, and at least have a little excitement to pass the day.'

He had described how a friend of his called Billy Pegler had laughed for joy as he had been slashed from one side of his neck to the other; and how he had still been laughing in bubbles of blood as he collapsed to the ground.

Eyre felt that he would almost be doing Arthur a service if he were to pick up his rifle and shoot the poor man dead before Chatto and Rose could take him back.

It took only four or five minutes for Arthur to be shackled, with circlets around his ankles, and handcuffs around his wrists, joined behind his back by a long running-chain. He stood beside Chatto's horse with his head bowed, averting his eyes from everyone around. He was an untouchable again, now that he was chained up; an old hand. He appeared to Eyre to have lost his humanity, and to have reverted to what Chatto believed him to be, a beast.

Christopher blurted out, in an agitated voice, 'Oh God, Eyre, is there nothing we can do?'

Without bitterness, Eyre said, 'You could have kept your eye on Rose, while I was warning off Chatto.'

'Eyre, I've *told* you, I'm not the kind of man who can point a rifle at anybody. and what would I have done anyway—even if I had seen him take out his pistol? Shot him, in cold blood? Killed him?'

Chatto came over and removed his hat. 'I have to take this man back to Adelaide now, Mr Walker, and thence to New South Wales, where the magistrates will decide what sentence to impose on him. Now, I would be quite within my authority if I were to require you to come back with me, too, and face charges of harbouring a convict. But as I understand it, this is Captain Sturt's expedition, and I have no desire to displease Captain Sturt. Therefore I will press the matter no further. But, if you and I should meet again, sir, under circumstances that are in any way similar; then, believe me, I will make sure that you pay the penalty for it. And that is as God is my saviour and judge.'

Eyre said, 'I should like to say a last word to Mr Mortlock, if I may.'

Chatto replaced his hat, and gave a white-lipped smile. 'Mortlock is not a "mister" now, sir; nor never will be, not again.'

'Nevertheless,' said Eyre.

Chatto stretched out a hand, to indicate to Eyre that he should do whatever he pleased.

Arthur was staring at the front fetlocks of Mr Rose's horse as if he had seen the animal dance, and did not want to miss it if it happened again, not for the world. When Eyre came up and laid a hand on his shoulder, he kept on staring; although a shudder went through his muscles like a man with a fatal chill. His shackles clanked dolefully, and Eyre could understand why men released from Botany Bay or Macquarie Harbour could never hear the sound of chain running upon chain without their teeth being set on edge.

Eyre said, softly, 'I fear that we've let you down.'

'Not your fault, Mr Walker,' Arthur replied. 'One of those things. Fate, in her winged whatsit. You did your level best, didn't you? Not your fault if Mr Willis doesn't have the necessary bottle. Not his, neither, some men are made that way. No—I was always at risk of being collared, right from the start. I should have known better than to try to make meself a respectable living. I should have known better than to get meself *born*, come to mention it.'

'As soon as we get back to Adelaide, I'll ask Captain Sturt to make representations through Government House to have you freed,' Eyre promised. 'If the expedition turns out to be a success, which I'm sure it will, then there isn't any doubt that they'll let you go. We'll be heroes.'

'Ah, heroes,' Arthur nodded. 'Well, I shouldn't bother

yourself too desperate, Mr Walker. By the time you get back, if there's anything left of you, there certainly won't be anything left of me. Not worth saving, anyhow. This time, I think that this is me lot. Called to lower service, as it were.'

He looked up at Eyre for the first time since he had been chained, and Eyre was shocked to see how drawn and grey his face had suddenly become, as if each link of each shackle had instantly aged him by another year. He could have been a man of seventy; or even older. There was the mark of pain on him already; the mark of a man who had been humbled to the ground, now facing the prospect of being humbled to the death. He knew what the prison authorities would do to him. How could he face it?

Eyre took Arthur's hand, and clasped it. In spite of the coolness of the morning, it was clammy with sweat.

'God go with you, Arthur. I shall pray for you.'

'Well, yes, sir, you might pray for me,' said Arthur. Then, through scarcely opened lips, 'But pray for yourself, besides. That Mr Chatto, he would have taken *you* today, too if he'd been able. He won't forget what you did to him yesterday morning. I know his type. He'll have you; even if he has to wait for the rest of his life.'

Eyre glanced over his shoulder at Chatto and Rose, who were standing a few yards away from the camp fire, talking to one another confidentially. Weeip had put the pot on the fire now, and the water was beginning to simmer for their morning tea. Presumably Chatto and Rose were waiting to have a cup themselves before they left for Adelaide. They had, after all, been riding since midnight at a fast trot, over the dry and dusty Adelaide Plain; and it would take them another four or five hours to get back, in the full heat of the day.

Eyre said to Arthur, 'Would you like some breakfast before you go? Some bacon, and a glass of rum?'

Arthur shrugged, and clanked his chains. 'I don't see that there's any point in it, Mr Walker, to be quite frank.

233

Whether I eat or not, what does that matter? I might just as well starve meself.'

'Arthur, you're going to need your strength.'

Arthur lowered his head, and then he said, 'You've been good to me, Mr Walker, that's all I can say. In twenty years you're the first man I ever met who had any time for me at all; the first man who wasn't a thief, or a convict, or a street beggar. The brewery sent for the peelers, as soon as I beat that foreman; and the peelers took me to the magistrate; and the magistrate sent me for transportation. I spoke up for meself; I told them that I was provoked. I told them that I wasn't the kind of man who broke the law heedless-like. But they sent me to Botany Bay, and from Botany Bay to Macquarie Harbour, and now they have me again, after all these years but. And out of the whole lot of them, you're the only man who helped me, and the only man who ever spoke up in my defence.'

Eyre was moved by what Arthur had said, and touched his arm. 'You're a man, Arthur, that's all; and every man is entitled to justice. That's what my father used to say.'

'Justice,' said Arthur. 'They'll kill me now. This is me lot, you wait and see.'

Weeip had made tea for Chatto and Rose, although he seemed disinclined to cook them any Scotch pancakes. Eyre went over to the fire, and said, 'Weeip—feed these gentlemen as they require. And make some pancakes for Mr Mortlock.'

'Yes, Mr Wahkasah,' said Weeip, and laid a flat iron sheet on top of the fire so that he could begin to cook their breakfast.

Chatto said to Eyre, as he drank his tea, and bit into his batter pancake, 'You surprise me, Mr Walker. You're not the man I thought you to be not when I first met you.'

'Oh?' Eyre asked him.

'You're more romantic; less practical. I don't know what you're doing on this expedition. I had imagined you to be harder; but you're not. You should sitffen up, you know,

Mr Walker, if you intend to survive what you have ahead of you.'

The sun was beginning to penetrate the mist, and the camp glowed with a supernatural light, yellow-silvery but still quite cold.

Eyre said, 'I have plenty of determination, if that's what you're talking about.'

'Hm,' said Chatto, wiping butter away from his mouth with a crumpled, blood-stained handkerchief. 'That's as may be. But determination and stamina, well, they're not the same thing. Never have been. To *think* you can do something; and to be *able* to do it—they're poles apart. I've found that out for myself.'

Eyre said to him, 'Where were you born, Mr Chatto?'

Chatto looked at him with suspicion. 'Is it anything to you, Mr Walker?'

Eyre shrugged. 'Not much.'

'Well,' said Chatto, 'I was born in Sydney, of exclusive stock.'

'Not an emancipist, then?'

Chatto said, with undisguised dislike, 'They should have kept them away. Not just by manners, but by law. Given them farms of their own, right out in the bush; anywhere to keep them separate from decent folk.'

'Are you trying to explain something to me?' asked Eyre.

'Explain something? What do you mean?'

'I don't know. You appear to be so angry.'

'Wouldn't *you* be angry, if your sister had been attacked and killed by convicts?'

For almost a minute, neither of them said anything. The fire popped and crackled, and Weeip turned over his Scotch pancakes, and the sun at last was bright enough to cast shadows across the ground; the pale, complicated shadows of pack-horses, and tents, and eight men, in various postures of fear and resignation. The shadow of Rose's rifle, too, as he kept Arthur casually covered.

Chatto said, 'My sister Audrey was caught one day in a side-alley off George Street. They assaulted her and strangled her and left her for dead. I was a clerk, Mr Walker, just like you; why do you think I decided to take up bounty-hunting? For Audrey's sake, God bless her, that's why I do it. To give her the satisfaction, as she sits there in Heaven Above, of knowing that every convict who escapes from New South Wales is always at risk. I became a bounty-hunter so that Audrey would smile, that's why. My dear and delicate Audrey. She has had her revenge, you know; but she will have more. She will have every convict who ever tried to escape his punishment. Every absconder; every ticket-of-leave man.'

He cracked his knuckles, one after the other; and then turned to Arthur, and said, 'Have you breakfasted? Mortlock?'

Eyre reached out and caught Chatto's sleeve. 'Mr Chatto, I appeal to you. Let this man go free. Tell them you found him dead. He can give you his rings to prove it.'

'Audrey begged for mercy,' said Chatto, sourly.

'What do you mean?' asked Eyre. 'How do you know?'

'I know because she was still begging for mercy when they found her; and she was still begging for mercy when I saw her in the hospital. She begged for mercy until she was dead, and that's the whole of it.'

Eyre said, 'Your own personal pain is no reason for taking this man back to Botany Bay. You know as well as I do that he will die there. At least give him this one chance to get away. He is doing nothing more heinous than helping us to track, and to put up tents, and to dig for water, when we need to.'

Chatto stared at Eyre with a face as grey as the front page of the *Southern Australian*.

'There is no question of it, Mr Walker.'

He raised his scarf over his face, and reached behind him to tighten the knot. And it was while he was standing in this position, with his elbows raised, that Eyre heard a sharp, vicious crack, off to his right; and saw Chatto's head blown noisily in half, right in front of his eyes, leaving nothing but one wildly staring eye, and a skull like a bloody soup-bowl. Chatto made no sound at all, but pitched backwards on to the dust, his arms still raised. Blood was sprayed for ten yards across the camp-site, in blobs and squiggles and exclamation marks.

Rose, alarmed, raised his rifle. But almost immediately there was another crack, and he cried, '*Ooff!*' and dropped backwards as if somebody has struck him in the chest with a ten-pound hammer. His right hand fell into the fire, and for a few moments it twitched and jumped like a redback spider.

Arthur said, 'Heads down!' and cautiously, bewildered, one by one, they sank on to their knees, and looked around with anxious faces to see who had been shooting at them. But whoever it was, he didn't seem to be intending to shoot any more; because a silence fell over the scrub; and there was no movement from any direction.

Christopher said, 'Dead as mutton, both of them.'

Eyre looked back at Chatto's awkwardly tangled body. 'Whoever he is, he's a marksman. And he has a heavy rifle, too.'

'Bush-rangers, do you think?' asked Christopher. 'There's a lot of expensive tools and supplies on those horses; not to mention the food and the water.'

Eyre lifted his head a little, and strained his eyes in the direction from which he thought the two shots had come. 'I don't know. It seems odd that he should shoot only Chatto and Rose, and leave the rest of us unharmed.'

Just then, as if he had materialised out of a sudden whirl of wind-blown dust, a man appeared, walking towards them, only about two hundred yards away. He wore a dusty bush hat, and a worn blue shirt, and brown leather boots. He whistled as he came, and as he did so, a horse suddenly rose up from behind the bushes, where it must have been lying down on its side. Christopher looked at Eyre and made a face.

Even before he could see the man clearly, Eyre knew who it was. He stood up, and waited for him with his arms folded, the wind blowing through his hair. Hesitantly, Christopher stood up, too; and Joolonga and Midgegooroo and Weeip came out from behind the packs of supplies. Joolonga said something to Midgegooroo, and the Aborigine mute dragged Rose's body away from the fire. The smell of charring flesh was beginning to grow unpleasantly strong, and Rose's hand had already been reduced to a small blackened claw.

The man whistled to his horse again, and the horse trotted over so that he could take its reins. Then he walked up to Eyre, and slung his rifle on to his back, and held out his hand.

'Hallo, Dogger,' said Eyre.

'Hallo yourself.'

Dogger looked down at Chatto and Rose, and then lifted an eyebrow. 'Not bad shooting, what do you think? Must have been all of three hundred yards.'

'You realise you've murdered them,' said Eyre.

Dogger smiled. 'I've brought along some brandy. It's French, none of your home-made hotch. Mr Abbott gave it to me, at the Queen's Head. What you might call a going-away present.'

'Dogger, this is no joke,' Eyre protested. 'These two men had papers from the Governor of New South Wales, not to mention the full authority of Colonel Gawler. If they don't come back, then the troopers are going to come looking for them. And they'll find them, too, if they have trackers as good as Joolonga.'

Christopher stood with his hands on his hips, staring at Eyre and Dogger in despair. 'What on *earth* made you shoot them?' he asked, almost petulantly. 'You could have come up behind them and made them lay down their weapons. You could have—well, I don't know, you could have hit them on the head, couldn't you? Good God, man, now we'll be wanted for murder, as well as aiding and abetting an escaped convict.'

'Old hand, I'd prefer, if you don't mind, Mr Willis,' said Arthur.

'Well, whatever you like,' Christopher replied. 'But what you call yourself doesn't mean much, not when it comes to the law. You can call hanging a judicial termination of life by means of glottal suspension from entwined hemp; but that doesn't make it any less unpleasant. I saw Michael Magee hung. That was two years ago—the first man they ever hung in South Australia, and believe me I never want to see another. He was choking and gurgling and crying out, and the hangman was swinging from his legs to try and finish him off. I don't want to see that happen again, and I very particularly don't want it to happen to me.'

Joolonga came forward, chewing a large wodge of tobacco. 'Excuse me, Mr Walker-sir, I think we can hide this killing.'

'Hide it?' asked Eyre. 'What do you mean?'

'We can cut the bodies, Mr Walker-sir, so that it will look as if they have been killed by tribesmen. Some bad Murray River blackfellows passed this way not long ago, causing some damage. The troopers will believe it was them.'

Dogger lifted his rifle off his shoulder, and propped it carefully up against one of their supply packs. 'He's right, you know. That's the best way to do it. I was going to suggest it myself, as a matter of fact.'

'Nonetheless,' said Eyre caustically, 'the fact remains that you killed them.'

Dogger sniffed, and walked around his horse to find his bottle of brandy. '*You* would have shot them, too, if you'd had the chance. It's a question of staying alive, that's all. And if you have to kill the other bastard to protect your own life; well, that's what you do. There isn't any room for fellows with too much religion; not beyond the black stump.'

He found the bottle, and pulled the cork out with his teeth. 'You can call on the Lord Almighty as often as you wish when you're out here, all alone; and there are plenty of times when you get the feeling that the Lord Almighty is listening to you. Even answering back, bless Him. But when you're out of water and out of luck, then there's only you. You and you and you alone; and sometimes not even a shadow to talk to.'

Eyre rubbed his eyes. The grey sand-flies were already swarming over Chatto's broken skull, and crawling like a living grey waistcoat over Rose's chest.

'All right,' Eyre said to Joolonga. 'Do what you have to.'

Nineteen

They saw the last of the ocean at Kurdnatta, on the third day out from Adelaide. They stopped to rest there at midday, under an extraordinary dark sky the colour of dark-grey mussel shells. Weeip and Midgegooroo went down to the beach to collect Goolwa cockles from the rocks; which they baked in a charcoal pit in the sand. The wind from the Gulf of St Vincent whipped the charcoal smoke through the grassy dunes, and blew a stray cinder into Weeip's eye.

Eyre sat back on a blanket staring out to sea. The waves sparkled in the sunlight like a dazzling treasure-chest filled with shining coins; and against their dazzle the naked figures of Weeip and Midgegooroo darkly danced, gathering treasure of their own. Flocks of muttonbirds, which had just begun to migrate fom the north in large numbers, fluttered and wheeled in the sky. Weeip kept his eyes open for exhausted birds which had fallen into the sea, and might be washed ashore.

Joolonga was silently sitting a few yards away on a sand-dune, his midshipman's hat perched on his head. He seemed to have been in an oddly subdued and uncommunicative mood since Chatto and Rose had been shot. He had cut off the remains of Chatto's head with a sharpened stone knife, and slashed Rose's plump white chest into bloodless ribbons, so that it would be impossible for anyone to tell that he had been hit by a rifle ball. Then he had broken the bones of both bodies with a wooden club, and burned them. The fire had still been blazing fiercely when they rode out of camp; and as they had ridden northwards the oily black smoke that had risen from it had reminded them for miles and miles of what they had done.

It was only when Arthur had begun to sing,

The miller, the dusty old miller
He carries his flour in a sack. . .'

one of his ribald songs from the East End markets, that the mood of the expedition had begun to lighten. Only Joolonga had remained silent.

'You shouldn't talk to a blackfellow if he's sulking,' Dogger had advised Eyre. 'He's probably thinking about one of his legends; some story from the dreamtime. What he had to do back there, burning those bodies, he probably thinks it was all told in a legend, hundreds and hundreds of years ago; and that he's going to have to pay for it, somehow. But don't worry. He'll get over it.'

Weeip, who had been listening, said, 'Joolonga believes that Wulgaru the devil-devil will chase him, because he cut off Mr Chatto's head.'

It had been accepted without any discussion between them that Dogger was to join them. After all, Dogger was an experienced bushman, and he had convincingly proved himself to be an excellent shot. He had also come supplied with all his own provisions. That was what he had been doing away from home on those last few evenings before Eyre and his companions had set off: preparing his packs and his food and choosing a horse.

'Right up until the last minute, I was still in two minds whether I ought to come with you or not,' he had explained over last night's camp-fire. 'But then I heard

Constance at the front door, talking to those bounty-hunter fellows. She was telling them that Arthur had been staying with us; and that he was about to leave on your expedition with you; and that if they wanted to catch him they should beetle around to Government House just about as fast as those spindly legs of theirs could carry them.'

'It was *Constance* who told Chatto and Rose where to find us?' Eyre had asked him, in astonishment.

'Why are you so surprised?' Dogger answered him, laconically. 'You know darn well that she didn't want you to go. She was always so afeared that you'd be killed by blackfellows, or bitten by a death adder, or that you'd run out of water and end up wearing nothing but your bones. She sent a boy to fetch Mr Chatto about ten minutes after you'd left the house. She told him she had some private information regarding Mr Mortlock here, but that she would only divulge it if the magistrate could be persuaded to keep you under a year's house arrest, for conspiracy, or whatnot. Anything to stop you going. She thought I wasn't around when she was a-talking to those fellows, but there I was up on the landing, and I'm like our friend Joolonga here. I was trained by practical experience. I can hear a bandicoot break wind from half-a-mile away; and I can certainly hear what Constance is a-whispering-of, even when she's out in the yard.'

'Well, I'm shocked,' Eyre had told him.

'Hm, no point in being shocked. A woman will do anything at all if she wants you serious enough.'

'You had every intention of coming along on this expedition right from the start, didn't you?' Eyre had asked. 'All that Constance gave you was a convenient excuse.'

'Constance is a convenient excuse in her own right, my friend,' Dogger had grinned. 'Is she a woman or is she a Yara-ma-yha-who?'

Weeip had giggled. Christopher had asked, with obvious impatience, 'What on earth is a Yara-ma-yha-who?'

Dogger's weatherbeaten face had crinkled up like a dry wash-leather. 'A Yara-ma-yha-who is a creature with such a big mouth that it can swallow a man up whole.' He had slapped his leg, and cackled out loud, and then he had said, 'That could call for a drink, couldn't it? What do you say?'

On the beach at Kurdnatta, among the drifting sands, they ate a meal of roasted muttonbird, baked cockles, which Weeip called '*pipi*', biscuits, and dried dates. Then they drank a little tea, and gathered up their supplies in preparation for their first strike inland.

Just before they mounted up again, Arthur came over to Eyre and said, 'Supposing they send the troopers after us?'

'Well,' said Eyre. 'Supposing they do?'

'You wouldn't want more killing, would you?'

'Not if I could possibly avoid it.'

'But you wouldn't let them take me?'

Eyre shaded his eyes so that he could see Arthur more clearly. The wind whistled through the spinifex grass, and blew the mane of Eyre's horse so that it stung his hand.

'I suppose I shouldn't have asked,' said Arthur, thrusting his hands into his pockets.

'No,' said Eyre. 'We have nature to contend with, just at this particular moment. Let's concern ourselves with troopers when we have to, but not before.'

Dogger was watching them, from a short distance away. With his long-barrelled rifle on his back, and his wide-brimmed hat tugged well down over his eyes, he looked like the archetypal Australian bushman. Eyre thought to himself that one day there would be a statue erected to men like him; and it would look exactly as Dogger did now, in bronze.

They rode slowly northwards under a high sun. There was no sound but the wind and the surf and the jingling of bridles. After a mile or so, Eyre turned in his saddle and listened and realised that he couldn't hear the surf any longer. Ahead of them lay miles and miles of yellow

243

grassy plain, dotted with saltbush and scrub, and far off to their right the first pink peaks of the Flinders mountains, mysteriously rising in the endless sea of the plains like enchanted and inaccessible islands.

In the distance, scores of big red kangaroos flew through the grass; sending up sudden bursts of pipits. There could have been more than a hundred of them.

Dogger drew his horse close up to Eyre's, and pointed towards the Flinders. 'Those are the mountains I was telling you about. There, you can see them for yourself now. That's where the Aborigines go for their ochre. It's sacred, as far as they're concerned. Magic. They dig it up, and then they mix it with water; or sometimes with emu fat; and they use orchid juice to stop it from running.'

He rambled on, occasionally taking a swig from his bottle of French brandy, telling Eyre about the day that he had ridden into the Flinders and seen a thousand emus gathered together at once. 'I watched them for hours. I thought perhaps the end of the world had come. The strangest sight I ever saw.'

Eyre said, 'What will Constance say, when she finds that you've gone?'

Dogger sniffed. 'Ah, she won't mind. Well, she may. But what can she do about it? Besides, I was beginning to get suffocated, back there in Adelaide. It was like having a pillow pressed over my face. Too cosy and too polite for my liking.'

He was silent for a while. Then he said, 'Besides, she never loved me. She never believed that I was good enough.'

'That's not what she told me.'

'You? You're her darling. As far as Constance is concerned, you're the best thing that happened to her since her cousin Ada drowned in a vat of maroon dye and left her fifty pounds.' He sneezed, and added, 'I'm not blind, you know, Eyre; and I'm not deaf, either, although I'm sometimes drunk. A man knows what goes on inside his own house.'

Eyre looked at him cautiously, uncertain if he ought to say anything or not. He decided that it was probably wiser to keep quiet. Whatever Dogger's suspicions about him and Constance, his desire to come north on this expedition had plainly outweighed any husbandly outrage he might be feeling. He seemed more contented now than Eyre could ever remember him; sitting easily in his saddle, his eyes narrowed towards the horizon with an expression of deep and happy hunger, as if he could devour the distance just by staring at it.

Gradually, the sun began to sink on their left, and their shadows began to lean to their right. The Flinders Ranges, pink during the hottest part of the day, now began to glow a curious iridescent mauve. Eyre could see clumps of native pines on the foothills, and white, contorted gums. The ground itself wriggled with dry creekbeds and eroded gullies, most of which were bushy with bright lime-green acacia. More kangaroos fled across the plain like frightened waiters.

The grass began to give way to mallee scrub and clumps of sharp spinifex. Joolonga urged his horse a little way forward to catch up with Eyre and Christopher, and said, 'We should make camp soon, Mr Walker-sir. We have ridden far today. Tomorrow the land will become more difficult.'

'Another half-an-hour,' said Eyre. 'The horses seem still quite fresh.'

Christopher said, 'The *horses* may still be quite fresh, but I'*m* absolutely exhausted. I feel as if my backside has grown to twenty times its usual size.'

'In half-an-hour we can make four miles,' Eyre told him. 'That will be four miles fewer to ride tomorrow.'

Arthur put in, 'That's four miles further away from Jack Ketch, as far as I reckon it.'

They stopped at last. The plain was dark and warm; although the sky was still luminous and light, and prickled all over with stars. The horses shuffled and scraped their hoofs; and Weeip knelt on the ground, busying himself with a firestick. Christopher had several times offered him lucifer-matches, but he had only stared at him mistrustfully, and shaken his curly head.

Eyre and Christopher walked around the campsite to stretch their legs. Eyre had sores on the insides of his thighs now, and his penis had become tender from grit which had lodged under the foreskin. There was a dryness in his mouth and throat quite unlike any dryness he had experienced before; he felt as if his tongue had turned to rough, brushed-up suede, and his sinuses had shrunk and shrivelled like cured tobacco-leaves. When he blew his nose now, his sinuses produced no phlegm. There didn't even seem to be any moisture between his eyeballs and his eyelids; and his eyes, like those of the rest of the party, were crimson from dust and glare.

'Somewhere out there is the man they call Yonguldye,' said Eyre reflectively, 'I wonder where he is tonight? I wonder if he's sensed that we're looking for him? They say that a Mabarn Man can feel you coming from twenty miles away.' Christopher slowly untied his scarf, with one hand, and then dragged it away from his dusty neck. 'I can't imagine how we're going to find him. One man, in country like this. It goes on for ever.'

Eyre was about to turn back to the fire when a slight movement in the darkness caught his eye. He gripped Christopher's wrist, and said, 'Ssh; there's something there.'

'As long as it's not a bunyip, or Wulgaru the devil-devil,' Christopher whispered; but all the same he stood still, and listened.

The fire crackled. Arthur was talking to Joolonga in an intensive murmur, something about 'I'll lay you odds. Well, I will. I'll lay you fifty-to-one.'

Christopher frowned. 'It's nothing. Come on, you're just tired. Probably nothing more frightening than a mallee fowl, raking a bit of extra soil on to its eggs. Got to keep the babies warm at night, after all.'

246

He strolled back to the fire, and asked Weeip, 'What's on the menu tonight, young man? I'm famished.'

'Me too,' said Arthur. 'I could eat a bloody horse.'

Dogger spat into the fire. 'Don't make jokes about it,' he said. 'One day you may have to.'

'Well, that's charm itself,' Arthur retorted. 'Gobbing in the fire like that. Good luck for you there wasn't no pot on it.'

'What are you, the Governor's chief advisor on campfire etiquette?' Dogger demanded.

'Oh, for God's sake stop arguing,' Christopher complained.

'Well, damn it, here's a man who's been flogged, and locked up in jail and here he is trying to teach me manners,' Dogger protested.

'My old mother taught me my manners, not the government of New South Wales,' Arthur shouted back at him. 'And you wouldn't catch my old mother gobbing in the fire. You wouldn't catch none of my family gobbing in the fire. My Uncle Joe fell in the fire once, and burned half of his ear off, but he never gobbed in it, not once.'

'What would you prefer?' Dogger snapped at him. 'Would you prefer me to throw *my* ear in the fire? Would that be polite enough for you? For Christ's pity, years in those prison made you soft in the head.'

Eyre said, 'Quiet,' and then, when the two of them continued to argue, he barked, '*Quiet!*'

They stopped bickering; and for one hallucinatory second, Eyre glimpsed four skeletons running through the scrub. He could hear nothing: no sound of feet running on hard-baked dust. No rustling of spinifex grass. Not even the soft clattering of spear-shafts. But he knew they were out there, daubed in their white pipe-clay bones; their faces reddened with the sacred ochre.

'Joolonga,' he called, quietly.

'Yes, Mr Walker-sir?'

Joolonga came up and stood beside him. He smelled strongly of fat and sweat and stale lavender-water.

'Joolonga, is anybody following us?'

Joolonga stared at him. The campfire was reflected in his eyes, two dancing orange sparks.

Eyre said, 'Are any blackfellows tracking us? Blackfellows painted like bone men?'

Joolonga looked out into the night. It was much darker now already, and the last luminosity was fading in the west, ushering in, for this day at least, the black wing of Narahdarn, the messenger of death. 'This is a *kybybolite*, nothing more,' he told Eyre, in a soft, hoarse voice. 'A place of ghosts, and unhappy spirits.'

'Twaddle,' snapped Eyre.

'No, Mr Walker-sir,' said Joolonga, calmly. 'There are men like ghosts; just as there are ghosts like men.'

'What are you talking about?'

'Yonguldye already knows that you are seeking him out, Mr Walker-sir. The bone-men you have seen are Yonguldye's messengers, the ghosts from Yonguldye's camp.'

'If they know where Yonguldye is, why don't they guide me to him?'

Joolonga shrugged, and took out his pipe. 'This journey means more than you understand, Mr Walker-sir. What you have decided to do has deep meaning both for your own people and also for the Aborigine. Both peoples see this journey with hope; both peoples see it with fear. Captain Sturt wants to find his inland sea, and his precious stones in the ground; but he is worried that the respect you will give to Aborigine magic may make it more difficult for him to take all of the land and the riches that he wants. Yonguldye is pleased that a white man is recognising the ancient beliefs from the dreamtime; but he also fears the other white men who will come after you. That is why his ghosts are following you. But, neither people can prevent this coming-together. It is something that *must* happen. It was prophesied in the dreamtime, and the story of it was written in the caves at Koonalda, in the desert called Bunda Bunda.'

Eyre felt as if the ground had shifted under his feet. Off-balance, perplexed, as if Joolonga's words had possessed the power to create a supernatural earth-tremor. The more he talked to Joolonga, the more unsure of himself he became; and the more he began to feel that as they journeyed forward into the interior, the further they were leaving behind them not just civilisation but time itself. Joolonga spoke like no Aborigine he had ever met before. It was not simply his wide European vocabulary that impressed Eyre: it was his ability to express Aboriginal ideas in white man's language, to make his own people understandable.

He had an inner perception, a clarity of thought, which even to Eyre was unexpected and disturbing. Eyre had never believed what most white settlers believed: that the Aborigines were idle, ignorant, savages; dirty and destructive; not even reliable enough to keep as servants. He had always seen magic in them, and understood something of their significance. But Joolonga was very different, and with each day they travelled deeper into tracklessness and timelessness, the difference became more apparent. It was like looking into the face of a wild animal, and suddenly realising that its eyes were knowing and human.

Joolonga said, 'Have you seen the bone-man before?'

Eyre nodded.

'Did they give you any signs? Any hand-signs? Or perhaps a bone?'

Eyre unbuttoned his shirt pocket and took out the stone talisman which the Aborigine warriors had given him on Hindley Street. He passed it to Joolonga, who made a protective sign with his hand before he touched it, rather like the sign of the cross. Then he examined it carefully, turning it over and over in his fingers.

'It is a magical stone,' he said at last. 'These marks on it show that it belongs to Yonguldye, the one they call the Darkness. The stone has the power to draw you towards its owner, It is quite like the *Kurdaitja* shoes, only it works the other way.'

Just then, Dogger came up, with his hands in his pockets. 'What's this, a Methodist prayer evening?'

'Not quite,' smiled Eyre.

'Well, tuck's ready when you are,' said Dogger. He caught sight of the stone which Joolonga was turning over in his hand. 'What's that, a *tjurunga*? Let's take a look.'

Without comment, Joolonga obediently handed the stone to Dogger, although he kept his attention fixed on Eyre. Dogger joggled the stone up and down in the palm of his hand, and then said, 'You know what this is, don't you? You know where it came from?'

Eyre shook his head.

'It's a shooting-star, or a piece of one. You can find them at the Yarrakina ochre mine, up at the place the blackfellows call Parakeelya. They think the stones were once the eyes of emus, back in the dreamtime, and that they give you power over all birds.'

Eyre looked at Joolonga. 'Didn't *you* know what it was?'

Joolonga's eyes were glittery but uncommunicative. 'I have never been to Yarrakina, Mr Walker-sir. I have never been further north than Edeowie.'

'But surely you've seen one of these stones before?'

Joolonga said nothing.

Eyre said, 'If this stone came from Yonguldye, then it seems likely that he must have been camped near Yarrakina. Perhaps he even sent it on purpose, to guide us.'

'Well, it's quite likely,' Dogger sniffed. 'The blackfellows travel from hundreds of miles away to dig out the ochre at Yarrakina. It's supposed to be first-class magic; the best ochre you can get.'

Eyre took the stone back, and dropped it into his pocket. 'How far is Yarrakina?'

'Couldn't tell you exactly,' Dogger admitted. 'I only went that far north because I was hunting emu.'

'You came all the way out here to hunt emu?'

'Well, I was a younger man then,' Dogger told them. He hesitated, and looked embarrassed, and then he said,

'Also, some sheep-farmer over at Quorn had told me that some emus have diamonds in their crops.'

'Diamonds?' asked Eyre, incredulously.

'That's what he said. He said he had met a bushman once who had shot an emu; and then, when he had cut it open, he had found a diamond inside it, a diamond as big as an egg. Well, a chicken's egg, not an emu's egg. And apparently the bushman had shot six more emu, and one of *those* had had a diamond in it, too. So he had ended up shooting two hundred of them, and making himself a fortune.'

'You really believed that story?' Eyre ribbed him.

Dogger scratched the criss-cross, weather-beaten skin on the back of his neck. 'Yes. I suppose I did. But who was to say it wasn't true? And when you've spent your whole life out beyond the black stump, well, you get to believe almost anything. But that's why I went up to Yarrakina. A blackfellow told me that there were thousands of emus there; he'd seen them whenever he went to mine for ochre. Only one thing, though: he warned me it was sacred ground there, especially around the ochre mine, and that if I didn't make sure I walked backwards, the monster Mondong would jump up and get me, and eat me up. They're very frightened of those ochre mines, the blackfellows. If you haven't been initiated, they won't let you anywhere near them.'

Joolonga said, 'That is simply because the ochre was left in the rock by our ancestral spirits.' His voice was flat and expressionless; neither mocking nor reverent.

Eyre looked towards the fire. 'You did say that Yonguldye had been heard of at Woocalla. Don't you think it would be better to go there first?'

'Of course, Mr Walker-sir. But my information was not new; and it is more likely that Yonguldye has moved on to Yarrakina; or perhaps beyond Yarrakina.'

'Nevertheless, it would be foolish of us to go past Woocalla; only to have to go back again.'

Dogger interrupted, 'Let's have something to eat. My belly feels like a *paringa*.'

Weeip giggled. *Paringa* meant whirlpool; and Dogger had already amused Weeip and Midgegooroo with his gurgling stomach. He seemed to Eyre to have an infinite capacity for food and drink which he shared with the Aborigines. Down at the beach, Weeip had eaten so many cockles that his stomach had protruded like a medicine ball; and Dogger had devoured almost as many—pushing twenty or thirty into his mouth at one go, and then swilling them down with tepid tea. Even Arthur had been revolted, and that was probably why he had complained to Dogger tonight about spitting in the fire.

They sat around and ate a meal of cockle broth, and four roasted mallee fowl. Weeip had kept the cockles fresh on their slow, hot ride north from the ocean by filling two sacks with damp sand, and then pushing handfuls of shellfish deep into the middle of them. The dampness had been sufficient to keep the cockles alive. Weeip said that his father used to bury hundreds of freshwater mussels in this way; and that he had been able to return to his larder months later to find them still fresh. Eyre found this fascinating; because he had heard that apart from smoking turtle meat for long canoe journeys, and sealing up wild figs in large balls of ochre, and leaving them in trees, Aborigines had almost no way of storing food at all.

After they had eaten, Joolonga went with Midgegooroo to prepare the horses and their packs for the next day's journey. Weeip, while he scoured their tin plates with handfuls of grass, and built up the fire to last them through the night, sang Aborigine songs in a clear, high-pitched voice.

'Wyah, wyah, deereeree
Tree-runner made a rainbow for the woman he loved
Together they walked in the sky
On the road of many colours.
Wyah, wyah, deereeree.'

It occurred to Eyre as he listened that this was the first

Aborigine song that he had heard Weeip sing. He twisted himself around so that he could see the boy better. Against the firelight, naked and skinny, except for his protuberant stomach, his hair bound tight now with kangaroo skin thongs, he looked quite different from the boy who had recited the Lord's Prayer in Adelaide. Savage, wild, with that extraordinary prehistoric sexuality.

Arthur said, 'Gives me the creeps, hearing them blackfellows sing.'

Dogger sniffed. 'It's not their singing I object to. It's when they start screaming for blood. I saw an old mate of mine killed in front of my eyes once, because he struck a lucifer match on some sacred rock, without even knowing what it was. The chief came up and my old mate said, "how d'ye do," and the next thing I knew it was wallop right over the head with a war club. And the scream that went up, from all the rest of the blackfellows there. I ran a straight mile and I didn't stop. That was in Whyalla not more than five years ago. You wouldn't believe it, would you? Just for striking a match.'

They drank tea for a while and listened to Weeip singing more chants. Eventually, Arthur threw away his slops into the darkness, and wiped his mouth with the back of his hand.

'I suppose we *are* going to come out of this alive?' he said, in a noticeably off-key voice.

Eyre looked at him in surprise. Even Christopher lifted his head from the book he had been reading.

'What makes you think that we won't?' asked Christopher. 'I mean, why shouldn't we? It's all gone rather well up until now.'

'I dunno,' said Arthur. Then, 'I had a nightmare, last night that's all.'

'Describe it,' Eyre encouraged him.

'Well, there's not much to describe, really. I just dreamed I was drowning, but I wasn't drowning at all, because it was too dry. It was like being in that what-do-you-call-it, quicksand. And all the time I could feel that something was pressing on me chest, so that I couldn't scarcely breathe.'

'I expect Midgegooroo came and sat on you in the night, thinking you were a sofa,' Christopher teased him.

'Well, you can laugh,' said Arthur. 'But I woke up in a muck sweat, and I was shaking like a horse with the blind staggers. Almost as bad as when I was in solitary.'

'You went through a terrible time in prison,' Eyre remarked. 'It isn't surprising that you have dreams about it. I'm surprised you stood up to it so well. Many men would have gone mad.'

'And did, Mr Walker. And did.'

A little after midnight, they rolled themselves up in their blankets around the fire, and tried to sleep. But although he was exhausted from the day's travelling, Eyre found it impossible to close his eyes. A dusty northerly wind had got up, uncomfortably warm; and it whistled in the spinifex grass. Fed by the wind, the fire glowed brighter, and its flames made breathy, feathery noises. Sparks flew across the scrubland, and were swallowed in the darkness. Eyre drew his blanket more tightly around him, and stared up at the stars.

He thought of Charlotte, and as if the ancient plains all around him were resonant with spiritual forces, he found that he could picture her with startling clarity, with those pretty blonde curls of hers blowing in another wind far away, and her eyes wide with affection. He could almost hear her speaking, and at times he was unsure if he could make out the words, 'Eyre . . . Eyre. . .' or if it was nothing more than the funnelling voice of the fire.

He wondered if he would ever see her again—if he would ever *live* to see her again. Would it really make any difference if he returned to Adelaide as a celebrated explorer? Would Lathrop Lindsay really take him by the hand and forgive him for everything—the secret courtship, the battered greyhound, and the apple trifle? Would she still love him, or would she have found herself another smart young suitor, a visiting baron from England or a wealthy stock-farmer from New South Wales?

Lying in the night, he felt painfully lonely for her; and he thought of the times they had walked out together, hand-in-hand, laughing, while Yanluga had sat on the carriage and whistled and waited for them. He thought of her body, too, of her full bare white breasts, and her slender waist, and of her vulva opening up for him like a sticky flower.

Supposing Lathrop forbade him to see her ever again, no matter what he had done? Supposing he died in the 'Ghastly Blank', like one of those boatloads of 'skellingtons' that the red-haired matelot had described to him. Supposing he were buried somewhere out in this wilderness in an unmarked grave, and Charlotte never even came to find out where he had died?

He slept for a few minutes, and then woke up again. He began to feel that the clock had deceived him; that an unseen corps of time- and scenery-shifters had been hustling around him while he slept; and that when he woke up the following morning he would find himself somewhere completely different.

From quite close by, Joolonga suddenly whispered, 'Are you all right, Mr Walker-sir?'

'Yes, thank you,' Eyre told him, quietly. 'I was just thinking, that's all.'

'This is not a place to think, Mr Walker-sir,' said Joolonga. 'There are too many ghosts and memories of ghosts, all waiting to rush inside your head. Remember what I told you; this place is a *kybybolite*.'

This time, Eyre didn't answer; but lay where he was; listening to the wind and the furtive noises of the night.

Twenty

In the morning, Arthur was hideously and spectacularly sick. He had only just climbed out of his bedroll, and stretched himself, when he jacknifed forward and clutched at his stomach.

Eyre said, 'Arthur? Are you all right? *Arthur!*'

Arthur did nothing but shake his head; and then suddenly brought up a splattering stream of dark brown bile and half-digested food. He retched again and again, and the fourth or fifth time he retched he brought up blood. He collapsed on to his knees, his face white and shiny with sweat.

Christopher exclaimed, 'For God's sake! What's the matter, Arthur? Arthur, are you all right?'

Midgegooroo hurried over to Arthur, and tried to lift him up, But Arthur was too bulky for him, and pitched sideways on to the dust and lay there shuddering and groaning.

Eyre knelt down beside Arthur and unbuttoned his shirt. 'Christopher!' he called. 'Fetch me a damp cloth, will you? Now then, Arthur, what's come over you? Do you think it's something you've been eating?'

'Perhaps it was the cockles,' suggested Christopher. 'There *are* people who come over all peculiar when they eat shellfish. My uncle Randolph only had to *look* at a whelk.'

'Arthur, do you think it was the cockles?' asked Eyre. But Arthur simply stared at him through pale misted eyes, and trembled, and said nothing.

'Well, whatever it is, he seems to have it rather badly,' said Christopher.

'Weeip, get me my medicine-chest,' said Eyre. 'Midgegooroo, bring me some water.'

Weeip ran over to the makeshift shelter in which they had stacked their packs, and began to search for the medic-

256

ine-chest. Meanwhile Midgegooroo came over with a leather bottle of water.

Joolonga knelt down in the dust beside Eyre, and examined Arthur closely. He peeled back Arthur's eyelid with his black fingers, and looked at the jerking, twitching eyeball as dispassionately as if he were inspecting a freshly opened oyster.

'Do you think we ought to give him any water, Mr Walker-sir?' he asked blandly.

'What do you mean?' Eyre asked him. 'He's feverish; he's been vomiting. He's going to need water, especially in this heat. And especially if he's eaten something that's poisoned.'

'Hm,' said Joolonga.

'What do you mean, "hm"?' Eyre demanded. 'Do you know something about this that I don't?'

'I know simply that fresh water is scarce, and that the next water-hole is many miles from here, especially if we go to Woocalla.'

'So?'

'So, it is wiser not to waste it on a man who will soon be dead.'

Eyre said fiercely, 'He has an upset stomach. It can't be unusual, especially when you're living off any bird or fish or animal you happen to come across. Would *you* like to be deprived of water, just because you had an upset stomach?'

'This man will die,' said Joolonga, baldly.

'You're a doctor, I suppose, as well as a constable?'

'I know the bush, Mr Walker-sir. I have seen hundreds of men die here. This man has the mark of death on him, and that is all I can say to you.'

Eyre beckoned sharply to Midgegooroo, who had been standing watching them in perplexity. Midgegooroo gave him the water-bottle, and Eyre opened it and touched it to Arthur's greyish lips. A trickle of water slid across his mouth and dribbled into the white stubble of his beard.

257

'He has the mark of death, Mr Walker-sir,' Joolonga repeated.

'All right, then, he has the mark of death,' Eyre retorted. 'But what's wrong with him? Why is he sick? All the rest of us are quite healthy. And if it had been the cockles, why wasn't he sick yesterday?'

'Perhaps the ghost-men pointed the bone at him, Mr Walker-sir,' suggested Joolonga.

'Pointed the bone at him? What kind of nonsense is that?'

Joolonga stood up. He was wearing his gilt-buttoned overcoat this morning, but no britches, and he had strapped his penis and testicles up against his belly in an elaborate cat's-cradle of bast fibre. He looked down at Eyre with that wise-animal expression of his, and said, 'To point the bone brings death. Yonguldye's bone is more magical than that of any other Mabarn Man. If that is what has happened to your friend here, then he cannot avoid death. He will die before the sun sets again today.'

Eyre said cuttingly, 'I respect your religion, Joolonga, but I have no respect whatsoever for malicious mumbo-jumbo. I want you to load up the horses, but leave one horse completely free of baggage. That horse you will cover with blankets; and on those blankets we will tie Mr Mortlock, in the most comfortable position we can.'

Arthur shuddered again, and moaned. 'No, sir,' he whispered. 'I'm not a bolter. Not me, sir.'

'Arthur,' Eyre coaxed him. 'Arthur, can you hear me? It's Eyre Walker, Arthur.'

Joolonga said, 'He will die, sir. That is a certainty.'

'Joolonga!' Eyre barked. 'Do as you're bloody well told!'

There was a taut, elliptical moment. Weeip raised his head from the fire, where he was boiling up oats and left-over mallee fowl into a kind of thin meat gruel. Midge-gooroo glanced uneasily at Joolonga, and then lowered his eyes. Dogger and Christopher stayed well back; Dogger because he was a stowaway of sorts, Christopher because he had no stomach for angry confrontations. The sun had risen now, and in that moment they stood in oddly theatrical poses, seven dusty men in a vast and dusty landscape.

Joolonga said something in dialect to Midgegooroo, and then strode off towards the line of pack-horses; angry and obviously affronted. Midgegooroo knelt down beside Eyre and touched his shoulder. His broad face was wrinkled with worry and disapproval, and he made a three-fingered sign across his chest.

'Weeip,' said Eyre. 'What is Midgegooroo saying?'

Weeip shook his head. 'They did not teach me finger-talk at the mission Mr Wakasah.'

Midgegooroo touched Eyre's arm again, respectfully but urgently, and made a jabbing gesture. Then he sketched a triangular shape in the air, on top of his head.

'Joolonga?' asked Eyre, recognising the triangular shape of the cock-eyed midshipman's hat. Midgegooroo grinned, and nodded, and repeated the jabbing gesture.

'Joolonga points?' Eyre frowned at him.

Midgegooroo nodded again, more frantically this time; and then reached down into the dust and picked up the wing-bone of one of the mallee fowl they had eaten last night. Again, he jabbed, this time at Arthur.

'Joolonga pointed the bone at Mr Mortlock?' Eyre queried.

Midgegooroo raised his hand in the one sign that Eyre recognised; the sign for 'yes'. But then he looked around to make sure that Joolonga was still occupied with the pack-horses, and that he hadn't seen anything of the strange one-sided conversation that had taken place between them. Weeip said nothing; but went back to stirring his mallee fowl gruel.

Arthur trembled again, and snorted. 'Not a bolter, sir,' he repeated. 'Not past Doom Rock, sir. Not worth it, sir, what? And end up an uncooked banquet for Skillings here, sir. Ha ha. Not worth it, sir.'

He seemed to contract every muscle in his body for a moment, and then he abruptly squirted green and foul-smelling diarrhoea into his britches and then squeezed again, and squirted some more.

'Good Heavens above,' said Christopher, ostentatiously hiding his eyes behind his hands.

'Get some water down him, for pity's sake,' put in Dogger. Otherwise the poor sod's going to dry up like a quandong; and that'll be the end of him. And give him something to bind his bowels.'

Eyre opened his medicine-chest; the same medicine-chest that had been prepared for him by the chemist at Bakewell, including everything imaginable for the treatment of sickness while abroad. There had been a bottle of tincture of Kino, which was the most effective treatment for diarrhoea that Eyre knew; but he had taken all of it himself during his first few months in Adelaide. He still had a full bottle of Dalby's Carminative, however; and he quickly poured out a spoonful of it and held it over Arthur's half-open mouth.

'Pinch his nose,' he ordered Midgegooroo; and when Midgegooroo did so and Arthur opened his mouth to breathe, Eyre poured the syrup straight down his throat. Arthur choked, and retched, and for a moment Eyre thought he was going to vomit again; but then he shuddered, and lay back on the ground, and appeared to fall into a deep and fretful sleep.

Christopher came closer now. 'Well, then,' he said, 'what are we going to do now?'

'Do you have any suggestions?' asked Eyre.

'Well, we could turn back, and take poor old Arthur with us, and hand him over to the authorities.'

'What about the expedition?'

'Oh, come on, Eyre; you know what I think about the expedition. Doomed from the very beginning, and too dangerous by half. Just look up ahead of us. What do you think you're going to find there? More of the same, if you ask me. Grass and scrub and kangaroos, *ad infinitum*; emus without end, amen. At least if we go back now, we'll have the chance to redeem ourselves, by handing over poor old

260

Arthur. Come on, Eyre. I told you right at the very beginning that it was a mistake not to call the police, that night he tried to rob us. And wasn't I right? And look where his new-found emancipation has led him to; a smelly death on a scrubby plain.'

Eyre screwed the cap back on to the medicine bottle, and put it carefully away. 'In my view,' he said, in that precise voice he could use when he was being a little too pompous; 'in my view, we ought to continue. In fact, that's exactly what we're going to do, regardless.'

Dogger took off his hat and squinted up at the sun. 'You'll kill him, you know,' he said, pragmatically.

'I'll kill him just as certainly if I take him back to Adelaide. That's if he doesn't die on the way. They'll chain him up, and they'll flog him, and then they'll put him in solitary confinement, and that will turn his mind for ever.'

He looked down at Arthur lying in the dust, eyes closed, still convulsing, white and sweaty and somehow shrunken, and all he could think of to say was, 'Poor bastard.'

'Perhaps we should put it to a vote,' said Christopher. 'You know, draw straws.'

Eyre shook his head. 'We're going on. I'm the leader of this expedition and that's my decision. If you don't approve of it, Adelaide is back that way, and you can take enough food and water to get you there.'

Christopher stiffened, and looked at Eyre with an expression which Eyre had never seen on his face before; offended, in a nakedly womanly way; like a wife whose dignity has been shaken by her husband's coarseness and lack of understanding. Eyre began to see then that Christopher was not a sodomite or an ogler of young boys, although he had several times seen him admiring Weeip's naked body. He was instead a man who sought the companionship of other men in the way that a good and loyal woman seeks the companionship of a husband. His love of Eyre was far more emotional than sexual; and Eyre's sudden rejection of him in favour of the expedition

261

and everything that it meant (Charlotte, Yanluga, fame and possible riches) was to Christopher a hurtful surprise.

Eyre realised that he would have to treat Christopher with care if he was going to retain his loyalty; and out here on the wild and empty plains with a self-willed Aborigine guide and a sick ex-convict, Eyre was going to need all the loyalty that he could muster.

'I'm sorry,' he told Christopher. 'I didn't mean to be so abrupt. It's just that we can't turn back now, not after we've come so far.'

Christopher tried to look aloof and displeased for a moment longer; but he was too sensitive and too good-humoured not to be able to accept Eyre's apology, and he made a considerable show of disassembling his frown, and unpuckering his mouth, and at last managing to smile. 'All right,' he said. 'I can't say that I understand what has driven you out here; not completely. Not at all, really. But if you think we ought to continue—well, let's continue.' He added wryly, 'At least until we're *all* dead.'

He came forward and rested his hand on Eyre's shoulder, and shook his hand. 'Do you have any idea what's wrong with him?' he asked, nodding towards Arthur.

'Well, your first guess was probably correct,' said Eyre. 'He could have eaten a bad clam; or perhaps one of the mallee fowl was diseased. Then again the water might have been poisoned.'

'What was Joolonga saying about him?'

'Some ridiculous Aborigine mumbo-jumbo about someone having pointed a bone at him. That's why I shouted at him.'

'They do say that Aborigine medicine-men kill their enemies that way,' said Christopher.

'And do you believe it?'

Christopher shrugged. 'In this country, I think I could believe anything.'

Arthur mumbled, 'Not a bolter, sir, I'll swear to that. Swear on the Holy Bible.' Then he suddenly convulsed again, and lumpy strings of bloody white mucus slithered out of his mouth and on to his shoulder.

Christopher looked almost as sick as Arthur. 'My God, Eyre, the man's *dying*. What on earth is the matter with him?'

'I just pray that it's nothing contagious,' said Eyre. 'Otherwise, this is going to be the shortest expedition into the Australian interior that ever was.'

Midgegooroo and Weeip tugged off Arthur's clothes; and washed him with what little water they could spare. All the time he rambled on about 'bolting', which Eyre presumed to mean escaping from Macquarie Harbour, and vomiting great ropes of mucus, mingled with raw membrane. It was as if his entire insides were being gradually gagged out of his mouth. His face took on a grey ghastliness that Eyre could scarcely bear to look at; and his eyes seemed blind.

They decided not to leave the camp until noon, to see if Arthur showed any signs of recovery. Weeip made a shelter for him out of twigs and scrub; and the rest of them sat around the fire and listened with increasing despondency to his ramblings and chokings.

'I don't know what on earth to give him,' said Eyre. 'I tried a carminative, but he must have vomited that back up by now.'

Dogger said, 'What else have you got in that medicine-box of yours?'

Eyre opened the polished mahogany lid, displaying the neat bottles of antimonial wine, blister compound, extract of colocynth, Epsom salts, powdered jalap, myrrh-and-aloes pills, powdered opium, opodeldoc, and Turner's cerate. Dogger picked out one or two bottles, and then said, 'I don't know. Constance would know what to dose him with, if she were here, Heaven forbid it. Perhaps we ought to mix them all together, and see what happens. He wouldn't be any the worse off.'

At noon, the temperature rose to 92 degrees Fahrenheit, according to their thermometer. Heat rose up off the plain in extraordinary transparent French-curves, and high above their heads, they saw flocks of seagulls flying northwards.

'There,' said Eyre. 'That's evidence for you. If seagulls are flying to the north, that must mean that water lies there; Captain Sturt's inland sea.'

'Or swamp,' put in Dogger. His face was sparkling with sweat.

Joolonga came over, and took off his midshipman's hat.

'Yes?' Eyre asked him, trying to sound as testy as he could.

'Mr Walker-sir, it is no use staying here. We must go on. Mr Mortlock will not get better for days and days; maybe weeks; that is if he ever gets better at all. If we stay here, we are only suffering for no reason, and exploring no further.'

Eyre stood up, and shaded his eyes so that he could look northwards. The scrubby bushlands wavered and danced as if he were seeing them through water, a world drowned in heat. He felt that everything was being relentlessly baked, punished by the sun to see what it was made of. Every breath he took was hot and suffocating and dusty; every move he made produced chafing and sweat. Now, at midday, even the red-capped robins had stopped shrilling and chattering in the bush, and there was an overwhelming hot silence. In the distance, the Flinders Ranges rose like the ramparts of some strange red city.

'All right,' said Eyre. 'You and Midgegooroo tie Mr Mortlock on to his horse. Make sure he's tied fast. Then we'll go.'

Arthur was muttering and shaking as Midgegooroo hefted him over his shoulder, and then lifted him up on to his horse. Joolonga tied him to the saddle, and then ran a leather strap under the horse's chest which he fastened tightly to each of Arthur's dangling wrists, Even if Arthur did slip off the horse, he wouldn't fall to the ground. He would be dragged along, instead, like a sack of meal.

And the trouble is, thought Eyre, that is exactly what Arthur has become. A sack of meal. A dead weight, to be dragged through the bush whether he likes it or not; and whether *we* like it or not. And if I catch this sickness, then I'll be the same. This is land in which only those who can keep moving can ever survive; a land in which a nomadic existence is not just possible, but essential. A land in which, when anybody is stricken by sickness, they are sick unto death.

In the same way that God had been practising creation when he had devised Australia, perhaps he had also been practising His punishments. Death by isolation; death by hunger; death by evaporation of the body and spirit.

It took nearly a quarter of an hour, but at last they were ready to leave. Midgegooroo had rigged up over Arthur's horse a kind of makeshift parasol, an unsteady contraption of tent-poles and calico, which would at least protect him from the worst of the sun. Arthur was slumped over the horse's back as if he were already dead, a string of spittle swinging from his parted lips, his eyes closed.

Christopher said, 'You don't think it would be kinder to leave him here? I mean, simply to let him—'

Eyre stared at him; thin-faced; his dark hair already streaked with blond from the sun; the untanned crowsfeet around his eyes making him look even older and more anxious than he actually was. 'I can't,' he said.

'If I did, I don't think I would ever be able to forgive myself.'

'What do you think the poor fellow is going to suffer now, on the back of a horse?'

'Christopher, for God's sake, there's always hope. There's always prayer. Why do you think I'm here at all? I'm here because I'm trying to redeem what I did to Yanluga; I'm trying to find him peace. Now you're asking me to leave Arthur to die, without the benefit of help or prayer.'

'It seems your religious upbringing had quite an effect

on you,' said Christopher, taking care not to sound too sarcastic.

'Well, perhaps it did,' Eyre told him. 'But I'm not ashamed of it, and I'm not ashamed of having hope. "The prayer offered in faith will restore the one who is sick, and the Lord will raise him up, and if he has committed sins, they will be forgiven him." That's James.'

'The brother of Jesus,' said Christopher.

'Chapter five,' Eyre retorted. Then, when Christopher was silent, 'Verse fifteen.'

Dogger whistled sharply from across the campsite. 'Come on, Eyre. If we don't go now, there won't be any use in going at all.'

'All right,' said Eyre. 'Come on, Christopher; we have to do our utmost for Arthur, no matter how sick he is. Just for pity's sake, let's stay together. I need your help; and Dogger's help, too. If we start arguing between ourselves, we'll be finished.'

Christopher said nothing more, but followed Eyre back to the line of horses. Eyre mounted up, and they set off again, heading north-north-west, towards the place called Woocalla, the water-hole where the kangaroos come to drink. The sun had fallen to the west of its zenith now, so that it shone directly in their eyes. All they could see was dust and dazzle, and willy-willys twisting and hurrying through the scrub. There was no sign anywhere of the ghost-men whom Eyre had glimpsed the previous evening; but then the bush was not a difficult landscape in which to hide. As they rode, they frequently surprised mallee fowl and pipits, and once or twice they sprang euros out of their squats in the tussocks of spinifex grass.

Dogger had often talked to Eyre about euros, and so he knew what they were when he first saw them: solidly built little hill kangaroos, with black-tipped hair and pale snouts. They hurried off in front of the slow-moving train of pack-horses like busy little clerks.

The afternoon was enormous and cruelly hot. For a while they chatted to each other; about Adelaide; about

Captain Sturt; about all the nauseating medical treatments they had been given as children. But as the temperature rose over 100, their conversation died away; and for almost two hours there was nothing but the jangling of buckles, and the squeaking of saddles, and the occasional snort from one of the horses.

Arthur made no sound at all. He lay strapped flat to a thick grey blanket under the lurching shadow of his rectangular parasol, his eyes staring at nothing at all. Midgegooroo was solemnly leading Arthur's horse; and occasionally during the afternoon Eyre rode up alongside and asked Midgegooroo whether Arthur had shown any signs of life; but Midgegooroo shook his head, and raised his hand in the complicated finger-language which meant 'no hope'.

There was a time, just before four o'clock, when Eyre felt as if God Himself were pressing down on them with all the heat and brilliance He and His angels could summon up. There didn't even seem to be any point in breathing. The air outside his body was hotter than the air in his lungs. His shirt and his britches were clinging wet; and the salt from the sweat which dripped from his eyebrows made his eyes sting.

Behind them, there was nothing but miles of wavering scrub. In front of them, a dusty and invisible horizon. All that reminded Eyre that there *was* an end to the world, after all, was the distant red line of the Flinders mountains, off to the right.

The heat separated them; and caused them to draw in upon themselves. They began to ride further and further apart; their heads bowed; until the expedition was strung out over a quarter of a mile. Their shadows walked beside them with irritating persistence, on and on, mile after mile, seven spindly Don-Quixote figures which lengthened even more absurdly as the sun burned its way down the sky.

Eyre found himself daydreaming, in a welter of heat and sweat. He daydreamed about Charlotte; and about returning to Adelaide with flags flying and people cheering, and riding straight up to Waikerie Lodge and claiming Charlotte, with a sweep of his arm, as his bride-to-be.

Then, unaccountably, he found himself thinking about the new wharf and the new sheds that Mr McLaren of the South Australian Company had been building at Port Adelaide. They must almost be finished by now, he thought. He remembered that Mr McLaren had promised a grand opening, with a regatta, and a band, and refreshments; and Eyre was quite sorry that he wasn't going to be there. The quiet, scratchy afternoons of clerkdom; with ledgers and ink and bills of lading; now, in the scrub, seemed idyllic. He thought of the times when he and Christopher had sat in Dougal's Oyster Saloon on Hindley Street, opposite Elder's store, sometimes eating two dozen oysters at a time, with black stout to wash them down. They had talked then of being wealthy and famous, but Eyre had never imagined that fame would have to be earned as hard as this.

Christopher rode up beside him, his face sugar-pink and sweaty. 'I hope we're going to be able to stand up to this heat,' he said, in a hoarse, dry voice. 'I'm beginning to feel as if I haven't got any more perspiration left to perspire.'

'It's very good for you,' Eyre replied. 'It cleanses out the body's impurities. Just like a Turkish bath, without any steam.'

'I'm not sure I'd rather remain impure.'

Eyre gave a wry smile, and shrugged.

'Did Joolonga say how far it was to Woocalla?' Christopher asked him.

'Not too long now. We should be there by evening.'

Christopher nudged his horse a little closer. 'He's not—he's all right, isn't he, Joolonga? You can trust him?'

'What makes you say that?'

'I don't know. He hardly speaks to me at all. I mean, I've tried to treat the chap decently, for all that he's a native. But he seems to have thoughts of his own.'

'Well?' asked Eyre.

'Well, I don't know. I've never thought it was too healthy for natives to have thoughts of their own.'

'I don't see that there's any way in which you can stop them.'

Christopher turned around in his saddle, and looked back at Joolonga, who was riding with his midshipman's hat pulled far down over his eyes, his blue uniform so dusty that it was almost white. Joolonga gave no indication that he knew that Christopher was watching him; and his expression remained as abstracted and as arrogant as ever. Weeip, however, gave Christopher a wave of his fly-whisk; and Dogger raised his head in interest to see what Eyre and Christopher were doing.

'Captain Sturt said he trusted Joolonga, didn't he?' said Christopher.

'He didn't say anything about him: except that he'd met him on his first expedition.'

'Well,' said Christopher, 'the fellow seems strange to me. Not altogether friendly. I don't know. It's difficult to describe, exactly. But I rather get the feeling that he's *watching over us*, don't you see, instead of guiding us. He's not what you might call co-operative.'

'He's self-opinionated, I'll give you that,' Eyre agreed. 'But I must say that I find him quite interesting. He's the first Aborigine I've ever met who can describe ideas, as well as people, and events, and places. He seems to have a grasp of what this expedition means; not only to his own people, but to ours, too.'

'Is that likely to have made him any more friendly?' asked Christopher. He took off his hat, and dabbed the sweat away from his forehead with a scarf that was already soaked in sweat.

'I'm not sure,' said Eyre. 'But he's no fool; and he knows a lot more about this country than we do. He also seems to know where we might find Yonguldye.'

'I'd rather trust Dogger's opinion on that,' said Christopher.

Eyre narrowed his eyes, and looked up ahead of them,

towards the horizon. The north-west wind had stirred up so much dust there that it was impossible to distinguish where the plains ended and where the sky began. There could have been mountains ahead of them, for all they knew. And now that the sun was sinking, the horizon began to glower and boil, a dark scarlet colour, and the empty sky above them began to rage with red.

Dogger had once said to Eyre, out on the verandah in front of Mrs McConnell's house, 'Don't ever ask me to tell you what the sunset's like, out in the bush. You wouldn't believe me if I told you, and if you saw it for yourself you wouldn't believe it. And besides, it happens every evening; and after a few weeks you begin to grow tired of reds and oranges and ochres; and you begin to dream about green.'

Eyre was beginning to understand what Dogger had been talking about. Ever since they had struck inland from Kurdnatta they had been living in a world of brick-reds and purples and dusty yellows. And the further north they travelled, the harsher and redder the landscape became; and the fiercer the sun. If there was an ocean in the centre of Australia, there was no question in Eyre's mind now that it could only be reached by days of hot and uncomfortable travel. Perhaps that would enhance the relief it gave them, when they eventually reached it. Eyre had already begun to have dreams about shining blue water, and nodding palm trees; and dhows sailing from the inland shores of South Australia to the tropical inland beaches of the north.

Perhaps the inland sea was further away than Captain Sturt had imagined it to be. After all, Joolonga had been as far north as Edieowie, and Dogger had actually visited the northern ramparts of the Flinders Range, and neither of them had seen the glitter of an inland sea, even from a distance. But the geological fact remained that scores of rivers drained inland, rather than out towards the ocean, and that if they drained inland then they must drain somewhere. And then there were the seagulls, which Eyre had seen with his own eyes. Seagulls, flying north.

Eyre said to Christopher, 'Don't worry too much about Joolonga. As long as he leads us to Yonguldye, we'll be all right. It can't be more than three or four days' riding now, to the inland sea. Then, if Joolonga proves to be troublesome we can dispense with his services altogether. Personally, I don't think that he's going to be particularly difficult. He's a man caught between two civilisations, that's all; and sometimes he has trouble convincing himself that he belongs to either. Hence, the arrogance.'

The sun had now plunged itself so deeply into the dust that it was no brighter than a sore red eye. They had reached a gully, where mulga and ghost gums grew, and Eyre raised his arm and called to Joolonga, 'This is it. We'll camp here for tonight. Then we'll make an early start in the morning.'

Joolonga came riding up, and circled his horse around in front of Eyre. 'We have travelled only thirty miles today, Mr Walker-sir. If we travel so slowly, our water will run out before we can reach a water-hole.'

'We will make up for any lost time tomorrow,' said Eyre. 'But for tonight, we will pitch our camp here. I think that Mr Mortlock has probably suffered enough for one day, don't you?'

Joolonga stared at Eyre defiantly, and then he said, 'Mr Mortlock is dead, Mr Walker-sir.'

Eyre said nothing. Instead, he stared at Joolonga in shock. Then he climbed down from his horse; and walked back to the heavy-set chestnut on which Arthur had been strapped, under his parasol. One of Arthur's arms dangled lifelessly; and his head was slumped to one side of the chestnut's neck at such an awkward angle that he had to be dead, because no living man could have endured it. Beneath him, his grey blanket was caked with dried mucus, which buzzed with flies; and flies clustered all around Arthur's mouth and nose, giving him the appearance of a man with a dark grey beard. The crimson sunlight

271

illuminated the spectacle of Arthur's death with grisly theatricality; as if it had been staged as a carnival sideshow, the Horrible Demise of Arthur Mortlock.

Eyre stood for a long time looking at Arthur's body, and his restless horse, and the makeshift shelter which had protected him from the sun during the worst of his suffering. Then at last he turned back to Joolonga, and said, 'We'll bury him here, tonight. Then we'll pitch our camp. Weeip—you make up the fire. Midgegooroo, you start digging a grave for Mr Mortlock. Joolonga—'

A moment's tight pause. Then, 'Yes, Mr Walker-sir?'

'Joolonga, you check through the stores. I want an inventory of what we've consumed to date, including how much water we've been drinking; and I also want an idea of how long you think our supplies are going to last.' He glanced towards Arthur's body. 'Taking into account, of course, that Mr Mortlock is no longer with us.'

'Yes, Mr Walker-sir.'

Midgegooro was unstrapping Arthur's body, and lowering him down the side of his horse to the ground.

Eyre said, 'You don't know how this happened, do you, Joolonga?'

Joolonga's face remained impenetrable; and very black; and there was something in his eyes that was so haughty and self-possessed and yet so strangely prehistoric that Eyre, for the first time in days, felt a prickle of coldness. He felt that Joolonga knew far more about Arthur's death than he was prepared to volunteer, whether it had been magical or not. Perhaps Joolonga knew more about the entire expedition, and where it was going, and what it could expect to find. Or, on the other hand, perhaps he didn't. Perhaps Eyre was simply allowing himself to be frightened by his own lack of experience, and by the prospect of leading six men to their deaths in a fiery and unfamiliar landscape. When they had ridden out of Adelaide, it had seemed inconceivable that this expedition could be anything more than a stiff ride into the South Australian countryside, with a few picnics along the way.

But now that Eyre had seen for himself the devastating distances; and felt for himself the sun bearing down on him at 110 degrees; now that he had peered until his eyes watered at horizons that refused to materialise, and mountains that refused to come any closer; now at last he knew that they were confronting far more than tiredness, and saddle-sores, and disobedient Aborigines. They were confronting the entire meaning of Australia. These plains, these mountains, these endless miles of scrub, these were Australia's unforgiving heart, and her uncompromising character. She was like an old, old woman, who no longer considered that she was obliged to grant favours to anyone; an old, severe woman who castigated her children, and her children's children, and especially the new children who didn't understand her cruelty at all.

On that evening when they buried Arthur, Eyre felt closer to turning back than he ever had before; or ever would again. Midgegooroo dug a shallow pit in the dry ground, and then wrapped Arthur in his blanket, and laid him down like a grey mysterious totem. They gathered around him as the sun boiled through the clouds, and hundreds of emus rushed away to the east, so that it looked as if the whole earth was moving.

Eyre recited the Lord's Prayer, and then he quoted from Job. ' "Why did I not die at birth, come forth from the womb and expire? Why did the knee receive me, and why the breasts, that I should suck? For now I would have lain down and been quiet. There the wicked cease from raging, and the weary are at rest. The prisoners are at ease together; they do not hear the voice of the taskmaster. The small and the great are there, and the slave is free from his master." '

'Food poisoning,' said Christopher, as they slid down the sides of the gully, back to the camp fire. Weeip was cooking beans again, and what he called 'fat flaps', or flapjacks.

'Perhaps,' said Eyre. 'But none of the rest of us have

caught it; and we've all been eating the same food and drinking the same water.'

'It could have been some disease that he picked up in prison,' Christopher suggested. He held out his hand to Weeip for a hot mug of tea. 'You know how malaria comes and goes; perhaps this sickness was the same kind of thing.'

Eyre looked around the warm twilit gully. The stars were out; the cicadas were singing; and the ghost gums were playing statues. There was a dry smell of scrub on the wind; and the spinifex grass whistled softly and eerily to itself. He thought: we could turn back now, saddle up the horses in the morning and head straight back to Adelaide. After all, three men had died already, Chatto and Rose and the long-suffering Arthur. Do the rest of us have to risk our lives, simply to find an Aborigine medicine-man for a boy already dead, and wealth for Captain Sturt? We could always say that we ran out of water; that we rode for hundreds of miles and saw no sign of anywhere to fill our bottles, let alone an ocean, and how could anybody think of mining or farming or driving stock through territory as harsh as that?

But the seagulls had been flying north; and what was more, he had given Yanluga his word. There would be no chance of his claiming Charlotte, either, unless he came back triumphant. His moral and political destiny were all invested in this one expedition. It was his one opportunity to fulfil himself, his one chance of greatness. The seagulls had been flying north and he would have to follow them.

He looked up and saw Joolonga sitting by himself on the opposite rim of the gully, hungrily spooning up heaps of beans. He stood up, and climbed across to him under a white moon the size of a dinner-plate. Joolonga glanced towards him as Eyre came across; but said nothing, and continued to wolf down his beans.

'Touching, wasn't it?' Eyre asked him, standing over him, one elbow resting on his knee.

'Touching, Mr Walker-sir?'

'The funeral. The Christian interment of Mr Arthur Mortlock, lately departed.'

'It was sad, Mr Walker-sir.' Joolonga washed down the beans he was chewing with a mouthful of tea. 'It is always sad when a spirit leaves the real world.'

Eyre watched him for a moment, and then said, 'Midgegooroo told me that it was you who pointed the bone at him.'

'Midgegooroo cannot speak, Mr Walker-sir,' replied Joolonga, placidly.

'Midgegooroo *can* speak, and you know it. He uses hand-language.'

'Perhaps there was a misunderstanding, Mr Walker-sir.'

Eyre shook his head. 'I don't think so. Midgegooroo has a way of making himself quite explicit.'

There was a very long silence between them. Joolonga continued to eat his beans, occasionally taking a sip of tea or a bite of hard biscuit; his eyes darting around in the gathering darkness like two elusive white animals.

After a while, Eyre said, 'I want to know the truth, Joolonga.'

'There are many different truths, Mr Walker-sir. One truth for the white man, one truth for the Aborigine.'

'And for you? Mr Betwixt-and-Between? What is *your* truth?'

Joolonga swallowed quickly, and sniffed, and then said, 'Mr Mortlock *had* to die, Mr Walker-sir. The decision was not mine. It was Ngurunderi, the spirit of death, who lives in the sky. He accepted the souls of those two white men, Mr Chatto and Mr Rose; and when Ngurunderi accepts the soul of a murdered man, he demands revenge for those who killed him. Otherwise, he sends Wulgaru the devil to exact the punishment himself.'

Eyre stared at him. 'You mean to tell me that you killed Arthur because you thought that those two bounty-hunters had to be avenged?'

'Not I, Mr Walker-sir. Ngurunderi.'

'And how exactly did—*Ngurunderi* make this requirement known to you?'

'There have been signs, Mr Walker-sir, ever since those men were buried.'

'What signs, precisely?' Eyre snapped at him.

Joolonga said, 'In the sky, sir. That is where Ngurunderi made his home. Two clouds, shaped this way; then a single cloud.'

Eyre was both furious and frightened. If Joolonga had really killed Arthur; then the rest of them were equally at risk. Who knows what exotic excuses he could find to murder Dogger, or Christopher, or Eyre himself, when they were sleeping? The expedition would have to be called off; and they would have to take Joolonga back to Adelaide as their prisoner. Unless of course, they summarily executed him here.

'Why in God's name didn't you tell me about any of this?' Eyre demanded. 'What earthly right do you think you had to take this matter into your own hands? You're a danger to yourself and you're a danger to all the rest of us, as well. Damn it, Joolonga, if you believed you saw a sign from Ngurunderi, why didn't you say anything about it? That's what you've been brooding about, isn't it? And now you've killed Arthur, and brought the whole expedition to a useless halt. It's over. It's finished. And you're responsible.'

'Ngurunderi would have stopped us himself, sooner or later, Mr Walker-sir. Far better to sacrifice Mr Mortlock, and spare the rest of us.'

'Joolonga, I don't give a damn about Ngurunderi. I don't give a damn for your hocus-pocus and I don't give a damn for you. This is a Christian expedition and we shall abide by Christian morality.'

Joolonga put down his dish. 'An eye for an eye, Mr Walker-sir? Isn't that what it says in your good book?'

'Joolonga—you were supposed to be our guide. You were supposed to protect us in the bush. You were not supposed to set yourself up as our judge and executioner.'

Joolonga raised one hand, the light-coloured palm facing towards Eyre. 'This is my country, Mr Walker-sir, and in my country I know how to protect the people in my care. Believe me, Mr Walker-sir, there was no other way. Mr Mortlock's spirit was forfeit. When men die wrongly, the one who brought about their death has to die, too. It is the balance of life.'

Eyre said, with a dry throat, 'How did you kill him? Come on, Joolonga, I want to know.'

Joolonga reached into the pocket of his coat and produced a packet made of tanned kangaroo-hide. He unwrapped it, and then held out on the palm of his hand a pointed white bone, almost pistol-shaped, highly polished. It looked like the shin-bone of a euro, or a small red.

'I said from the first, sir, that he had the mark of death on him.'

'You didn't say that it was you who had pointed the bone.'

'Would you have believed me, Mr Walker-sir, if I had told you that this bone had brought about Mr Mortlock's sickness? Do you believe me now?'

'Give it to me,' said Eyre.

Joolonga carefully laid the pointing-bone on to Eyre's palm. Eyre felt the weight of it: it seemed to be unusually heavy for a bone so small. And even through the kangaroo-hide wrapping, he was sure that it felt cold. A dry, ancient artefact from a magical age. As cold as the night. As frigid as the Southern Cross.

'That was all you did to Arthur? Point this bone at him?'

'That was all that was necessary, Mr Walker-sir.'

Eyre slowly stood up straight. He didn't know what to say. Joolonga had suddenly confronted him with one of the greatest tests of his religious convictions since he had decided not to take holy orders. He had set out on this expedition with the unusual but firm belief that *all* faith, no matter how it was expressed, found equal favour in the eyes of God—that God's power and influence could be called upon in any language, by any ritual, and that God would answer any prayer, regardless of whether it was addressed to Yahweh or Allah or Baiame.

As long as those who called for help were ready to acknowledge the moral supremacy of a higher Being, then all of God's strength could be theirs.

Eyre had believed that Yanluga's spirit could be laid to rest by Yonguldye the medicine-man. But could he now bring himself to believe that Joolonga had killed Arthur Mortlock simply by pointing a bone at him? If he could, then Joolonga was a fearful threat to all of them, and to the whole expedition. Or perhaps he wasn't—because if he *had* killed Arthur, then everything he had said about Ngurunderi, and the necessity for avenging the killings of Chatto and Rose—well, it was conceivable that all that had some basis in reality, too.

If on the other hand Joolonga *hadn't* killed Arthur, he could still be very dangerous. After all, he had pointed the bone at him with the *intention* of killing him; and he seemed quite pleased that Arthur had died. Next time, he might try murdering his white companions with something less innocuous than a kangaroo's shin-bone—like a knife or a rifle.

Then there was the possibility that Joolonga was lying, and that he had deliberately poisoned Arthur's food. There were plenty of virulently poisonous fruits in the scrub, especially the brilliant red macrozamia nuts, and certain yams. Joolonga may even have stolen poison from Eyre's medical supplies. There were small bottles of salt of lemons and pearlash in his box, both of which could bring on bloody vomiting, and even madness.

At last, however, Eyre gave Joolonga back his bone. 'I'm going to put you on trust,' he said quietly. 'I cannot arrest you here, nor can I put you in irons. You would just become an encumbrance. Nor would there be any point in shooting you, since we need your guidance to continue. And we *are* going to continue. We are going to pursue this expedition of ours to wherever it may lead us. We are going to find Yonguldye and we are going to find the inland sea; and we are not going to return to Adelaide until we do. We have a great destiny to fulfil, and we shall fulfil it with glory.'

Joolonga watched him, warily. 'Yes, Mr Walker-sir,' he acknowledged.

'*Yes*, Mr Walker-sir,' Eyre repeated. 'Because you are going to behave yourself from this moment on. No more insolence, no more contemptuous behaviour, no more mumbo-jumbo or pointing of bones. If you try to harm any one of us in any way, then I warn you now that I will personally kill you, at once. You are a guide, and you will guide us, and that is all.'

'You accuse me of Mr Mortlock's murder, Mr Walker-sir?'

'Yes, Joolonga, I do.'

'Then what will you do when we return to Adelaide?'

'I will have you arrested and tried.'

Joolonga said, 'You are a brave man to tell me that, sir. Either brave or foolish.'

'Not as foolish as you think, Joolonga. If you see us through this expedition, and bring us back safely, then it may be possible for me to forget the way in which Mr Mortlock died; and simply to say that he was suffering from food-poisoning.'

Joolonga sat back, hugging his knees, and slowly grinned. 'You are an interesting man, Mr Walker-sir. You seem to be one who dreams, and yet your dreams move mountains. Perhaps we are all dreaming with you.'

Eyre said nothing; but slid cautiously back down the gully to the camp-fire, where Dogger and Christopher were finishing their supper.

'I was just telling Joolonga to buck his ideas up,' said Eyre.

'About time, too, coal-black bastard,' sniffed Dogger.

'I find him impossible,' said Christopher. 'He's the strongest case for keeping the blackfellows uneducated that I've ever come across. Obstinate, wilful, bad-tempered, and bloody ugly.'

'Don't imagine the blackfellows think very much of *your* looks,' grinned Dogger, nudging Christopher in the ribs. 'Whenever they see a bright-red fizzog like yours, they say, "Time to wake up, it's sunrise." They do have a sense of humour, you know.'

Christopher said, 'Are we going to go on, now that Arthur's dead?'

Eyre nodded. 'There's nothing to go back for; and every reason for going on.'

'And you're sure you can trust Joolonga? You seemed to be having rather a testy discussion with him up there.'

'I was simply reminding him that, out here, the first duty of each of us is to his companions, and to the whole expedition.'

Dogger spat into the fire. 'Eyre's right, you know. You don't have to worry about trust in the outback, Joolonga needs us just as much as we need him. The only time that you ever have to worry about trust is when you've run out of everything—food, horses, water, and leather boots. That's when you start looking at each other and imagining each other as cutlets and chops.'

His spit sizzled in the fire, and he suddenly realised what he'd done. He looked up towards the night sky, and took off his hat, and said, in an apologetic voice, 'Sorry, Arthur. Forgot myself there, for a moment.'

Twenty-One

By noon the following day, the temperature had already risen to 100. They rode single file through a distorted landscape of brindled scrub and twisted bushes, under a sky that was as blue as a sudden shout.

Joolonga rode ahead, with Eyre a little way behind. Somehow, their talk yesterday evening had excited a fresh awareness between them; and although Eyre remained as suspicious of Joolonga as ever, he began to sense that the Aborigine guide was just as determined to see this expedition through as he was himself; and that for their different reasons they both needed to see this extraordinary act of social and geographical drama brought to whatever conclusion history might demand.

It might end in the bush, with exhaustion, and bones. It might end in frustration and giving-up. It might end in magnificent triumph. But both of them had made up their minds with equal strength that it would succeed.

Dogger said to Eyre, as they sat under the patient shade of their horse a little after midday, swatting at the flies which crawled all over their faces and arms, 'Do you know something, Eyre? About an hour ago, I asked myself a question.'

'What question was that?' Eyre wanted to know. He took a carefully measured mouthful of warm leathery water, swilled it around his mouth, and then swallowed it.

'I asked myself: Dogger, I asked, what in blazing hell are you doing here, sitting on this horse, sweating your way through the bush like a boiled bandicoot, when you could be back on Hindley Street in the comfortable arms of Mrs McC., well-drunk on ice-cold beer, and with a belly full of pot-pie? That's what I asked myself.'

Eyre looked at him, brushing away again and again a persistent fly that seemed determined to land on the same spot on the side of his nose, whatever happened. 'What was the answer?' he asked Dogger, with a smile.

'The answer was, I don't know. I suppose I'm like the sailor; who every time he went to sea, he was homesick; and every time he came home, he was seasick.'

From the shadow of his horse, where he was lying with his head back on his carefully rolled-up jacket, with the casual air of a reclining picnicker, Christopher said, 'I think I'd give a year of my life to be back at the racecourse now, eating an ice, and watching Mr Stewart's Why Not in the three o'clock. It would be a fine thing to see a decent elegant horse again, instead of these equine elephants.'

At that very moment, there was a loud clattering noise; and Christopher shrieked, and sprang up from under the horse, flapping his hands at his shirt and britches. 'Bloody thing pissed on me! Of all the bloody nerve!'

Eyre and Dogger laughed until they were weak, rolling and kicking around in the dust. Eyre at last stood up, coughing the dust out of his lungs, and put his arms around Christopher's shoulder. 'My dear chap. Don't you know that you should never malign a horse within earshot.'

'And especially not within pizzle-shot,' put in Dogger. 'By God, I've seen some fellows jump. But you!'

They rode on, into the afternoon. As they rode, the land subtly changed from mallee scrub to flat salt marshes, dried out in glittering swirls of pink and white, like ground glass, and dotted with tussocks of tough grass. The wind persisted hot north-westerly, keeping the temperature high, and a flock of bustards rose against it, and then circled lazily in the air.

By mid-afternoon, the land began to rise a little, and they were riding again through scrubby savannah, with an occasional scattering of stunted mulga trees on the low horizon. The spinifex grass was so sharp that sometimes it drew blood from the horses' legs; and the ground between each clump was uncompromisingly stony and hard. But shortly after four o'clock they reached a twisting gully; and at the far end of it was a small reflecting pool of water, its sides stained like a geological rainbow with the various minerals which had evaporated from it during the dry season. A frightened collection of red gums grew around the pool, and their branches were thick with zebra-finches.

Joolonga dismounted, and led his horse down to the edge of the water. Eyre followed him; then Christopher and Dogger. Weeip and Midgegooroo began to unpack some of the leather water-bottles, so that they could replenish their supplies.

The water in the pool was low, and tasted metallic; but it was cooler and fresher than the water they had been drinking from their bottles. Dogger knelt down by the edge of the pool and drank until water gushed out of the sides of his mouth; then washed his face in it.

Eyre said to Joolonga, 'No sign of Yonguldye.'

Joolonga replaced his midshipman's hat and looked around. Then he beckoned to Eyre, and the two of them climbed up the far side of the gully until they reached a second ravine, which must have been carved out centuries ago by the water which once flowed through these plains. There were signs of an Aborigine encampment here: a fire which had been left to burn after the nomads had left, and which had blackened the grass all up one side of the ravine. Bones, pieces of wood, and three shelters made out of mulga branches and woven grass.

Eyre looked back. The heads of the horses drinking at the pool were reflected like the heads of turned-over chess-pieces. Weeip was sitting by the far edge, filling up two or three water-bottles at once, while Christopher watched him contentedly, his hands in his pockets; and Dogger lit up his pipe.

'How long ago did Yonguldye leave here?' Eyre asked Joolonga. 'I mean—this was Yonguldye's camp, wasn't it?'

Joolonga nodded. 'Yonguldye was here. There, on the stone, are the marks of his totem.'

Eyre could made out nothing except a few criss-cross

streaks of ochre, but he was prepared to take Joolonga's word for it.

Joolonga said, 'He is not long gone. See the footprints are still clear. Here, and here. The north-westerly wind has been blowing hard enough to have swept these footprints away in a week or so. Perhaps he was here two days ago; perhaps only yesterday.'

'As recently as that? Are you sure? Then we've only just missed him.'

'The ashes of the fire are still fresh,' said Joolonga. 'If we are quick, we may catch up with him tomorrow. If not tomorrow, the day after that.'

Eyre cupped his hands around his mouth and called down to Christopher and Dogger, 'Halloo! Some luck, at last! Joolonga says that Yonguldye was camped here only two days ago. We could catch up with him by tomorrow!'

'Thank God for that,' said Christopher. 'Then we can all go home.'

Eyre turned back to Joolonga but he could see by the fiercely amused expression on Joolonga's face that he was not thinking of returning to Adelaide yet, any more than Eyre was. There were other mysteries to be solved, before they could head back south again. There were other discoveries to be made.

'Which way do you think he went?' Eyre asked.

Joolonga pointed north-east, across the salt marshes, towards the brick red line of the north Flinders mountains. 'The ochre mine,' he said. 'Mr McConnell was quite right. But we have only ridden half a day out of our way; and at least we know that we shall not have to retrace our steps. We have water, too; and we can find more water at Edieowie.'

Eyre said, 'All right. You can set up camp now. And before we leave in the morning, I want to make sure that every water-bottle is filled right up to the neck, and that the horses have all been watered. And one thing more. I want the rifles loaded, and holstered beside our saddles. One for Mr Willis and one for me.'

Joolonga looked back at Eyre with one hand raised against his eyes to shield them from the setting sun. 'Yonguldye will not harm you, Mr Walker-sir. Not as long as you have Joolonga with you.'

'Nevertheless, I want the rifles loaded and holstered; and properly loaded too.'

'Yes, Mr Walker-sir.'

'*Yes*, Mr Walker-sir,' Eyre repeated, just to remind him that he was on probation.

They were reasonably lucky with food that night. Midgegooroo speared a bandicoot that had come to the waterhole to drink; and they roasted it and ate it with salted beef and pressed apricots, and tea. Eyre thought that it tasted rather like lamb; although Christopher said that it was easily the most repulsive meat that he had ever tasted. It had probably been the sight of the small furry animal twisting and jerking on the end of Midgegooroo's spear that had upset him. He sucked a barley-sugar to take the taste away; while Weeip, to complete *his* meal, dug scores of fat white grubs from between the roots of the gums, and crammed them into his mouth as eagerly as if they were sweets.

Eyre stood beside Weeip as he dug deftly with the end of a pointed-stick. It was almost dark now, and the surface of the pool had turned to glutinous blood. 'They didn't teach you to eat those at the mission,' he said.

Weeip shook his curly head, and looked serious. 'The Lord is mice pepper,' he said. 'I shall knot one.'

Eyre squatted down beside him. The point of Weeip's stick flew into the loose-packed soil and quickly winnowed out the grubs with extraordinary speed; although Eyre was growing used to the boy's dexterity. He had seen him two days ago pick up a handful of ants and sand; let the sand slide slickly through his fingers, and then press the whole handful of ants straight into his open mouth, and crunch them between his teeth. The way in which he had done it had been so matter-of-fact, so practised, that for a moment Eyre hadn't thought that it was anything unusual.

Christopher looked determinedly in the opposite direction whenever any of their three Aborigines began to eat anything which he considered to be disgusting. He particularly complained about the way in which Midgegooroo would sit by the camp-fire, and suddenly scoop out of the flames any ghost-moths which had fluttered too close; plucking off their wings and devouring them ostentatiously.

Joolonga had told them that in the mountains of the far south-east, Aborigine tribes would soon be gathering for the aestivation—the summer equivalent of hibernation—of the Bogong moth. He called it 'the summer sleeping'. The moths would swarm together in rock crevices, thousand upon thousand of them, and the tribesmen would either scrape them down with a stick or, if they were nestling in very deep crevices, smoke them out. They would cook them quickly on a hot flat stone, brush away the burned wings, and eat them. The moths were tiny, no larger than peanuts, but full of fat; so that at the end of the season the tribesmen would come down from the mountains glossy and plump.

'It is a time for friendly tribes to meet together; to tell stories, and to trade, and to hold a great corroboree,' he had explained.

Eyre had looked up, interested. 'Captain Sturt mentioned corroborees. They're dances, aren't they? Religious meetings.'

'A corroboree can be held for any reason,' Joolonga had informed him. 'To celebrate a boy's initiation; or to tell sacred stories from the dreamtime or to give thanks for food. Sometimes a corroboree may be held because it has rained, and there is plenty of water. But many of the corroborees are secret, and may only be danced by initiated men. No white man or woman will ever see those dances; nor the magic that is performed there.'

'If the magic has anything at all to do with eating moths, I think I prefer to be exluded,' Christopher had remarked, wrinkling his nose.

Now Eyre watched Weeip dig out a whole handful of ten or twelve fat white grubs, which slowly twitched and wriggled in the palm of his hand.

'What do they taste like?' Eyre asked him.

Weeip poked at the grubs, and then looked up at Eyre with his wide reddish-brown eyes. 'Coomoorooguree,' he said, simply.

Over at the camp-fire, Joolonga laughed. 'He says they taste like grass-tree grubs. He is a connoisseur of grubs.'

'Let me taste one,' said Eyre.

'I cook it on the fire for you?' Weeip asked him.

Eyre said, 'Don't bother. I'll eat it the way you're eating them.'

'Oh God, as if I didn't feel sick enough already,' Christopher groaned. Dogger took his pipe out of his mouth and laughed like a dog barking. 'Trying to eat like a real bushman, are you?' he said. 'Wait until they give you that juice they squeeze out of green ants.'

Weeip dropped the grub on to Eyre's hand, and Eyre felt it squirm against his skin. It was semi-translucent, ringed with faint brownish markings, and there was a pattern of dots at one end of it which could almost have been an insect-like face. It seemed very much bigger and fatter now that he had offered to eat it.

Grinning, his own mouth full of grubs, Weeip watched and waited for Eyre to put it between his lips.

'Come on, Eyre,' Dogger coaxed him. 'Nothing ventured, nothing gained. You don't want some salt-and-pepper with it, do you? Or a dash of Worcestershire sauce?'

Eyre tilted his head back, closed his eyes, and opened his mouth. Then without any more hesitation, he clapped his hand over his mouth and let the grub tumble on to his tongue.

For one moment, as the grub twitched and wriggled against the insides of his cheeks, he felt a shudder of convulsive disgust. His stomach, already overfilled with half-digested bandicoot and dried apricots, let out an

287

audible groan. But then he sternly commanded his regurgitative muscles to behave themselves, and ordered his front teeth to bite through the slightly membranous exterior of the grub, into the grape-like insides.

The taste of the grub was bland, not dissimilar to undercooked pork fat, and Eyre supposed that it would be quite acceptable if you happened to be particularly short of food. The consistency of the flesh, however, was repulsively stringy and jellyish; and when he had finished chewing the grub and swallowing it, he had to sit down on a fallen gum-tree for four or five minutes, trying to discipline himself not to think about those ringed markings, or that insectlike face.

'Well?' asked Christopher. 'You haven't said much. Not even *delicieux*!'

'It's good Aborigine manners to belch out loud if you enjoyed something,' grinned Dogger.

'I think I'd bring it all up if I belched,' said Eyre.

'I have more here, Mr Wakasah,' enthused Weeip, who had been busy with his digging-stick. He opened up his cupped hands to reveal twelve or fifteen fresh, twitching grubs.

Dogger, without a word, opened up his satchel and took out a silver flask of home-distilled rum. Eyre took a long, sweet, fiery swallow; and then gargled with it.

'I don't think you're hungry enough for an Aborigine diet yet,' said Dogger dryly. 'Most of what they eat is what you might call an acquired taste.' He took a pull on the flask of rum himself, and sniffed. 'I remember we were down on the beach once, not far from Wallaroo, and a whale had been stranded there. Pilot whale, huge bastard. It must have been rotting for weeks, but about a hundred blackfellows found it, and hacked it to pieces, and roasted it there and then. Great rejoicing there was, that day. The stink would have blown you all the way to Tasmania and back.'

They bedded down early that evening: Eyre wanted to make an early start to track down Yonguldye. The moon and her reflection moved gracefully to rendezvous behind the black bank of the water-hole; and the insects began their repetitive timekeeping.

Twenty-Two

Eyre slept dreamlessly for two or three hours; and then suddenly woke up, his eyes wide, listening. The insects had stopped singing, and all he could hear was the wind, low and sibilant, like the breath of a hesitant flute-player. Everyone else was asleep, as far as he could make out; although the horses were shifting restlessly beside the gum trees. He sat up, and looked around. The water-hole was as dark as a memory, pricked with stars. The gums performed a motionless mime, white-faced dancers in the prehistoric night.

Then, he heard chanting. Very low, and quite far away; but vibrant enough to carry. He listened for a minute or two. Sometimes the chanting was blown away by the wind, but when the wind dropped he heard it quite clearly. It was accompanied from time to time by a sharp wooden clapping, and by a hollow pipe-like sound which inexplicably made the hair around Eyre's scalp prickle up like pins.

He shook Christopher's shoulder, and whispered, '*Christopher*!' But Christopher was determined to carry on sleeping, and all he did was roll on to his back, open his mouth, and begin to snore. Eyre whispered, '*Christopher*!' again, but when it was obvious that he was going to arouse no response, he quietly drew back his own blankets, and eased himself away from the camp-fire, which had now burned down to nothing more than hot grey ash.

Dressed in nothing but his shirt, he crossed to the other side of the gully, and climbed up it so that he could see out across the plain. Off to the north-east, over the peaks of the northern Flinders range, large clouds were banked, although there was no likelihood that they would bring any rain. Directly to the north, there was a tiny blue glitter; the light of a distant camp-fire. It was from there that the chanting was coming; and the clapping of sticks.

Eyre looked back at the gully. None of the others had stirred, and he decided not to wake them. Dogger and Christopher always made such a performance of unrolling themselves in the morning, scratching and yawning and stumbling around, and so Eyre preferred to investigate this chanting himself; quietly. He would have liked to have taken a rifle with him, but unpacking it and loading it would have made too much noise.

He crouched low, so that he would remain unseen behind the mulga bushes and spinifex grass, and headed diagonally away from the gully, towards the eastern side of the distant fire. The wind was a light north-westerly, and so from the eastern side he would be able to hear the chanting at its clearest. Apart from that, Aborigines could pick up scents as sharply as hounds, or so Captain Sturt had told him, and so he decided that it would probably be more prudent to stay downwind.

He ran stealthily and quickly through the grass. His feet were cut and his legs were stung, and he began to wonder whether it would have been more sensible simply to fire off a few rifle shots from far away, and scare the chanting tribesmen from a safe distance. But he thought; you never know with blackfellows. If he were to frighten them, or if he were to interrupt one of their sacred rituals, they might well take it into their heads to come after him, and pay him back with a swift death-spear in the heart; or some more arcane revenge, like that which had befallen Arthur Mortlock.

The thought of Arthur still alarmed him. He would probably have nightmares about Arthur gagging and vomiting for the rest of his life; however long *that* would last. And most disturbing of all was the thought that Arthur might actually have died from the magical effects of Joolonga's pointing-bone, no matter how unearthly or preposterous that seemed. Eyre had heard of Mabarn Men who could actually shout their enemies to death; by letting out a long and terrible roar that ruptured their hearts and stunned their minds.

As Eyre made his way closer to the fire, the chanting died away; and a ragged chorus of cries and responses was taken up, like a primitive version of a Church of England collect. The responses were accompanied by a loud sporadic clapping that sounded like boomerangs being slapped together. A voice shouted a hoarse incantation, and there was an answering cry that ended with an Aborigine word that Eyre recognised, '—*wynarka!*' It meant 'Stranger'—and judging from the ferocity with which it was cried out, these blackfellows plainly felt very little affection for the 'stranger' about whom they were singing.

Eyre crouched and half-crawled his way up behind a mulga bush, and pushed the branches apart with his hand so that he could see the corroboree more clearly. As far as he could make out, there were ten or twelve blackfellows there, gathered around the fire, all of them naked, all of them painted with horrific masks of white pipe-clay. Their hair was elaborately pulled up into high top-knots, and there were rows of wallaby's teeth hanging across their foreheads. Two of them were sitting cross-legged on the ground; one of them clapping two boomerangs together to produce the sharp wooden rhythm that had first woken Eyre up, the other playing a large wind instrument that looked like a decorated tree-trunk, but which obviously must have been hollow. The booming, flutey song that this instrument produced was the most scaring noise of all; it didn't even sound as if it could have been created by a human at all, but rather by the wind, blowing through some lonely curve of eroded limestone, or by a breathing

Bunyip, or by some other strange creature from Australian legend.

Eyre watched the ritual for nearly half-an-hour. The blackfellows sang and clapped, and then they took each other around the waist and danced in a circle, swaying and shuffling, and humming in an undertone which was even deeper and more vibrant than the voice of the wooden instrument. Eyre began to wish very much that he hadn't ventured out this far, because he was now faced with the difficult task of returning to the gully without being noticed. The sky was lighter now, and the singing and the humming and the clapping had died away; and he was much more likely to be seen or heard. And there was no doubt about it: the collection of weapons which lay stacked beside the fire included not only spears with pirri points, but 'death-spears' with rows of sharp quartz flakes stuck along the sides of them with gum—spears which could inflict terrible wounds and which could usually be removed from a victim's body only by being pushed right through.

'The Lord is mice pepper,' he breathed to himself, a self-mocking repetition of the prayer which Weeip had told him. Then he stealthily backed away from the mulga bush, and then began to hurry like a frightened hunchback towards the edge of the gully.

He was panting as he ran; and his footsteps sounded thunderous as he weaved through the scrub and the spinifex grass. He kept imagining that he would hear the noise that the north Australian Aborigines described as *bimblegumbie*—the sound made by a spear launched from a woomera—and that seven feet of quartz-tipped kalyra-wood would stick into his back and bring him down before he could even tell Christopher that he loved Charlotte irrationally but passionately, and that she could have his bicycle, if she wanted it.

He was almost there. He could see the gums that surrounded their makeshift encampment. But just as he was about to slide down the slope towards the *billa*, something attenuated and dark rose out of the bushes beside him and made him shout out, 'Jesus!' in uncontrollable fear and surprise.

'*Quiet*, Mr Walker-sir,' said Joolonga's urgent voice.

'Quiet? You scared me half to death.'

'I saw you had gone, Mr Walker-sir. Weeip was supposed to be keeping watch but Weeip was asleep. I was coming after you, in case you needed me.'

'You could have given me a heart-seizure, you black rogue. Have you heard all that singing and chanting? Have you heard those fellows? Out there, by the fire. They've been singing and dancing away there for hours.'

'Yes,' said Joolonga, enigmatically.

'Well, do you know what they're doing?' Eyre asked him, as they made their way down to the water.

Joolonga squatted down by the oil-black surface of the pool, scooped his hand into the water, and splashed his face; then the back of his neck. His eyes glittered in the night like coins glimpsed at the bottom of a sunless well. 'They are holding a corroboree, Mr Walker-sir. A sacred dance to celebrate the coming-alive of a dreamtime story. It is here, tonight, that the coming-alive of the story begins.'

'Out here? What are you talking about?'

'Out here is where it was always foretold that the story would begin.'

'I'm not at all sure that I understand you.'

Dogger rolled over testily in his blankets, and called out, 'If you two want to spend the night nattering, why don't you do it somewhere out of earshot? I'm uglier than both of you put together: I need my beauty-sleep.'

Joolonga stood up, and beckoned Eyre to follow him further down the gully, until they were out of sight of the camp behind an outcropping of rock, overgrown by mulga bushes. Then Joolonga lit up his crab's-claw pipe and filled the night air with the strange pungency of his tobacco. 'I can safely tell you now, Mr Walker-sir. Before tonight, you may not have understood why this expedition was so important to us; and you may have declined to embark on it, in spite of how you felt about young Yanluga.'

'Go on,' said Eyre, warily.

'Well, Mr Walker-sir, it was always said in the dream-time that the spirits of the dead would one day return from the place of the setting sun. When the first white men came here, most of us believed that they were the ghosts of our forefathers, since they came from the west, and their skins were white. Dead people, you see, were thought to shed their earthly skin when they rose up to the skies. In the early days, white men were always called *djanga*, which is the same word we use for "spirits of the dead".'

'Well?' said Eyre, a little testily. 'What does that have to do with this expedition?'

'Simply that it was always foretold, Mr Walker-sir, that one of the *djanga* would visit Tandarnya, which is what we call Adelaide; and that he would accidentally take the life of a blackfellow whose name in the story is Utyana, which means a boy who has not yet been initiated. But the *djanga* would seek atonement for what he had done; and would seek out a clever-man in order to be forgiven for taking the boy's life. He would have to journey for many weeks across the plains in order to find the clever-man; just as you have been obliged to.'

'If this mythical spirit is supposed to be me, I think you're forgetting that it wasn't *I* who killed Yanluga; it was Lathrop Lindsay, and those hounds of his.'

Joolonga looked unperturbed. 'You have said yourself, Mr Walker-sir, that if you had not gone to meet with Mr Lindsay's daughter that night, Yanluga would still be alive. It was always foretold that you would cause his death, Mr Walker-sir, and no matter what you did, no matter how you tried to avoid it, the foretelling had to come to pass.'

'Rubbish,' Eyre snapped. He was silent for long, deafened seconds, while Joolonga attentively smoked. Then he said, 'How does the story end?'

Joolonga spat into the darkness. 'In the story, the *djanga* comes across the trail of the clever-man at a place where the kangaroos come to drink. That is why we have come here to Woocalla. I think that Mr Dogger is probably right, and that Yonguldye is already at Yarrakina, the place of the ochre-mine; but it was necessary for us to come here in order to fulfil the story. That is why my brothers are out there tonight, dancing. They know that the foretelling will soon come to pass. They are celebrating.'

'Does the story say what happens when the *djanga* meets the clever-man?'

Joolonga nodded. 'It is known all over South Australia as the Story of the Spirit's Gift; for when the *djanga* meets the clever-man, he gives him in atonement all the knowledge of the spirit-world, so that living men might at last know all the strange and marvellous secrets of the land beyond the setting sun. These days, however, the blackfellows realise that the story foretold the landing of the white man, rather than the return of ghosts from the world above, and they believe that the chosen white man will give to the clever-man all the magical knowledge that makes the white man so superior; and that the clever-man will pass this magical knowledge from tribe to tribe, so that at last the blackfellow will be able to stand as an equal to the *djanga*; and protect his lands and his secret places from the white man's thievery.

'You, Mr Walker-sir, are the *djanga* for whom the Aborigine people have been waiting for hundreds of years, ever since the dreamtime. On your shoulders, the future of the Aborigine people completely rests; and they look to you for their salvation. Do you now see why you have been followed and protected by Aborigine warriors ever since the day of Yanluga's death; ever since you first declared that you would give him the burial which you believed he deserved?'

Eyre smeared chilly sweat away from his forehead with the back of his hand. The sky was far lighter now; and the *billa* shone like a cold memory, its surface circled only by the beaks of early-rising zebra-finches which had come down to the water's edge to drink while it was cool.

Eyre said, 'Listen to me, Joolonga. I determined to come out on this expedition firstly to do my duty by Yanluga; and secondly to make my name; so that I can claim the bride I want, and the fortune I want. But those two goals are the beginning and the end of it; whatever interpretation you and your Aborigine chums wish to put on it. I am a Christian, and I am as a moral as the next man, although I have no pretensions to holiness. But, damn it, Joolonga, I am not a messiah. Nor ever shall be.'

'Captain Sturt doesn't seem to agree with you,' said Joolonga, with a sly smile.

'Captain Sturt? What does Captain Sturt know about it?'

'Everything, of course.'

'You mean he knows about the legend of the *djanga*?'

'Of course,' Joolonga nodded. 'That is why he chose you to lead this expedition. Do you think there could have been any other reason for choosing an inexperienced shipping clerk to plunge straight into the deserts of South Australia? Captain Sturt came directly to talk to you at the Spring Ball, do you remember? Why do you think he picked you out so readily?'

'*You*,' said Eyre, 'are the black devil.'

'No, Mr Walker-sir; I am Captain Sturt's man.'

'But how did Captain Sturt come to hear so quickly of what I wanted to do? How did he know that I wanted to find Yonguldye? And what possible good could it have done him, even if he *did* know?'

Joolonga waved a mud-wasp away from his ear. 'You remember Captain Henry, who took you home after Yanluga was killed? He heard what you promised Yanluga, and heard it clearly, and he believed right away that you were the *djanga* of whom the foretelling had always spoken. Captain Henry is a Wirangu, sir, and in his own time was a clever-man of a kind. He was very excited. He told Yagan, who is the head man of the Aborigines who camp by the Torrens River, in Adelaide, and Yagan in his turn told me. Yagan has believed all his life that the blackfellow must find a way to live with the white man, but that he must have strength, and knowledge, and understand the white man's power, in order to survive. Otherwise, he will be like nothing better than a possum attacked by dingoes. Torn apart, ripped to pieces, out of weakness and ignorance.'

Eyre said nothing. He felt both angry and humiliated. Angry most of all that Captain Sturt should have deceived him; but deeply humiliated that he hadn't been chosen for this expedition because of his determination to find Yonguldye or because of his confidence and clear-headedness, but because he had appeared to a few superstitious blackfellows to be the thunderous coming of some mythical messiah; a magnificent but stupendously ignorant delusion which Captain Sturt had obviously done his best to exploit to the very limit. Captain Sturt had known his Aborigines better than he had let on; and his white men, too.

Joolonga said, casually, 'I told Captain Sturt all about you; and Captain Sturt contrived for you to meet him at the Spring Ball.'

'How?' Eyre demanded.

'A friend of Captain Sturt's talked to *your* friend, Mr Willis. I think the friend persuaded Mr Willis that Captain Sturt would soon talk you out of any ideas of looking for Yonguldye. And, I think there was some money.'

Eyre felt as if the flesh were being boiled of his bones. '*Why*?' he hissed at Joolonga; too furious and too shocked even to shout.

Joolonga shrugged. 'Finance, Mr Walker-sir. That is the word for it, isn't it? South Australia is almost bankrupt: the whole colony. Lately, Captain Sturt has lost thousands of pounds of his own money in sheep and wheat farming; while Colonel Gawler has already drawn £200,000 on the London Commissioners to build new roads and houses in Adelaide, and they say they will order him back to England if he draws any more. South Australia has no money, sir, and things go from bad to worse, and worse to terrible.'

'And that is why Captain Sturt has decided to make the best of me, is it? That is why he sent me off to meet with the Aborigine clever-men, and find out anything I could about opals, or copper, or cattle-trails to the north; anything that would pull his financial chestnuts out of the fire? And in the guise of a dreamtime spirit!'

Eyre stood up, and he was shaking. 'My God,' he said. 'Captain Sturt knew how much I respected the Aborigine religion. He knew what guilt I felt for Yanluga's death. And yet he calmly deceived both me and blackfellows who take me for their *djanga*. They were out there all night, around their fire, dancing and singing and celebrating! You saw them yourself! They believe that I'm that legendary spirit of yours! They believe that I can help them against men like Gawler and Sturt and Lathrop Lindsay! And *you*, Joolonga, what the hell do *you* believe? Not in your own people; that's quite obvious. Not in your own religion and your own legends. Nor do you believe in me; or you wouldn't have tricked me for so long. Is it money you believe in? Is that it? Is that all? God, man, you have no morals at all!'

Joolonga tapped out his pipe. 'I have beliefs, Mr Walker-sir.'

'Oh, yes? What beliefs?'

'I believe that we must fulfil this expedition: that we must follow Yonguldye to Yarrakinna.'

'Even though you know damned well that whatever riches Yonguldye points us to; no matter how many stock-trails to the north he tells us about; in return I can give him nothing? What magical secrets do *I* know? You would deceive your own people so flagrantly?'

Tightly, Joolonga said, 'My own people, as you call them, Mr Walker-sir, are already doomed. They were doomed from the moment the first white man set foot on Australia. My own people are a sad, poor, filthy, people. They should have died out hundreds of years ago; before

298

the white man ever saw them. Perhaps they should never have been.'

'You don't believe that.' Eyre challenged him.

'What I believe is unimportant,' said Joolonga. 'The man who was Joolonga died many years ago. He cannot rise again. It is not foretold.'

Eyre looked up at the pale, sand-coloured sky. His anger at Captain Sturt's deception had died down a little; although he knew it would continue to grate inside him like a fractured rib, until he could face Captain Sturt again and have it out with him, shout for shout. His most critical dilemma now was not whether he ought to take revenge on Captain Sturt or not, but whether he should call off the expedition altogether. Whether he ought to return to Adelaide without wealth, without glory, and without any kind of discovery to honour his name; to face both a political and a financial scandal, not to mention disgrace in the eyes of everybody he knew, especially Charlotte; or whether he ought to press on, and find Yonguldye, and accomplish everything that both Sturt and the Aborigine people expected of him regardless of how he had been tricked; and regardless of how the Aborigines would eventually suffer. And, by God, how they would suffer, especially if Captain Charles Sturt had anything to do with it.

Joolonga had already taken sides. Joolonga had chosen inevitability. Why struggle to win a battle that has already been lost? Yet, in spite of himself, Joolonga still guarded some silent and secret faith in Ngurunderi, and Baiame, and the other dreamtime gods; and that faith gave Eyre an inkling of hope that if he continued the expedition, they would be able to bring to Yonguldye's *noora* not magical knowledge, perhaps; not even the promise that the black-fellows would be able to protect their hunting-grounds and their sacred places from the ravages of the whites but the possibility that they might at least be able to survive and eventually flourish in what was one day going to be predominantly a white man's country.

Dogger, from around the bushes, shouted, 'Eyre? What the *hell's* going on? Where are you? Not taking your morning shit already?'

'*Coming!*' Eyre called back, as lightly as he could. Then, to Joolonga, 'I'm not sure why you felt it necessary to tell me all of this. But, I appreciate your frankness. At least I know now why I'm here.'

Joolonga said flatly, 'It was necessary for you to know sooner or later. Captain Sturt said that I should tell you the night before we expected to reach Yonguldye's encampment. However, I saw that you were seeking an explanation for that corroboree which was held during the night; and that unless you were given an answer, you might decide to return to Adelaide.'

'What makes you think that I'm not going to return to Adelaide even now?'

'You are a young man, Mr Walker-sir. You have ideals that older men no longer have; and you are ready to believe things which older men no longer believe. But I have seen that you make your mistakes once only; and that you learn as quickly as a dingo. You know that you will go on, if only to prove to Captain Sturt that you can do everything he expected you to do, only better. Ahead, there is a chance of fame and wealth. Behind, only confusion and disgrace. This is not a country which rewards those who surrender, Mr Walker-sir, no matter what the perils may be.'

Eyre said, 'Very well, we're going on. But let me warn you, Joolonga, everything I said to you yesterday still applies. I've had enough of your secrets, and enough of your arrogant manners. We're going under *my* terms, not yours, and certainly not under Captain Sturt's. When we catch up with Yonguldye, it will be my decision how we approach him; and I will want nothing more from you than to act as my interpreter. Because, by God, if you cross me once more, Joolonga, I will have your head off for it.'

Joolonga bowed his head, and then trod heavily away to sort out the horses. Eyre stayed where he was for a while, breathing deeply, and wondering what in all Heaven he ought to do. The sharpest pain of all was that Christopher should have talked about him to Captain Sturt's friend before the Spring Ball; and that he should actually have taken money to persuade Eyre to come along with him that night. No wonder Christopher had seemed so angry when Captain Sturt had done nothing at all to dissuade Eyre from setting out to find Yonguldye. No wonder he had tried to say that night how much he loved Eyre; and how much he revered him.

It had been the love of Judas; the reverence of guilt.

Twenty-Three

They crossed the salt lake towards Parachilna like slowly-moving figures in a sparkling dream. The sun shone with such shattering brilliance on the swathes of dried-out, coloured minerals that made up the lakebed; almost blinding them; that Eyre devised himself a pair of spectacles made of smoked pieces of bottle glass and wire; and rode through the days of heat and dust like Mephistopheles.

He hardly spoke at all to any of his companions; and in return they kept well away from him, Dogger and Christopher and Midgegooroo and Weeip riding in a small, close bunch, with the pack-horses on either side of them, although Joolonga rode closer to Eyre, and a little off to the right, as if he were privy to his secrets, if not his thoughts.

During the whole length of those glaring days, Eyre could think about nothing but Captain Sturt, and how he had betrayed him; and Christopher, too, and how Christopher had hurt him more than Eyre could have imagined possible. He ate in silence at their evening fires; and slept apart in his bedroll. In the morning, with the sun rising over the crust of the lake like the unwelcome visitation of some incandescent Presence from heaven itself, he would mount up and ride ahead of them again, silently, blind-eyed, his face wrapped in scarves against the saline dust. Dogger began to talk of sunstroke, and bush-madness, and of turning back. But Christopher perversely began to talk about Eyre as if he were a doomed young knight from medieval days on a quest for the Holy Grail; and far from faltering, his enthusiasm for the expedition grew even more complicated, and more involved.

They reached Parachilna on a surprisingly mild evening, when a light dusty wind was blowing, and there were clouds moving along the horizon like sailing-ships in a nearby harbour. The rusty-coloured peaks of the north Flinders rose all around them now, the dry, wrinkled peaks of a once-forested mountain range. Eyre dismounted, and began to walk his horse up a twisting creek-bed; and there was no sound but the clinking of fragments of slate disturbed by its hoofs, and the *whirrr-whirrr-whirrr* of the cicadas.

Dogger gave his horse to Midgegooroo to lead, and hurried up the creekbed to overtake Eyre before they started climbing up the more gentle slope ahead of them.

'Eyre,' he said, taking hold of Eyre's bridle. 'Eyre, you can't continue like this. Come on, mate. You've got the rest of us to think about, apart from yourself.'

Eyre was silent for a while, standing very upright, his face floury with dust. His eyes were invisible behind the two darkened curves of smoked glass; like the eyes of an insect.

'I suppose you want me to sing and joke,' he said, at last.

'Well, why not?' Dogger told him. 'This is a miserable enough business as it is, without a little fun. And damn it, Eyre, you used to be fun. What about those evenings on Hindley Street? Two jugs of beer and you and me were laughing fit to bust our trousers. What happened to all that?'

'I don't know,' said Eyre. He truly didn't know. He felt as if all the fun had been evaporated out of him, by the sun; as if now he had been kippered into mirthlessness, sexlessness, and irascibility; a leathery ascetic in search of a dried-up ideal. He no longer knew why he was here; or what moral principle he was trying to uphold. He had lost his faith in Christopher; his trust in Joolonga; and his enjoyment of Dogger.

Dogger said bluntly, 'If you don't snap yourself out of this, old mate, I'm turning back. I know this territory, as far as here. I came out here once, looking for emu. But I'm not going any further; not unless I get some sign from you that things are jogging along as they ought to be. I'm game for adventure, Eyre. But I don't intend to die for no good reason; and especially not without a smile on my fizzog. Anyone who comes out beyond the black stump with a mien as miserable as what yours is; well, mate, they're certain dingo-fodder, that's all, and I didn't spend twenty years hunting down dogs to end up as dog's breakfast, nor dinner, nor *hoose-doovries* neither.'

Eyre lowered his head, and brushed white dust from his curls with the back of his hand. Then he carefully took off his dark glasses, and looked at Dogger, and grinned.

'You're right,' he said. 'I've been a sour and miserable bastard, and I'm sorry. But let's go on.'

'We can turn back if you want to. Nobody will think the less of you.'

Eyre shook his head. 'I've forgotten why I'm here. The whole desert is so overwhelming that I don't think I really care any more. But let's go on.'

'And you'll smile, now and then?' urged Dogger.

Eyre nodded.

'Not just at me and Weeip; but at Christopher, too. You've been giving *him* a pretty uncomfortable time, these past three days. Come on, Eyre, you know it.'

'I'll do my best.'

Christopher caught up with them, leading his horse with difficulty up the narrow, fragmented creek-bed. He frowned at Eyre from beneath the brim of his wide kangaroo-skin hat, and there was a look in his eyes which was a mixture of admiration and despair; a look to which Eyre was bound to respond. Bound not only by their friendship; but by plain human dignity; and by the circumstances in which they now found themselves, hundreds of miles from anything but scrub and salt and mountains as dry as a nine-hour sermon.

Eyre let go of his bridle, and came forward over the clattering slate, and put his arms around Christopher, and held him close; and then turned to Dogger, and held out an arm for him, and embraced him, too. And the three of them stood under the violet evening sky, on the side of a rust-red mountain, holding each other in the comradeship that would one day be known in the outback as 'mateship'; the love man-for-man that is blatantly forged on the battered anvil of self-preservation; the love that knows neither dignity nor suspicion; that asks no questions; and expresses no desires; but which fades in city streets as rapidly as an uprooted desert rose.

Joolonga watched this embrace dispassionately from the ridge above the creek-bed, among the vivid-green acacias. Weeip and Midgegooroo stood by their pack-horses, equally expressionless, both of them chewing on pitjuri leaves, which always made them placid and detached.,

At last, Eyre said, 'Let's get ahead. It's going to be dark before long and I want to find a decent place to camp.' He felt more encouraged now, especially since Christopher had made it quite clear that he would follow him and support him wherever he went. 'Joolonga,' he called, 'do you think there's any chance of catching up with Yonguldye before nightfall?'

'I smell an encampment close, Mr Walker-sir; big one. See, there is smoke over the ridge there.'

'Do you think it's a good idea just to go barging in to a

strange community of blackfellows?' asked Dogger. 'I've heard that some tribes are quite partial to explorer casserole.'

Eyre put on his dark glasses again. 'We'll carry the rifles with us; just in case. Midgegooroo, unpack three rifles for us, will you; three; and make sure that they're properly loaded, the way I showed you.'

He felt in his pocket and made sure he had one essential item: his magical *mana* stone. Weeip came up and brought them water. There were streams running through the Flinders, which the Aborigines called *aroona*; streams which bubbled up from underground springs and danced their way down between the limestone rocks, sometimes forming pools of stunning clarity. The water attracted seabirds, grey teal and white-faced tern, as well as wallabies and euros and emus, so there would be plenty of fresh food for them to eat while they were here.

Eyre led them up the creek-bed until they found themselves in a wide gorge, with overhanging rocks rising up on three sides; and extraordinarily, like a silently-shrieking governess throwing herself from an attic window, a single ghost-gum growing out from the rocks almost thirty feet above their heads.

Eyre said, 'We'll leave the horses here. Weeip, you keep watch on them. Joolonga, Midgegooroo, you come up with us. If we can find Yonguldye, we'll come back and fetch the horses; if we can't, we'll settle here for the night. Weeip?'

'Yes, Mr Wakasah?'

'Light yourself a fire. If we don't find Yonguldye, we'll be hungry by the time we get back.'

'Yes, Mr Wakasah. And—Mr Wakasah?'

'What is it, Weeip?'

Young Weeip covered his face with his hands, so that his dark eyes sparkled through the gaps between his fingers. 'Don't bring back the devil-devil, Mr Wakasah.'

Eyre knelt down beside him. Weeip kept his hands over his face, and his soft curly hair blew in the evening breeze.

'You're not scared of the devil-devil, are you?' Eyre asked him, kindly.

Dogger laughed; and snorted. But all the same, he looked around the gorge with sudden apprehension, as if Weeip's fear had attracted the first flickering coldness of Koobooboodgery, the night spirit. Christopher coughed into his hand.

'I feel the devil-devil, Mr Wakasah. Something bad here. Yea though I walk through the alley of the valley of death.'

Eyre glanced up at Joolonga. 'Joolonga?' he asked. 'Do you sense anything?'

Joolonga took off his midshipman's hat and raised his flat nose to the wind. He remained like that for a few moments, his face concentrated and fierce, but then he said, 'Only fires, Mr Walker-sir. No evil spirits.'

'Well, then,' said Eyre, and stood up. 'Let's go and see if we can find our man. You know, I'm almost sorry I didn't bring my bicycle. Can you imagine what a rip it would be to cycle all the way down that creek-bed?'

Dogger picked up his rifle, and slung it on to his back. 'Surprising how a few hills can cheer a fellow up, isn't it? It's the flatness that makes you feel like giving up, and killing yourself. One old dogger I knew, Bill Hardcastle, he used to curse the desert for hours on end, because it was flat. You never heard such language in your whole life; and every insult for flat that you could think of. He used to say that it was all God's fault, the desert. God ran out of ideas, he said, and said to the Angel Gabriel, what shall I do with the rest of this world? And Gabriel said, "Oh, I shouldn't bother if I were you; leave it flat." So that's what He did. Mind you, he could catch dingoes, could Bill; even the ones that could sniff out a trap from a mile away. He'd set up scarecrows and windmills alongside his traps; just enough to catch the dog's attention, so that the dog wouldn't notice where it was walking. Then snap, and the dog was caught. God's featureless folly, that was one of the names he called the desert. Poor old Bill.'

'Why "poor old Bill"?' asked Christopher.

Dogger spat inaccurately at a lump of euro dung on the rocks. 'Gave up dogging, did Bill, went back to Melbourne, and tripped over a mounting-block by the side of the road and broke his neck.'

With Joolonga leading the way, and Eyre close behind him, they climbed the side of the gorge. The rock was flaky in places, and once or twice Eyre missed his footing and skidded backwards, sending showers of stones down on Christopher's head; but at last they crested the gorge and found themselves walking along a high spine of mauvish-coloured limestone, with the higher peaks around the Yarrakinna ochre-mine rising off to their left, blood-red against a blood-red sky.

They crossed a low, gentle valley of lemon-scented grasses. Here and there, they came across clumps of the startling red-and-black flowers which had been named for Captain Sturt—Sturt's desert pea. They had petals like the gaudy hoods of elfish cardinals, hung up in the vestry.

The air was aromatic with eucalyptus oil and the dryness of emu bushes but now Eyre, too, could pick out the distinctive smell of cooking-fires. Joolonga was twenty or thirty paces ahead of him now, his head down, following the tracks of Yonguldye's people through the grassy sand.

Christopher said, 'I hope we know what we're getting ourselves into.'

Eyre ran his hand through his tangled curls. 'Don't worry about it, old chum. I've talked to Joolonga, and Joolonga says that the Aborigines really want us here. To them, this expedition is vitally important. Apparently, it was foretold in the dreamtime; and it has some sort of magical significance for them.'

'I'm still not desperately happy about it,' remarked Dogger, laconically. 'They're a funny lot, these bush black-fellows. Different from the tame characters you see around town. Funny ideas; and very quick to take the huff.'

The ground had been steadily rising, and the grass becoming increasingly sparse, until they were walking on

307

bare limestone again; over ridges that had been scoured by sand and worried by water. At last, they saw the bright blue haze of cooking-smoke rising up ahead of them; and Joolonga turned to Eyre and raised ten fingers twice, which meant twenty fires, at least.

'Quite a gathering,' said Eyre. 'It seems as if we're expected.'

Christopher held back. 'Eyre, listen—we ought to approach these people with the greatest of caution.'

Eyre walked back and took hold of the straps of Christopher's satchel, and drew him forward. 'They're not going to hurt us, I promise you. Tell him, Joolonga. They think that I'm a messenger from the spirit world, or something like that. Everything's going to be perfectly all right.'

Dogger said to Joolonga, 'What's your opinion, squash-face? You're supposed to be the guide. Do you know these people? What are they, Wirangu?'

'Some Wirangu, some Nyungar, maybe some from Murray River.'

'Are they friendly, or what? And what's all this about our friend here being a messenger from the spirit world?'

'It is what they believe, Mr Dogger. It is a long-ago story which they now seem to think has come true.'

'And has it?'

'We must see, Mr Dogger,' said Joolonga.

At that moment, so silently that even Joolonga was startled, three skeleton-figures rose up from the rocks nearby; three Aborigine warriors smeared with grease and pipe-clay and ochre, their hair wound with twine and decorated with scores of wind-twirled emu feathers. Each of them carried a long spear and a woomera; with clubs tied around their waists. One of them also had a dead tern hanging around his waist, a bird he must have caught while waiting and watching for Eyre's expedition to make its way up the mountains.

'Christopher, Dogger,' said Eyre, and beckoned them to stand closer to him. All three of them raised their rifles, and cocked them ready for firing. Midgegooroo remained where he was; but Joolonga raised one hand and stepped forward, until he was fewer than ten paces away from the nearest tribesman. He spoke quickly, first in Nyungar, which was the nearest that South Australia's tribes had to a common language; and then in Wirangu. The tribesman did not deign to reply at first, but looked haughtily from Joolonga to his three white companions, and then to Midgegooroo.

'What did you say to him?' asked Eyre.

'I said that you were the chosen *djanga*, and that you were seeking to talk to Yonguldye the Mabarn Man.'

'Tell him again,' said Eyre.

'Wait,' advised Joolonga.

They stood their ground. It was beginning to grow dark now; and against the gradually thickening sky, the three Aborigine warriors looked as wild and primaeval as Cro-Magnon men. One of them pointed with his spear at Midgegooroo, and indicated that he should move closer to Eyre and Christopher and Dogger; and this Midgegooroo reluctantly did. Eyre lifted his rifle-stock up to his shoulder, and took aim at the tribesman who stood furthest off to the left. He was silhouetted sharply against the last of the daylight, and made by far the easiest target.

'Be careful, Mr Walker-sir,' said Joolonga. 'If you should shoot by mistake, there is no telling what they might do.'

'Tell them again that I am the *djanga* who has come to talk to Yonguldye, Eyre insisted. 'And also tell them that we are all *ngaitye*. We are all friends.'

Joolonga hesitated, but then rapidly spoke to the tribesmen again.

'If you want my opinion,' said Dogger, 'We should drop the lot of them here and now, before they know what's hit them; and then leg it back to the horses at top belt.'

'Ssh,' said Eyre. 'He's answering.'

Now, the leading tribesman was saying something to Joolonga. The language sounded to Eyre like Wirangu, although he couldn't be certain. There was a distinctive guttural clacking about Wirangu which Eyre recognised from the way in which Yanluga used to talk to his horses. The tribesman seemed to feel very vehemently about what he was saying, because he kept rapping his throwing-stick against the shaft of his spear, and ducking and nodding his head. Sometimes his voice was a breathy murmur; at other times he was shouting as if he were apoplectically furious that they had arrived here without asking his permission. All the time Joolonga remained impassive, his hat set very straight on his head, one arm tucked into his impressive coat like Napoleon, but trouserless, with his scrotum and his penis elaborately wound up with twine.

At last the tribesman's haranguing appeared to be over. He stepped back two or three paces, and stood quite still, the wind ruffling his feather head-dress. Joolonga made two or three quick gestures in sign-language, and then walked back to Eyre. To Eyre's surprise, Joolonga's forehead and cheekbones were shining with sweat, and he was shivering.

'What was all that about?' asked Eyre.

'He says that we must follow him, but that he expects us to observe certain proprieties.

'What proprieties?'

'We must leave all of our clothing here; and our weapons.'

'What?' demanded Dogger. 'You expect me to walk baby-bum-naked into a camp full of mad Aborigines, without even a rifle to guard my particulars. Come on, Eyre. This is ridiculous.'

Eyre looked towards the tribesman who had spoken to Joolonga. 'Ask him what his name is,' he said.

'Joolonga turned around and called out to the tribesman, who lifted his spear and said, 'Parilla.'

Joolonga translated, 'That is his familiar name, not his family name. It means "cold", or "the cold one".'

'Well, you can call *me* the cold one if I have to go down and meet those blackfellows without my clothes on,' put in Dogger.

But Eyre called out to Parilla, in a challenging voice,

'Parilla! You go without clothes! But what man would ever go without his weapons? Not you! Well, nor will we!'

Anxiously, gabbling sometimes, Joolonga translated. Parilla listened seriously, occasionally nodding his head; and then he turned and spoke to his two lieutenants. Joolonga murmured to Eyre, 'This could mean some trouble, Mr Walker-sir. Parilla is a fierce tribal warrior; he does not like to be ridiculed, especially by a white man. It seems to me that he does not believe that you are the *djanga*; or even if he does, he feels enmity towards you.'

Without any warning at all, Parilla stooped, picked up a stone, and hurled it straight at Eyre's face. Eyre didn't even have time to think about dodging away; but the stone was thrown so accurately that it did nothing more than graze his cheekbone, and flick an instant line of bright red blood across his skin.

There was a clockspring silence between them. Joolonga backed away a little. Christopher raised his rifle now, and aimed it directly at the second tribesman. Even Dogger kept quiet, except for a spasmodic sniff, and warily flicked his eyes from one warrior to another.

Below them, off to the right, where the cooking-smoke was coming from, they heard the first cry of a great chant. To Eyre, the sound was completely electrifying; because it must have come from the throats of a hundred Aborigines; and it made the entire evening vibrate, as if the limestone bedrock of the Flinders mountains themselves were humming like a tuning-fork. A flock of fairy martins, hunting insects in the dusk, swooped and turned as if the sound of human voices had deflected them in flight.

Eyre lifted his rifle again and pointed it at Parilla's head. the Aborigine remained motionless, his expression unreadable beneath the thick pipe-clay and ochre that striped his cheeks and his forehead. The rifle was heavy and Eyre knew that he would have to be quick before his aim started to waver. He was no marksman; and although the distance between them was only fifteen paces, it was so gloomy now that it would be easy to make a fatal mistake.

311

Dogger said, 'We'd be well advised to walk quietly away now, Eyre. I'm not funning with you.'

Eyre said, 'If we walk away now, they'll never let us go. And besides, we still have our duty.'

'I rather think our prime duty is to stay alive,' said Christopher, with deep unhappiness.

Eyre ignored him. He had been challenged by Parilla; only a glancing, childish blow with a stone; the kind of blow with which the tribesman would have teased an uninitiated youth. But he had done it to see whether Eyre really was the *djanga* he proclaimed himself to be, or just another scavenging white man. Eyre had no way of knowing it for certain, but he sensed that if they tried to retreat without accepting Parilla's challenge, they would be speared where they stood, like Weeip's writhing bandicoot.

Joolonga blurted, 'Mr Walker-sir—' But Eyre squeezed the rifle's trigger, and there was an abrupt loud report, as if two boomerangs had been slapped together right next to his ears, and a spurt of bright orange fire from the pan; and then a cloud of brown smoke.

Everybody turned to stare at Parilla in shock. But the Aborigine warrior was still standing, although he was swaying slightly in delayed reaction to being fired at. The most remarkable sight, however, was his head-dress of emu feathers. The shot had blown it completely to pieces, leaving his thickly-greased hair standing on end in a parody of utter fright, and the air around his head full of whirling, floating feathers.

The echo of the shot came back from the distant mountains, and far away there was a flurry of birds. But then came the laughter: first from Midgegooroo, then from Dogger and Christopher, and finally from Parilla's own tribesmen. The laughter subsided for a moment, but then Parilla himself reached up gingerly and patted his hair; and he began to laugh, too, an odd clacking high-pitched chuckle.

'By God I think you've rediscovered your sense of humour,' said Dogger, wiping his eyes with the back of his sleeve. 'Look at the poor bastard. He looks as if he's seen a devil-devil.'

Only Joolonga remained unsmiling. Eyre had taken on the challenge of Parilla against his advice, and won it; without bloodshed, and without any loss of dignity on either side. Joolonga stood to one side, his hands crossed behind his back so that they lifted up his coat-tails, and flapped them up and down like a cockerel's tail, intermittently baring his stringy brown buttocks.

The shot attracted more Aborigines, painted and feathered just as Parilla and his companions were. Parilla spoke to them in a harsh, imperative voice, and they stayed back in a respectful circle, waiting to see what would happen next. The chanting from the encampment continued, however, deep and melodious; so deep sometimes that it seemed below the range of human hearing. Two or three of the tribesmen who had come to join them on the ridge shouted back their responses towards the camp-fires, and there was whooping and rapping of sticks and boomerangs, until the night echoed and clattered and screeched.

'What are we supposed to do now?' asked Christopher, apprehensively.

'Now we do what they asked us,' said Eyre. 'We take off our clothes, and we follow them down to the encampment. But we don't let go of our rifles; and Midgegooroo can still bring his satchel of ammunition. Here, Midgegooroo, you might as well reload this one while we're undressing.'

'I'm damned purple if I'm going to undress,' said Dogger, ferociously.

'In that case, you can go back to the horses and wait with Weeip.'

'What, and miss the fan-dancing?'

Joolonga came over and said, 'You were lucky with this one man, Mr Walker-sir. He can laugh at himself. But there are many others who do not have the same facility.'

'Like you, for instance, my dear Joolonga,' said Eyre, unbuttoning his cuffs.

Joolonga gave a bitter little smile, and shook his head. 'I can laugh when the occasion warrants it, Mr Walker-sir. But tonight we must go warily, and treat our new acquaintances with respectfulness.'

Eyre stepped out of his britches, and unfastened his long cotton underwear, already stained and marked from days of sweaty riding, and from being washed out in nothing but muddy pools of stagnant water. He shook his shirt over his head, and then he was naked, very thin now, with protuberant ribs and a slightly curving stomach, and reddened thighs from the constant chafing of the saddle. Dogger, once he had struggled out of his combination underwear (A.L. Elder's finest), looked like a displeased Mr Punch. Christopher slowly took off his britches; but kept his shirt on. Parilla said something angrily to Joolonga, pointing and waving at Christopher, but Christopher said: 'Tell him I'm sick. Tell him I've got a rash. If I get the sun on my back, it'll kill me.'

'Come,' said Joolonga; and they followed Parilla and the other tribesmen down the sloping side of the limestone ridge, towards a second, less prominent outcropping.

Eyre felt curiously light-headed, walking through the night stark naked with these fierce and primitive-looking tribesmen escorting him on either side. But on the other hand he felt there was a naturalness to being naked in these surroundings; a oneness with the warm air and the raw rocks and the spiny grasses that stung his bare ankles. There was an ancient eroticism to it; the same blatant and unashamed sexuality that had first struck him when he landed in Adelaide last year. His penis half-stiffened as he walked, but it neither upset him nor embarrassed him.

During his days of isolation from Christopher and Dogger as they had crossed the salt lake, he had come to the understanding not so much that he should be more mistrustful of others, but that he should invest more trust in himself. That was why he had been able to turn to his companions at last and embrace them. That was why he had been able to face up to Parilla so confidently. And that was why he could walk naked through the mountainous night with all the confidence of a warrior. Christopher had sensed the change in him, without even realising that it was his own betrayal of Eyre that had brought it about.

They reached the brink of the second outcropping; and Parilla said, in Wirangu, 'Behold.' And what they saw beneath them was so breathtaking and so moving that Eyre could only turn to Christopher and shake his head in astonishment.

The ground dropped steeply away below their feet into a deep layered gorge, scoured out of the limestone over thousands and thousands of years by a rushing array of waterfalls. The reddish crags on either side were in darkness now that night had fallen; but their terraces and balconies and water-hewn pulpits were sparkling with hundreds of cooking-fires and torches, so that the gorge had taken on the appearance of the grandest of civilised theatres, La Scala in the middle of the Australian outback, with chandeliers and footlights and carriage-lamps. Among these lights, shadowy primitive figures came and went, scores of them, and it was these figures who sang so resonantly as they roasted their meats or fed their dingo-pups or prepared their children for the night's sleep. It was the greatest gathering of Aboriginal tribes that any of them had ever seen; or even heard about. And the warmth of these people's humanity, the power of their family closeness, were overwhelming, rising from the glittering depths of the gorge as distinctly and as strongly as the smoke from the cooking-fires, or the vibrant harmony of the ancient songs. They were innocent feelings, yet proud; and under these skies on this most timeless of nights, they brought Eyre for the first time to an emotional rather than an intellectual understanding of the people who had lived in Australia for three million years.

'If all the centuries during which Australia has been inhabited were condensed to a single hour,' Captain Sturt had told Eyre, the night before they had set out, 'then the Aborigines would have lived here alone for fifty-nine minutes and twenty seconds; and the remainder of the time would represent the white occupation.'

There had been Aborigines here in the Pleistocene age. There had been Aborigines here when the deserts were thick with trees, and giant kangaroo roamed the grasslands. There had been Aborigines here when the lakes of South Australia were vast sheets of water, teeming with fish, instead of crusted salt flats. And there were still Aborigines here, gathered together on this warm spring night to celebrate the coming-alive of one of their oldest legends.

Eyre found that there were tears in his eyes. 'Smoke,' he told Dogger, but Dogger understood, too, in his rough-and-ready way.

Parilla called to Joolonga; and Joolonga said, 'This way. There is a path down the side of the hill.' As the chanting swelled from the gorge below them, they climbed their way down through the rocks; at one point crossing a narrow waterfall, their fingers slipping on the lichen-covered rocks, the cold water splattering their naked bodies.

'I could murder a beer,' said Dogger, longingly. His belly was raw and scratched from scraping against the rocks as he shuffled from ledge to ledge. Eyre couldn't help glancing at his genitals: they looked like a mallee fowl sitting on her nest of gingery-brown vegetation, waiting for her eggs to hatch.

When they reached the floor of the gorge, they were immediately surrounded by a crowd of curious Aborigine men and women and children. The fires flickered and smoked, the chanting and the boomerang-banging continued as loudly as before; and all around them was chattering and laughing and scuttling; and a constant carnival of white-painted faces, scarred and decorated shoulders and chests, beads and feathers and shining teeth, wide eyes and wildly decorated hair, bare breasts and dancing feet. Dazed and dazzled, they followed Parilla to the centre of the ravine, where the greatest fire of all was burning, a huge stack of dried gums and emu bushes, spitting and sparking and roaring, and there, tied with twenty or thirty wallaby skulls and stuck with hundreds of emu feathers, stood a large shelter, or *tantanoorla*, of branches and brushwood.

'Parilla says that this is the shelter of Yonguldye the medicine-man,' said Joolonga.

'Well, then,' replied Eyre, 'I think you can announce us, don't you?'

'There is one thing to remember, ' said Joolonga. 'When Yonguldye asks you where you have come from, you must answer "Goondooloo".'

'What does that mean?'

'It is a name in the legend, that is all. But he must believe that you have come from there; otherwise our lives may be in danger.'

Joolonga told Parilla to call Yonguldye. Parilla shook his head, and launched into another of his long clacking lectures; but then knocked the end of his spear two or three times on the rock, and nodded, and went inside the shelter.

'What did he say?' asked Eyre.

'He said that Yonguldye is the greatest of all medicine-men, and that he must be treated with great respect because his revenge is very terrible and we will all have our heads cut off and our bones broken and be fed to the dogs.'

'That's reassuring,' said Christopher. He glanced beside him at a particularly inquisitive black girl, who was staring unashamedly at his nakedness. He crossed his hands over his genitals and the girl giggled at him.

Yonguldye kept them waiting for almost five minutes. They scarcely spoke to each other at all as they stood there; their faces and chests scorched by the raging fire, their backs chilled by the cool night air which was now beginning to flow into the valley. Eyre glanced at Christopher, but Christopher had his head bowed as if he were thinking deeply, or praying.

At last, however, there was a sharp clamour of sticks and boomerangs, and Parilla reappeared from the *tantanoorla*, raising his spear high into the air. A shout rose up from all the blackfellows clustering around them, and a chant of 'Yonguldye! Yonguldye!'

Yonguldye appeared before them with massive ritual dignity. He was a very tall, old Aborigine with a gigantic head-dress of fur and feathers and wallaby teeth that looked like some monstrous mythical creature which had decided to perch on top of him, and remain there to keep watch on his enemies. His face was painted grey with pipe-clay, with a broad ochre band across his forehead, and his withered chest was covered in curving and twisting *ngora*, or decorative scars. His penis was contained in a rolled-up piece of ghost-gum bark, tied around his waist with twine, which gave his protuberant belly the appearance of a brandy-barrel, complete with spigot. He was almost completely toothless, except for the stumps of his two top canines, which gave his face an even more devilish appearance.

Joolonga raised his hand and greeted Yonguldye in sign-language. Then he spoke to the medicine-man in a tone which Eyre had never heard him use before, low and quick and muttering, with none of his usual posturing or arrogance. Now and then he wiped sweat away from his upper lip with his hand. Eyre caught the words *'djanga'* and *'tyinyeri'*, which meant child; and *'milang'*; but Joolonga was speaking so quietly and so rapidly that it was impossible for him to follow the meaning.

Eventually, Yonguldye stepped forward, and stood before Eyre with half-closed eyes, scrutinising him in the firelight. He had a strange smell about him, Yonguldye, like herbs and sweat and lemon-grass.

'So,' he said. 'You are the *djanga*.'

'Yes,' said Eyre, as firmly as he could.

Yonguldye raised his hand and touched Eyre's shoulder. 'You feel like man.'

'Nevertheless, I am the *djanga*. I come from Goondooloo.' Eyre hoped that he had remembered the correct pronunciation.

Yonguldye lifted his head towards the sky, and peered up at the stars. 'You speak like man,' he said. 'You speak like white man.'

'All men speak like white men in Goondooloo,' Eyre smiled, with as much confidence as he could manage.

'Hm,' said Yonguldye. He lowered his head again, and stared at Eyre with renewed ferocity. 'Why does *djanga* carry—' he was lost for the right word for a moment, and then he said, '—*oodlawirra?*'

'Weapon,' whispered Joolonga.

Eyre lifted up the rifle. 'For hunting.'

'*Djanga* no eat.'

'Ah, but sometimes the *djanga* wants to shoot a wallaby or two just for the sport of it; and give it to his friends and relatives. A kind of a gift, if you understand me. The dead nourishing the living.'

Joolonga translated, and Yonguldye seemed to be satisfied with that answer, for he walked all the way around them, nodding and sucking noisily at his gums, and then with a hand like a galah's claw, he beckoned them to follow him into his shelter.

Dogger hesitated at first, but Eyre took his arm, and they bent their heads down and made their way under the clattering skulls around the entrance into the darkness of Yonguldye's lair.

The stench inside the shelter was overpowering. Grease, and sweat, and aromatic herbs, and a smell like decaying fish, which turned out to be an overripe sea-bird which Yonguldye must have been keeping for his breakfast. There were already five other tribespeople inside the shelter; a thin-ribbed boy whom Eyre guessed to be Yonguldye's assistant; and four women; one of them grey-haired and elderly, with a face which looked as if it had been squeezed in a wine-press; the other three far younger. The youngest of them all, who couldn't have been much older than fifteen, was unusually attractive, with very long black curly hair tied with twine, and that rare glossy look about her skin which the effects of harsh sunlight and an irregular diet had not yet dried away. Her face was as Aboriginal as any of her tribe but it was unmarked and unpainted, except for two tiny scars on her cheek and the more he looked at her, the prettier Eyre thought that she was. Her breasts were very large for her age, high and brown-nippled; although there was only the lightest fan-like growth of dark hair between her thighs. Christopher noticed the way that Eyre looked at her, and made a point of crossing the shelter in front of him, to obstruct his view.

'Sit,' said Yonguldye, and they eased themselves awkwardly down on the heaps of greasy-smelling kangaroo hides with which the floor of his shelter was carpeted. 'Food, and water?' he asked, and Joolonga nodded in appreciation, although Eyre realised with chagrin that because he was supposed to be a *djanga*, returned from the dead, he would not be able to eat anything.

Yonguldye knew very little English. Most of it he had picked up during the bad dry of 1838, when he and his tribe had been forced to camp close to a mission at New Norcia in order to survive the summer. He quickly lapsed into Nyungar, and Eyre had to depend on Joolonga's translation to follow the conversation. He felt uneasy about that: Joolonga seemed to be in a peculiarly uneasy mood this evening, snappy with Eyre and exaggeratedly subservient towards Yonguldye.

'You have come to ask me to journey to Adelaide and bury the boy Yanluga according to proper ritual?' Yonguldye asked Eyre, through Joolonga.

'That's right,' Eyre told him. 'He was given a Christian burial; but his soul will never join his ancestors unless he is given the rites in which he believed.'

'You were responsible for his death. Why should you be so concerned about his burial?'

'Because it is my duty.'

'And not simply because you are frightened that his spirit will never give you rest?'

'I am already at rest.'

Yonguldye nodded in assent. This was obviously a good reply.

'Will I be rewarded for journeying to Adelaide?' he wanted to know.

'Whatever you want. Food, clothing, knives.'

'Who will give me these things?'

'Captain Sturt. In fact, Captain Sturt will give you many more things if you help him further.'

Yonguldye looked suspicious. 'What further help does he want? This is not part of the legend.'

Joolonga interrupted here, and raised a hand towards Eyre to warn him not say any more. Yonguldye listened carefully to what Joolonga was saying occasionally sucking back the saliva from his toothless gums, and grunting to indicate that he understood.

'What's going on?' asked Eyre.

Joolonga said, 'Yonguldye has agreed to travel to Adelaide to perform the proper burial rites over Yanluga's body. He thanks you for your concern for Yanluga's soul. He says that you are obviously a wise and compassionate *djanga*.'

'Anything else?'

'He has agreed that in return for your magical knowledge, he will help us to locate a place he knows where there are firestones to be found.'

'Firestones?'

'Opals, Mr Walker-sir. He says there is a place near Caddibarrawinnacarra where firestones can be found; but this is a difficult place to reach, and he will have to guide us there. He cannot describe it to us.'

'Where the hell's Caddibarrawinnacarra?' Dogger wanted to know. 'I've never heard of the place.'

'Beyond,' said Joolonga. 'Yonguldye says *kononda*, which means northwest'.

'There's nothing out there but fried *charra*,' growled

321

Dogger. For Yonguldye's benefit, he had deliberately used the Aboriginal word for 'emu shit'.

'Nonetheless, Yonguldye says the firestones are there; very many of them. Tomorrow he can show us some of the firestones that his own people have dug up.'

Eyre said, 'What about the route to the inland sea? Does he know anything about that?'

Joolonga spoke to Yonguldye for three or four minutes. There was more nodding between them, and then Joolonga said, 'He knows of a route northwards, and he says his ancestors came that way, but he has never been further north himself than the place where the magic kangaroo came to slake its thirst.'

'Where's that?' asked Dogger, with a sniff. 'The Queen's Head Tavern in Kermode Street?'

'No, a place called Callanna,' said Joolonga, humourlessly.

Eyre put in, 'If the magic kangaroo came there to drink, then surely there must be water there.'

'Probably just a waterhole,' said Christopher.

Joolonga spoke to Yonguldye further, and this time Yonguldye rose up on to his knees, his ghost-gum spigot sticking straight out from between his legs, and stretched his arm wildly towards the north, again and again, and talked in a furious babble.

Joolonga said, 'Yonguldye has seen the ocean himself from Callanna. He looked in the distance and it was there. The sea-birds were flying that way, and he is sure that the shoreline can be reached in less than a day's walking.'

Eyre looked around at Christopher and Dogger and his eyes were bright with pleasure. 'Well, my friends,' he said. 'It seems that we may be able to achieve everything we set out to achieve. Yanluga's burial, Captain Sturt's opal mine, and the discovery of the great inland sea. We're going to be rich and celebrated yet.'

'If only you could drink to that,' said Christopher.

'Yes,' agreed Eyre. 'If only I could.'

Twenty-Four

That evening, the gorge rang with the chanting and singing of the greatest corroboree that had been held in South Australia since the days before the white men came. That, at least, was the opinion of the old grey-haired woman who turned out to be Yonguldye's senior wife, and to whom he always referred as *unkeegeega*, which, whether he meant it ironically or not, meant 'young girl'.

Eyre saw nothing that evening of the pretty young girl who had been sitting at the back of Yonguldye's shelter, but that was hardly surprising. He was surrounded all evening by warriors from six or seven different tribes, all of whom seemed to feel that sitting close to the mythical white-skinned *djanga* was a matter of great prestige; and all of whom were very curious about his paleness, and his uncircumcised penis. None of them spoke any English whatsoever; and so Eyre was restricted to smiles and nods and indulgent shakes of his head.

The food came first. Roasted emu, bloody and scorched, but smelling delicious to men who hadn't eaten fresh meat for days. Mallee fowl, their eggs served raw. Skinks, stripped of their legs and peeled of their skins, and dangled over the fire on spits. And with all of this feast, plenty of cold fresh water and Bunya Bunya pine-nuts.

Only Eyre had to remain hungry and thirsty; sitting cross-legged in the centre of his circle of inquisitive protectors; while Christopher and Dogger and Midgegooroo sat around a fire not far away, laughing and talking with a small group of Aborigines who had travelled here from Streaky Bay, and devouring as they did so whole breasts of emu until their faces glistened and the fat ran in rivers down their stomachs and into their pubic hair.

Later, the women silently withdrew to their shelters and to their own cooking-fires; and the men performed a sacred dance. Joolonga told Eyre that this was the dance usually

323

seen at funerals, when the body had been interred, and fires were burned for days on end, while the family looked around for magical signs explaining what had caused the death.

The men looked ferocious and other-worldly in the firelight. Most of them had circles of white painted around their eyes, and skeletal outlines painted on their bodies. They jumped and shuffled and spun around; shaking their spears and swinging their clubs; while scores of sticks were tapped and beaten, and boomerangs were clapped together, and hollow wooden flutes blew that deep, vibrant song that now and forever would make the hairs rise on the back of Eyre's neck.

Sparks flew from the cooking-fires into the darkness; dancers whirled and shouted; and from the entrance to his shelter, Yonguldye the Mabarn Man watched the corroboree with the air of an elderly hawk, watching his revelling young.

After the dancing was over, the tribesmen gathered around, and Yonguldye stepped forward and spoke to them. His speech was long, and involved, and sounded very discursive, because Eyre saw several of the tribesmen yawning and looking impatiently around. It amused him to think that even in a primitive society which had remained almost completely unchanged since the dawn of time, there were still men who gave tedious speeches, and still men who had to stand around and listen to them.

Over and over again, Yonguldye talked about the *djanga*, and shook his bony arm towards Eyre; and every time he did so, there would be a responsive murmur from the assembled tribesmen. It sounded like *'moomoomoomery'*, and incongruously it reminded Eyre of Mrs McMurtry, Lathrop Lindsay's cook on the day that he had gone around to Waikerie Lodge to take Charlotte for a romantic constitutional.

Eventually, Yonguldye untied from his belt a kind of rattle, made of the skull of a young rock-wallaby hafted with gum on to the leg-bone of a kangaroo. Inside the

324

skull there must have been pebbles, or dried macrozamia nuts, because when Yonguldye shook it there was a hollow, echoing sound, like a man desperately trying not to die of cholera. As soon as he shook it, a short imperative burst of noise, all the tribesmen sank silently to their knees, two hundred bowed black heads against a background of twisting orange camp-fires, and Yonguldye hopped and rattled and danced, and uttered a long, sharp, dry-voiced incantation.

'He is calling on Baiame to bless this meeting,' said Joolonga. 'He is telling the people here that this night will be remembered for all time, just as the gods of the dreamtime are always remembered.'

Eyre said nothing, but watched as the tribesmen began to disperse, and return to their shelters and their fires, some of them high up in the rocks, others beside the creek which splashed through the centre of the gorge.

Yonguldye called to Joolonga, and Joolonga said, 'He wants to talk to you before you sleep.' Eyre thought: thank God he doesn't think that spirits stay awake all night. Together they crossed the rocky ground to the entrance of Yonguldye's shelter, and there Yonguldye stared at Eyre and said, in what sounded like formal and dignified language, 'The story is complete. You have returned from the sunset and now you are here. Tomorrow you will give me all the magical knowledge that you possess; and we will take back all the lands and the sacred places that we have lost.'

Yonguldye paused, and then he said, 'You have the stone?'

Eyre beckoned Midgegooroo, who came forward with his satchel. Eyre reached inside it, and produced the engraved tektite which had been given to him on Hindley Street.

'You are truly the *djanga*,' said Yonguldye. 'Look—there is a shelter for you where you can sleep tonight. Tomorrow we will talk more. Tomorrow we will celebrate your coming, and your departure.'

Christopher and Dogger had been taken to a humpy shelter on the far side of the gorge. If Eyre knew anything about Dogger, he had eaten and drunk far too much, and had already fallen asleep. Christopher he knew would be awake, and fretful. Christopher always was. But tomorrow they would be able to set out on their journey to find the opal mine; and beyond, to the great inland sea; and that was exciting enough to overwhelm any apprehension that Eyre felt about their safety among the Aborigines. Tomorrow, they would set out on the journey that would make them great men; the journey that would discharge his moral debt to Yanluga; and which would win him Charlotte back. They would be heroes: Walker, Willis, and McConnell. Names to be taught in schools for the rest of recorded time.

Eyre's shelter was constructed of gum branches and brush, woven together, Like Yonguldye's, it was filled with kangaroo skins, in which Eyre could wrap himself up and sleep. His rifle, which he had left in Yonguldye's shelter during the corroboree, had carefully been laid at the far end of the shelter, still loaded, and respectfully polished for him.

Exhausted by a day of travelling and an evening of Aborigine celebration, Eyre crawled naked into the shelter and lay down on the coarse-haired kangaroo skins. He thought of going to talk to Joolonga about what they would be doing in the morning; and whether Weeip was safe, all alone on the far side of the ridge. But even with his face pressed against stinking kangaroo leather, his eyes began to close, and within four or five minutes the tapping rhythm of the boomerangs which was still going on outside began to fade from real perception, and reappear in his dreams.

He dreamed of murmuring voices, and silhouettes of blackfellows, like the strange lithographs of W.H. Fernyhough; black profiles and stylised poses. He heard rattling and shaking, and the whistling they called *bimblegumbie*. And all the time there was the over-and-over motion of boomerangs, vertiginous and sickening, like riding on a swing-boat at a fair.

He awoke with a shock. Someone had touched his thigh. He twisted his head around so quickly that he tugged the muscle, and hurt himself.

Black against the midnight sky was the shape of a girl, on her hands and knees. She had crawled into the shelter and woken him; and now she was waiting anxiously to see what his reaction would be. He recognised the long soft curly hair. He recognised the sightly slanting eyes. He also recognised the faintly herbal smell of Yonguldye's shelter, which she carried on her skin mingled with the aroma of sour grease and young-womanly perspiration.

'What do you want?' he whispered. Then, when she didn't answer, '*Minago*?' which was the same question in dialect.

She covered her mouth with her hand, to tell him that he should be very quiet. Then she wriggled up close to him, and lay down beside him on the kangaroo skins, and whispered back, 'My name is Minil. I speak English-language. They taught me English-language at mission-school. I was the class top at English-language.'

'If you speak English, what are you doing here?' Eyre asked her.

'I was at the mission-school at New Norcia when Yonguldye and his people stayed there. When they left, I followed them. I wanted to find my own people. No longer cooking and washing and learning Holy Scriptures. I wanted to be free like Yonguldye and his people.'

'But?' asked Eyre.

'But?' Minil frowned. 'I didn't say but.'

'You *say* no but; but there is but in your voice.'

Minil was quiet for a moment; then she said, 'Yonguldye is a strange cruel man. Now I wish to leave him, go back to mission-school. Mrs Humphreys.'

'Are you married to Yonguldye? Are you one of his wives?'

She shook her head. 'He does not like me. He says I

327

have devils in me. But he makes me work hard, cooking for him, making magic powder. Cure powder, for sick. Sometimes insect drink.'

She hesitated, and then she said, 'Wait,' and wriggled her way back to the entrance of the shelter. She came back straight away, with a wooden bowl full of water and a large curved piece of flaking bark, in which she had wrapped four or five large chunks of cold roasted emu breast.

Eyre propped himself up on one elbow, until his head was almost touching the main supporting branch of his shelter. But he was too hungry to worry about whether or not he might destroy his temporary palace. He crammed the half-cooked meat into his mouth, chewing it as quickly as he could; and then washed it down with gulps of cold spring-water. He belched twice; but he couldn't have felt less ashamed. He had sat there all evening, stark naked, watching hundreds of other people eat. Now it was his turn.

Once his hunger had begun to abate, however, and his chewing had slowed down, he turned to look at Minil with suddenly awakening suspicion.

'I'm a *djanga*,' he said. 'You realise that I don't usually eat this stuff. I'm only doing it so that I won't hurt your feelings. You realise that, don't you? Normally, in the spirit world, we survive on . . . well, on clouds, air, things like that.'

'You are not a *djanga*,' said Minil. Her nipple was pressing against his right arm, and he was beginning to feel surges that had nothing at all to do with Yonguldye, or Captain Sturt's opals, or tonight's corroboree.

'Of course I'm a *djanga*,' he insisted. 'It's in the story. The *djanga* returns to earth from the land where the sun sets; accidentally causes the death of a young Aborigine boy; and goes to the clever-man to seek forgiveness. That's me; that's why I'm here. Seeking Yonguldye's forgiveness.'

328

'Yonguldye knows that you are not a *djanga*,' Minil told him.

'What?'

'Yonguldye knows that you are not a *djanga*. He knows that you are nothing but a white man. You cannot be a *djanga* because *djanga* never eat.'

Eyre chewed even more slowly. 'Sometimes we do,' he said, in a petulant voice. 'Just to keep in practice.'

'Perhaps,' said Minil. 'But you are not one of them. And anyway Yonguldye believes that the old story foretells the landing of the white men, not the coming of the dead. A white man will kill an Aborigine boy; perhaps by mistake, perhaps not. But he will travel through the desert seeking a medicine-man who will forgive him for what he did.'

'All right, it's the same story,' said Eyre. 'The only discrepancy is that I'm a white man; a white man who eats cold roasted emu; and not a ghost.'

'What happens in the end is the same.'

'I don't think I understand you.'

Minil reached down and touched Eyre's bare thighs. Then, quite matter-of-factly, she grasped his penis, which was already erect, and began with a gentle black hand to stroke it up and down. Eyre knew that he should have told her to stop; that he was a *djanga*, and that *djanga* had no sexual feelings. But he found himself powerless to say a word. The feeling was too compelling. Apart from which, he didn't want to upset her until she had told him why Yonguldye didn't believe that he was a real spirit, returned from the dead.

Minil said, 'Yonguldye talks tonight to your man Joolonga; and your man Joolonga talks to you. But what Joolonga says to you is not the same as Yonguldye says to him. Joolonga says, "This is the white man who killed the boy in Adelaide. He is come here just like the story. He seeks forgiveness just like the story. Everything he knows I will give to you, if you tell me where to find firestones, and if there is sea to the north where men can sail." '

329

Eyre looked down. In the shadows of the shelter, he could just make out the black outline of Minil's hand, massaging him, and the whiteness of his own skin.

'I don't—' he began, but then he collected himself, and said, 'I don't see that it makes very much difference—whether Yonguldye believes that I'm a spirit returned from the dead or not. He's agreed to give poor Yanluga all the proper Aboriginal burial rites. He's told us where to find the firestones; he's even directed us towards the inland sea. I mean, I can't tell him much in return. I don't have a lot in the way of magical knowledge. But he's fulfilled *his* part of the bargain, and so I'll certainly do my best.'

Minil suddenly took her hand away, leaving Eyre highly aroused and crucially frustrated. 'If you really were a *djanga*, Yonguldye would not even dare to ask you for magical knowledge. He would be too frightened that you would drag him away to the land beyond the sunset. But, you are a white man, and he wants the white man's knowledge, and he is not frightened to take if from you. It is the white man's knowledge that he thinks will make him strong; and the leader of all the medicine-men, of every tribe. As well as that, he wants to stop the white men from exploring his country; to keep them away from his sacred places. He wants to use the white man's knowledge against the white man himself.'

Eyre said, 'Really, Minil, no matter *what* I tell him, he's never going to be able to keep white settlers out of his territory. Not for very long.'

'He thinks that he will.'

'Well, let him think it. As long as Yanluga gets his burial, and Captain Sturt gets his opals.'

'But I am trying to say to you that he will kill you for your knowledge. Tomorrow, he will kill you.'

'*What*? What are you talking about?'

'Yonguldye believes that if he strikes you down, and breaks open your head, and eats your brains, that he will take all your knowledge, all of it, even those things that you would try to hide from him.'

Eyre's erection shrank away like a frightened skink retreating into the sand. 'I can't believe that,' he told Minil. 'Eat my *brains*? But Aborigines aren't cannibals.'

'It is the way that Yonguldye believes he will learn everything you know.'

Eyre slowly chewed the last stringy mouthful of emu meat; although now he didn't feel hungry at all. He began to see at last what game Joolonga had been up to, right from the very beginning of their expedition; and, even more alarmingly, what game Captain Charles Sturt had been playing. There *was* an ancient Aboriginal story about a *djanga* returning from the dead and killing a boy; and although what had happened to Eyre had differed from the legend in several material ways, it had been close enough for Joolonga to excite the blackfellows around Adelaide into believing that at last it was coming true. Aborigine messengers must have taken the news to Yonguldye days and days ago; and to the kings of other tribes as well; and so this corroboree at Yarrakinna had been swelled not only by the tribes who normally would have come here at this time of year, but by scores of curious Aborigines who wanted to witness the great coming-alive of a celebrated myth.

It was the way in which Captain Sturt had so inventively used the legend that disturbed Eyre the most, however. Impending bankruptcy had obviously made the good Captain unusually sharp-witted. Sharp-witted enough to instruct Joolonga that he should tell Eyre about the legend just before they caught up with Yonguldye; so that Eyre would be prepared for Yonguldye's worshipful welcome; but also sharp-witted enough to conceal from Eyre the frightening truth about the legend which Minil had now revealed to him. In the days before the arrival of the white man, the Aborigines had thought that the *djanga* would be a real ghost; but over the past fifty years they must have come to believe that he would be a white man, and that his appearance would signify the moment when they would at last learn the secret of white supremacy.

All of the complicated conversations which had taken place between Eyre and Yonguldye throughout the evening had been a sham. Yonguldye had known very well that Eyre was no resurrected spirit, and that Joolonga was tricking him. Between the two of them, Yonguldye and Joolonga had been doing nothing less than preparing Eyre for the final ceremony which would take place when the sun arose tomorrow morning. His sacrifice to the cause of Aborigine resistance.

Presumably Dogger and Christopher would be murdered as well: and even poor Midgegooroo.

Sturt's cunning appalled Eyre. Sturt must have known from his earlier encounters with Aborigines that there were opals to be found somewhere in the southern plains; and that a route could one day be found to the great inland sea. There was probably silver and gold, too, although Yonguldye didn't know where it was, or was not prepared to disclose it. But now Sturt had discovered exactly where the opals lay, and how to reach the sea, by offering the Aborigines the life of a fellow white-man. Sturt would reap all the profits, and the glory. He would probably hold a memorial service for those brave adventurers who had lost their lives in order that South Australia and Captain Sturt, could become rich again. And he would have risked nothing, not even the possibility of real resistance from the Aborigines, because of course Yonguldye would learn nothing at all from beating Eyre's brains out.

Eyre said to Minil, 'I must leave here at once. Do you think we can escape without being noticed?'

'There are watchers.'

'Well, we'll just have to take our chances, then. Listen, go across to the other shelter and wake my companions. Tell them they are in terrible danger. Don't try to explain why. Just bring them back here, and then we will try to get away.'

'I must come with you.'

'It's too dangerous. They will probably try to kill us.'

'I do not care. I must come with you.'

Eyre laid a hand on her shoulder. 'Go and find my companions first. Please. It will be daylight very soon.'

Minil touched his cheek with her fingertips. Then she nodded, and wriggled silently out of the shelter, and off to wake Christopher and Dogger. Eyre meanwhile sat up in the shelter, and retrieved his rifle, and made sure that it was ready to fire if necessary. His mouth felt very dry, 'like a lizard's gizzard', as Dogger used to say; and his stomach kept grumbling because of the half-chewed emu meat he had swallowed.

It seemed to Eyre that almost half-an-hour passed before the crouching shapes of Dogger and Christopher came into sight through the encampment, closely followed by Minil and Midgegooroo. They huddled up close to the entrance of Eyre's shelter, shivering in the pre-dawn chill. Dogger had had the sense to make himself an improvised *buka* by tying a kangaroo-skin around his shoulders.

'What's up?' asked Christopher. 'One minute I was dreaming about horse-racing; the next thing I knew I was being prodded through the dark by your lady-friend here.'

Eyre said quickly, 'It's too difficult to explain in detail. But Captain Sturt and Joolonga have betrayed us; and Yonguldye intends to kill us tomorrow morning. We're going to have to try to get away from here right away.'

'But they'll see us. We're going to have to climb right up that ridge again, in plain view.'

'Then we'll have to take a hostage,' said Eyre.

'Who do you have in mind?'

'The most valuable man in the tribe, of course. Yonguldye himself.'

'Now I know you're funning,' said Dogger. 'Let's get back to bed.'

Eyre said, 'It won't be as difficult as you think. Yonguldye knows the power of a rifle. He also speaks enough English for us to be able to make it clear to him what will happen if he doesn't co-operate.'

333

'Well, I can think of more pleasant ways of going to the great green pasture beyond the mountains,' said Dogger.

Christopher shivered, and raised his head, and said, 'It's getting light. Whatever we're going to do, we'd better do it right away.'

Eyre eased himself out of his shelter, dragging his rifle after him, and then stood up. Only a few yards away, the great fire that had burned during the corroboree outside the entrance to Yonguldye's *tantanoorla* was nothing more now than a huge heap of hot blowing ashes. Eyre said, 'Wait here,' and made his way barefoot across the rocks to the skull-hung entrance to Yonguldye's den. He glanced back for a moment at his friends, squatting apprehensively on the shadowy ground, all watching him; and then he crouched down and managed to penetrate the darkness of the shelter without making any of the skulls rattle.

It was so black inside the *tantanoorla* that Eyre had to rely on feel, and on the sound of Yonguldye's snoring, in order to make his way to the far end, where most of the kangaroo hides were piled. He was fairly certain that the great Yonguldye would have reserved for himself the warmest and most comfortable place to sleep. He edged his way forwards on his elbows and knees, holding the rifle clear of the ground in his right hand, and groping around in front of him with his left.

The smell of sleeping bodies was so rancid that Eyre had to suppress an upsurge of bile. Added to the usual grease and sweat, there was a stench of meat, and farts, and foul breath. And all around him there was the thick breathing of Yonguldye's wives, a chorus of congested bellows.

He touched something in the blackness. It felt like a foot. He circled around it warily; but as he did so, he partly lost his balance, and had to jab out with his left hand to prevent himself from tumbling over. His hand went straight into soft flesh: a woman's stomach. There was a jerk, and a screech of surprise; and a sudden harsh cry that could only be Yonguldye's.

Eyre stumbled up on to his feet, knocking his head

sharply against the main branch which supported the shelter. But then he threw himself forward, his left hand flailing around to find Yonguldye, and after two or three wild lunges he caught hold of a bony shoulder; and then a greasy, wrinkled-skin chest. He rolled himself forwards and sideways over the kangaroo-skins so that he was clutching Yonguldye from behind; and he rəmmed the muzzle of his rifle right up into Yonguldye's skinny back.

The medicine-man screamed with fury and fright, but Eyre shouted at him even more loudly, '*Keep still! Keep quiet! This is a rifle! Keep quiet or else I'll kill you!*'

Yonguldye twisted and struggled, but Eyre held him tightly around the neck with his elbow; and then gave him a hard punch in the small of the back with his knee. 'You want to die, Yonguldye?' he yelled at him. 'You want to meet Ngurunderi?'

The name of the god beyond the skies silenced the medicine-man almost at once. He lay still, panting a little, and Eyre could feel his withered skin sliding up and down over his protuberant ribs as he breathed. Now that he was at the very end of the shelter, he could see the triangular light of the dawning day at the entrance, and the startled outlines of Yonguldye's wives, one of whom was whimpering, and twisting her hair in anxiety.

'Very well, now,' said Eyre. 'I want you to make your way outside. Outside, do you understand me? But don't try to run away, or call for anybody to help you, because I will shoot you dead. Is that clear?'

Yonguldye said, 'A curse on you.'

'Save your curses for when I've gone,' Eyre told him. 'Now, let's get going.'

Grumbling and coughing, Yonguldye crawled out of his *tantanoorla*, and stretched himself in the pale blue light of early morning. All around the gorge, last night's fires were smouldering, so that the mountains were hazy with fragrant smoke; and the gathered tribes of Wirangu and Nyungar lay scattered on the ground in their skins and their shelters like the casualties of a massacre. But the massacre was only sleep, and soon the tribesmen would be rising again, and Eyre would have almost no chance of escaping from the gorge whatsoever.

'Hurry,' he told Yonguldye, and prodded him towards his own small shelter, where Dogger and Christopher were waiting with Minil and Midgegooroo. Behind them, Yonguldye's wives crowded fearfully at the entrance to his *tantanoorla*, watching as their husband and Mabarn Man was taken away from them. Yonguldye lost his footing on the rocks, and Eyre prodded him again. 'Quick, or I'll kill you here and now, and take my chances.'

Yonguldye hesitated and stiffened when he saw Minil crouching there with Eyre's companions; and said something blistering to her in Nyungar. Minil turned her face away from him, and refused to answer, and Eyre said, 'Come on, Yonguldye. We don't have any time for recriminations.'

'Funny-looking bugger, isn't he, without his hat?' Dogger remarked.

Yonguldye haughtily ignored this gibe. His sparse woolly hair was knotted all over with bows of possum-skin twine, giving his head the appearance of a black decorated pineapple. He looked fiercely from one of his captors to the other, and Eyre was quite sure that he was silently wishing sickness and death on them all. Personally, Eyre preferred to risk any kind of curse, rather than submit to having his brains beaten out.

'Come on,' he said. 'Dogger, you go first; then Minil; then Christopher and Midgegooroo. I'll keep our friend Yonguldye with me as a shield.'

Tribesmen were beginning to wake and rise as they made their way through the encampment. Some were blowing on fires to breathe them back into life; others were going down to the creek-bed with gourds and skin bags to fetch water. They passed one family who were all asleep except for one of the wives, who had been woken up by her hungry dingo pup. She was yawning as she suckled the brindled wild dog at her breast.

Somehow, they seemed to pass through the smoke almost unnoticed as if they were ghosts. Perhaps nobody recognised Yonguldye without his head-dress. Perhaps Eyre and Christopher and Dogger were so dirty now that on first inspection they passed as blackfellows. It was only when they began to climb the rock-face back up towards the ridge that they heard a cry of distress, probably from one of the medicine-man's wives; and then a general clamour of alarm.

Eyre looked back quickly. He could see Joolonga in his midshipman's hat, running towards Yonguldye's shelter. All over the floor of the gorge, and up on the balconies of rock above them, tribesmen were rising and calling and taking up their spears.

'Now you will die,' crowed Yonguldye, toothlessly.

'Now you keep quiet and climb as fast as your skinny legs will carry you,' Eyre retorted. He could see that Dogger had passed the waterfall now, holding his kanga-roo-skin *buka* in front of his belly in a rather matronly way to protect it from the abrasive rocks, and that Minil was close behind him, climbing with all the agility of a young rock-wallaby.

Eyre was necessarily slower. Yonguldye was elderly, and climbed the slippery rocks with difficulty; and Eyre had to keep the rifle pointing at his back. By the time Eyre had crossed the waterfall, grunting with the effort of levering himself over the green and greasy rocks, Joolonga and a rush of tribesmen had arrived at the foot of the rock-face, brandishing spears and clubs and fighting boomerangs.

Eyre twisted himself around, and called out, 'Joolonga!'

'Where are you going, Mr Walker-sir?' Joolonga shouted back.

'For a long walk, Joolonga; and I'd prefer not to have your company.'

'You must come back down, Mr Walker-sir. There is no escape that way.'

'We'll see.'

'These people will kill you, Mr Walker-sir. Yonguldye is their clever-man. You cannot take him with you.'

'I have no intention of taking him with me. He is my hostage, that is all. As soon as I am clear of the mountains, I will let him go.'

'I am only thinking of your own well-being, Mr Walker-sir.'

'I am very touched,' Eyre shouted back. 'I suppose you were thinking of my well-being when you brought me here. I suppose you were thinking of how salutary it would be for me to have my brains knocked out, and eaten for breakfast by this aged buzzard in return for his opals, and his route to the inland sea.'

'Why do you make such accusations, Mr Walker-sir?' called Joolonga.

'Because I know now what you and Yonguldye were saying last night.'

'Who told you, sir? That girl? That girl knows nothing; she is mad from sickness.'

'She may be, Joolonga; but in my opinion she's a lot less dangerous than you are.'

Eyre began to climb further, pushing Yonguldye ahead of him. At last he reached the crest of the ridge. Christopher and Minil and Midgegooroo were already halfway across the grassy slope up to the next ridge, heading back towards the creek where they had left Weeip the night before. The morning was quite bright now, and the first stab of sunlight appeared between the broken stumps of the mountains. Yonguldye limped as he walked, and groaned as if his feet hurt, but Eyre kept pushing him on with the muzzle of his rifle, and saying, 'Faster, come on, you can walk faster than that!'

As they reached the top of the next ridge, four or five Aborigines appeared on the lower ridge behind them, rapidly followed by more. Eyre shouted to Dogger, 'It's all right. They won't try to attack us as long as we have Yonguldye!' But even before he had finished speaking, there was the whop-whop-whop sound of a boomerang, then another, and two of them flew overhead like giant sycamore seeds and landed close by, in the grass.

It was then that Yonguldye dropped flat on his face on to the ground. Eyre seized hold of his shoulder, and tried to pull him upright, but the medicine-man crouched down and refused to get up.

'Do you want me to kill you?' Eyre screamed at him. But then he realised what Yonguldye must already have realised: that he was almost certainly incapable of shooting him in cold blood.

'Get up!' Eyre hissed at him. 'Get up, or I'll blow your head off your shoulders!' But still Yonguldye huddled amidst the lemon-grass, all ribs and bony spine, like an elderly kangaroo. Another boomerang flapped over Eyre's head, and this time he heard a cry. He looked up and saw that the boomerang had struck Christopher on the back of the leg, and brought him down.

'For God's sake, get on to your feet!' he shouted at Yonguldye; but the medicine-man only covered his ears with his hands, to show his contempt for all of Eyre's desperate threats. Eyre was about to leave him, when there was a tremendous report, and his rifle went off in his hands, recoiling so violently that it jumped out of Eyre's grasp and tumbled into the grass. Yonguldye let out a high, effeminate shriek, and jerked and writhed on the ground in agony, and then lay still, shuddering a little, like a lizard which Eyre had once accidentally crushed beneath the wheels of his bicycle.

Eyre left him, and ran through the scrub towards Christopher, who was trying to stagger up on to his feet. Eyre weaved and dodged from side to side as he ran, in case any more boomerangs were being thrown after them. But long before he could reach the limestone outcropping where Christopher had fallen, he heard another sound, far more frightening than the flackering of boomerangs. It was the humming of spears, launched from woomeras; and the next thing he knew, the sky was dark with what the Aborigines called 'the long rain' a torrential shower of quartz-tipped death-spears.

Three spears clattered on to the rock beside Christopher, who had fallen back down again now, clutching his leg. Another sang past Eyre and stuck into the ground, quivering.

Eyre shouted, 'Christopher! Christopher, get up!' But it was plain that Christopher's leg had been too badly bruised by the boomerang for him to walk; it was even possible that the bone was broken.

It was then that Midgegooroo appeared over the brow of the ridge, running low and quickly. He looked like a dark scuttling crab against the pale pink limestone rock. Eyre watched in relief and gratitude as he picked Christopher up without any hesitation at all and lifted him bodily on to his broad black back. He heard Dogger whistle shrilly in encouragement as Midgegooroo reached the brow of the ridge again, and shouted out, 'Back to the horses! Dogger, I've lost Yonguldye! Cover me!'

But then a death-spear came flying through the air as accurately as if it were a black pencil-line being swiftly drawn against the pale blue of the sky with a ruler. It struck Midgegooroo right in the back, missing Christopher by inches, and Eyre, who was much closer now, heard the crunch of quartz-tipped spear-wood dig right into his flesh.

Midgegooroo staggered, and let out a hoarse, high cry; but somehow he kept on balancing his way across the bare limestone ridge, with Christopher still dangling over his shoulders, until he had reached the other side, where the rocks fell away, and he was out of spear-shot. Then with the death-spear trailing noisily against the ground behind him, he slowly sagged to the ground like an emptying sack, letting Christopher fall awkwardly against an outcropping of rocks and bushes.

Minil, who had been halfway down the creek-bed to the place where they had left Weeip, turned and climbed back up the hill, kneeling down beside Christopher and feeling his leg, to find out how bad his injury was. Eyre was surprised to see that she completely ignored Midgegooroo, as if he were dead already; but then Eyre supposed that with a death-spear lodged in his back, that was probably true. He said, 'Dogger! Open fire! Hold the bastards off!'

Dogger knelt down on the limestone, and took aim at the Aborigine warriors who were now running towards them across the grass. He was an experienced shot, even if he was rusty, and the leading warrior fell into the bushes without even a shout. Eyre clambered over towards Midgegooroo, and eased the satchel of ammunition from around his neck; trying not to look into Midgegooroo's grey and desperate face, or at the bloody froth which bubbled at the corners of his mouth. He slung the satchel over to Dogger, and called, 'See if you can get another one in!'

Dogger reloaded with relaxed skill; and when the Aborigines were less than fifty paces away, he fired again, hitting another one right between the eyes, so that the blood sprayed up from the top of his head like an ornamental fountain. The other warriors hesitated, and retreated a few steps, while Dogger loaded up for the third time.

Eyre, keeping his head low, knelt down beside Midgegooroo and said, 'You're going to be all right. Don't worry. Once we get the spear out of you, you'll soon recover.'

Midgegooroo's expression was sweaty and strained, an agonised gargoyle. He shook his head again and again, and said, 'No, sir. No, sir.'

Dogger fired one more shot, which went wide. Eyre heard the bullet singing off the distant rocks.

'We'd better make ourselves scarce,' said Eyre. 'Here—give me some help with Midgegooroo.'

Dogger came over at a low crouch. He turned Midgegooroo over a little way, and examined the spear. The entire head was buried in Midgegooroo's back, and sticky blood was coursing over his black muscles, and on to the grass. As gently as he could, Dogger tugged at the spear, but Midgegooroo whimpered with such pitiful agony that he let it go. Dogger looked at Eyre, and said, 'Death-spear, no doubt about it.'

'What can we do?' Eyre asked him.

Dogger shook his head. 'Not much, except push the whole thing all the way through him. There are teeth on the end of this thing, flakes of sharpened quartz. You can't pull it out the way it went in, not without tearing half his back off. I've seen it before. An old chum called Keith Cragg, out at Broken Hill. We had to push the spear right through his lung to get it out; and he only lived for half-an-hour after that. Kept coughing up blood and singing about his wife. Couldn't stand the name Madge ever after.'

'What then?' said Eyre, urgently, lifting his head so that he could see how close the tribesmen were approaching. Then he turned back to see how Christopher was getting on. It looked as if Minil had managed to help him on to his feet, because now he was hopping down towards the creek-bed, with his arm around Minil's shoulders.

Dogger sniffed, and wiped sweat from his forehead with the back of his hand. 'Can't see much option,' he said.

'What do you mean?'

'Well, either we leave him here; or we put him out of his misery.'

'*What*? We can't kill him.'

'That lot will do worse. Especially since we seem to have done for their clever-man.'

'For God's sake, the gun went off by accident.'

Dogger shrugged. 'They don't know that.'

Eyre said, 'We have to try. We can't just leave him.'

Dogger peered with infuriating thoughtfulness in the direction in which Christopher and Minil had just disappeared. 'Listen, old mate,' he said to Eyre, 'why don't you go and make sure that your chum's all right. That boomerang gave him a fair knock. And then there's your girlfriend, too.'

'You'll shoot him, that's why.'

Dogger rubbed the back of his neck. 'Well, you're right

342

about that. I thought perhaps you wouldn't want to see it.'

Impatient, angry at Dogger's defeatism, Eyre worked his way around Midgegooroo's shivering body until he was right up behind him. He rested the shaft of the spear on one bare knee, and grasped it in both hands as if he were cracking firewood. 'We're not going to give in,' he told Dogger, fiercely. 'If this were *you* lying here, with a spear in your back, I believe you'd thank me for what I'm going to do now.'

'Not I, friend,' said Dogger. 'I'd curse you all the way to Purgatory and back.'

Eyre pressed down on the spear's shaft with all his weight, trying to break it across his knee. Immediately, Midgegooroo threw up his arm and screamed. Dogger said, 'For pity's sake, Eyre, leave the fellow be.' But Eyre was determined. He pressed down on the spear again and again, until he heard the wood cracking, and at last the shaft broke off, leaving only six or seven inches protruding bloodily from Midgegooroo's back.

'Now,' he said, 'up with him, and let's get him down to the horses.'

Midgegooroo was roaring with pain, his eyes bulging and his mouth stretched open like a frilled lizard. But Eyre seized the Aborigine's arm, and bent forward, and lifted him up on to his back; and Dogger, with a quick spit of disapproval, took hold of his other arm, and made sure that Eyre wouldn't drop him.

Hunched over like gnomes or goblins, they hurried down towards the creek-bed; while a fresh salvo of death-spears came whistling over the ridge and rattled against the rocks all around them. One came so close that it scratched Eyre's calf, and almost tripped him over. Dogger, glancing back, said, 'They'll catch us if we don't run faster. For God's sake, Eyre, lay this fellow down and let's get away while we can.'

Eyre, panting under the weight of Midgegooroo's cold and sweaty body, could do nothing more than shake his

343

head. Then he began to slither down the loose shale of the creek-bed; half-tumbling, half-staggering, with the acacia branches whipping at his bare arms, and the rocks tearing at his bare legs. He managed the last few yards at jarring over-and-over roll, bruising his back and his hip; and Midgegooroo fell off his back and tumbled even further, at last lying concussed against a purple-flowered emu bush, his face grey.

Eyre stood up, just as Dogger came slithering down behind him. Two or three stray spears hurtled over the brink of the creek, and fell noisily down between the over-hanging banks.

Weeip and Christopher were ready with the horses; Minil was already mounted up. Without a word, Dogger and Eyre dragged Midgegooroo over to the nearest horse, and while Christopher held the animal's reins, and shushed it, they hoisted him across the saddle, and quickly tied his wrists and ankles to prevent him from sliding off. The broken-off spear protruded bloodily from his back and gave him the appearance of having been nailed on to the horse. His muscles quivered, and he let out a deep bubbling groan, but then he lapsed into unconsciousness again.

'Come on, let's get away from here,' Eyre ordered, and they turned their horses and began to pick their way back down the narrow waterway, riding as quickly as they could, but all of them aware that until they reached the open plains, they were far slower on their horses than a running man; especially a running Aborigine.

Dogger tried several times to reload his rifle as he rode, but it was impossible, and he scattered half-a-dozen balls on to the ground, as well as losing most of his priming-powder to the early-morning wind. Eventually, he cursed, and gave up, and slung his rifle back over his shoulder, and concentrated on making his way down the mountain-side as fast as he could.

At the foot of the mountains, they had to cross a maze of wrinkled gullies, where the water that ran down from the higher peaks had washed down with it thick clay sediments, and then eroded them into a complicated pattern of passageways and dead-ends. Their horses' hoofs slipped on the crumbly yellow earth; and for one moment Eyre thought that his horse was going to slide sideways down one of the gullies, taking him with it; but with a flurrying scrabble of hoofs, the horse managed to regain its ground.

Behind them, startling them, they heard a great warbling cry, and a rattling of spears and boomerangs. Eyre twisted around in his saddle, and saw at least twenty Aborigine warriors running across the clay towards them, jumping from ridge to ridge and runnel to runnel, shrieking and calling, and occasionally pausing to fit a spear into their woomeras and launch it off.

Eyre shouted, 'Dogger! Stop here, and reload! One more good shot should keep them back!'

Dogger circled his horse around, and then dropped down from the saddle. While Eyre and the rest of the party began to make their way out of the clay gullies, he calmly loaded and primed his rifle, sniffed, adjusted his hat, and knelt down beside his horse's right flank; taking aim not at the leading Aborigine but at another, much further back.

Two spears landed close by, but he ignored them. He waited for the moment when the Aborigine at whom he was aiming was right at the top of the last steep slope, and then he fired. There was a flat *crack*, and a cloud of blue smoke drifted unhurriedly away from Dogger's rifle. The tribesman staggered, slipped, and then fell spectacularly head-over-heels all the way down the zig-zag creek-bed, spraying blood over the rocks as he went. He landed disjointedly at the bottom of the slope like one of the dancing beeswax figures at Mushroom Rock.

Dogger remounted, and cantered after Eyre across the powdery clay, letting out a high, harsh whoop. Behind him, the Aborigines threw another heavy shower of spears, but most of them fell short; and the tribesmen had been too frightened by Dogger's marksmanship to risk running very much closer. Even when it was launched from a woomera, a spear could only travel a hundred and fifty paces with any accuracy and force, whereas even an out-of-date muzzle-loading rifle like the Baker could bring a man down from over twice that distance.

At the top of the creekbed, Eyre saw Joolonga, his distinctive midshipman's hat silhouetted against the brightening eastern sky. As Dogger drew level with him, Eyre said, 'Look!' and pointed Joolonga out; and Dogger reined back his horse and squinted back towards the mountains, his face as creased and wrinkled as the dry gullies they were riding over.

'I should have picked *him* off, too,' sniffed Dogger. 'He's a dangerous fellow, your Joolonga. Educated savages always are. They gain the knowhow, but they never lose the wildness. Can't trust them, not an Irishman's inch.'

'He's clever just the same,' Eyre replied.

'Well, that's all very well; but my mother always used to say that you ought to give men like that legroom in case they kicked at you; and throwing room in case they chucked a stone at you; and that you should never tell them how much money you were carrying or introduce them to your wife.'

'Wise lady, your mother, by the sound of it,' Eyre smiled. For the first time since they had undressed yesterday evening, he was conscious that they were naked. 'It's probably a good thing that she can't see you now.'

Dogger slapped his big round beer-belly. 'Let's put a mile or so between us and these savages; and then let's get some britches between ourselves and these saddles.'

Christopher was waiting for them a little way away; holding the reins of Midgegooroo's horse. It was impossible to tell whether Midgegooroo was alive or dead; he hung over the saddle with his arms and legs trailing, and his entire bloody back was smothered with flies. Minil was riding next to him, and Eyre could see by the expression on her face that she didn't expect him to survive. As Eyre came closer, she said, 'This man was very brave. He was

346

like one of the saints they told me about at the mission. St Philip, or St Jude.'

'If we can dig that spear out of him, he may live,' said Eyre.

'No,' said Minil. 'He is dead already.'

Twenty-Five

They camped at noon in the hot purple shadow of a limestone outcropping ten miles west of Parachilna. The temperature was 113 degrees Fahrenheit, and all around them the flat salt lake appeared to move up and down in slowly-undulating curves, as waves of superheated air flowed over it. The rust-coloured peaks of the Flinders also rose and fell, as if they were observing them through water. Eyre had the extraordinary sensation of being on a ship again, although he knew it was only an optical illusion.

The dryness was stunning. Two of their seven horses sank to their knees when they set up camp: and one of them, a three-year-old chestnut which had carried their main bags of water all the way from Adelaide, lay on his side after a while and began to pant and tremble.

'What do you think?' Eyre asked Christopher.

Christopher shrugged. 'There isn't very much we can do, except put him out of his pain.'

They deliberately avoided talking about Midgegooroo. He was still alive, although he had lost so much blood that he was barely conscious. Dogger had speculated that some herb or other had been rubbed on the tip of the spear to prevent the blood from clotting; certainly it had run out of

Midgegooroo's back in a wide sticky river, and they didn't even have enough water to spare to be able to wash him clean. He lay on his stomach in a small crevice in the rock, his eyes wide, scarcely breathing, his back teeming with huge grey sand flies.

They had dressed now: Eyre in his wide kangaroo-skin hat and bush-jacket and wide cotton ducks; Christopher in his white shirt and riding-britches; Dogger in his familiar faded trousers and shiny-toed suede boots. Eyre had offered clothes to Minil, and she had happily accepted a blue shirt and a silk scarf; although she had tied the sleeves of the shirt around her waist, so that only her bottom was covered, and crossed the scarf between her breasts, so that it did nothing more than lift them up even more prominently. She had combed her hair back now and tied it with twine; and Eyre was struck by the gracious black profile which this revealed, and by the flared curve of her bare shoulders. It unsettled him slightly to watch the way in which she allowed flies to settle on her, to walk across her cheeks or cluster on her back, and make no attempt to flick them away, as Eyre always did; but she had a hypnotic naked beauty about her which appealed to him more every time he looked at her.

Whether she was aware of what he felt, or not, he found it impossible to tell. She made no obvious effort either to ignore him or encourage him. She was sitting now in the shadows, her eyes closed, her forehead sparkling with sweat, her thighs unselfconsciously parted so that he could see how the grains of salty sand clung to her vaginal lips. He found he had to look away; and think of anything else instead; of the expedition; of what Captain Sturt had done to him; and of Midgegooroo.

They were four hundred miles from civilisation on a roaringly hot salt lake, with one desperately wounded man and another who could only limp; and only two young Aborigines who were little more than children to guide them.

They drank hot water from their flasks, and ate two

grey-faced terns which Weeip had snared the previous evening and charred over his camp-fire. It was Eyre's instinct to eat only a little, and to save the rest for later, but Dogger reminded him that the meat wouldn't last the day, not in this heat.

'Eat like an Aborigine,' he told Eyre. 'Cram as much into your belly as you can, because whatever you save will be stinking by nightfall. You can't keep anything fresh, not in the outback. I think the only food that I've ever seen the blackfellows store is wild figs, which they roll up in balls of ochre, and hide in the trees. The rest of it, they keep in here,' he said, pointing to his stomach.

They talked about Joolonga and Captain Sturt. Minil told them exactly what Joolonga had been discussing with Yonguldye; how Yonguldye wanted to break open the white *djanga's* head at once and take all the magic that was stored there. Apparently Joolonga had been arguing that if he allowed Yonguldye to kill Eyre so soon, he would no longer have any guarantee that Yonguldye would direct him to the place where the firestones could be found; or north to the inland sea.

Surprisingly, Yonguldye had been determined to travel south to Adelaide to give Yanluga's body a traditional Aborigine burial, as he had agreed. It was a crucial part of the coming-alive of the legend that he should do so. Presumably he would have asked Joolonga to take him to Captain Sturt, and Captain Sturt would then have arranged the burial with Lathrop Lindsay.

Christopher said, 'I really find this all rather hard to swallow.'

Dogger sniffed, with a dry catarrhal thump. 'You're dealing with people who believe in magic here, matey. I've heard tell of that story of the white *djanga* myself, although the one I heard had a slightly different twist to it. I think the *djanga* ended up eating the clever-man, instead of the other way about. And there was something about a waratah tree in it.'

'But it's quite extraordinary that the news of it should

have spread so quickly . . . and that we should have travelled all the way out here and found Yonguldye ready for us.'

'Not at all,' said Dogger. 'Once old man Lindsay's blackfellow had decided that Eyre here was the one true *djanga*, and told his friends, that story would have spread like a bushfire. The trouble with you, Mr Willis, is that you think that all blackfellows are as good-for-nothing as those idle buggers you see hanging around Adelaide, getting drunk on twopenny rum and running odd-jobs. Well, you're wrong, sir; eighteen hundred percentile wrong, because the chaps you come across out here beyond the black stump, they're clever and they're bright and if they want to carry a piece of important news from one end of this desert to the other in three days flat, then they'll do it. Look at the way they've been following Eyre around, ever since they decided that he was their man, taking care of him, making sure that he got out here safe and sound. If those fellows Chatto and Rose had tried to take him back to Adelaide, I reckon they wouldn't have gone for more than a mile before the blackfellows used them for spear practice. Mind you, I think they could do with some, the way they've been flinging them at us.'

'But can you really believe that Captain Sturt arranged all this?' Christopher demanded. His cheeks were red and flushed from the heat, and his eyes were bloodshot. 'It all seems so, well, *underhand*. So ungentlemanly. For a man of his stature to send another chap out to be killed by savages . . .'

'Christopher,' said Eyre, quietly, 'I know about the money. Joolonga told me.'

Christopher opened his mouth, and then closed it again. He flushed.

Eyre said, 'I know you didn't realise what Captain Sturt really had in mind. Well, I assume you didn't. Perhaps he didn't have *anything* in mind. Perhaps he knew nothing about all this ritual brain-eating and whatever; and perhaps Joolonga's been lying to me. But, if Captain Sturt is capable of paying one friend to betray another—well, I would say that he's capable of almost anything.'

Christopher said unevenly, 'It was five pounds. I don't even know why I took it. But Captain Sturt did solemnly promise me that he would try to persuade you not to go off looking for Yonguldye.'

'Although of course he did exactly the opposite.'

'I still couldn't tell you, though, could I? How could I protest that he hadn't kept his word to me, when I had taken his money? What would you have thought of me? My God, what do you think of me now?'

Eyre looked at Christopher; and then looked away. 'Not much,' he said.

'I suppose if I were to say that I had nothing but your best interests in mind . . . that I was thinking of nothing else but protecting you . . .'

'Oh, for God's sake, Christopher, protecting me from what? From myself? From the Aborigines? If you ask me, the only person I need protecting from is you.'

Christopher's reddened eyes brimmed with tears. But then he sniffed loudly, and took a deep breath, and brought himself under control.

'Well, well,' said Dogger philosophically, and then, for no reason that anybody could think of, 'Rats in the cupboard.'

Eyre could think of a dozen cutting and hurtful things to say to Christopher; but there was no point in adding to the humiliation which he already felt. Besides, Christopher's suffering seemed trivial beside that of Midgegooroo, who was groaning again now, and calling out.

Eyre glanced at Dogger with a questioning expression.

'You're in charge,' Dogger conceded. 'Whatever we do, it's all up to you.'

'But you've seen wounds like this before.'

'I've seen worse. I've seen chaps with spears through their faces; and no way of getting them out. You should have left him, you know. He would have been dead by now; but at least you would have spared him all of this.'

351

'He stayed loyal to us; we had to stay loyal to him,' Eyre argued.

'Making him suffer like a dying dog isn't a very noble piece of loyalty, I wouldn't have thought,' said Dogger.

'Well, what do you suggest we do? Shoot him?'

'No,' said Dogger. 'I suggest we face up to what we've started to do, which is try to keep him alive; and the only way we're going to have any chance of succeeding in that particular mission is by taking that spearhead out of him.'

'You mean pushing it right through him,' said Eyre.

'I mean pushing it right through him,' nodded Dogger.

Eyre stood up, and went over to the shadow where Midgegooroo was lying and knelt down beside him. A shower of flies rose into the hot afternoon air, and Eyre had to keep brushing them away.

'Midgegooroo?' he said, gently.

Midgegooroo's eyes flickered, but he said nothing.

'Midgegooroo?' Eyre repeated.

Again, nothing but a flicker. A fly crawled into Midgegooroo's open mouth, and out again.

Eyre sat back. 'Well,' he said, swallowing dryly, 'I think you're right. We're just going to have to try it. Weeip, will you bring my medicine-box?'

Weeip ran over to the pack-horse which was lying on the ground and unbuckled its pannier. In a moment, he came back to the rock carrying the polished wooden case, and set it down beside Eyre, wide-eyed. 'You cure Midgegooroo?' he asked, impressed.

'I don't know,' said Eyre. 'I can only do my best. Would you like to untie a scarf from my saddle-pommel, and see what you can do to keep the flies off while we operate.'

'Operate?' said Dogger, wryly. 'That's a fancy word for pushing a spear through somebody.'

'Just give me a hand, will you?' asked Eyre testily. 'And Christopher, could you hold his ankles? I think he's probably going to kick quite a bit.'

Between them, they lifted Midgegooroo out of the shadow of his crevice and laid him on his side on a crumpled green horse-blanket. Midgegooroo's eyes were still open, but Eyre wasn't at all sure that he was actually conscious. He didn't appear to be focusing on anything or anyone; and his breathing was rough and shallow, as if he were asleep, but having nightmares. His face had always looked very primitive to Eyre; very pug-like and Aboriginal; but now it was so ashen and stretched with pain that it scarcely seemed human. It reminded Eyre, chillingly, of some of the gargoyles on Durham cathedral.

Dogger said, 'Are you quite sure you want to do this? It isn't going to be easy; not on us, and especially not on him. It would be twenty times kinder to do away with him quickly.'

'We can't kill him, for God's sake,' Eyre retorted.

Dogger shrugged. 'If you say not. You're the one who knows everything about immortal souls, and stuff like that.'

'He's a human being,' Eyre reminded him.

'Well, exactly,' said Dogger, equivocally.

Eyre hesitated, and looked around, They were all watching him—Christopher and Dogger and Weeip and Minil—and none of them was able or prepared to take the decision for him. He was the leader of the expedition. Midgegooroo's life was in his hands; and the hands of God.

The day felt so immensely hot that he couldn't think. The heat was almost audible, an endless terrible drumming on the back of his neck. He realised that the atmosphere was so dry that he wasn't even sweating any more. His tongue lay in his mouth like a lizard, and swallowing required a complicated contortion of his throat muscles, as well as an act of will.

'I think we'd better begin,' he said, and opened the hot brass catch on his medicine-box, and took out surgical spirits and soft linen cloth. Weeip flapped the clustering flies away while Eyre cleaned as best he could around the lips of the wound, which were already stiff with crusted blood, and bobbled with whitish flies' eggs. Midgegooroo

353

remained limp and silent as Eyre was doing this, except when Eyre cleaned very close to the broken-off shaft of the spear. Then, his hand flailed out, and he clasped Eyre's knee; and let out a faltering breath, and a single word that sounded like 'yungara . . .'

'He's asking for his wife,' said Dogger.

Weeip piped up, 'Midgegooroo have wife Mary-mary. Mary-mary died last Christmas, very sick.'

Eyre finished cleaning the wound, and wiped his dry forehead with the back of his hand, abrading it with salt grit.

'Right, Mr McConnell,' he said. 'Do you have any idea how this kind of thing is done?'

Dogger cleared his throat. 'You grab hold of the spear, and you push. It's as simple as that.'

Eyre took a painful swallow of hot air, reached around Midgegooroo, and clasped the spear in his right hand. Instantly, Midgegooroo screamed like a slaughtered cat, and jerked upwards, and thrashed his legs, and Eyre whipped his hand away from the spear and knelt there, shaking. 'Jesus,' he prayed. 'If I ever needed help, I need it now. Please help me to save this man's life; and please guide me so that I don't hurt him so much.'

Christopher was white. 'Please, Eyre, if you're going to do it, then do it.'

Eyre nodded. He firmly grasped the spear again; and again Midgegooroo shrieked so harshly that Eyre could imagine the flesh being stripped away from his larynx. But this time, Eyre kept on: pushing and twisting the spear-head into Midgegooroo's back, cutting through muscle and membrane and liver. Midgegooroo writhed like a beetle on a hotplate; and his screaming became so intense that he ceased to scream at all, but uttered an endless soundless cry that was more terrifying than all the screams of hell.

The point of the spear burst bloodily through Midge-gooroo's chest, with a sound like a dinner-fork piercing the taut skin of a turkey. By now, however, the broken-off shaft was so deeply buried in his body that Eyre no longer had any purchase on it; and he was unable to grip the sharpened head and drag it through the front. He said to Dogger in a mouthful of jumbled words, 'Pass me that ramrod, from your rifle. Yes, the ramrod. Quickly.'

Dogger grimly did as he was told; and then Eyre lodged the end of the ramrod against the end of the spear, and gave one fierce push. The spear head cut its way out from under Midgegooroo's ribs, dragging with each quartz barb a shred of bloody muscle or black liver; and then at last it was out. Midgegooroo shuddered once, and then lay still, with his face pressed against the ground.

Christopher gingerly released his ankles. 'Is he dead?' he asked.

Eyre felt his wrist. His pulse was uneven, almost undetectable, but he was still alive.

'He can't last,' said Dogger.

'Perhaps if we could get him back to Adelaide,' suggested Christopher.

'I doubt it he'd survive it,' said Dogger. 'Look at the poor bastard; he's almost dead now. And what are we talking about—eight days on horseback at least. More like nine.'

'In any case,' put in Eyre, 'I wasn't planning on going back to Adelaide.'

Christopher stared at him; and slowly took off his hat. '*What?* But what are you going to do?'

'I'm going to go on.'

'What are you talking about, go on? Go on to where?'

'Go on to the inland sea, where do you think?'

'But we no longer have the guide, or the supplies. Look at us—one poor fellow nearly dead—two young children—and my leg's coming up like a balloon after that boomerang hit it. How can you possibly think of going on?'

Dogger thrust his hands into his britches pockets, and whistled a dry little tune. 'In for a penny, in for two or three hundred pounds,' he said, and then whistled some more. The sky above their heads was utterly cloudless, and the thermometer was creeping up to 115 degrees.

Eyre cleaned Midgegooroo's wound again, making sure that he squeezed out as many of the flies' eggs as he could. Then he padded both the entry wound and the fresh exit wound with folded gauze; and with Christopher's stunned and resentful help, he tightly bandaged the Aborigine's chest.

Christopher said, 'It's madness. We'll die.'

Eyre began to pack away his medicine-chest. 'There's an inland sea there, Christopher. Once we reach the sea we'll be safe.'

'But we don't have anybody to guide us.'

'The sea lies to the north. Due north. You heard what Yonguldye said.'

'But why, for Heaven's sake? Don't you think we've all suffered enough? I just assumed that we'd be heading straight back to Adelaide. I ask you, my dear chap, why should we carry on? Our sponsors have betrayed us; our guide has nearly had us sacrificed; what earthly reason do we have for continuing?'

Eyre made sure that Midgegooroo was as comfortable as possible, and then he stood up. 'I want that inland sea to be called the Walker Sea, that's why. I want this salt-lake to be named Lake Eyre; and I want that mountain to be called Mount McConnell; and that outcrop to be called Willis Hill. I want this place to be known as Midgegooroo; and we'll find other places and call them Weeip and Minil. We've sweated and fought our way as far as here; let's go back with the fame and the glory. Let's make our mark on this continent. What do you think would happen if we crawled back with our tails between our legs; whining that Captain Sturt had tried to feed us to the Aborigines? We'd be laughed out of Adelaide. No, Christopher, we've got to go back and announce that we've discovered the inland sea and maybe the opal mine, too; and then we'll see what our fine Captain Sturt has to say for himself; yes, and Colonel Gawler, too.'

Christopher walked two limping paces away from Eyre; then he turned around and kicked Eyre's medicine-box all across the sand, scattering bottles and tweezers and tablets.

'Are you mad?' Eyre shouted at him.

'You're asking me if I'm mad?' Christopher shouted back. 'What's the use of keeping a medicine-chest if you've condemned us to death? What's the use of salt tablets for men without water? Or laxatives if we don't have any food? By God, Eyre, we're going to be the healthiest corpses in the desert! Skeletons with rosy cheeks! You and your vanity! You and your damned vanity! I always knew that it would be the end of me! I always knew!'

Eyre took a deep breath, and held it. Then, without another word, he knelt down and began to pick up his bottles. Laudanum, syrup of Toulu, acid of sugar. He had almost finished collecting up the liver-pills when he saw that the tiny amber-glass jar of corrosive sublimate appeared to be empty. He picked it up and held it against the light. Absolutely empty; even though he knew that there must have been two or three drachms in it when they started out on their expedition. Usually, he kept it right at the bottom of the chest, since it was so intensively poisonous, and scarcely ever useful; but Christopher's kick had sent it flying out.

He thought of Arthur; and the sudden way in which Arthur had started vomiting those long stringy white masses of bloody mucus. He had suspected Joolonga before of poisoning Arthur; but the events that had followed had put the matter out of his mind. This empty sublimate jar was proof; at least as far as Eyre was concerned. The pointing-bone may have held some strange and dangerous properties; but none of them could have been half so strong as two drachms of corrosive sublimate. The only question that really remained unanswered was why Joolonga had considered it necessary to put Arthur to death. He had said, of course, that it was to protect them all from the vengeance of Ngurunderi. But nothing that Joolonga had said or done had turned out to be what it appeared to be. Eyre decided to reserve judgement; but to remain suspicious.

He also decided to say nothing to Dogger and Christopher, not yet. He didn't want them thinking that he had turned completely mad.

'Listen,' he said, closing the medicine-chest, 'if the inland sea is as close as Yonguldye said that it is, we should reach it in two or three days. But, if we turn back, we'll have at least a week of hard travelling; and nothing to show for it. Besides, Joolonga will probably still be after us; and the first thing that he will expect us to do is turn south. We'll ride straight into him, more than likely; and then where will we be?'

'Pickled,' said Dogger. 'And that's a dead bird.'

'Nevertheless,' Christopher retorted, 'I still think that it's foolishness, to carry on. Pride, and foolishness. My vote is that we try to make our way back to Adelaide.'

Eyre handed his medicine-chest to Weeip, to pack away, and then stood and looked at Christopher for a very long time, his hands on his hips, trying to give Christopher the opportunity to change his mind. But Christopher did nothing more than wipe his face with his red-spotted belcher and stare defiantly back at him. Eyre knew that Christopher would have to go; and Christopher knew it, too.

'Very well,' said Eyre. 'You and Weeip can leave us here and head southwards. Take Midgegooroo with you. I'll give you fresh bandages and spirits to clean his wounds with. If you're careful with him, he may survive. Use your compass, that's all you have to do; and head directly south. When you reach the ocean, follow it south-east, along the coastline.'

Dogger said, 'You seem to be assuming that I'm going along with you, you and your donah.'

'I had hoped that you would,' said Eyre. 'You're the only experienced man we have left.'

'Nobody has any experience when it comes to the inland sea,' said Dogger.

'Of course not,' Eyre agreed. 'But at least you know how to survive.'

'If I knew how to survive, I wouldn't have come with you at all,' Dogger told him. 'I wouldn't have shot those two gents, just for the sake of a grumpy old yoxter like Arthur Mortlock; and nor would I have followed you out as far as this. If I knew how to survive, I'd be back with Constance, well-pissed on home-made beer and tickling her garden-grove.'

'Are you coming?' Eyre asked him.

Dogger took off his hat, mopped away the sweat, and then replaced it. 'You know damn-well that I'm coming. If there's an inland sea, I want to wash my feet in it.'

He hesitated, and sniffed, and then he said, 'God almighty, if I took my boots off now, I reckon every one of those flies would jump off poor old Midgegooroo there and cluster on to my feet like berries.'

So, as the sun tilted away from its glaring zenith, and the shadows around the outcropping began to give Midgegooroo a few inches more protection, it was decided. Christopher and Midgegooroo should ride south to Adelaide, with Weeip as their guide and interpreter. Once in Adelaide, they would go to Captain Sturt and raise fresh supplies, which they would arrange to be taken to a spot on the salt-lake sixteen miles due east of Woocalla, buried under a stone cairn. These supplies would enable Eyre and Dogger to survive on their return journey, when they would probably be desperately short of almost everything, especially water. That was, unless they found the inland sea, and the freshwater rivers which must be feeding it, and the naturally irrigated forests which probably lined its shores. In that case, they would be bringing their own water, and their own supplies, and news of the greatest graphical triumph since Australia had first been discovered.

Eyre and Dogger would take the lion's share of the

supplies, as well as most of the water; and with Minil to help them in any encounter with Aborigines, they would strike due north, until they reached the ocean; and then south-west, to see if they could locate the source of Yongul-dye's opal diggings at Caddibarrawinnacarra.

By mid-afternoon, when they had finished dividing most of their supplies, it was clear that the sickest of their horses was finished. Dogger loaded up his rifle and shot it. The animal quivered and then lay still in the sunlight. The sound of the shot echoed through the burning afternoon like the clap of a stage-manager's hands.

Dogger came back with the rifle over his arm. 'Weeip,' he said, 'cut that poor old chap up before you go; and we'll share as much of his meat as we can carry.'

But Weeip was frowning towards the eastern horizon. 'No time, Mr Dogasah.'

'What's the matter? What do you mean, no time?'

Weeip pointed. Far, far away, a row of tiny black shapes moved in the wavering afternoon heat; like ants in syrup. And off to their right, carried above the hot distorted layers of air by the north-westerly wind, there was an ochre-coloured cloud of dust.

'Blackfellow,' said Weeip. 'Very many, running to fight.'

Dogger walked over to his horse, and took a shiny brass telescope out of his saddle-pannier. He slid it open, and peered for a long time in the direction of the Flinders mountains.

'Well?' said Eyre.

'They're coming after us, all right,' said Dogger. 'We're going to have to leave here right away.'

'And the horse?'

'Sorry, matey, we'll just have to leave it. No choice. Pity, though, I'm quite partial to horse-meat and pickles.'

Eyre and Christopher self-consciously said goodbye to each other. Eyre shook Weeip's hand and promised him a medal if they ever discovered the inland sea. Only Minil stayed aloof from their fond farewells; squatting on top of the limestone rock watching the gradual approach of the tribesmen from Yarrakinna.

'Well,' said Dogger, raising his flask of home-distilled rum. 'God loves you. Inside and outside.'

Eyre stood by his horse watching Christopher and Weeip ride off towards the south. Behind them, slung over his saddle, lolled the body of Midgegooroo, probably more dead than alive; but now heavily dosed with laudanum to dull the pain of his wound. Eyre stayed where he was until Christopher's horse appeared through the heat-haze to be ankle-deep in water; then Weeip's; and he didn't turn away until all three of them had begun to run and flow like a rainy painting.

'I wonder if we'll ever see *them* again,' said Dogger, pragmatically.

'I don't know,' said Eyre. 'But did you notice something, he didn't even turn around to wave.'

'Waving,' said Dogger, 'is for regattas only, and ladies on quaysides or clerical gentlemen on the top of God-permits.' God-permits was what Dogger always called stage-coaches, because their timetables carried the qualification '*Deo volente*'.

Eyre realised with some surprise that he was hurt by Christopher's temperamental departure. But at last he beckoned Minil down from her perch, and mounted up on to his horse with a squeak of hot leather, and said, 'Come on; we have some history to make.'

'Vultures to feed, more like,' countered Dogger.

Twenty-Six

It was cold, that night, out on the salt-lake. Dogger decided it was a dog-and-a-half night, not quite a two-dog night; but Eyre found it impossible to keep warm, and huddled in his blankets sleeplessly watching the moon curve from one side of the horizon to the other. The Aborigines often used their tame dingoes as bed-covers, and considering how hot and furry the animals' bodies could be, a dog-and-a-half night meant that it was almost down to freezing.

The next morning, they breakfasted on sugary tea and semolina, and set off early. There was no sign of Joolonga behind them, but Eyre knew that their former guide could follow their tracks as easily as if they had strewn him a paperchase.

The lake was flat for as far as they could see in every direction; and it glittered like ground glass. Their horses' legs soon became encrusted in salt, and they left a powdery trail behind them that even Eyre could have followed.

From time to time, Dogger turned his horse, and took out his telescope, and peered behind them at the distant waves of heat. But it was only towards late afternoon that he beckoned to Eyre, and handed him over the telescope, and pointed south-south-east.

'See them?' he asked.

The eastern horizon was beginning to darken; and the dust and the heat gave it a grainy appearance in which it was hard to distinguish anything. Eyre saw several black shapes that could have been Aborigine tribesmen, following them; or then again they could have been vultures, circling over a dead kangaroo.

'I see *something*,' said Eyre, hesitantly.

'You see Joolonga and Company,' Dogger asserted.

'How do you know?'

Dogger tapped his head. 'Long experience, chum.'

Minil reined her horse around and stood beside them.

362

She still wore Eyre's shirt as an apron in reverse, but she had unwound the scarf from her chest and now wore it on her head, tied loose at the back to keep the sun off her neck.

'If they catch us, they will surely kill us,' she said.

'We'll just have to make sure that they don't, then, won't we?' said Dogger, and turned his horse to ride on.

Towards nightfall, however, Eyre's horse suddenly lurched, and almost threw him out of the saddle. Eyre clicked at it to rear itself up, but then it lurched again; and Eyre looked down and saw that its hoofs had penetrated the crust of the salt-lake, and that it was buried up to its cannon-bones in thick grey mud.

'Dogger!' he called, and immediately dismounted. His own feet crunching on the salt, and made impressions in its surfaces as if it were the frosting on a soft cake. Dogger swung out of the saddle and came cautiously across, leading his horse on a long rein. Eyre said to Minil, 'Stay where you are, Minil; don't come any nearer.'

'*Koolbung*,' Dogger explained to her. 'Salt swamp.'

Eyre soothed and rubbed his horse's nose, and managed gently to coax it to step backward out of the mud. It shook itself and snorted, but the experience had obviously made it nervous.

'How deep do you think this mud is?' asked Eyre.

Dogger shrugged. 'Can't tell. The only other salt swamp I've ever been through, it swallowed a horse and a hay-cart, right up to the driver's hat.'

'Don't tell lies,' Eyre retorted. 'That's the same story they tell about Hindley Street, during the wet.'

'All I'm saying is, we can't tell,' Dogger repeated.

'Maybe we can ride around it,' Eyre suggested. 'After all, if there's mud under the surface, that's probably because there's a deeply buried watercourse down below. Perhaps it comes from the inland sea.'

'Yes, and perhaps it doesn't,' said Dogger.

'Well, wherever it comes from, it can't be limitless. No

wider than a river. So let's try riding westwards a few miles, and then strike north further along.'

Dogger took a measured swallow from his water-bottle. 'All right, then. I suppose it's worth a try. But we're better off camping right here for the night, where we know we've got solid ground to sleep on. We've still got some of that dried suet left, haven't we; and some dried plums. Maybe I'll boil up a hooting pudding.'

'What is "hooting pudding"?' Minil asked, curiously.

'My old mother used to make it, in the days when we were stony,' said Dogger. 'There were so few plums in it, they used to hoot to each other to let each other know where they were.'

Eyre looked southwards. 'You don't think there's any danger that Joolonga might catch up with us?'

'There's always a danger that Joolonga might catch up with us; but we'll be in a worser fix if we try to ride through that *koolbung* in the dark.'

They tethered the pack-horses and set up their hump-backed canvas shelter. Eyre lit a fire out of gum branches which they had brought with them; and the broken pieces of the box in which they had been carrying their dried fruit. Dogger's pudding would use up the very last of the fruit, and other essential stores were running low. There were only ten pounds of flour left, now that they had divided it with Christopher and Weeip and Midgegooroo, and they were also short of sugar, tea, and dried fish. Almost the only food which they had in plentiful supply were hard navy biscuits; but without an equally plentiful supply of water to wash them down with, these were harshly dry, and painful to swallow.

'We still have the horses to eat,' said Eyre, as they sat around their small, windblown fire.

'That's if Joolonga gives us long enough to butcher them,' Dogger replied.

Minil, her eyes sparkling in the reflected light from the fire, said, 'The Nyungar believe that food will always be given to them when they need it. Drink, too. They say when they leave each other "never-starve"; it is a kind of goodbye, like "God-be-with-you." '

'Or, the Lord is mice pepper, as Weeip used to say,' smiled Eyre.

Dogger's pudding was so stodgy that when Eyre had finished it, he felt as if his stomach had been stuffed with kapok. He lay back on his blankets and looked up at the wealth of stars which sparkled overhead, and thought of Charlotte. Somehow, her face seemed less defined now; and he couldn't imagine her voice any more. But he still missed her. He still missed her softness and her silly innocence; he still felt aroused by her slyness and her smiles.

And while he thought of her, the cold pale moon rose again over the salt-lake; transforming it into a landscape of white and silver, a place of death from which only the spirits of those who had crossed it would ever return. A land without flesh, the Wirangu called it; and now Eyre understood what they meant. The body could not survive here; only the *djanga*.

He felt a dull, uncomfortable pain in his stomach. Perhaps he ought to walk out across the lake a way and try to empty his bowels. On a flat and treeless salt-swamp like this, privacy was impossible; and the most they could ever do to maintain their modesty was to turn away. He grimaced, and broke a little wind. No wonder Dogger's mother had called it hooting pudding. In actual fact, it was more like trumpeting pudding. On the other side of the shelter, Dogger broke wind too, and Eyre thought here we go, a musical evening; just when I'm really exhausted. He giggled, and then wished he hadn't. It wasn't very leaderly.

He slept and dreamed of Adelaide. When he woke up, he thought he was back at Mrs McConnell's, and for a moment he couldn't understand where he was. Minil was lying next to him, and when he sat up with a startled jerk, she said, 'What is it?' in a hot whisper; and then, '*Naodaup?*'

'I'm all right,' Eyre whispered back. 'I had a dream, that's all. I had the idea that I was somewhere else.'

Minil touched his shoulder. 'You're cold, that's why you dream.'

He twisted himself around in his blankets. 'I'll be all right. It was probably that hooting pudding.' He picked up his watch and peered at it in the darkness. Three o'clock in the morning. Another hour or so before it would be light enough to travel on.

Minil said, 'The other man, Christopher. . .'

'What about him?'

'I don't know. He is very strange. He seems to like you and yet also to hate you.'

'Well, he has own his particular way of looking at things. I don't think he really hates me. It's just that he wants me to be somebody else; somebody different. And when I'm not . . . well, it makes him angry.'

'You do not make me angry.'

'Why should I?'

'Sometimes white men make me angry. They call me "black polish". Sometimes they touch me. Mr Harris at the New Norcia mission used to touch me. But you are not like Mr Harris. You are like Prince Rupert.'

'Prince Rupert?' Eyre asked her, amused.

Minil lifted the side of Eyre's blanket and snuggled in close to him. Her skin was very soft and warm; a little greasy, but no greasier than Eyre's, who had been washing in no more than a pint of water for the past two days. She smelled of fat and woodsmoke and some musty but quite appealing fragrance that reminded Eyre of rosemary. Her breasts squashed against his arm, and she happily and immodestly thrust one thigh between his legs.

'What made you say Prince Rupert?' he said, although he didn't much care what the answer was. His penis had risen almost immediately, and touched her curved belly with a blind kiss. In response, she reached down and cupped his testicles in her hand, and gently rolled them.

'The Black Prince,' she whispered, as if that settled everything.

He lay on his back on the rumpled, uncomfortable blanket; and she climbed on top of him, not kissing him, but biting his shoulders and his neck and even his cheeks with her sharp, filed teeth. Her breasts swung against his chest, and he held them in his upraised hands, so heavy and full that they bulged out from between his fingers. Her nipples knurled, and he twisted and caressed them, and then pinched them hard, so that she pressed her hips against him, and shuddered, and let out short high gasps of pain and excitement.

She was fierce: she bit and gnawed at his nipples until he cried out loud, and he was aware then by the restless snuffling from the other side of the shelter that they had woken Dogger. But somehow, knowing that Dogger was listening made their coupling even more exciting; and when at last she grasped his erection in both hands and pressed it up against her warm, swollen vulva, it was all he could do not to spurt out immediately, and anoint their stomachs with semen. But he made himself think of how low their stores were; and how long it was going to take them to find the inland sea; and so when he slid inside Minil's body, so deeply that she bent her head forward and quaked with the feeling of it, he was able to thrust into her again and again, lifting her up with his hips so that he penetrated her even more deeply, but still keep his climax at bay.

'*Kungkungundun* . . .' she whispered; and he knew from Yanluga that she was calling him 'loved one'.

He kissed her then; the bridge of her nose; her forehead; her lips; and she accepted his kisses with shy passion.

'Loved one,' he breathed back at her, in English.

There was a moment when their bodies juicily slapped together; when her vagina squeezed him, slippery and hot; and when his penis began to jolt out the first tremblings of sperm. That was the moment of ultimate selfishness; when the demands of pleasure contracted tight inside their own minds, and they both sought that bright white concentrated spark that would release all their feelings.

But, unexpectedly, Minil began to cry out first; and shake and shake and claw at Eyre's shoulders with her long broken fingernails until he knew that he must be bleeding. He had never known a girl reach any kind of climax before; and for a moment it put him off his rhythm; and his own ejaculation began to slide away like the mercury down a thermometer.

But then Minil thrust her hips at him again, and roused him up, and the wetness that ran down his buttocks made him feel that he had excited and satisfied her fully; and that gave him a pride that fuelled up his passion again. He suddenly groaned, and ejaculated right up inside her, right up against the neck of her womb; and it was then that she fell forward on him, and hugged him, and wiggled and wriggled her hips against him, and kissed him, and rolled her face against his, so that he could feel the tears, and the decorative scars on her cheeks, and her sharp teeth biting at his lips.

It occurred to him as they lay together afterwards, and Minil slept, that he may already have made her pregnant. She looked disturbingly young lying there against his arm, her mouth slightly parted as she breathed. She also looked remarkably black. But he didn't mind her blackness at all. It was rather like an exotic varnish on a body that was already beautiful.

Dawn cleared the skies again, and for an hour the air was remarkably limpid, so that they could see for miles. Ahead of them, the salt-lake looked flat and firm; although they already knew how deceptive it was. Behind them, they could see for the first time the encampment of the Aborigines who were following them: a strung-out row of improvised shelters and smouldering fires. Dogger spent a long time scrutinising the Aborigine camp through his telescope while Eyre tried to shave with nothing but soap moistened with spit. It was a slow and painful process; but Eyre was determined to be civilised, and not to grow a beard. Every now and then Dogger said, 'Mmm,' and Eyre said, 'Ouch.'

After a while, Dogger said, 'Have a gander at this,' and passed the telescope to Eyre. 'Look to your left,' he said, 'the big umpee second from the end.'

Towelling himself with one hand and holding the telescope with the other, Eyre inspected the Aborigine encampment. There were more than a dozen shelters altogether, and another score of blackfellows had probably slept out in the open, wrapped in their *bukas*. When he swung the telescope towards the left-hand side of the encampment, however, Eyre saw a larger shelter, and this shelter was decorated with feathers and skulls.

'That looks like a medicine-man's hut,' Eyre remarked, He turned to Dogger, and said, 'Joolonga?'

Dogger shook his head. 'Wouldn't have thought so.'

'But I shot Yonguldye.'

'Perhaps you didn't. You know how the balls tend to drop out of these old Baker rifles, especially when you shake them around. More than likely you did nothing worse than burn his bum with a charge of powder.'

'Then they're really after us,' said Eyre. 'Yonguldye too.'

'I would have thought so, yes,' sniffed Dogger.

'And they'll still be determined to sacrifice us,' said Eyre.

'Well, they'll still be determined to sacrifice *you*,' agreed Dogger.

'Thanks very much,' Eyre snapped.

'Don't mention it,' said Dogger, cheerfully.

Eyre finished wiping his chin, and put on his hat. Dogger said, 'You've humiliated Yonguldye, that's the worst thing. Humiliation is worse than death; at least as far as a clever-man is concerned. You can bet your hat that he's wearing the *Kurdaitja* boots; and you can bet your hat that he'll follow you now to the ends of Australia, wherever they may be.'

Eyre returned the telescope. 'It's time we left then, before they break camp.'

Minil came up. This morning she was wearing Eyre's

shirt tied around her shoulders, and her scarf arranged in peaks, like the wimple of a Brigittine nun. She came close to Eyre, but didn't touch him; but all three of them knew now that the triangle between them had changed during the night; and that Dogger was now the outsider. She said, 'Will we have time for breakfast?' But Eyre shook his head. 'We'll eat a few biscuits while we ride. I want as much distance between us and those blackfellows as we can possibly manage.'

'I heard you say Yonguldye,' said Minil, simply.

'Dogger thinks he may still be alive,' Eyre explained. 'One of the shelters has skulls on it; or what look like skulls.'

'Yes,' said Minil.

'Yes, what?'

'Yes—I too think that Yonguldye is alive. I feel it. He has a very strong—' she waved her hand around her head to try to describe mental power. 'When he calls me, even when he is far away, I am sure that I can feel it.'

'You feel that now?' Eyre asked her.

She stared at him. Her eyes were reddish-hazel and very wide. 'Yes,' she whispered. 'Yonguldye is still alive.'

All that day they rode westwards, skirting the edge of the salt swamp. The sun rose hot and white over their heads, and their shadows shrank beneath their horses as the thermometer rose to 112 degrees. Eyre wore his smoked-glass spectacles; but during the fiercest hours, just after noon, he felt as if the world were nothing but glaring white; white on white; and when he turned around to make sure that Dogger and Minil were following him, he thought that they looked like ghosts, bleached-out apparitions on a bleached-out landscape.

He drank as little as he possibly could; for their flasks were low now and there was no sign of a water-hole. But three mouthfuls during the course of the day was far too little to prevent his mouth from drying up, and his skin from cracking. At times he felt so hot and exhausted that he could have dropped off his horse and laid down on the salt and let the sun slowly bake him into a gingerbread man, stiff and smiling. A happy, mindless end. And there were plenty of times when he felt like giving it all up, and turning south.

They ventured again and again into the salt swamp; at least once every two miles. But each time their horses broke the crust of the lake, and began to sink. Then they spent valuable time coaxing the horses out of the mud, and calming them down, before they set off westwards once more, searching with increasing desperation for a northern passage.

At three o' clock in the afternoon, Dogger passed the telescope to Eyre without comment. Eyre focused sharply, about a mile-and-a-half away; and there was Yonguldye, in his tall head-dress; and beside him was that familiar midshipman's bonnet that belonged to Joolonga.

'We may have to stop and fight,' said Dogger.

'They will kill us,' said Minil, with frightening certainty.

Eyre focused the telescope again. Behind Yonguldye there was a large band of Aborigine warriors; fifty or sixty, judging from the spear-points which rose from the dust.

'We don't have a chance,' he told Dogger. 'Not out here, in the open. We're going to have to think of a way to balance the odds.'

'We've got rifles,' said Dogger.

'Not enough,' Eyre asserted. 'All they have to do is run into spear-range while we're reloading, and that will be the finish of us.'

'Well, don't ask me,' said Dogger.

They rode westwards for three or four more miles, but now it was clear that the Aborigines were catching up with them. Eyre observed the Aborigines through Dogger's telescope every five minutes or so; and they were running at a steady, even, lope. They must have scented that Eyre and Dogger and Minil were very close now; some of their sharpest-eyed warriors may actually have seen them, even through the dust and the distorted waves of heat.

Eyre drew his rifle out of its saddle-holster and made

sure that it was loaded; this time checking that the ball was still in place. Dogger did the same; and also unsheathed a large cane-cutting knife with a curved blade, which he tucked into his belt.

'What's that for?' asked Eyre.

'Topping and tailing,' said Dogger, without smiling.

Eyre looked all around for any kind of cover; any slight hillock or outcropping of rock where they could dismount and make a stand against Yonguldye. But the salt-lake's surface remained relentlessly flat and featureless, swirled with pink and grey; and he began to realise that if they were going to fight, it would have to be man-to-man, and face-to-face, and that they would unquestionably die. He muttered a prayer under his breath, and then part of the 59th Psalm: 'Deliver me from my enemies, O my God; set me securely away from those who rise up against me. Deliver me from those who do iniquity; and save me from men of bloodshed.'

Yet still, throughout the grilling afternoon, through the whiteness and the heat and the saline dust, Yonguldye and Joolonga followed him, guided by their native instincts and by the bloody *Kurdaitja* shoes, emu feathers stuck together with human blood, perhaps Yonguldye's own blood, or the blood of a tribesman who had been especially slain for the purpose.

At last, as the sun began to glower down through the crimson dust of the day, Eyre and Dogger were able to see their pursuers without using their telescope; and the trail of dust that the Aborigines left hanging in the air behind them was like the red steer, which was what the bush settlers nicknamed a bush-fire.

'They're going to catch us,' Dogger said, philosophically.

Eyre pulled up his horse, and sat in the saddle for a long time, looking behind him. At last he said, 'Could a man walk across that swamp, without sinking?'

'I haven't a clue,' said Dogger. 'You want to try it?'

'Yes,' said Eyre, and dismounted. He sat down on the ground and tugged off his boots, and then he began to walk due north, feeling the crusted ground gradually giving beneath his feet. He was able to walk nearly a hundred paces before the crust broke, and thick grey mud began to squidge up between his bare toes.

He walked further; and the salt crust broke again and again, until he was up to his knees in mud. At last he was floundering, and unable to walk any further. He fought against the warm mud clinging to his legs, but the more he struggled, the more deeply embedded he became. At last, panting harshly, he managed to drag himself clear, and crawl on his hands and knees back to firmer ground.

'You are so dirty,' smiled Minil. 'You look like the Mud-Man.'

'You certainly do,' agreed Dogger. 'And what have you proved? Yonguldye's only about a mile away now; they'll be with us in ten minutes.'

Eyre said, 'Don't argue, just listen to me. We'll ride on a little further, until we reach a place where the ground's unbroken; then I'll tell you what to do.'

They rode on for another half-mile, even though their horses were exhausted and stumbling. Then Eyre told them to draw up, and dismount, and unbuckle their saddle-panniers. Dogger frowned, and shrugged, but did as he was told. Eyre took their rifles, and their ammunition, and as many water-bottles as he could carry, and shared them out between them. Then he said, 'We have to buckle the saddle-panniers on to our feet, like big flat shoes.'

Dogger stared at him. 'You haven't got sunstroke, have you, chum? You want us to buckle these things on to our *feet*?'

'That's right,' Eyre nodded. 'Look, just watch me,' and he sat down and strapped one of the wide leather panniers to his right foot, buckling it tightly.

Dogger rubbed the back of his neck. 'I've seen some lunatics in my time, but this just about takes the biscuit.'

'Don't be ridiculous,' said Eyre. 'I got this idea from one

373

of my father's parish magazines. We can walk across the salt swamp without falling through.'

'Like Christ walking on water?'

'No, of course not. Like Eskimos walking on snowshoes. The Eskimos wear wide flat shoes to spread their weight, so that they don't sink down through the snow. We can do the same on top of the salt swamp.'

Hesitantly, still sniffing and grumbling, Dogger eased himself down on to the ground and strapped his panniers on to his feet. He stood up, and danced a little shuffling trot, and said with distaste, 'I feel like a duck. What are my mates going to say if I die with a couple of satchels on my feet?'

'They'll say "clever, but unlucky",' Eyre replied. 'Now, let's walk out as far as we can.' He took Minil's bare arm, and began to guide her out on to the crust of the salt swamp.

The sun had turned bloody now, and was almost gone. They walked clumsily across the salt swamp, tiny figures in a red-and-purple panorama that stretched as wide as any of them could see. Eyre felt the ground give beneath his feet as he dragged his panniers along; but it didn't break. Soon they were more than a half-mile out on to the crust, in an evening that had now turned to boiling plum.

The wind smelled of brine, and dry dust, and distant mountains. The last vultures of the day spun lazily over their heads, looking for any stray creatures that might have died on the salt-swamps just before nightfall.

Eyre slowed down at last, and stopped, and said, 'Here. This should do us.'

Dogger looked around. 'This place is as flat as any other place; and any other place is as flat as a churchwarden's pancake.'

'Didn't you feel those last few hundred yards?'

'What do you mean?'

'Didn't you feel how soft the ground was?'

Dogger peered back. 'Yes. I suppose it was. But what does that have to do with anything at all?'

'Watch,' said Eyre. 'They're coming.'

Already, Yonguldye and his warriors had reached the edge of the swamp, where Eyre and Dogger had tethered the horses. Now, with Yonguldye leading them, his huge head-dress bobbing and waving in the evening light, they were running due northwards, to catch up with their magical prey. They wanted the *djanga* for their sacrifice. They wanted Yonguldye to have Eyre's brains, and devour them, so that at last they could stand equal to the white man, and keep him away from their sacred *corroboree*-sites, and their *bora*-grounds.

Eyre and Dogger had four rifles between them, all loaded. Eyre said, 'I'll fire first; then, when I'm reloading, you fire. And so on. But we may not need to kill very many!'

'I'm glad you're so confident,' said Dogger.

The sight of the Aborigines running towards them in the twilight was mystical and frightening. The tribesmen's eyes were surrounded by huge circles of white pipe-clay, and their bodies were outlined like boogie-men. This evening, too, they were completely silent, except for the clattering of their spears and the slapping of their bare feet on the salt. No fighting cries; no anger; no chants. Just fifty of them, running nearer and nearer; a dark and complicated outline of spears and head-dresses and running legs.

Eyre touched his cracked lips with the tip of his dry tongue, and lifted his rifle to his shoulder. He took aim at Yonguldye's head, and held it as best he could. Yonguldye was taller than most of his tribesmen, and so he made an easier target; but all the same he was bobbing and weaving as he ran, and Eyre knew that he would be very difficult to hit. 'Save me from men of bloodshed,' he repeated to himself.

Dogger said, 'God almighty, Eyre, they're going to murder us.'

Eyre, at that moment, felt equally frightened. The back of his neck prickled coldly, and he found it almost impossible to maintain his aim on Yonguldye. Any second now, he thought numbly, it's going to be the death-spear through the ribs, or into the belly; and after having seen how poor Midgegooroo had suffered, he knew what he would do next. Thrust the muzzle of his rifle into his own mouth, and pull the trigger. At least it would all be over in one catastrophic blast.

A spear whirred overhead, then another, and a third landed crisply in the salt soil not five feet away. Eyre fired; and his gunpowder flashed brightly in the gathering darkness; and he saw Yonguldye's head-dress collapse out of sight. Then Dogger fired, so loudly that it made Eyre's head sing, and another Aborigine went down.

Eyre took another rifle, and lifted it up; but at that moment he heard a cry from two or three of the Aborigines; then more cries, and shouts of panic. Their running feet had broken through the crust of the salt-swamp, and they had staggered headlong into the mud. Eyre fired at a knot of them who were struggling to free themselves; hitting one of them in the shoulder, but causing shouts of terror that far outweighed the value of the shot. Four or five more spears whistled around him, but now Dogger fired again and Eyre began to reload; and the Aborigines began to turn back in confusion.

For a few minutes, it sounded like a major battle. Six or seven tribesmen were stuck waist-deep in the mud, while at least twenty others tried to drag them out. The rest were running away; while Dogger and Eyre fired their rifles into the air, and screamed and yelled and shouted. 'Bunyip! Bunyip! and 'God Save The Queen!' Even Minil joined in, dancing and shrieking and banging two ramrods together.

Quickly, fearfully, the last tribesmen slithered out of the salty mud and ran away; grey ghosts in a thickening night; until only three of them were left. Yonguldye, lying flat on his back, his mighty head-dress plastered with blood; a young warrior whose spears remained unlaunched; and Joolonga.

Eyre and Dogger and Minil shuffled back across the salt,

with their saddle-panniers on their feet. Joolonga stood by
their horses and watched them with arms folded.

'Well, Joolonga?' said Eyre, unbuckling his panniers.

'Well, Mr Walker-sir. It seems you were wiser than I
first imagined.'

Eyre nodded towards the last of the running tribesmen.
'Will they be back?'

'I don't believe so, Mr Walker-sir. Not without Yonguldye the great Darkness to guide them.'

Dogger kept his distance from Joolonga, his loaded rifle
over his arm. Minil crouched down and began to scoop a
pit in the sand where they could light a fire.

'You deceived me, didn't you?' Eyre asked Joolonga.
'You knew that Yonguldye wanted to put me to death.'

Joolonga said nothing, but took off his midshipman's
hat, and nodded.

'Did Captain Sturt know about this?' asked Eyre.

Joolonga closed his eyes, and swayed a little. 'I am
wounded, Mr Walker-sir.'

Eyre handed his rifle to Minil, walked up to Joolonga,
and opened the Aborigine's decorated coat. There was
blood all over his chest; like a waistcoat of scarlet silk, and
with each beat of his heart, there was more. Eyre looked
straight into Joolonga's eyes. 'You'd better lie down,' he
said, quietly.

Joolonga half-smiled. 'No need, Mr Walker-sir. Quite
soon, I shall fall down.'

Eyre was silent for almost a whole minute. He glanced
towards Dogger but Dogger could only shrug. He turned
back to Joolonga, and repeated, 'Did Captain Sturt know
what would happen if we found Yonguldye?'

Joolonga closed his eyes. 'Nobody knew, Mr Walker-sir;
not even I.'

'But Minil heard you talking to Yonguldye about sacrificing me, and eating my brains.'

'Minil?' frowned Joolonga. His voice slurred; and his lips
were sticky with blood.

'This girl; Yonguldye's protégée.'

'I shall have to sit down,' said Joolonga. Eyre took his arm, and helped him into an awkard sitting position, one leg raised, his back propped against one of their saddle-bags. He lowered his head for a while, so that his chin was resting on his blood-soaked tunic; and he snored blood-clots through his nose. Then he raised his head again, and said, 'Yonguldye wanted only your knowledge.'

'By killing me? By eating my brains?'

Joolonga shook his head. 'This girl does not understand Wirangu well, Mr Walker-sir. There are words which sound like Nyungar words, but have different meanings. Yonguldye would not have killed you, Mr Walker-sir; he was going to initiate you into the brotherhood of his tribe, so that he could share your mind. He did not say "eat your brains". He said "devour everything you knew." '

Eyre said tauntly, 'Are you sure?'

Joolonga nodded.

'You're not lying to me? Because, by God, if you are—'

Joolonga lolled his head back and looked up at Eyre with glassy eyes. 'Why should I lie to you, Mr Walker-sir? I shall soon follow Ngurunderi to the place above Nar-oong-owie, the island of the dead.'

Eyre glanced over towards Minil, who was deftly rubbing a fire-stick in order to start up their evening cook-fire. He said to Dogger, 'Give her a chuckaway, would you?' Then, to Joolonga, 'You lied to me about Arthur Mortlock. Why should I believe you now?'

'Mr Mortlock, sir? I said before. It was necessary for him to die; otherwise we would have been cursed by Ngurunderi. It was my fault, for burying those two bounty-hunters according to Aborigine custom. I am to blame. As it was, I think I was too late to save us.'

'But you poisoned him.'

'No, Mr Walker-sir.'

'You must have done. He died because he was given corrosive sublimate.'

'No, Mr Walker-sir. All I did was to point the bone.'

'How can a man die, just because you pointed your bone at him? Come on Joolonga, you're far more civilised than that!'

Joolonga coughed, and a great black gout of blood splashed out on to his gold braiding.

'Am I, sir?' he asked, in a gluey voice. 'I pointed the bone at him, and he died. Is that not proof enough?'

A billow of aromatic smoke engulfed them for a second; and an ash blew into Eyre's eye. Rubbing it with his finger, he asked Joolonga, 'You're serious, aren't you? I mean, you believe it. And did you really believe that I was the *djanga*?'

Joolonga's head fell forward again. The blood was so thick in his lungs that it was almost impossible for him to breathe. But after a moment or two he raised his head once more, and said, 'Whether you believe you are the *djanga* or not, Mr Walker-sir; you are the white man who came looking for Yonguldye because you wanted to atone for killing Yanluga.'

He hesitated, and then he said, 'Whether you believe you are the *djanga* or not, Mr Walker-sir; you are the man in the story. Captain Henry believed it, and from the moment Captain Henry believed it, and passed it on, it became true.'

Eyre knelt close beside him; felt the warm wet stain of Joolonga's blood through the knee of his britches. 'Joolonga,' he said. 'For God's sake, explain it to me. I don't understand.'

Joolonga almost managed a smile. 'It is easy to understand, unless you are white, Mr Walker-sir. The truth is that you are the man in the story; you have become a part of the dreamtime; Australia has made you her own.'

He caught his breath; and caught it again. But there was too much blood in his lungs now; and all he could do was to give one last desperate choke, splattering blood all over Eyre's shirt and trousers; and roll sideways on to the ground, as if he were dodging away from a blow, and lie with his face against the salt.

Dogger came over and looked down at him.

'Well?' he wanted to know. 'Did you believe any of that?'

'I'm not sure,' said Eyre. Stiffly, he stood up; then looked down at his bloody hands, and wiped them on his shirt. 'I always thought that men made up stories; rather than the other way about.'

Dogger put down his rifle, and stretched, and scratched his belly, and yawned. 'I don't know. They're a rum lot, these blackfellows. Old George Hubbard used to say that they'd all be better off dead. Well, save them some suffering. And, besides, who wants to end up as the figment of some savage's imagination?'

Eyre felt a grey wind across the salt-lake. He looked around, and although the body of the young Aborigine warrior was still there, lying twisted just where Dogger had shot him, the body of Yonguldye was gone.

'Dogger,' said Eyre, and nodded towards the broken surface of the swamp.

Dogger stared for a moment, not sure what he was supposed to be looking at; but then he spat, and said, 'Hell! The wily old bugger's made off!'

They crouched down by the spot where Yonguldye had fallen. Some of his blood-crusted emu feathers were stuck to the salt. Dogger traced the marks in the ground with the tips of his fingers, and said, 'You hit him, all right, but not too badly by the looks of it. He must have made off while we were talking. They can walk silent, some of these blackfellows, and some of them say that they can make themselves invisible.'

Eyre took off his hat and wiped the grit away from the band. 'Well,' he said, 'that means that Yonguldye's still out there; either looking for us because he wants to make friends, and devour my knowledge; or else because he wants to sacrifice us to the great god Baiame, and eat my brains.'

Dogger jerked a thumb towards Minil, who had begun to boil up a thick barley soup. In the intermittent firelight, her face was quite impassive, a mahogany mask. 'It all depends on your point of view, doesn't it, chum? I mean, I'm the last man around to be a spoil-your-sport; but it does strike me that you ought to be taking her carefully; with a pinch of salt, if you know what I mean. If old squash-face was right, and *she* was wrong, then the consequences could be rather uncertain, if you understand me.'

'I'm not sure that I do.'

'Well, I'm not either,' said Dogger. 'But what I'm saying is, take care, and keep your powder dry.'

But it wasn't only the question of Minil that was troubling Eyre that evening; it was the question of Arthur Mortlock. For if Joolonga hadn't poisoned him; who had?

Twenty-Seven

Again and again, for over a week, they tried to strike out northwards, towards the shores of the inland sea. One afternoon, they managed to ride almost six miles further northwards than they had before, and Eyre was convinced that at last they had found a way through the salt swamp. Dogger even began to whistle, and Minil called to Eyre that as soon as they reached the other side of the salt-lake she would cook them a special meal to celebrate.

But then their horses' hoofs began to break through the crumbly crust again, and within ten minutes they were plunged belly-deep into thick, oozing mud.

Eyre shouted, 'Let's try to ride on! Perhaps the horses can find a footing!' But after quarter-of-an-hour of thrashing and wallowing, they were forced to dismount, and drag their frightened, miserable mounts out of the mud again; and stand filthy and bedraggled by the edge of the swamp looking northwards through the trembling heat at the distant horizon that Australia seemed to be determined to deny them. The 100-degree heat dried the mud on their clothes and on their horses' flanks in a matter of minutes; and so they looked like powdery white effigies of themselves; a monument to forlorn hope.

Through Dogger's telescope, Eyre could make out the faintly purple peak of two distant mountains. He pointed them out to Dogger, who collapsed the telescope with a soft brassy whistle of air, and then shrugged. 'You saw them first, you can name them,' said Dogger. 'How about Mount Constance and Mount Charlotte?'

'What would you call them?' Eyre asked Minil, who was standing a little way away from him, shading her eyes.

'I would call them *manaro*,' said Minil. 'That is north-language for breasts.'

'And what about you?' Dogger asked Eyre.

For the first time in days, Eyre gave way to frustration and bitterness. 'Mount Deception; and Mount Hopeless,' he said, and turned away.

Dogger said, 'Eyre—' But Eyre snapped, 'Never mind. We'd better mount up and make our way back.'

The following morning they tried for the last time to make their way northwards. It was one of the hottest days they had yet experienced, and they were becoming dangerously short of water and food. Eyre rode ahead wearing his smoked glasses, straining his eyes for any glimpse of hills or trees or even a gradual rising of the ground—anything to indicate that they could find a way across the terrible glittering surface of the salt-lake.

All the time, discreetly, Dogger kept a watch behind. Dogger knew Aborigines of old, and he was convinced that Yonguldye would be following them. It was Dogger's opinion that even if Yonguldye hadn't wanted to kill them on their first night at the *corroboree*, he would most certainly want to kill them now. They had slaughtered his tribesmen and wounded him twice and more importantly they had humiliated him in front of his people.

They paused for half-an-hour just before noon, and Minil brewed up a pot of tea. Now that she and Eyre had become lovers, of a kind, Minil seemed to consider that it was her duty to serve Eyre like a wife; and she did whatever she could to clean his clothes and cook him food and make him comfortable. Dogger had been a little peeved by this arrangement at first; but he was humorous and adaptable, and he soon accepted it. Eyre was grateful to Dogger for not making his usual relentless fun out of it; although he was still given to grumbling out loud whenever Minil was riding Eyre with too many screams and cries. He would bark, 'Keep that damned galah quiet, will you?' from the other side of the camp-fire.

Eyre was unsure whether he believed Minil or not. But, for the time being, her believability was unimportant. As long as she could cook for them, and help them to feed and water the horses, and as long as Eyre had a warm companion for the night, nothing else mattered. He would sometimes watch her, though, through the long glaring hours of the afternoon, her bare black back shining in the sunlight, her buttocks spread wide across her saddle, and he would wonder what and who she was; and whether she had a part in the dreamtime story, too. Then from time to time she would suddenly turn and smile at him, calm and erotic, and that smile would do nothing at all to make the mystery any more explicable.

They rode north until three o' clock; and then again the salt-lake began to deteriorate under their horses' hoofs, and one of the pack-horses sank to its knees and knelt there sweating and trembling, unable or unwilling to move any further.

Eyre sat on his horse in his smoked-glass spectacles, caked in white salty mud, his head bare under the relentless sun. 'This is where we have to turn back,' he said, in a voice that was little more than a hoarse croak.

Dogger stared at him silently; and then dismounted. 'Minil,' he called. 'Give me a hand with this horse.'

Together, while Eyre watched them, Dogger and Minil cooed and coaxed the stricken horse back on to its feet again. It still seemed bewildered, because it walked around and around in circles, until Minil was able to seize its bridle, and even then it kept twisting its head around as if it were wildly disoriented.

'Brain's gone,' said Dogger, tugging his hat further down over his eye. 'Thinks he's back in some pasture somewhere. Seen it before. Horses trying to chew the ground because they imagined it was grass.'

'Still, we have to turn back,' Eyre repeated.

'Yes,' said Dogger.

They both looked for the last time towards the north. In the gruelling afternoon heat, they could see the tantalising ripples of a horseshoe-shaped lake, glassy and clear, reflecting the peaks of Mount Deception and Mount Hopeless with crystalline clarity.

'That's your inland sea,' said Eyre, with cracked lips. 'A mirage. A dream. And nothing else.'

'Well, it's probably there all right; two or three hundred miles further north,' said Dogger. 'But the question is: how does anybody get to it?'

'Come on,' Eyre told him, and the three of them gathered their reins and began their long retreat south.

After an hour or so, Dogger said, 'What about the opals? Are we going to go and look for the opals?'

Eyre said nothing, but continued riding southwards, with his back to the glory of which once he had felt so sure. But now there was to be no glory, no great discovery; not even a clever-man to bury Yanluga according to the rites of his religion. He closed his eyes as he rode and tried to think about anything and everything else, in order to suppress the sharpness of his defeat. He thought of Charlotte, and of Adelaide, and of riding his bicycle again, if the piccaninnies hadn't stolen it. But again and again the bitterness of having to turn back rose up in his gullet

384

like a cat's-cradle of regurgitated brambles. He cursed Captain Sturt and he cursed Joolonga and he cursed himself for being taken for a fool. He couldn't bring himself to curse Minil, although he began to feel that he ought to.

Neither could he bring himself to curse God.

That night, as they sat around their campfire, Minil said, 'We have no flour left. Tomorrow we must find fresh meat. Kangaroo, maybe. Emu.'

Dogger finished his mouthful of pasty, half-burned bread, and swilled it down with warm water. 'Won't be too soon for me, my lady.'

'I don't think I've seen a single kangaroo since we left Parachilna,' Eyre remarked.

'Don't you worry,' Dogger reassured him. 'We'll soon be back in Kangaroo country; and even if we can't catch any for the first couple of days, we can always survive on lizards until we do. Nothing like a good grilled goanna; what do you say, my lady?'

Minil knew that he was teasing her; for she leaned forward and kissed him with surprising demureness on his grey bearded cheek.

'Well, now,' said Dogger, his eyes bright. 'You'd better watch yourself now, Eyre old chum. Don't want your lady straying to an old dinger-hunter like me.'

On the morning of the following day, their sick pack-horse suddenly staggered and collapsed. They drew up, and dismounted, and Dogger felt the pulse in its neck. 'He's almost gone,' he said; and then 'He's gone.' The horse lay on the sandy ground with its purple tongue protruding and its eyes staring at nothing at all. Eyre looked away, thinking: my God, what has my conceit and my vanity brought to all of these people and all of these animals? Nothing but suffering and death. He began to feel like a Jonah, a curse on everything and everybody who had anything to do with him. It probably wouldn't be long before Dogger and Minil would be struck down with heat-stroke, and exhaustion; and then his devastation of all those whom he had ever loved or liked would be complete. And there would be no chance of him ever returning to Charlotte.

Dogger said, 'We'd better make the best of this poor beast. Are you any good at butchering; Eyre?'

'For God's sake,' said Eyre. 'Haven't you had enough?'

Dogger stood up. 'Now, listen here,' he said, and his voice was a rasp. 'You just stop behaving like Hunt's dog; which would neither go to church nor stay at home; and we'll all get on much better. It wasn't your fault that there were more salt swamps out there than you could manage; and it isn't your fault that we're having to go home with our tails between our legs. So let's make the best of what we have; and the best of what we have today is fresh horse-meat.'

Throughout the stunningly hot afternoon, Eyre cut up the dead pack-horse with a sharp sailor's-knife, hanging out some of the dark-red strips on a length of twine in the hope that they would be dried by the sun; and dividing the rest into bloody steaks. By the time he had finished there must have been more than 100 pounds of meat stacked up on every available plate and cooking-pan they had, clustered with grey sand-flies, but ready for a massive feast.

Minil built a fire out of dried bushes and twigs, and during the whole long evening they sat with lumps of horse-meat speared through by twigs, and roasted them in front of the glowing ashes.

Dogger said, 'Remember what I told you about surviving in the outback, old chum; eat whatever you can, and as much as you can, whenever you can get it; because you never know when you're going to get it next.'

Eyre's chin was glistening with fat and blood, and he didn't know whether he wanted to vomit or die, but he managed to eat nearly five pounds of meat before he lay back, his hands clutching his distended stomach, and decided that even Purgatory would be better than another mouthful of horse-meat. Dogger and Minil continued wolfing for another half-hour or so; but eventually even

Dogger had to admit that he didn't care whether he saw another horse in his entire life or not, and lay back on his blankets with a curse on all four-legged animals, and a ripping belch, and in five minutes or so was fast asleep.

Eyre was exhausted, both by days of riding and by disappointment, and he found it increasingly hard to keep his eyes focused on Minil as she sat by the fire. He dozed, and dreamed, and woke up; and she was still sitting there, naked, tearing voraciously at handfuls of horse-flesh, her attention focused on feeding, and nothing else; the single-mindedness of a wild animal. When she had sex with him, she thought of nothing but sex. When she drank, she thought of nothing but drinking. Now she was presented with nearly seventy pounds of uneaten horse-flesh, she thought of nothing but feeding.

The grease ran down her chin and over her breasts. Her eyes were half-closed but totally concentrated on what she was doing. As he watched her, Eyre began to feel very lonely, because he knew that he could never get to know her, not closely, not a girl who saw daily life as a continuous struggle to ward off the dangers of tomorrow. Minil was probably right and he was probably wrong; particularly in the outback of Australia; but all the same he would rather invest his trust in God, and the fairness of destiny, than in nine pounds of half-raw horse-meat.

He slept, and dreamed of Mount Deception and Mount Hopeless; and that future citizens of Australia would damn him for giving them such defeatist names. But then he woke up and thought that nobody would ever find out what he had christened them, because he would never reach Adelaide alive, or, if he did, it would be in deep disgrace, a waster of money and a wanton killer of innocent Aborigines. And if Captain Sturt had to wear the green bonnet simply because Eyre had failed to penetrate northwards to the inland sea, or discover any opals or gold and silver; then he could imagine what an outcast he would become. 'Not-Fall-Over' indeed. How could anybody have called him that?

He slept again; and woke up again; and when he woke up Minil was still squatting by the fire, devouring raw crimson lumps of horse-meat. Eyre looked at the stacks of meat remaining on the plates, and saw that she must have consumed nearly twenty pounds. Her stomach was bulging out as if she were pregnant, and glossy with fat; but she continued to pull at the meat with her sharpened teeth as if she were ravenously hungry.

He propped himself up on his elbow, and watched her in silent fascination. She had given up bothering to cook the meat, and now she was cramming everything she could into her mouth: bloody lumps of raw horse-liver, stringy shreds of neck; even lungs, like pale gory balloons.

Towards dawn, he lay back and dreamed of Yonguldye, disfigured and wounded, and hunting him to the ends of the desert. He woke up again with a peculiar jolt, and Minil was lying by the ashes of the fire, asleep at last. He crawled over towards her, and covered her with a blanket. He didn't know whether to kiss her or not. She seemed like a girl from another age altogether; not repulsive; not frightening; but utterly different from anyone he had ever met before, even Yanluga.

For a moment, he lifted the blanket again and looked at her. Her face, pouting and black, with its decoratively scarred cheeks, one hand touching her lips the way children do. Her breasts, swollen and shiny with grease. Her hugely distended stomach; and her unconsciously parted thighs, revealing labia as pink as parakeelya petals. He covered her up, and went over to the fire to brew himself a small pot of tea. Perhaps she disturbed him because she was the personification of Australia, this continent that he had so badly wanted to conquer, and failed.

Perhaps, on the other hand, she disturbed him because in an extraordinary way he had fallen in love with her; or at the very least, felt deeply reluctant to be parted from her. Unlike Charlotte, she had seen him both at his very best and at his very worst; and had accepted him without question. Charlotte had always adored his fashionable clothes, his silk neckties and his fancy patterned waistcoats. Minil had first met him when he was naked.

Charlotte had been delighted by his cheek and by his confidence. Minil had seen him stare at the endless salt-lakes of the Southern Australian outback, and give in.

What love do I owe, he thought to himself; and to whom? Do I owe anything to anybody? And he tried to think of his father in Derbyshire, and what his father would have said; and it was peculiarly dizzying to think that his father was probably awake now, and going on his rounds, all those thousands of miles away, on a winter's afternoon; safe and slow through the rain-dewed Dales of England.

He was woken up by the sun, lancing under his eyelids. He blinked, and raised his head, and his neck was stiff as a board. Dogger was already awake, frying up some slices of horse-meat with pepper and salt. Minil was squatting not far away, her hand covering her face, which meant that what she was doing was private. Dogger called it 'picking daisies'. Eyre stood up, and limped towards Dogger on a leg that fizzed with pins-and-needles.

'Good morning, chum,' said Dogger. 'Fancy a slice of beast-of-burden?'

Eyre shook his head. 'I feel as if I've eaten the whole of that horse, tail-first.'

'I think Miss Minil beat you to it,' grinned Dogger. 'Have you seen the size of her belly this morning?'

'I watched her in the night.'

'Well, I don't know how they do it, these Day and Martin's.'

Eyre said, 'Don't call her that. Do you mind?' and there was enough sharpness in his voice to make Dogger look up. Day and Martin's was a popular brand of boot-polish, and a name commonly given to blacks. Dogger prodded his frying meat, and made a face; but he was too much of an old hand to argue. Arguments caused bitterness; and even the best-equipped and most well-fed of expeditions could be ruined by bitterness.

'When you've finished eating, we'll go on,' said Eyre. 'We should reach our cache of food by nightfall tomorrow, if we make good time.'

'Always supposing there *is* a cache of food there,' said Dogger.

'Of course there's a cache of food there. Christopher promised.'

'Well, Christopher is Christopher, my old chum,' said Dogger, 'but food is food.'

'It will be there,' Eyre asserted.

Dogger said, 'You're a greater morepork than I thought you were.'

'What does that mean?'

Dogger grinned. 'It simply means that you'll always believe the best of people who are out to do you down; and the worst of people who like you. It's a common-enough disease. Poor old Joolonga had quite a dose of it, as far as I could see.'

'And what have you ever done?' Eyre demanded. 'You came along on this expedition uninvited, and since then we've heard nothing from you but philosophic advice, and salty aphorisms, and twopenny-halfpenny mottoes.'

'Did I ever offer anything else?' asked Dogger.

Eyre stood in the morning sunlight looking at Dogger carefully. His shadow stretched thin across the salt-lake; his hair was ruffled by the wind. 'You're trying to tell me something,' he said, at last.

Dogger turned his meat over, and sniffed at it with exaggerated relish. 'Only a twopenny-halfpenny motto,' he said.

'Tell me,' Eyre insisted.

Dogger sniffed. 'What about a rhyme?' he suggested.

'A rhyme?'

'What about, "When you fear the pointing-bone, Fear much more the John-and-Joan." Now, that's good, don't you think. You never knew I was a poet, did you?'

Eyre tugged at his curls, and then propped his hands

on his hips, and then turned away. 'God in Heaven,' he said.

Dogger forked out some curled-up horse-meat, and began solemnly to chew.

'God in Heaven,' said Eyre again; and then, 'Do you really think that?'

'Well, I didn't do it,' said Dogger, 'and I know you didn't do it; and nor do I believe that Weeip or Midgegooroo had any hand in it. So who does that leave?'

Eyre walked a little way away and stared for a long time at the western horizon. He knew what Dogger was saying; he had thought the same thought himself. 'John-and-Joan' meant 'homosexual'; and there had only been one homosexual on this expedition; and that was Christopher. The man upon whom they were relying so heavily for their next cache of supplies. The man who, for whatever motive he may have done it, was circumstantially most likely to have poisoned Arthur Mortlock.

Twenty-Eight

The following day, another of their pack-horses collapsed, this time with a splintered fetlock joint; and Eyre shot it straight away. Everything that the horse was carrying they had to discard; all their tenting equipment, all their spare clothing, their pick and their shovel.

They left the horse's body lying where it was, and rode on; while up above them the vultures began to collect, like flies on a dirty window.

The weather was unexpectedly cool, and the skies were overcast with thin woolly clouds. They enjoyed the relief from the overpowering sun; but the coolness brought higher humidity, and when they made camp for the night it was clear that all the half-dried horse-meat they had brought with them was begining to spoil. Eyre ate as much of it as he could, but he gagged on the last gamey piece, and gave up. The day after was blazing again, up to 115 degrees. They threw all their remaining meat away, and decided to ride as long and as hard as they could, until they reached the cache of provisions which Christopher was supposed to have left for them. Eyre had calculated that even if Christopher had taken ten days to return to Adelaide from Parachilna, he should have taken no more than another five days to reach the agreed spot, sixteen miles west of Woocalla.

They reached the cache late in the evening, under a sunset of trumpeting crimson. Eyre had seen from some way away that something was wrong; and that the stores had been disturbed.

'Maybe it's only dingers,' Dogger had suggested; but when Eyre dismounted and walked across to it, there was no question at all who had been here. Barrels of flour had been dug up, and emptied all over the sand. Biscuits, tea, sugar, and salt were flung around everywhere; not stolen, but wantonly destroyed. Most serious of all, three large barrels of water had been deliberately split open, and left to drain into the dry soil. There was no message, no letter, not even a marker to show who had left the cache, and for whom.

'I suppose the nearest water-hole is Woocalla itself,' said Eyre.

Dogger nodded, and couldn't even spit. 'We could try heading due south, to see if we could make it to Adelaide without taking on any water at Woocalla, but in this heat I doubt if we'd get too far. It's not us I'm worried about so much, it's the horses. And the last thing I've got a fancy to do is to walk there.'

'We'll go to Woocalla,' said Eyre. 'If we ride for most of the night, we should be there by morning.'

Minil asked, 'No rest tonight?'

Eyre shook his head. 'Definitely, no rest.'

They turned westwards, and rode through the thickening sunset with the sun glaring right into their eyes like the open furnace of an iron-foundry. At last, however, it was dark; although still stifling; and they rode through scrub and spinifex grass, their horses stumbling with almost every step, and they felt as if they were going to have to ride like this forever.

Just before dawn, after the moon had gone, they rested. They lit a fire, and brewed a little scummy tea; and then, when it was light, they set off again, leaving their fire burning in the way that Aborigines always used to. Aborigines believed that fire cleansed and fertilised the land; and so they would often burn hundreds of acres at a time, a style of agricultural husbandry which enraged the white settlers, especially the sheep-farmers. Sheep were too stupid to run in front of a fire; they invariably stood still as the flames approached, and allowed themselves to be roasted alive. 'I've been through some red steers,' Dogger used to say, 'when there so many sheep being burned that you only had to sniff and you could imagine yourself at Charles's Chop House.'

They reached Woocalla a little after ten. But as they neared the water-hole, with its white gum trees and its mulga scrub, Eyre lifted himself up in his stirrups and peered carefully ahead.

'What's the matter?' asked Dogger.

'I'm not sure. Just a feeling.'

'Aha. You're beginning to grow into a bushman. What kind of a feeling?'

'Well, look, there are no birds around the water-hole, like there usually are; and no animals. Not even an emu. Now, what could be keeping them away?'

'The same buggers who broke into our provisions, I'd guess," said Dogger.

'That's what I'd guess, too,' agreed Eyre.

Minil said, 'You think they wait for us?'

'This is the nearest water-hole. They must have been fairly sure that we'd head straight here.'

Eyre said to Dogger, 'Give me your rifle. The big one.'

Dogger drew his long hunting-gun out of its canvas holster, and swung it over. 'It's all primed and loaded,' he said. He didn't say that this was the first time he had ever allowed anyone else to use it.

Eyre lifted the heavy gun and aimed low towards the mulga bushes around the water-hole. He fired, a great bellow of a shot that echoed for miles; and foliage burst in all directions.

Immediately—even before the echoes had died away—twenty or thirty black warriors rose from the rim of the water-hole, raising their spears and their war-clubs; and they screamed at Eyre with a high, unearthly ferocity.

'Aha,' sniffed Dogger. 'I do believe they're trying to tell us something.'

'Where's the next water-hole?' Eyre wanted to know.

'Due west is the only one I've heard of,' said Dogger. 'A place the Aborigine hunters call Mulka.'

'West? But we want to go east.'

'There's nothing that way; not east; not within living distance.'

'All right,' nodded Eyre. 'In that case, we'd better go west.'

'We've got to get past these blackfellows first.'

Four or five Aborigines were already running towards them, screeching and waving spears. Eyre nudged his horse to the right, and clicked at it, and gradually they began to circle away from the water-hole, hoping that the tribesmen would be satisfied by having chased them away. But the tribesmen suddenly realised what they were doing, and changed course so that they could cut them off.

'Guns,' said Eyre, and handed Dogger's rifle back to him. They drew up for a moment while they loaded with powder-and-ball; and then Dogger said, 'Ready, let's give them a go.'

They rode towards the running tribesmen at a fast walk;

Dogger and Eyre and Minil and their two remaining pack-horses. Two or three spears were flung up towards them, but they fell short. As his first target, Eyre picked a warrior right in the middle of the crowd of tribesmen, lifted his gun to his shoulder and fired at him. He missed the man he was aiming for; but another warrior off to his left fell flat on his back in an explosion of blood and lay on the ground spreadeagled.

Now Dogger fired, and another Aborigine cried out, and dropped to his knees. Then, before they knew it, they were riding through them, with spears clattering all around, and Eyre grasped the barrel of his rifle and swung the stock around him like a club. It connected twice: once with another club, jarring Eyre's shoulder; and once with a warrior's jaw, smashing out his teeth with a noise like a breaking plate.

Their second pack-horse was brought down by four spears thrown almost simultaneously; one clean through its neck and the others bristling into its flanks. Most of their ammunition was strapped to this horse, and Eyre turned and watched it collapse to the ground with a feeling of alarm and helplessness. But there was no possibility of riding back to salvage anything; as it was, they would be lucky to escape with their lives.

One spear struck a glancing blow against the croup of Eyre's horse, and slid underneath the back of his saddle, piercing the leather and grazing his thigh. A second missed his head by less than two inches, and fell noisily in front of him, almost tangling his horse's legs and tripping it up.

But then, 'We're clear!' cried Dogger, and whooped, and waved his hat.

Minil was already well away, fifty yards off to Eyre's right. She was far lighter than both of them, and her horse was fresher. But all of them had passed through the gauntlet of Aborigine warriors unscathed, and as they turned around, it seemed that the tribesmen were reluctant to run after them.

'I think they've had enough lamb-and-salad for one day,

don't you?' shouted Dogger. And he lifted his hat again, and crowed, 'Brayvo, Hicks!'

As he did so, a heavy death-spear arched high through the air, seeming to travel so slowly at its zenith that Eyre glimpsed up and saw it hanging suspended. But then it appeared to accelerate, and by the time it reached them it was travelling so fast that Eyre turned his head too quickly and lost sight of it. It was only when he looked back again, perplexed, that he saw that it had pierced Dogger between the eyes and impaled his head, and that Dogger was sitting upright in the saddle with both his arms raised in a kind of stunned supplication; like a martyred saint, or a strange variety of balancing-act at a circus.

Eyre couldn't even speak. His horse carried him on; but Dogger remained where he was, his arms still raised, the spear still growing out of his forehead. Eyre thought: *Constance, oh God. What am I going to say to Constance?* And then he saw Dogger topple and drop to the dust, and the Aborigines running towards him, waving their clubs and their boomerangs.

His first angry temptation was to ride back, and swing his way through the tribesmen with his rifle-stock and his knife. But that would mean certain death for him, too; and apart from the plain fact that he didn't want to die, who would be able to go to Constance and tell her how Dogger had fallen? And how courageous Dogger had been; and how consistently reassuring, and what a friend could really be, when you really needed one; a mate; out beyond the black stump.

They rode westwards now with their single pack-horse and the sun behind them. Minil said nothing to Eyre and Eyre remained silent with shock and grief. But Minil seemed to know roughly the direction in which the water-hole called Mulka lay, because she walked her horse ahead of him west-north-west, and she kept her eye on the sun as the day progressed.

By noon, they were far out over a dry lake, shadowless, under a crucifying sun. Minil stopped, and climbed down from her horse, and shared out between them a few dry biscuits and a half-mouthful of water, which was all they had left. The horses shivered and sweated, and flared their nostrils at the scent of moisture, but if Eyre and Minil were to survive, there was to be none for them.

Eyre stayed in the saddle, slowly and dryly chewing his biscuit. Minil stood beside him, in her scarf head-dress, with Eyre's shirt tied around her shoulders. She said, 'Will you say a prayer for your friend?'

'A prayer?'

'He always told me that you were a man of God.'

Eyre wiped the sweat away from his face. 'He told you that? When?'

'One evening, when you were sleeping; and we were awake.'

'Well, you could hardly call me a man of God. Especially not now.'

Minil traced a pattern in the fine white dust that clung to Eyre's riding-boot. 'He said that he envied you.'

'He didn't have any reason to do that.'

'Oh, but he did, He always envied you. He said that you were the kind of man who makes days begin and years go by; whether you want to or not.'

Eyre coughed, and almost choked on his biscuit. 'Well, I don't want to, as a matter of fact.'

'What are you going to do now?'

'Go on,' said Eyre. 'Go on until we reach the water-hole. Then, drink.'

Minil smiled. 'Dogger was right. You are becoming a bushman.'

They rode on, and gradually the sun descended in front of them to scorch their faces and blind their eyes. By five o' clock, however, they reached a series of deep water-holes in the bed of the dry lake; and there they tethered their horses, and let down their water-bottles and water-bags on lengths of bridle and twine, all knotted together, and brought up gallons of water that was fresher and cooler than any that Eyre had tasted in weeks. They drank until the water poured out of their noses, and they felt as if they would drown in the middle of the desert. Then they watered the horses, and splashed their coats with hatful after hatful of fresh water, and rubbed them, and patted them, until at last the horses shook themselves, and stood calm and refreshed. There was even a scattering of tussocky grass around the edges of the water-holes for them to eat; but Eyre made sure that they were well-tethered before he let them graze. The water-holes were sheer and very deep, and if a horse were to fall down one of them, they would never be able to get it out again, even if it survived.

His caution proved itself only a few minutes later; for an emu came to the water-holes to drink; and while Eyre and Minil were sitting watching it, it toppled with a feathery squawk of fear and annoyance into one of the narrowest of the holes. It thrashed and cried, but couldn't extricate itself. Eventually, when it sounded as if it had grown tired, Eyre went across to the hole with his rifle, and shot it. Smoke rose out of the limestone well like a magic trick; soon to be followed by a dead female emu, dangling from the end of an improvised lassoo.

They had a feast that night. Eyre said it was for Dogger; a last offering from the mortal world. Minil dug a deep pit in the hard ground with a stick; lined it with brush and twigs and burned the wood until it glowed. Then she dragged the emu into the hole and buried it, leaving only its neck and its head protruding. Two hours later, steam began to puff out of the emu's beak, and Minil pronounced the bird cooked. Actually, it was half-raw; but they were ravenous, and ate the whole breast between them.

They made love that night, too, out in the open, for they had lost their *umpee*. And it was love, rather than coupling; warmth and companionship, rather than erotic excitement. Both of them were naked in the warm night air; with nobody around them for miles amd miles; only the scratching of the night-creatures for company, the Kowaris and fat-tailed dunnarts, searching for insects and other small mammals; and the explosive constellations of southern stars over their heads.

Afterwards, as they lay cuddled together under their horse-blanket, Eyre said, 'Was it true, that Yonguldye was going to kill me?'

Minil stroked his face with her fingertips, tracing the outline of his lips, and his nose, and his bristly chin. 'Did Joolonga say that it wasn't?'

'He said they wanted only my knowledge. Only what was inside my brains not the brains themselves.'

'And what do you believe?'

'I don't know. There doesn't seem to be any way of telling, not for certain.'

Minil kissed him. 'You are in the desert,' she said, softly. 'There is nothing certain here; only thirst.'

'Who are you?' he asked her; not for the first time.

'I am someone looking for something that is probably lost for ever,' she said.

'Yes,' he answered her. Then, 'Yes', again; because at last he began to realise what she meant. There would be no peace for the Aboriginals now; their innocent centuries of living alone in Australia could never return. All that lay ahead for them now was retreat; retreat from their old fishing- and hunting-grounds, retreat from their sacred places, retreat from their magical and mysterious way of life, even a backing-away from their own souls. No wonder such an electrified ripple of excitement had run through the Aborigine community when Captain Henry had announced that the *djanga* had at last arrived. Eyre had been seen as their very last hope against a bewildering and increasingly destitute future.

Whether Yonguldye had really intended to eat his brains or not, Eyre very much doubted whether he would have escaped from Yarrakinna alive. For when he failed to give Yonguldye the great knowledge and power of the white invaders, as he inevitably would have done, the wrath and disappointment of the Aborigines would have been catastrophic, especially for him. In one way, perhaps it was better for the Aborigines themselves that he had escaped, because as long as he remained alive, their hope of standing up against the white man would remain alive with him.

Eyre slept. When he awoke, there were dingoes prowling around their camp attracted by the smell of the half-charred emu. He called, 'Dogger?' and almost at the same time remembered that Dogger was dead.

Still, he said it again, a whispered name in the vastness of the cold Australian night. 'Dogger? Can you hear me, Dogger?'

But of course there was no reply.

Twenty-Nine

They had no choice now but to strike out west. There was little doubt in Eyre's mind now that Yonguldye was following them; and that it had been Yonguldye and his tribesmen who had destroyed Christopher's provisions. So if they tried to return to the water-hole at Woocalla, and then make their way south to Adelaide from there, the risk of running straight into Yonguldye would be dangerously high.

They knew of no more water-holes beyond Mulka, but Eyre could see that the ground was rising ahead of them; and in all probability they would be able to find an *aroona*, or a water-pool.

They rode for hours in silence across miles and miles of dry mallee scrub; and as they rode they were smothered in grey sand-flies, in their hair, on their faces, crawling inside their clothes. Eyre tried at first to keep them out of his mouth by tying a handkerchief across the lower half of his face, but the flies always found a way of working their way underneath it, and time after time he would snap it away from his face in disgust.

When they stopped at a little after one o' clock to eat as much of the emu as they could manage, and swallow a mouthful of water, Eyre found that he was crunching mouthfuls of flies as well as meat, and spat his food out on to the ground. But Minil seemed to be quite unperturbed by the glistening, clustering insects that clung around her lips; and giggled at Eyre for being so sensitive.

They rode on and on; Eyre using his compass to tend slightly southwards in the hope that eventually they would reach the coast. He estimated that if they continued on this bearing, they would probably see the Indian Ocean within four or five days, at Fowler's Bay, or Cape Adieu, or fairly close by; and with any luck at all they would be able to camp there and wait for a whaler or a merchantman to pass, and pick them up.

Minil said, 'If we ride westwards, we will come to my home.'

Eyre wiped the sweat from his face. 'Home? You mean New Norcia? That must be a thousand miles. I don't have the slightest intention of riding for a thousand miles.'

'I walked a thousand miles, when I came to Yarrakinna with Yonguldye.'

'You walked all the way across this desert?'

Minil nodded. 'There are many places to find water, for those who know.'

'All I want to do is find a ship,' said Eyre.

'You really want to go back?'

'Is there anything wrong in that?'

'I don't know. It doesn't sound like you; to give in.'

Eyre slapped flies away from his mouth. 'What are you talking about? Give in? You saw for yourself that we couldn't ride any further northwards through those salt-lakes. And if we couldn't ride through them, certainly nobody could ever run a road through them, or a railway-line, or drive stock through them.'

'But what about *this* way?' asked Minil.

'What about this way?'

'You could drive stock this way perhaps. Or just a road.'

Eyre stared at her. Her bright eyes were giving nothing away; no clues about her seriousness, nor why she was provoking him into thinking about carrying on westwards. But perhaps she saw in him something that he couldn't see in himself; a stamina and a sense of persistence that only needed the right cause, and a great enough inspiration.

'You can go back to Adelaide with nothing,' she said. 'Or, you can go back with a new stock-route to the west. Isn't that what you told me? That the farmers of Adelaide need to send their sheep and cattle to other parts of Australia, so that they can survive?'

Eyre said, 'Who was your teacher, at New Norcia?'

'Mrs Humphreys. She was teaching me ever since I was a baby.'

'Well, she taught you remarkably well. But your intelligence is your own; and you've got plenty of that.'

She said, 'Do you love me yet?'

'Do I *love* you yet? What a peculiar question!'

'I will stay with you for ever,' she said. 'If you want me to.'

Eyre laid his hand on her shoulder, and then brushed away the flies and kissed her. While they kissed, the flies crawled all through their hair and over their faces, but they did not part their lips from each other until they had shared everything they had grown to feel for each other since they had first met, in Yonguldye's shelter.

'No matter what happens to us, I will always love you,' said Eyre.

'You don't have to make that promise. I don't expect it.'

'Nonetheless, you have it.'

They rode on through a long and hazy afternoon. Now and then Eyre looked behind them, to see if there was any sign of Yonguldye and his warriors; but there was none. He wished very much that he had Dogger's telescope with him, and Dogger's long gun; and he wished very much that he had Dogger, too. But their lives were now reduced to nothing more than riding westwards, and surviving. There was no time for sentiment, and very little time for mourning. They were a dark, emaciated white man and a naked Aborigine girl, riding through a world of scrub and dust and relentless beige, and that was the sum of their existence.

Days passed; more days of dust; and they found no more water-holes. Every morning the sky-spirits lit the sun-fire; and every afternoon the scrub wavered with heat so great that the goannas and the skinks remained motionless, as if stunned by the 120 degree temperature, and even the vultures looked as if they were flying through clear syrup.

Still there was no sign of anybody pursuing them, and they were now as far from Parachilna as Parachilna was from Adelaide, and Eyre was sure that they would soon reach the coast.

But every morning the sun came up behind them, and there were no more water-holes. Their bottles were almost empty, and they had no water for the horses. They threw away everything they could, to save weight. They left their saddles behind in the dust, like abandoned tree-stumps. They left the two extra rifles, and Eyre's spare boots and even, at last, Eyre's copy of Captain Sturt's *Expeditions*.

They lay at night under their blanket, shaking with cold, and scarcely speaking to each other.

'When we reach the coast,' Eyre told Minil one morning, 'if we don't see a ship straight away, we'll turn back eastwards towards Adelaide.'

Minil said nothing. But both of them had begun to accept that staying alive was their only priority, and that the route to Western Australia could wait for another explorer, at another time.

By noon that day, they had run out of water completely.

Eyre turned his water-bottle upside-down, and a drop fell on to the palm of his hand, as precious as a diamond, and gradually evaporated in the heat. Minil looked up towards the sun, her eyes squeezed almost shut, and said, 'We have to go on.' The shine which fresh meat and fresh water had given her skin had now faded to a dull cocoa-brown; and her ribs and pelvis were showing, as if death were making a premature announcement of his imminent appearance.

They went on. Their last pack-horse was close to collapse, but Eyre was reluctant to butcher it in case they needed it later. Fresh meat lasted only a day or two in this heat, with all these flies; and although blood might see them through one more waterless day, it quickly congealed and went bad.

The following day was Christmas Eve. Eyre sat silent on his horse, his eyes closed, feeling the sun drum and drum and drum against his skull. Even inside his eyelids, the day was vivid scarlet, and too bright to look at. He thought: I shall probably die on Christmas Day, and that will prove what an Anti-Messiah I turned out to be. Everybody expected so much of me: destiny, history, the opening-up of a continent; and here I am, stupid with sunstroke, lolloping through the scrub on a half-dead horse without a saddle. *Brayvo, Hicks!* Dogger had cried, as the death-spear slammed into his forehead and right through his brainful of memories and laughter and drunken nights. At least he had died quickly; at least he had gone without any chance to grumble or regret, a cantankerous invalid on Hindley Street, without beer or horses. But he never got to see Constance again, and when he had been sitting on his horse dying in those last few instants he must have realised that; and what a woman Constance was.

Eyre thought: Christmas Day, whoever would have believed it? All these years, all through childhood, all through catechism, all through college, I've been destined to die on Christmas Day. By God, if I had known, I would have dreaded each succeeding Christmas, instead of merrymaking, and eating too much, and dancing like a damned doomed marionette.

He saw Minil pitch off her horse like a falling shadow out of the corner of his eye. She dropped face-down on to the scrubby ground, and lay there still, while her horse came to an exhausted and obedient stop.

Eyre slid down from his mount, and walked quickly across to her in sweat-filled boots. He knelt down beside her, and gently turned her over, and she looked up at him with flickering eyelids, muttering and chattering with blistered lips.

'Minil,' he croaked. 'Minil, what's the matter?'

She lapsed into unconsciousness again, twitching nervously now and then as if she were dreaming.

'That's it,' he said to himself, out loud. 'That's it, that's damn-well it. She's going to die.'

He stood up, and took off his hat, and he was so dehydrated that he couldn't even bring tears to his eyes. But then he knelt down again, and slapped her face, one way and then the other way, and shouted at her in a high, broken voice, 'Minil!'

She wasn't dead; but he knew that she must be close to it. Her breath fluttered as delicately as a zebra-finch caught in a thorn-bush. He rolled back her eyelid and her eyes were white. She muttered, and jerked, but she didn't wake up.

He bent over her for a long time, fatigued and trembling and stricken with the pain of losing her. But then he sat up straight, and thought: I must find water. Where am I going to find water? If I try to take her any further, she'll be dead by the time the sun goes down. She'll probably be dead within the hour, in this heat. But supposing I leave her here, and go looking for water on my own?

He knew how desperate a chance it was. His only experience of bush-craft was the experience he had acquired on this one expedition. There was a high risk that he would go looking for water and never be able to find her again. And there was also a risk that when he was away, Yonguldye and his warriors would catch up with them, and kill her. But all he could do was trust in God, and his own judgement, and try to survive.

Carefully, he rolled her over on to a spread-out blanket. Then he propped up their second blanket on a dry branch, so that it formed a canopy over her head. She lay still, her mouth open, breathing faintly and roughly. God, he thought, how can I leave her? This may be the very last time I see her alive. But I must.

He remounted his horse, and rode westwards again; turning around from time to time to fix his bearings on the improvised shelter he had made. But after an hour, it was out of sight; and there was nothing but the rippling heat and the mallee scrub and the sky like a punishment above his head.

He thought of nothing sensible: the heat was too powerful. He rode with his thighs chafing against his salt-caked britches, his hat pulled low over his eyes. He didn't even have the strength to curse any more. He was sure that the sun was actually driving him mad, and that if he survived this journey it would only be as a lunatic, kicking and gibbering and nagging forever about roasted emu and weeks without water.

In a wandering, discursive way, he began to wonder what he was actually doing, riding westwards under this pitiless sun looking for water. Surely the most sensible thing to do would be to keep on going. Even if he did manage to find a water-hole, it would take him at least another two hours to ride back, and by then Minil would be dead. She was probably dead already.

It disturbed him that he could think about Minil so callously. But then it occurred to him that he must be very close to death himself, to be thinking so selfishly about his own survival.

He peered ahead through the sloping, glistening heat. There were imaginary lakes all around, lakes which could never be reached. He began to think that even when he eventually reached the sea, he would find out that it was nothing but a mirage, and that he would still be riding across dry sand.

What he didn't yet know was that he was riding thirty miles too far north to reach the sea, and that he and Minil had entered the eastern extremities of the land which the Aborigines called Bunda Bunda, and which the Europeans would one day christen the Nullarbor Plain; Nullarbor being dog-Latin for 'no trees'. The plain stretched all the way from Southern Australia, eight hundred miles to Western Australia, treeless, relentlessly flat, and with no running water from one side to the other. In the heat of Christmas Eve, it was more than the human imagination could bear.

Eyre began to think of Minil. At this moment, if she were still alive, she was the closest companion he had; or had ever had. They had now shared all the physical intimacies which any man and woman could share. But Minil remained strangely aloof; rather in the same way that Joolonga had done; and he still found it hard to understand her or what she was expecting out of her life. She had evidently been very grammatically schooled at New Norcia, and she had told him that she had always worn European dresses there, bonnets and parons and petticoats. And yet, for all of her education, she had gone with Yonguldye into the outback, leaving her dresses and her Christian upbringing behind her.

It showed Eyre just how strong the mysterious magic of Australia must be, that when Aborigines were classroom educated and taught how to question the world around them, the first question which they seemed to be drawn to; magnetically and inevitably; was the question of their own origin, their own being, and the reality of the dreaming. Cynical and sarcastic as he often was, Joolonga had plainly come to consider that the myths of the dream-time had a greater strength and relevance to life in Australia than any of the beliefs which the white settlers had brought with them from the old country. The myths of the dreamtime were everlasting and immutable; they

407

could not be adapted to suit the greed or the convenience of the believer. Joolonga's only tragedy, like Minil's, was that in rediscovering his own religion through European education, he had lost his natural and intuitive link with native magic; his ability to commune with the spirits of the sky, and the spirits of the rocks, and most importantly of all, the spirits of his ancestors.

Perhaps this link was what Minil had been hoping to regain when she had followed Yonguldye; and perhaps she had come into Eyre's shelter that night because she had realised at last that she could never regain it. Take me back, she had asked him; back to the white man's mission. There could have been no greater pain than living in a world of strange and limitless magic, but never being able to share in it.

Eyre could see now why Yanluga had pleaded with him to be buried according to Aborigine custom. It had been a last attempt to join in his people's spiritual heritage; even if it was after death.

'What are we *doing* to these people?' Eyre said, and surprised himself by saying it out loud.

He opened his eyes, which had gradually been closing as he was riding. About seventy-five paces ahead of him was a low limestone outcropping, on which four or five princess parrots were perched, pink-throated and yellow-chested. There were thick tufts of grass around the rock, and even a stunted gum. My God, thought Eyre, a water-hole. I can't believe it. I've actually found a water-hole.

He climbed stiff and awkward down from his horse, and hobbled like a very old man through the grass and scrub, until he reached the edge of the hole. It was dried up now, filled with sand, but when he knelt down and pressed his hand against the ground, he could feel that it was still slightly damp. He went back to his horse and took out of his saddle-bag the only implement he had which would serve as a spade: his curved brandy-flask, long ago emptied of brandy, but which he had kept with him as a water-bottle.

Watched by the inquisitive parrots, he began to dig into the sand. He was weaker than he had realised and he had to pause every few minutes to rest. But gradually the sand he was digging grew cooler and damper, and after an hour the bottom of his narrow excavation began to fill with clouded water. He lay flat on his stomach with his head down the hole and drank the water mouthful by mouthful, even though it was gritty and salt-tasting and even though he had to wait for minutes on end after each mouthful while the hole slowly refilled itself.

After he had drunk as much as he could manage, he dug the hole wider and deeper, and led his horse to it. The horse lapped at it for almost half an hour, while Eyre managed to dig another hole a little further away, and slowly fill up his water-bottle. He glanced up at the sinking sun: he would just be able to get back to Minil before it grew dark, and the water in his bottle would be enough to last them until they could ride back here tomorrow morning. Then: well, they couldn't be too far from the sea now. Another day's riding, perhaps. And if they were able to hail a ship, or find themselves a few fish, or washed-up mutton-birds, or cockles perhaps they might even think of going on, of doing what Minil had suggested, and finding a stock-route to the west. Destiny had brought him this far. Who knew where it might take him now? And it was extraordinary how much more alluring and accessible fame and glory both seemed to be, now that he had quenched his thirst. Minil had been right: it wasn't in his nature to surrender, and discovering a stock-route to Western Australia would make his name for ever.

It would also, he sincerely hoped, bring him Charlotte.

He looked around for his brandy-flask, to fill that up as well; but he couldn't find it. His horse must have trampled down the sand when he was drinking, and buried it. He dug for a while with his hands, but it was growing much darker now, and it looked from the clouds that they were building up in the north-west as if it was going to be a cold and windy night.

He rode back through the gathering dusk, clutching his one full water-bottle close to his stomach. His exhaustion had begun to overwhelm him now, and he had to make a sharp effort to wake himself up every few minutes, and check his compass bearing. His long shadow rode in front of him, across the dark orange scrub; and in the distance, towards the south-east, he saw four or five kangaroos bounding like rocking-horses against the thunder-black eastern sky.

The sun sank at last and the wind began to get up. Eyre dozed as he rode; only managing to jerk himself awake when he was on the point of overbalancing and falling off his horse. As he dozed, he dreamed, and sometimes he found it impossible to distinguish between the dream and reality.

It was only his horse drawing up beside Minil's horse and nuzzling it that at last woke him up. The sky was lighter now, with the moon just about to rise, and he could make out the dark triangular shape of the blankets under which he had left Minil. He clicked encouragingly to Minil's horse, and then dismounted. It was then that he realised with a physical shudder of horror and distress that he was no longer carrying the water-bottle.

'Oh my God,' he said to himself. He looked desperately around, to see if he could see it anywhere close. But he had just crossed miles of scrub and rough grass in the dark, and he could have dropped it anywhere.

Shaking, he went across to the shelter and lifted back the blankets so that he could see Minil. He thought she was dead at first, but when he bent down and listened against her lips, he could hear her breathing in shallow and uneven gasps, interspersed with occasional reedy whines, as if her lungs were congested.

'Minil,' he called her, and rubbed her hand. 'Minil, it's Eyre. Minil for God's sake, wake up.'

There was no response; except for a thin, dry cough. Eyre tried opening her eyelids with his thumbs, but even when she stared at him, it was obvious that she was unconscious, and that she couldn't really see him. 'Minil,' he repeated. 'Minil, you must wake up.'

He knew that she was close to death. She was so cold that he could hardly bear to touch her. Her body seemed to have shrunk even in the few hours that he had been away looking for water. Her hips protruded bonily, and her breasts had shrunk, so that they were soft and flabby.

He dragged together as much brushwood as he could find, and lit a fire. It flared up quickly in the northwest wind, and he had to stack on more brush every few minutes to keep it going. Then he walked back the way he had come, back towards the water-hole, following his horse's hoof-marks in the dust, searching everywhere for his lost water-bottle. He would have cried if he hadn't already been so exhausted, and angry with himself.

At last he walked back to the fire. The warmth seemed to have roused Minil a little, because she opened her eyes and whispered his name. He crouched down beside her, and took her hand between his.

'Koppi unga,' she said, so quietly that he could scarcely hear her. He knew what the words meant. Yanluga had said the same thing to him when he was dying. 'Bring me water.'

He licked his lips. 'There is no water. Not unless you can ride.'

He tried to lift her up into a sitting position, but she fell back on the blanket, her arms tangled uselessly.

'Minil,' he insisted, 'there is no water. We're going to have to ride and find it.'

He thought: I can lift her up, and tie her on to her horse. But will she survive another two or three hours, jolting on the back of an animal that itself is already on the verge of collapse? And will I be able to find the water-hole again in the dark? He felt that he had as good as killed her already, with his carelessness.

'Water,' she begged him.

'Minil, there isn't any. I found some, I filled the bottle, but I dropped it, somewhere in the scrub.'

411

She stared at him. 'Where is the water?' she whispered. 'How far?'

'Two, three hours. A little more.'

She said nothing for a very long time. Eyre watched her, while the brushwood fire died down behind him.

'Take me there,' she said, at last.

Eyre lifted her up, and half-dragged, half-carried her over to her horse. On the third attempt, he managed to lift her up on to its back, and she leaned forward, clinging on to the horse's neck, while Eyre tied a blanket around her, in the style of a *buka*.

There was no question of letting her ride by herself; she was too weak, and a fall from the horse's back would probably kill her outright. So Eyre walked beside her, leading his own horse and their one spare pack-horse by the reins.

The wind was stronger now, and as they left their make-shift camp, the brushwood fire was blown away across the scrub in fiery tumbling circles. Eyre pulled his hat down further over his eyes, and leaned forward against the wind and the cold and the stinging dust.

They walked for nearly five hours. The wind was at gale-force now, and it shrieked and howled across the plain of Bunda Bunda like Koobooboodgery. One blessing, thought Eyre: the wind and the sand will cover our tracks, and make it more difficult for Yonguldye to find us. But what will there be for him to find? Bones, and dead horses; nothing worth plundering, nothing worth punishing.

By the time the next day dawned, he knew that he had missed the water-hole; possibly by yards, possibly by miles. He stood on that endless expanse of scrubby plain and looked around him in the light of the early-morning sun, and nothing seemed familiar. He didn't even know where to begin looking for it.

He gently lifted Minil down from her horse, and laid her on the ground on her blanket.

'Are we near the water?' she asked him, in a peculiarly clear voice. But she looked much worse than she had yesterday: her eyes were dull and her thin arms were drawn across her chest as if even the act of lying down were painful.

'Not far now,' Eyre lied.

'You said two hours. Surely we have gone further.'

'I've, er . . . I've, er, lost my way . . . just once or twice . . . that's why. But, it won't be long now.'

He looked towards the sun. It was blazing brightly now, rising over the plain with bare-faced ferocity; causing every living creature at which it stared to scuttle for shadow, and protection. Eyre remembered that it was Christmas Day; and he knew that he would never survive it. Neither would Minil. She was already half-delirious, and her eyes kept closing in pain and fatigue.

'We have to go on,' said Eyre.

Minil shook her head. 'No more strength, Mr Walker.' She could still tease him, even now.

'We must go on. We can't just lie down here and die.'

'You go on. Let me stay here.'

'Minil, I need you. You must try.' But his voice sounded broken and weak and unconvincing, like an old man trying to persuade his sick dog not to give in. Minil would die first, probably within a matter of hours, when the sun grew really hot, of dehydration and heat exhaustion; and then Eyre would die shortly after. This patch of mallee scrub would be his last resting-place; and he didn't even know where it was. He looked around but there were no vultures; not yet; although he thought he could see some wild dogs in the distance. He just prayed that they wouldn't start to tear him apart until he was really dead.

Minil opened her eyes again, and lifted one hand to touch her lips. 'Water,' she said. Eyre didn't know what to say to her. 'Water,' she repeated. 'Water.' A soft and plaintive chant to her own extinction. 'Water.'

He sat up straight. He had remembered something that Captain Sturt had told him, about the way in which men had survived when they were stranded without water in the deserts of Western Australia. He pressed his hand over his dry lips for a while, thinking; but then he made up his mind. If it would keep Minil alive for long enough for them to find the next water-hole, then there could be no vulgarity about it, and no indignity.

He stood up, unbuttoned his shirt, and loosened his belt, stepping out of his britches. His body was bony and dry-skinned and still pale, although his hands were as brown as gloves. He dropped his clothes to one side; and then slowly and carefully sat himself astride Minil's face, taking care not to kneel on her.

She opened her eyes again and looked at him. '*Urrabirra*,' he said, throatily. It meant 'drink'.

She reached up weakly and touched his bare stomach. She understood. Then she took him in her hand, and guided him between her lips. She closed her eyes momentarily to show him that she was ready.

There was very little; a sudden gush; but then in spite of everything he had drunk yesterday he had been very dehydrated. She drank thirstily, however, and even when he had finished she held him in her mouth, sucking from him the last possible drop. He eased himself up at last; and left her to rest, covering her over with a blanket; but he felt that in an hour or two she might have sufficient strength to ride for just a few miles more.

Those few miles more might lead nowhere. They might lead to another place just like this. Heat, and scrub, and flies, and imaginary oases. But on the other hand they might take them to the next water-hole, and save their lives. There was always hope. After all, there was nothing else.

He waited for her under the sun. At last, after an hour, he woke her and lifted her back on to her horse. Then they went on, south-westwards, into the hottest Christmas Day that Eyre had ever experienced.

Thirty

They saw the Aborigines from well over two miles away; thin black figures standing ankle-deep in a reflecting lake. They could have turned due south, and tried to escape, but Eyre knew that it was no use. So he kept on walking, straight towards them, and the Aborigines stood and waited for him with their spears and their clubs, a black etched pattern of naked figures against the hot horizon, as if somebody had been shaking a nibful of India-ink on to a sheet of glass.

They reached the Aborigines, and Eyre drew the horses in close and stood with his head bowed, waiting for them to approach him. He had no idea how they had overtaken him. Perhaps they had been running through the night. But he had no more strength to elude them; no more will to fight them. He could scarcely stand, and his horse was trembling and foaming dry foam at the mouth, and almost ready to collapse.

One of the Aborigines came forward, a dignified old man with a big pot-belly and a grey curly beard. He laid his hand on Eyre's shoulder, and said something in a dialect which Eyre didn't understand at all.

Eyre said, 'Where is Yonguldye? Let me speak to Yonguldye.'

The old man frowned, and shook his head.

'You are not Yonguldye's people?' Eyre asked him.

Again, the old man shook his head. He turned back to the blackfellows standing behind him, and said something long and excitable and emphatic. One or two of them answered him, and one began to point towards the north-east, and say over and over again, 'Yarrakinna, Yarrakinna.'

Eyre tried to step back to tell Minil that they had met up with a tribe that seemed to know nothing of Yonguldye, or what had happened at the great corroboree; but as he turned he felt the ground rising beneath him like the rising crust of a loaf; and suddenly he was deaf and stunned and lying on his side in the dust, although he was not at all aware that he had fallen, and there was no pain, no bruising; only the strange hot silence and the bare feet of blackfellows all around him.

'We have been travelling for many days without water,' he thought he said, although he couldn't hear his own voice. Then there was nothing at all: no sound, no sight, no feeling. His world dwindled away to a single speck of light, and then was swallowed up.

He was woken by the sound of tapping; the rhythmic tapping of musical sticks. He opened his eyes and saw that it was sunset, and that the sky was streaked with dark curls of cirrus. He was lying on a kangaroo-skin blanket; and not far away a fire was burning.

Stiffly, he raised himself up on to one elbow, and looked around. He was lying in the middle of an encampment of about twenty or thirty Aborigine men and women and children. The men were sitting in a group, tapping with their sticks, and humming. The women and children were squatting around the fire cooking sand-lizards. Two kangaroos were being roasted in pits filled with hot ashes: Eyre could see their leg-bones sticking up out of the ground. An elderly man was obviously in charge of this part of the cooking, for he sat scowling between the two ash-pits, and every now and then he would shout at the children who came hungrily sniffing around, and flick at them with a long whippy stick.

After a while, one of the younger men noticed that Eyre was awake, and came over to kneel down beside him.

Eyre said, 'Minil, the girl. Is she all right?'

The young man grinned, revealing several missing teeth, and pointed towards the far side of the fire. There, covered up by blankets, Minil was sleeping; watched over by an old woman.

'Thank God,' said Eyre.

'Thank God,' the Aborigine repeated.

Eyre pointed to his lips. 'Do you have any water?'

The young man grinned again, and produced a shaped wooden bowl, filled with muddy-looking water. Eyre took it, and finished it in three large swallows. It wasn't enough to quench his thirst, but it seemed impolite to ask for any more, particularly since the families may not have had very much to last themselves the night. Muddy water meant there had been hours of painstaking digging at water-holes. That much he knew from experience.

Soon the elderly chief who had first greeted him came over, and shyly shook his hand. He gave a long speech, occasionally turning towards the fire, and pointing towards the roasting kangaroos, and Eyre understood that he was being invited to stay for a while, and share in the meal. 'You're very kind,' acknowledged Eyre, nodding and smiling. 'I have been trying to reach the sea. Fowler's Bay, perhaps. Yalata, isn't that what you call it?' He made his fingers walk across the kangaroo-hide blanket, and said, 'Yalata.'

'Ah, Yalata!' said the old man, beaming back at Eyre, and clapping his hands. Then he pointed towards the south-west; in a far more southerly direction than Eyre had imagined that Fowler's Bay would actually lie.

'Thank God,' the young man repeated.

The old man placed his hand over his bony chest, and said, '*Ngottha* . . . Winja.' Then he said, 'Winja,' again, and beamed some more. Eyre took this to mean that his name was Winja; and in return laid his own hand over his chest, and said, 'Eyre.'

For some reason, this caused great hilarity, and the young man fell on to his back in laughter, and kicked his legs. Even old Winja cackled uncontrollably, and had to wipe his eyes. He called out to the rest of the Aborigines there, and tapped his finger on Eyre's shoulder, and said, 'Eyre.' And there was even more laughter, and tapping of sticks, as Eyre's name was repeated all the way around the encampment.

The younger man recovered his composure enough to point to his own chest, and announce himself as 'Ningina.'

Ningina brought Eyre another bowlful of water, and watched him carefully while he drank it. It was only then that he decided that Eyre was fit enough to come across the camp and see Minil. He held Eyre's elbow solicitously, and talked to him all the time, as if he were a child taking his very first steps. In fact Eyre's knees felt so watery that he was glad of the encouragement. He squatted down beside Minil, and reached out to touch her forehead.

Minil stirred, and opened her eyes. Eyre suddenly felt overwhelmed with affection for her, and gladness that she was alive; and by sheer relief that Winja and his people had saved them from the desert. His throat tightened, and the first tears that he had been able to cry since they had started out on their expedition burst into his eyes.

'We're safe,' he told her. 'These people have saved us.'

Minil closed her eyes again and slept. Eyre was led back to the fire, where a *buka* was draped around his shoulders, and he was given some of the first of the kangaroo meat. He ate it very slowly; watched all the time with unblinking intentness by tribespeople all around him, who appeared to regard every movement of his jaw as being of almost magical interest. The meat was fresh, and well-cooked; and although Eyre's stomach had shrunk during his days without food, he forced himself to eat as much of it as he was offered. He remembered what Dogger had told him about surviving in the outback; and he had been through too much hunger to want to suffer like that again. He even sucked the grease from his hands.

Later that evening, Minil woke again, and one of the women fed her with dried quandong fruit and kangaroo-fat mixed with ground grass-seed into little flat cakes, and gave her repeated drinks of water. She came and sat by the fire with Eyre, tightly wrapped in a blanket; and Winja and Ningina soon came to join them, noisily chewing *pitjuri* leaves blended with ashes. Minil was a Nyungar, and could not translate everything they were saying, but they

418

managed to communicate haltingly; and Winja's natural good humour filled most of the gaps in their conversation with nods and smiles and cackles of laughter.

As she spoke, Minil repeated everything she said to Eyre, so that he could pick up as many Aboriginal words as possible, and occasionally join in. Both Winja and Ningina seemed to think that Eyre was irresistibly comic, and whenever he spoke they would hiss with suppressed amusement, and clutch their hands over their mouths to stop themselves from laughing out loud. Winja explained to Minil that they were not being disrespectful, but there was a long-standing joke in their tribe that somehow involved *earea* bushes, although they couldn't make it comprehensible to a white man. Minil tried to explain the joke to Eyre by saying that his announcement when he had first spoken to Winja was roughly the equivalent of having said, 'You, Winja, chief of your people—me, small bush.'

The conversation grew more serious, however, when Minil told Winja about Yonguldye, and what had happened at the Yarrakinna corroboree. 'Yonguldye is not dead, not as far as we know, and he is still following us with the *kurdaitja* shoes . . . his people have already killed Mr Eyre's good friend, and one of his black trackers. This is why we are travelling westwards. Partly, to find a new road to the west. Partly, because we cannot go back.'

Winja said, 'There is no road to the west.'

'*You* are travelling west,' said Minil.

'We are following kangaroo.'

'Somewhere, there must be a road to the west.'

'We have never seen one. There is no water until you reach Gabakile.'

'How far is that?'

Winja spat *pitjuri* juice, 'A whole lifetime if you die on the way.'

They talked well into the night. Winja had heard the ancient story of the *djanga* who returns from the land beyond the sunset, although the version he knew was slightly different; in that the *djanga* assuaged his guilt by asking the medicine-man to bring the boy back to life, and whispering all the secrets of death in the boy's ear. He gave the story one more twist, however, which may have explained why Yonguldye had been so determined to track Eyre down. In Winja's version of the legend, the *djanga* had to be prevented from returning to the skies, because then he would have told all the other spirits that mortal men now knew the secrets of the dead, and the other spirits in jealousy and anger might well have hunted down as many men as they could find, and kill them, as a punishment. 'The spirits will say, "if these men know the secrets of the dead, then let them die also." '

Eyre said, 'Do you believe that I could be the *djanga*?'

There was more laughter, and thigh-slapping. 'You! You are a bush! How can you be a *djanga*!'

But then Winja said, more seriously, 'You are a white man; not a *djanga*. We live well with the white people. We travel from the Murray River to the Swan River, to meet our kinsmen and to trade skins and flour. We also trade with the white people. We do not want any difficulty with the white people. Last year, two of my people were wrongly accused of burning a house; one of them was hanged. I do not want this to happen again. From what this girl says, you are an important man in Adelaide; therefore, we will take care of you, and make sure that Yonguldye does not harm you. I understand about the legend of the *djanga*; but life is changing. I do not believe that the black people can ever stand up against the white people. That is a lost dream. The best we can hope for is that we can live together side-by-side and that the white people respect our hunting and fishing places, and our sacred grounds. Already they have destroyed many of my kinsmen's fish-traps. Already many of our sacred places have been occupied by farms and settlements. But, we wish only to live our lives in peace.'

That night, Eyre and Minil slept together under a hide blanket close to the fire. They did not make love; they were too ill and too exhausted; but they held each other close, and kept each other warm, and when dawn came they were both much calmer and more collected, and they greeted each other with a kiss.

'I am beginning to see who you are,' said Eyre.

'Yes,' said Minil.

'You and I are just the same. I didn't understand that at first. We both went out into the wilds to look for ourselves; for what we were. You went to look for your people and I went to look for glory.'

Minil kissed him again, his lips, his cheeks, his closed eyelids.

'What do you think we found?' she asked him.

Eyre stroked her bare shoulder. 'I think we found that there is more than one truth. The truth of the desert is quite different from the truth of the town. All of the myths and the legends are alive out here; they all have reality and meaning. But back in Adelaide they will be nothing but traveller's tales. When you return to New Norcia, and put on your pinafore again, will Mrs Humphreys believe that you lived with Yonguldye, the terrible Mabarn Man? Will she believe what happened here, in the desert? Magic can only exist where people believe in it.'

Minil smiled. 'I do not understand you when you talk like this.'

'No,' said Eyre. 'But it doesn't matter.'

Winja happily agreed that Eyre and Minil could travel with his people as far westwards as they wanted to go. He declared that he was not at all frightened of Yonguldye; and that if Yonguldye and his warriors caught up with them, there would be a great *pungonda*, and that Yonguldye would be sent back to wherever he had come from. Ningina in particular seemed to relish the idea of a *pungonda*, and showed Eyre his axe, which was made of hard stones stuck to a kangaroo-bone with gum, and hung ostentatiously around his waist in a belt of oppossum-fur.

'Bong,' he said, and demonstrated the axe's use with a mock-blow to Eyre's head.

After gorging themselves with cold kangaroo-meat, the small tribe set off towards the south-west. Winja and Ningina led the men out in front, with their spears and their clubs, looking out for game. The women followed behind, carrying on their heads and on their shoulders their dilly-bags and wooden bowls, and digging-sticks, and the children who were too young to walk.

They were a strange but beautiful group. As they crossed the scrubby plains, Eyre rode behind them and admired their unselfconscious elegance, the dark curves of their bodies, the easy movements of their buttocks and legs. And the women walked with impeccable balance, even though some of them had bags and bowls and children to carry; their bare breasts pendulous and their stomachs protruding, but graceful beyond anything he had seen at an Adelaide ladies' tea-party.

For Eyre's sake, and Minil's sake, Winja ordered his families to rest halfway through the day; and they drank a little water and ate lizards and a paste of green ants. Eyre was too hungry to be squeamish. Last night's heavy meal of kangaroo meat had begun to restore his stomach to working-order, and it was demanding more. The lizard-flesh, singed over a small fire, was quite tasty. Firm, and slightly nutty, like smoked chicken.

That night they reached a water-hole, and made camp. Ningina had been unlucky, and had caught only a stray joey; but the women had brought in a collection of hopping-mice and lizards and a mallee fowl with a broken wing.

And so for three days they travelled this way, slowly heading south-west; while Eyre and Minil became gradually more accepted into the family, and Eyre began to speak a hesitant version of Winja's language.

On the morning of the third day, however, Ningina crawled into their shelter and said, 'We have caught sight of the warriors who are following you. They are less than two hours away. Soon there will be a great *pungonda*.'

Thirty-One

It was well past eleven o'clock before Eyre caught sight of them clearly. There must have been fifteen or twenty of them, well strung out, walking swiftly and with great deliberation. Soon he could see their spears, balanced over their shoulders, their hardwood shafts catching the high sunlight. Then he saw the great head-dress that belonged to Yonguldye, the Darkness, and he knew that his nemesis was at last going to catch up with him. He might have cheated death on Christmas Day, but sooner or later he was going to have to face up to Yonguldye.

Minil, sitting on her horse in a kangaroo-hide *buka* decorated with ochre, said, 'What can we do? We can't let Winja and Ningina fight our battle for us.'

'They want to,' Eyre reminded her. 'It's a question of honour. Well, I'm not certain that honour's the right word; but it's certainly a question of pride.'

'It seems terrible, to risk their lives.'

'I can give myself up.'

Minil stared at him. 'No,' she said. 'They'll kill you. I couldn't bear it.'

'Then we have no choice but to protect ourselves as best we can. And when I say ourselves, that means Winja and Ningina and all of their people.'

Eyre rode forward, between the walking women, and caught up with Winja.

'I wish to ask you a question,' he said, in Aborigine.

'Ask it,' said Winja.

'Do you truthfully wish to fight against Yonguldye, just for me? There is no thought in my mind that you are a coward. I wish only to protect your women and your children.'

Winja looked up at Eyre narrowly. 'You still do not understand, do you?'

'I do not know what it is that I am supposed to understand.' He stumbled over this phrase, and had to say half of it in English.

But Winja said, 'We found you; and saved your life. Your life therefore belongs to us, and the choice of whether to protect it or not is ours alone. We have decided. We will protect you; and the girl Minil. Some time in your future life you will return the favour. But for now, be prepared only to fight alongside kinsmen.'

Eyre shaded his eyes against the sun. 'There's some cover up ahead; a few rocks. Not much, but enough to give us some advantage. He translated what he had said into Winja's language, as best he could, using the word *bojalup*, which meant 'place of rocks', and ducking his head to illustrate 'cover from spears'.

The rocks were very sparse; only a scattering of limestone spheres littered across the scrub. They looked as if some giant god from the dreaming had tired of playing marbles, and thrown his handful across the desert. In fact, they were the remains of a ridge that had been undermined by water and by gritty wind. Winja and Eyre gathered the women and children as far behind the rocks as they could, with Minil to supervise them; and then they went to the front of the outcropping to arrange the men, with their spears and clubs.

Eyre said, 'Look—we will stand here, right out in front of the rocks—then, when Yonguldye and his warriors begin to throw spears—we can run back.'

'Run back?' frowned Ningina.

'Not out of fear. Out of wisdom. They will run after us in among the rocks, and then we can trap them, and kill them.'

'I do not want to run back,' said Ningina, pouting. 'I have never run back from my enemy.'

Winja glared at him. 'You will run back when you are told to. Are you my *ngauwire*, my son?'

'Yes, *ngaiyeri*.'

'Then you will run back.'

Eyre loaded his rifle while they waited for Yonguldye to

catch up with them. He would probably only have time for one shot; but this time he hoped he would be able to hit Yonguldye somewhere fatal. It was a miracle that Yonguldye had already survived what must at the very least have been a severe powder-burn, and then a glancing rifle-ball to the side of the head. Perhaps there was something in his magic, after all. Perhaps, like the fabled Mabarn Men of the past, he was invincible, and possessed of eternal life.

The sun began to fall to the west; and this to Eyre was another advantage. Yonguldye and his warriors as they approached would have the glare of the early afternoon in their eyes, as well as a quarry that was going to behave completely uncharacteristically, and run away. Running-away was not a recognised tactic in Aborigine battles; the tradition was to stand firm with club in hand and fight blow-for-blow until you or your enemy dropped dead.

Yonguldye looked unnervingly threatening as he approached. His huge black emu-feather head-dress dipped and blew with every step he took; and he walked with a long, awkward limp that must have been caused either by the two shots that Eyre had fired at him or by the exhausting length of his pursuit. At first, because of the rippling heat, Eyre was unable to see his feet; but as he came nearer, only a hundred yards away, he could distinguish the dreaded *kurdaitja* shoes, of emu feathers and human blood, the shoes which unerringly guided a Mabarn Man towards his victim. Yonguldye had followed Eyre for hundreds of miles now, through the heat and dust of high summer; and he had found him.

Eyre stepped forward with his rifle raised. Winja caught his arm, but Eyre said, 'No. Let me speak to him.'

Yonguldye stopped, and raised one hand in the sign that meant greeting. He was wrapped in a kangaroo-skin *buka*, the fringes of which were tied with coloured threads and rows of tiny bandicoot skulls, which rattled as he walked. The rest of his skulls and magical apparatus were being carried by two young boys who stood at the back of the group.

Eyre could see now that Yonguldye's face was scarred on the left side; a half-healed bullet wound which had tattooed his skin with black powder. The powder burns which Eyre had inflicted on him at Yarrakinna were presumably concealed beneath his *buka*. Yonguldye's expression however was haughty and disdainful; the look of a man of power and influence. A man who had proved himself to be the greatest of all clever-men: unstoppable and impossible to kill.

Eyre called, 'What do you want, Yonguldye?'

Yonguldye kept his hand raised. Some of his warriors shifted uneasily around him, and one or two of them lodged their spears into their woomeras. Behind him, Eyre could hear Winja's men moving forward a few paces, to protect the white man whose life they now owned.

Yonguldye let out a great harsh crowing, which made Eyre's back tingle with alarm. Then he spread his arms wide, and came out with a long screeching chant, punctuated by raucous and repetitive cries, which sounded like an imitation of a red-tailed cockatoo.

Winja called back something in return which sounded to Eyre like mockery. He couldn't understand any of the words, but Winja's tone was 'Come on, then, puffed-up one, come and fight if that's what you've walked all this way for.'

Yonguldye stopped screeching and crossed his arms over his chest. Then he said in broken English—English which Minil must have taught him, 'You, *djanga*, have killed many. You too must die.'

'You would have killed me first, Yonguldye. You and Joolonga.'

'Joolonga led you to find me. But now you must die. The story must finish.'

'The story is only a story, Yonguldye. I am not the *djanga*.'

Yonguldye shook his head, and all his skulls and his

426

beads shivered as he did so. 'The message came. I was in Woocalla; two men came from Tandarnya and spoke.' For a moment he couldn't think of the words; but at last he said, 'The *djanga* has returned, they said. He is here and he will come to find you. The story has come to be.'

'Why do you want to kill me?' Eyre asked him.

'You must not go back to the land of *tinyinlara*.'

'But I have not yet told you what is in my head.'

'You kill too many,' said Yonguldye. 'In your head is death. I will learn what is in your head when you are killed.'

'So it's true; you want to eat my brains.'

'The story says that you will give your head. The story must come to be.'

Eyre lifted his rifle and pointed it straight at Yonguldye's chest. 'I am not the *djanga*. And I am telling you now, unless you go back to where you came from, you and all your warriors, I will shoot you, and kill you, right here, and right now.'

Yonguldye looked at Eyre with eyes as dull and primaeval as grey creek-washed pebbles. Then he lifted a single finger; and immediately, one of his warriors leaned back, his spear poised in his woomera, and launched it towards Eyre's head. Eyre caught sight of the flash of movement out of the corner of his eye, and heard the whistling called *bimblegumbie*, and dropped smartly to one knee, and fired his rifle towards the knot of warriors. The shot was overcharged, and deafeningly loud; and a cloud of blue smoke rolled through the Aborigines like a frightened ghost. One of them cried out, and spun to the dust; and then Eyre was running back towards Winja and Ningina, shouting, '*Back! Back!*' and waving his arm at them to retreat.

Winja ran back towards the rocks straight away; but Ningina hesitated. Two spears whistled dangerously close to him; but then Eyre seized his arm and pulled him along after him, into the ambush they had prepared. Winja had already scrambled up on to the rocks and was standing there with his spear drawn back to catch the first of Yonguldye's men as they came running and whooping after them.

Eyre leaped up on to the rocks beside him, and picked up the stone-headed club that Ningina had lent him. Yonguldye, startlingly, was right behind him, and swung at him with a kangaroo-bone axe, tearing the leg of his britches and grazing his left calf. Then the rocks were crowded with howling, keening warriors, and a sudden burst of spears clattered down all around them like a hailstorm, followed by racketing stones and tumbling axes.

Eyre leaped higher up on to the rocks, but Yonguldye climbed up after him, his sharp teeth bared, his face contorted with concentration and anger. His huge emu-feather head-dress fluttered and blew in the afternoon wind, and the skulls around his *buka* set up a shaking, shattering noise, like the death-rattle of a dying man. Carefully, feeling the rocks behind him, Eyre backed away until he was right up against a sheer wall of eroded limestone.

Yonguldye hit out at him again; once, twice, and the kangaroo-bone axe made a soft *whew* sound as it flew past Eyre's arms. Eyre swung back at him; and their weapons jarred and clashed together, and for one moment they gripped each other and wrestled hand-to-hand. Then Eyre let himself drop back against the rock, and as Yonguldye lunged towards him, his axe raised, Eyre pressed his back against the rock to support himself, and kicked out at Yonguldye with both legs. His boots hit the medicine-man hard in the pelvis; and with a desperate shout, Yonguldye fell backwards off the rocks, and tumbled like an overbalancing emu on to the dusty ground. Eyre jumped after him, and struggled astride him, pinning him down. Then he lifted his club threateningly over Yonguldye's head, and shouted at him, 'Yonguldye! Listen to me!'

Yonguldye stared up at him, wild-eyed. Eyre's heart was galloping, and he felt that he could hardly breathe.

'Call your people off!' Eyre demanded. 'Call them off! Tell them to put down their weapons!'

Yonguldye spat, and struggled, and cursed Eyre in a

hissing stream of Wirangu that Eyre began to think would never stop. All around them, Winja men battled with Yonguldye's warriors; and even as Eyre knelt in the dust, pinning Yonguldye down, a spray of warm blood spattered over them both, and a man shrieked with agony, and fell heavily to the ground close beside them, bleeding and jerking.

Without any further hesitation, Eyre knocked Yonguldye in the side of the face with his stone club as hard as he could. Yonguldye grunted with pain, and twisted his head away, in case Eyre hit him again.

'Tell your people to drop their weapons!' Eyre shouted at him. 'Tell them to stop fighting! Otherwise, damn it, I'll beat your brains out!'

Yonguldye hesitated for a moment, and then closed his eyes; and let out a hoarse, commanding roar. It was so harsh and so supernaturally loud that it made Eyre's head ring; but then he had heard about medicine-men who could simply shout their victims to death. He looked up, and the fighting had suddenly stopped. The Aborigines eyed each other cautiously; and then Yonguldye spoke his command again, more softly this time; and one by one, clubs and spears and fighting boomerangs dropped to the ground.

Eyre climbed up off Yonguldye's body, and brushed down his shirt. 'That's it.' he said. 'That's the finish of it. No more story. No more coming after me with those *kurdaitja* shoes. It's finished, do you understand?'

Yonguldye was helped to his feet by two of his warriors. He stood and faced Eyre with undisguised malevolence; scowling like Kinnie Gerthe cat-demon, whose single pleasure was to eat men alive. Winja came forward and stood next to Eyre, as protective as before, holding his bloody club raised as an obvious warning that the battle was over; and that Yonguldye's men should not make any attempt to renew it.

'Are any of your people hurt?' Eyre asked him.

Winja said, 'Ningina has been wounded in the leg, but that is all. We have killed two of theirs.'

Eyre said to Yonguldye, 'This is what happens when you try to make a story come true. Men die. This bloodshed is your responsibility.'

Yonguldye held his hand to his reddened cheek. 'Truly you are the *djanga*.'

No, Yonguldye, I am not the *djanga*.'

'It is spoken that the true *djanga* will always deny his real name,' said Yonguldye, in Wirangu this time. Winja translated as best he could, into his own language.

Eyre said to Winja, 'Tell this medicine-man that he must go now and never trouble me again. Tell him that I am not the *djanga*, but that I will kill anyone who suggests that I am; or comes anywhere near me. Tell him that if he continues to track me, he will meet an extremely sticky end.'

'Stick-ee end?' frowned Winja.

'Yes. Tell him I will turn him into a grub and eat him for breakfast.'

Winja explained all this to Yonguldye, shouting to make himself understood in the same way that an English traveller would have shouted at a French douanier. Yonguldye listened with rage and mystification, glaring at Eyre as if he wished that death-spears could fly from his eyes and strike Eyre dead where he stood. At last, with an irritable chop of his hand, he indicated to Winja that he had heard enough. Then he limped forward two or three paces, and inspected Eyre even more closely, his face smeared with sweat-runnelled *wilga*, his eyes bloodshot.

'You are the *djanga* of the story even if you will not say so. You are the dead one who has come to give us knowledge. But you will not. Why?'

'Yonguldye, I am not the *djanga*. I am a perfectly ordinary human being, not a ghastly white spirit from beyond the sunset.'

'You have betrayed us!' screeched Yonguldye, with

430

spittle flying from his lips. 'I curse you! I curse you! I curse you!'

Shaking with anger, he plucked a shell-bladed knife from out of his possum-fur belt, and brandished it under Eyre's nose. Winja immediately stepped closer, his spear raised towards Yonguldye's chest, but Yonguldye waved him away again with that same impatient chop. 'We have waited for your coming for countless years,' he said, half in English and half in Wirangu. 'Now you have betrayed us; and left us naked in the face of the white-faced people who would steal our lands and break our fishing-traps and take our women. You have the secret. Why will you not give it to us? Is this a punishment? What have we done?'

Winja translated as much of Yonguldye's fulminating speech as he could follow. Eyre listened with apprehension; and with some sadness. There was nothing he could do for Yonguldye. There was nothing he could do for any of the Aborigine people. He was barely surviving himself.

He said at last, 'Go, Yonguldye. I will take your message to the white people; and do whatever I can.'

Yonguldye roared at him in utter frustration and fury. Then, turning the shell-bladed knife towards his own body, he ripped a deep diagonal cut all the way from his left nipple to his right hip, almost cutting the nipple right off. Blood ran down his belly in a bright red curtain, and rivered down his thighs. But then he transferred the knife to the other hand, and cut himself again, slicing a cross from one side of his body to the other.

The pain of his cuts must have been mortifying; but he threw down his bloody knife and stood facing Eyre with raw defiance on his face and both fists clenched like a madman. The lower half of his body glistened with running blood, as if he had been wading in it.

'If this is the end of our people; if we are betrayed even by the spirits; then so be it. We will fight to the very end of our existence, and that is the word that you can carry back with you to Ngurunderi.'

Winja translated a little of this, but very perfunctorily.

Winja himself believed that the fight against the white man was already lost; and that Yonguldye was trying to live in a world which had long ago come to an end. He also respected Eyre, and was anxious not to upset him by saying anything slighting about white people, or (if he did happen to be a spirit) about spirits.

But Eyre approached Yonguldye, trying hard not to look down at his terrible self-inflicted wounds, close enough to shake hands with him, and said, 'You are a proud and terrible man. You are a great wizard and a great chief. The greatest of all Mabarn Men.'

Yonguldye stared at him with those dark, unreadable eyes, and said nothing. Out of his shirt pocket, Eyre produced the mana stone which had been given to him by the Aborigine warriors on Hindley Street. With considerable ceremony, he held it out on the open palm of his hand, and offered it to Yonguldye.

'Your people gave me this totem. Now it is imbued with my magic. Let it now be your totem, as a gift from me. I cannot give you any more.'

Yonguldye swayed. The blood on his body had now begun to congeal; and Eyre could see that the cuts, although gory, were not fatally deep. They had not been an attempt at suicide. Rather, they had been meant as a gesture that Yonguldye could inflict on himself greater pain than anything that Eyre could force him to suffer; that he was master of his own fate.

Eyre continued to hold out the mana stone, and said, 'Please.'

Yonguldye took the stone, and held it up between finger and thumb, turning it over, and examining it, although at the same time never letting his eyes stray very far away from Eyre. At last he slipped the stone into a small bag he was carrying around his waist, and bowed his head.

'The future has now been altered,' he said. Winja translated this as, 'from tomorrow, all the days will not be the shape they were expected to be.' Yonguldye went on, 'There will be storms. This has been foretold. There will be rain in places where there has never been rain before. The moons which live beyond the horizon will appear whole; instead of being cut up into stars by the giant who watches over them; and they will circle the world. But what these days will hold for my people, that is uncertain. The story did not happen as it was meant to happen. Therefore, everything will be different.'

Eyre realised that in his anger and his humiliation, Yonguldye was trying to rationalise what had happened. He could not bring himself to believe that Eyre was not the expected *djanga* after all; because when would a white-faced man ever again cause the death of an Aborigine boy, and come journeying through the outback looking for absolution as Eyre had? Not for years, perhaps not ever, whereas Yonguldye badly needed to believe that his people would learn the magic knowledge of the white people now, and have the strength and the knowledge to stand up for what they believed to be rightfully theirs.

He was still furious at Eyre; still bitter and grieved about the men who had died; but in spite of his anger he had to accept his defeat at the hands of the *djanga*, or else he would be unable to believe in the *djanga* at all, and that would mean despair.

'I will go now,' he said to Eyre, with terrifying gravity; and still bleeding he turned and beckoned to his warriors. The sand beneath his feet was speckled dark with blood. But without any further ceremony, he limped away towards the east, under the hot mid-afternoon sun. Neither he nor his warriors looked back; and none of them made any attempt either to pick up their weapons or to bury their dead. Let the dead bury their dead. Let the *djanga* take the responsibility for the havoc he had wrought.

Ningina came hobbling up. The spear-wound in his thigh was now wound tightly with bloodstained hide. He shaded his eyes and watched the wobbling black figures of Yonguldye and his warriors grow steadily smaller.

'You should have killed that medicine-man,' he said. 'You would have been a great hero.'

'No,' said Eyre. 'This is not a time for heroes.'

'What do you mean?'

'Eyre took off his hat. Behind him, there was the *pick-pick-pick* of digging-sticks, as Winja's people dug graves for their dead enemies. It was 109 degrees, out here on the treeless plain called Bunda Bunda, and it looked as if the heat had liquefied the whole world. A molten blue sky, and a desert that rippled like the surface of a muddy lake. Through the liquidness, Yonguldye and his men walked and walked and walked, heading towards a new destiny; and leaving littered behind them the remains of their very last dream.

Thirty-Two

They journeyed west through the desert, following the kangaroo. Week after week, under skies that were devastatingly blue, living on charred meat and half-cooked lizards and whatever water they were able to suck out of the mud.

Eyre discarded his soiled and tattered shirt; and his back reddened and peeled and burned and then tanned as dark as wood. He was surprised to see, one morning, the birth of an Aborigine baby, slithering out of its mother's vulva as pale as a white baby; and he realised then how close to the European races the Aborigines were. Just because they had migrated to this strange desert continent, millions of years ago, and just because they had adapted to heat and drought, and a nomadic way of life, that had not denied them their ancestry, nor their intelligence, nor their racial heritage.

Eyre, as he rode along with them, thought of the words that Captain Cook had written, only seventy years ago, when he had tried to describe the natives of 'New-Holland' to his English readers:

> They may appear to some to be the most wretched people upon Earth, but in reality they are far happier than we Europeans. The Earth and the sea of their own accord furnishes them with all things necessary for life, they covet not Magnificent Houses, Household-stuff &c, they live in a warm and fine Climate and so they have very little need of Clothing, for many to whom we gave Cloth left it carelessly upon the Sea beach and in the woods as a thing they had no manner of use for. They think themselves provided with all the necessarys of Life and that they have no superfluities.

For Eyre, these weeks of journeying across the land of Bunda Bunda with Winja and his people was like an extraordinary but revelatory dream. He hardly ever thought about Captain Sturt, or Christopher, or even of Charlotte. He was completely preoccupied with hunting kangaroo, with helping to skin and roast whatever game they could find; with digging for water and building fires. After five weeks, he went naked, and tied his trousers around his neck to protect his shoulders from the sun. There seemed to be very little point in being the only dressed-up man in a friendly company of people without clothes. Winja's women laughed openly at his white bottom; until Winja shouted at them, and threatened to prod them with his spear. Winja still thought a great deal of Eyre; especially after the way he had defeated Yonguldye; and he would not have him insulted.

Eyre and Minil grew closer all the time; for both of them were discovering the simple truth of survival in the outback; and at the same time the complicated truth of

Aborigine beliefs. A love developed between them that no longer required explanations or understanding. It consisted of touches, and close embraces, and looks, and kisses, and of holding each other in the night, when the moon was high and the wind was freezing cold. Sometimes it expressed itself in affectionate silence, when they rode together during the day, with their last solitary pack-horse following obediently behind them. Two naked people, a man with a wide-brimmed hat and a girl with a tight kangaroo-skin headband and wild black hair, on horses, on the hottest of all imaginable days. At other times, it expressed itself in violent lovemaking; when Eyre would force Minil on to her back and raise her legs high in the air and lance her and lance her deep into her vagina until she tore at his hair and screamed out loud, regardless of who could hear or who could see.

It was a life of incendiary passion and unreal tranquillity; when the days and the weeks no longer mattered, and were no longer counted; when Eyre rediscovered his basic thirsts and his fundamental hungers, his throat and his stomach and his penis; but with a force and a dignity that gave new meaning to everything he felt. Nothing could be cruder than to have to squat in the sand, in front of the girl you loved and the people you knew, and excrete. But nothing could be more spiritual than to sit with them around their various wind-blown fires; just before the sun had set across the plain; and offer prayers to the greater Gods who had created the world, and all the abundance that it could offer.

They reached the coast one morning in March, on a cool and breezy day when Eyre had decided to put on his shirt; although he still wore his trousers tied around his waist. They came across it quite suddenly. One minute they were walking through thick mallee scrub; the next they were standing on the edge of a cliff overlooking the shore.

After so many months traversing the desert, Eyre was peculiarly moved by the sight of the sea. He climbed slowly down from his horse, and walked to the very edge of the cliff, and looked down at the tumbling, seething surf as if he had never seen anything like it before. Winja stood a little way off, watching him with quiet paternalism, as if he in his turn had been waiting for this moment, and expecting what Eyre's feelings would be. Minil came up, too, and stayed close to Eyre, holding his arm, and for a long time they watched the long curve of the ocean, from east to west, and the gulls which dived and screeched for Goolwa cockles.

Some of Winja's men clambered down to the shore, where they found a dead pelican lying among the rocks, its beak rising and falling in the tide. Whooping, they brought it up to the clifftop, and hacked it open, so that they could drag out its entrails. Tonight, the families would all share a treat: pelican's intestines filled with heated fat. Eyre watched them cutting open the bird, and the white feathers flying in the wind, and smiled.

'You have become one of us,' said Winja, quietly.

'No,' said Eyre. 'I can never become one of you. I only wish that I could. Even poor Joolonga could never become one of you; not again. I have to go on; to finish this journey. I have learned now that God wills it, whoever God may be.'

'God is in your heart,' said Winja.

Eyre took Winja's hand, and squeezed it hard. 'God is in you, Winja. God is in all of us. That's what my father used to say, and it's true.'

The sea surged and splashed below them. Far away, beyond the ocean, lay Antarctica. Behind them stretched the hot and desolate land called Bunda Bunda. Eyre felt as if he had arrived at last at the conjunction of the Lord's hugest and most impressive creations. This was not the place where He had run out of ideas. This was the place where He had foregone conventional beauty in search of truth, and found it. It was apposite that it had cost Eyre such suffering to reach this place; because no truth could be reached without suffering. Eyre got down on his knees, and closed his eyes, and while Minil laid her hand on his shoulder, he repeated the words of Psalm 86. 'Give ear, O Lord, to my prayer; and give heed to the voice of my supplications! Teach me Thy way, O Lord; I will walk in Thy truth. Arrogant men have risen up against me, and a band of violent men have sought my life. But Thou, O Lord, art a God merciful and gracious, slow to anger and abundant in loving kindness and truth.'

That afternoon, on the beach, while the women baked cockles in the sand, and the men fished, Eyre baptised Winja and Ningina in the foam; and there was singing and stick-clapping, and the fires were lit for a family corroboree.

Winja said, as they sat around the fire eating the cockles, 'Tonight we must begin your *engwura*, Eyre. You have become one of us; but you are still an *utyana*, an uninitiated youth. Your *engwura* is your initiation ceremony. You must be a man, not only among the white-faces, but among the black-faces.'

Eyre scooped another cockle out of its shell. 'Can't we leave it until tomorrow? It hurts, doesn't it?'

'What is pain?' asked Winja.

'Pain is when your body hurts,' Eyre answered him, tartly.

Winja pressed both hands against his head. 'Your body will hurt, but inside your head you will feel nothing but peace.'

Eyre frowned, and Ningina laughed. Eyre turned to him crossly, and said, 'I suppose *you* weren't nervous, when you were about to be initiated?'

'I was shaking!' laughed Ningina. Everyone around the fire joined in, and some of them threw pebbles at Eyre and cried, '*Utyana! Utyana!*'

Eyre said to Winja, 'Are you seriously inviting me to be initiated?'

Winja nodded. 'Seriously. You are one of us. It was Baiame's will that we met you in the desert.'

Eyre glanced at Minil. Minil looked remarkably pretty tonight, with her headband, and her patterned *buka* drawn over her shoulders, and a string of red-painted beads decorating her plump bare breasts. He felt that she had found contentment now: with an Aborigine family to satisfy her need for freedom, and to get back among her own people; but with Eyre to love her and to give her the European sophistication which Winja's people lacked. He felt regretful in a way that she had found such contentment, because it could never last. Winja and his families would have to be on their way, and Eyre would have to return to Adelaide; and where would that leave Minil? Eyre could sense the pain that would inevitably end their relationship; he could sense it already, now that he was down by the sea, and closer to civilisation. He just hoped that it would not be so great that neither of them could bear it.

He looked at Minil laughing and clapping her hands by the fire. He smelled the brine from the ocean, and the sizzling aroma of charcoal-roasted cockles. He saw the clouds overhead, fine and golden-grey. And he wished then that this moment could last for ever; that it would never pass, and that he would always be here, on this evening, for the rest of his life.

But the night came; and passed; and in the morning the sun stretched itself across the ocean. Eyre noticed, however, that Winja's people were not making their usual preparations for travelling on. Instead, they were lighting fresh cooking-fires, and the women were preparing food, and the children were playing in the scrub. Winja came up to Eyre wearing a heavily decorated *buka*, and said, 'Today we have decided to rest and hunt. Perhaps you will take your gun and see if you can find kangaroo or *toora*.'

Eyre ate a sparse breakfast; and then took his rifle and the rest of his ammunition and set off alone towards the north-west to look for game. He was glad of the opportunity to think in silence. Usually, whenever they went hunting, Ningina came with him and chattered incessantly about the fights he had had with other tribes; and the time that he had outrun a big red, and jumped on to its back.

The morning was clear and sharp, and there was a fresh autumnal wind blowing inland from the sea; although once he was below the line of the cliffs, and walking through the scrub, the desert was more sheltered, and very much hotter.

He spent hours stalking a *toora*, a scrawny-looking mallee hen, and twice fired at it and missed. At last he caught it by throwing a stone at it, knocking it stunned and fluttering on to the ground, and then clubbed it with the stock of his rifle. It wasn't much to bring back to several families of hungry people, but it was better than nothing. There had been plenty of days when he and Ningina had gone out all day and come back empty-handed, except for a few lizards. The sun was beginning to go down, so he made his way back to the cliffs, following his own tracks in the dust.

Winja and Ningina and two other tribesmen were waiting for him a little way out of camp. As he came closer, Eyre was surprised to see that they were fully painted with pipe-clay and *wilga*. Winja called to him, 'How was your hunting?' and Eyre lifted up the *toora* to show what he had caught.

At that moment, all four of the Aborigines ran forward and seized him, snatching away his rifle and his game, and running with him as fast as they could back towards the camp. Eyre shouted, '*Winja! What the hell's going on! Ningina!*' but neither of them took any notice. He struggled and kicked and tried to leap away from them, but their grip on his arms was too firm, and they were obviously determined not to let him go.

As they ran through the camp, past the flickering fires and the brushwood shelters, the women and children came hurrying out, shrieking and ullulating, and calling out, '*Don't take him! Don't take him!*' in Wirangu. Some of the women tried wildly to snatch at his arms, but Ningina and his men pushed them away. Even Minil came struggling forwards, shrieking, '*Don't take him! Don't take him!*

Don't kill him!' but Winja pushed her out of the way with his spear-shaft.

The men hurried with him down the sloping pathway that led to the seashore, leaving the women behind. Eyre fought and twisted, but most of the time his feet weren't even touching the ground, and he was taken down to the beach with his legs kicking in the air, like the *toora* he had just managed to catch. He was badly frightened: it occurred to him that Winja and his people had been keeping him all this time as a living totem, as a human good-luck charm, and that now they were going to please Baiame by sacrificing him.

Perhaps they had come to believe what Yonguldye had said about him: that he was the true *djanga*, and that somehow he had betrayed the Aborigine people by not giving them the magic knowledge which had been promised by myth and by legend. Perhaps they believed that if they killed him, the true gods would look on them favourably, and protect them from white men and devil-devils. Yonguldye had wanted his brains; perhaps Winja had decided that he too had an appetite for the white man's magic.

Panting, terrified, coughing, he was dragged along the sand and around a rocky limestone headland, until he reached a cove that was out of sight of the main encampment. Here, there was a huge fire burning, its flames rolling and flaring in the dusk; and all the men of the tribe were gathered, their faces painted with circles and stripes; so that they looked like a rabble of horrifying demons, hot from hell. Eyre shouted, '*No!*' but the men forced him down on to the sand, first on to his knees, and then flat, face-down.

Winja came up and stood over him. 'Eyre-Walker, you are about to die. Everything you have been, up until now, has been a way of getting ready for this death. All of your life; all of your thinking; all of your friendships. All your prayers, too, have been directed to this one moment.'

Eyre was turned over on to his back. He looked up at

Winja; and to his surprise, the grey-bearded old man was smiling at him.

'This is your *engwura*, your initiation ceremony. Tonight, the Eyre-Walker you once used to be will die; and the new Eyre-Walker will be born. You will take a new life, and a new name.'

Eyre said, 'You scoundrel, Winja.' His relief was enormous.

Winja prodded him in the shoulder with the point of his spear. 'Tonight is not a night for you to be disrespectful. Tonight you are a boy. Only when you are initiated will you become a man. Now, you will lie there, and Galute will paint your body with the totem of our people.'

Eyre lay flat on his back on the sand while Galute and Ningina stripped him completely naked and rubbed his skin all over with pelican-fat. Then, with tongue-clenching care, Galute began to paint Eyre's skin with moistened pipe-clay and ochre, an inverted white crucifix pattern with red stripes and triangles on it. Galute painted his face, too, a mask of white with diagonal red arrows, which tightened as it dried and made Eyre feel that his whole face had turned into a clinging, rigid mask. Finally, Galute painted pipe-clay into his hair, so that it looked like a wild configuration of plumes. When Galute had finished, Eyre lay back with his arms raised, looking up at the stars and the sparks that blew from the fire, while Winja and Ningina led their people in a long song that told of the boys who came for their initiation, and discovered the secrets of the tribe.

Out of a kangaroo-skin package, they produced flat, boat-shaped wooden *churingas*, attached to long twists of twine, and as they sang they spun these around and around over their heads, producing an eerie droning noise. Winja said to Eyre, 'The women and children believe when they hear this noise that they are hearing the voices of the dead. Only initiated men know that it is the sound of the sacred *churingas*.'

The singing and the chanting continued for hours; until

at last Galute returned, this time with a knife and a wooden bowl of ashes from the fire.

'We will mark you now with the marks of a man,' he said. Eyre watched him with a tingling feeling of anticipated pain. He could have stood up now, and refused to take part in any of Winja's initiation ceremony; but he knew that it was going to be an important step forward in his life; and that it was probably going to be the ultimate expression of his radical belief that every race and every religion must be respected, no matter how bizarre it might seem to be to those brought up on the Prayer Book.

While another young man tightly held Eyre's wrists, Galute produced a sharp shell knife, and knelt down beside him. 'This is the mark of a great hunter,' he said, and before Eyre could wriggle, he sliced his shoulders, left and right, in two swift stinging strokes. Eyre bit his tongue to keep back his pain, and most of all to stop himself from crying out loud. But then Galute said, 'This is the mark of the warrior,' and cut his chest in a herringbone pattern, one deep incision after the other.

'Now the mark of Pund-jil, the great god, who caused men to wander throughout the world.' And Galute slashed his thighs.

The *churingas* whirled around and around, and the evening was overwhelmed with their endless humming, and with the sound of the surf breaking on the shore. Eyre lay mute and helpless while Galute rubbed ashes into his bloody wounds; although the stinging was almost more than he could bear; and the edges of the cuts flapped open in a way that made his nerves shrink like sea-anemones.

He closed his eyes and tried not to think of the pain. The pain seemed to wash in with the surf, in waves of scarlet. And all the time the *churingas* droned and droned, and the sticks tapped, and Winja sang his songs of Baiame and Yahloo the moon goddess, and the days in the dreamtime when men had walked the earth like gods.

Winja told him how their families had first been born. Eyre could understand very little of it: it was a lengthy and complicated fable involving all the gods who had helped and guided them. He told of the first *churingas*, and how these thin pieces of wood, when they were twirled around and around in the air, could bring back the voices of spirits and demons. He told of suffering and drought; of days when there were so many kangaroo that the desert had rippled like the sea; of moons and lyrebirds and Bunyips and wallabies. He told of pain and punishment; of joy and laughter; and above all of friendship and love. It was desperately hard, surviving in the desert, and the love that grew between both men and women was defiant and beautiful.

Eyre saw pictures in his mind. Dark figures, dancing through a dark night. He heard noises, too; hollow hums and strange sibilant whirrings. And when they approached him at last with the circumcision knife, he was prepared for what they were going to do. He lay back on the sand, watching as they lifted the blade, and as they blessed it; and when they knelt down beside him, and took his soft penis in their hands, he closed his eyes and offered no prayers to the Lord, but only to those spirits who would now accept him as a man and a warrior, to those ancient gods whose land he had chosen as his home, and these people he had chosen as his kinsmen.

Galute pinched his foreskin, and drew it out as far as he could. Then he inserted two fingers inside it, stretching it wide, and began to cut through it with his knife. Little by little, the skin bloodily came free, until the purple glans was naked. Eyre no longer thought of the pain. The pain was too dull; too much; too insistent. He looked at Winja and gave him a slow, bleary smile. Winja nodded, and held up the little fold of skin which Galute had cut off.

'You must swallow this,' he said; and offered it to Eyre on the ends of his fingers, with a wooden bowl of water.

Eyre raised his head, and opened his mouth, and accepted on his tongue the soft salty-tasting envelope of skin. He was beyond nausea now; beyond anything but going through this initiation ceremony until the end; until it was over. Winja pressed the water to his lips, and he drank, and swallowed.

But now came the greatest of all tests. Galute inserted the point of his shell-knife into the cleft of Eyre's already-blooded penis, and made the first cut downwards, to open out the urethra in the same way that Joolonga's urethra had been opened out; and Midgegooroo's, and Weeip's.

Agonising as it was, Eyre's penis rose into a stiff erection; and Galute held him tight in his fist like a spear-shaft. Then, without hesitation, Galute cut deep into the underside of his flesh, right down to his tightened scrotum. He splashed the incision from his bowlful of water to make sure that it was clean; and then stood up, and lifted both hands, and cried out loudly, 'This is a man now!'

Eyre felt hot, and then chillingly cold. He couldn't feel his genitals at all. The tapping of sticks faded; the surf sounded as if it were pouring all over him. And the drone of the *churingas* went on and on; until he couldn't decide if the droning was inside his mind or outside on the sea-shore. He shivered with a pain that he was too far gone to understand. All he wanted to do was to sleep, and to forget it forever.

Winja covered him gently with a *buka*. However harsh the initiation ritual might have been, Winja knew how to cope with the bodily shock that always followed. Keep the initiate warm and quiet for at least a day; and then gradually begin to tell him what had happened; and why; and all the stories and fables that were connected with his new totem. There were hours of stories to tell, and Winja knew them all, just as his grandfather had told them; and his grandfather's father; right back to the days of the giant kangaroo.

Eyre slept fitfully for a while; then woke in agonising pain that made him cry out. The night passed in torrents of suffering, and there was nothing he could do but lie crouched-up on the sand and endure it; while the chilly wind blew from the Indian Ocean, and the fire popped and crackled and died down, and the sun gradually rose again from the eastern horizon.

They kept him hidden away from the rest of the tribe for two weeks, while Winja told him all the stories of the dreamtime, and how their people had come to be. He was shown all the magical artefacts; all the *churingas*, all the totems, and the significance of each was explained to him in detail. He woke, slept, dreamed, and suffered. But gradually his wounds healed themselves, and he was able to walk again, sometimes down to the seashore to watch the surf deluge through the rocks; sometimes along the cliffs, with the gulls screaming over his head.

One morning he examined his penis and saw that it had stopped suppurating; and that the lips of his ceremonial incision had crusted with healthy scabs. The fountain of urine that sprayed out whenever he relieved himself was still a surprise; but at least it no longer stung him, and he was almost completely recovered. His mind was still detached, still swimming in a half-world of legend and pain, but gradually he found that he was able to focus more clearly on what had happened to him, and understand what it was that he had become, and also what it was that he could never become. He would never become a true Aborigine, he knew that. He had no desire to be. But he would always be one of their kinsmen; a *ngaitye* both physically and mentally, a friend, and no matter what happened to him during the rest of his life, nobody would be able to take that away from him. He had achieved at last what he had set out to achieve, when he had first left Adelaide on this long expedition. He had become a man, and he had discovered his soul, and what it meant to him.

Winja had said, 'Your body will hurt, but inside your head you will feel nothing but peace.' And that was true.

They brought him back to the encampment on the clifftop twenty days after he had left to look for the *toora*; and he was greeted by the women and children with shouting and clapping and singing. And there, at the far end of the camp, standing in front of her shelter naked, in spite of the wind, was Minil, her hands raised, her face shining with welcome.

They roasted kangaroo that night, and mutton-birds, and cockles, and Government House for all its pomp could never have laid out such a feast; nor excited such happiness. And any whaler passing close to the shore would have seen six or seven fires on the clifftop, and heard tapping, and music, and the voices of those to whom Australia had always belonged, and always would.

Thirty-Three

In the morning, standing amidst the smoke of the burned-out fires, Winja said, 'This is where we have to part.'

Eyre said, 'You're not going west any further?'

Winja shook his head. 'The wet season is coming. We will go back towards Yalata.'

Eyre looked at Ningina. It was a grey, overcast morning. The sea shushed dolefully against the rocks. 'You understand that I have to go on?'

'Yes,' said Ningina. 'We always knew that. We always knew that we would have to say farewell to you, sooner or later. You were not born one of us. You have become our kinsman. But you have other duties, in another world.'

Eyre looked out over the ocean. Today, it was relentlessly dull. A few gulls circled and swooped, but they were silent. The wind nagged at the clifftops, and rustled through the scrub, like a cold hand rubbing up a dog's coat the wrong way.

'I shall miss you for ever,' he said.

'No,' said Winja, taking his hand. 'It is we who shall

miss you for ever. You came from the desert; you return to the desert. We knew always that you were not a spirit, but a man. You were also one of us, even before you met us. It was prophesied when you were born that you would become one of us, and you will stay in our minds for ever, as one of our stories. Our ancestors will speak of you long after all of us have joined Ngurunderi. Eyre-Walker, who came from the east, and vanished in the west; and who defeated with one blow the great Mabarn Man Yonguldye.'

He paused, and then he said, 'There is one thing more. You are one of my people now; and therefore your son is one of my people; and your son's son.'

'I have no son,' said Eyre.

'You will,' replied Winja, looking towards Minil, 'and when you do, your son must be ours. You must return him to the tribe so that he may grow up amongst his kinsmen, and learn our ways, and undergo his *engwura*.'

Eyre held Winja close. 'My son is yours,' he pledged him. 'You gave me my life, you looked after me and protected me, you accepted me as one of your people. The least I can do is observe your laws.'

'Do not forget, then,' nodded Winja. 'On the first hour of the first day of the boy's second year, we shall be waiting for him. Our arms will be open to welcome him, and make him ours.'

'I promise it,' said Eyre.

Less than an hour later, Winja and his people were ready to leave. They stood watching as Eyre and Minil mounted their horses, and turned westwards; but it was only when they were almost out of sight, a line of black silhouettes on the clifftops, that they set up a hair-raising ululation, a warbling primaeval cry that swelled and faded on the wind, and raised their spears in salute.

Minil said, 'I am sad to leave them.'

But Eyre could say nothing except, 'Let's go,' because his feelings of pain and separation were even sharper than Winja's initiation knife.

They rode west for week after week; and gradually the

weather began to break, and the winter rains came. For days they were riding through a bright yellow landscape of mud and puddles; and then there were torrential storms, with the rain hurtling out of the sky at them like watery spears, leaving them drenched and bedraggled and silent. There was almost a whole week of sunny humidity and steam; when it was hot, but impossible to see the horizon, but then the clouds rolled back again, and the rains cascaded down, cold and unforgiving, until their *bukas* were soaked all the way through, dark and heavy, and they felt as if they had never seen a desert in their lives.

Eyre lost count of how far they had travelled. Every evening, he went to catch game; and now that the wet season had arrived, he was usually lucky. They sat close to damp, smoky fires, trying to roast bandicoots and lizards; and then they huddled up close together under whatever shelter they could improvise, while the rain clattered down, and the clouds fled past, and the whole world seemed to be flooded. Minil prayed every night to Birra-Nulu, the flood-sender, the wife of Baiame, that they should not be overwhelmed and drowned, but Birra-Nulu seemed to take very little notice of Minil's prayers; because by the time June arrived, they were riding through gullies that were waist-deep in muddy water, under skies that were as black as blankets.

Eyre's initiation wounds healed, although they were still quite tender; and by the beginning of July they were able to make love again. Some intensity, however, had gone out of their coupling, some feeling of closeness. Perhaps it was the nearness of civilisation, the anticipation that within a few days now, their extraordinary journey would be over. After their third unsatisfying bout, Minil twisted herself up in her wet *buka* and tried to sleep, while Eyre sat by the fire and chewed *pitjuri*.

'What will happen when we reach Albany?' Minil asked.

'What do you mean, what will happen?' The rain dripped off the leaves of their makeshift shelter.

'Do you want me to stay with you?'

'I don't understand. Haven't I said so?'

'You said that you loved me.'

He looked at her; and then held out his hand to her. 'I do. You know I do. Nothing's changed.'

'Something has changed.'

Eyre took the wad of wet *pitjuri* out of his mouth, and threw it aside. He wiped his lips with the back of his hand. 'My feelings for you haven't changed, if that's what you're trying to suggest.'

'Still, something has changed. I feel it.'

'It's just the weather,' said Eyre, trying to sound light-hearted.

Minil sat up, and leaned close to him. For a long time she said nothing at all, but then she stroked his arm, and asked, 'Do you really want me to stay with you, once this journey is over?'

'I'll have quite a few things to do,' said Eyre. 'I'll have to look for a new job, to begin with; and perhaps a new place to live.'

'Will you let me live with you?'

'I can't. Not to begin with. I only have one room, at Mrs McConnell's. But I expect that I can arrange something for you.'

Minil said, 'You are trying to tell me that you do not want me any more.'

'Of course not. That's ridiculous.'

'No. You are trying to tell me that when you are back among white people, you cannot have an Aboriginal girl with you. It would not be right. Other white people would not like it.'

'Minil—' he said, but she quickly shook her head.

'I have felt your love drawing away from me, mile by mile. I have already started to accept it. When you did not think that you would ever see your Charlotte again, you loved me. I was glad of your love; and I still am. But now you are thinking of returning to your friends, to your own people, and I will have to let you go.'

Eyre said, softly, 'Nothing will ever change the fact that I love you.'

'I know,' she said. 'But many people who love each other cannot live with each other.'

After that, Eyre could think of nothing more to say to her. He was still trying to work out inside his own mind what he was going to do; and he knew that to make her any more promises now would be futile and hurtful.

He had not yet allowed himself fully to face up to the truth that even this long and torturous part of his expedition had degenerated into failure. He had been trying to discover a stock-route from Adelaide to Albany; and all he had found was a wild and inhospitable coastline and a desert without water or trees or grazing. He had dreamed as they journeyed through the land of Bunda Bunda that he would be welcomed as a hero when he returned, but the closer he came to Albany, the more threadbare the dream became. He had found only that it was impossible to reach the inland sea, if there really was one; and that the Western desert was impassable to cattle. He had found no opals, no silver, and no lakes that could be used for irrigation. He hadn't even discovered any new plants or insects.

In the process of failing so completely, he had lost the lives of two black trackers and one of his dearest friends, as well as a dozen Aborigine tribesmen. Worse than that, he had squandered all of Captain Sturt's finances, and thrown away all his valuable equipment: guns, books, compasses, tents, saddlebags, shovels and picks.

Up until recently, he had fondly pictured his return to Waikerie Lodge, to claim Charlotte; but on this chilly rain-soaked night on the coast of Western Australia, crouched under a shelter of sticks and leaves with an Aborigine girl, the prospect of that, when he thought about it seriously, was dismally remote.

He would be lucky to be noticed when he finally trudged back into the municipality of Adelaide. He would be even luckier to find any employment. And there was a considerable risk that Captain Sturt would have him locked up for fraud and incompetence and God knows what other charges he could devise. Then there was the matter of Arthur Mortlock to be considered, and the deaths of Messrs Chatto and Rose. He hadn't thought about that for weeks now; but it had returned to worry at him like a bad tooth.

There was a choice, he supposed. He could stay in Western Australia, or even take a ship back to England, if he could somehow raise the money. But he knew that he would have to return to Adelaide to settle matters; whatever the outcome might be. And he did want to see Charlotte again, if only through the palings around her house, from a distance, as an elegant young fantasy that might have been his.

He slept, and snored, and had nightmares. He saw a man with a beard, smiling, and a baby who cried. Towards morning, the rain began to trickle in underneath him. He opened his eyes and saw Minil looking down at him, her face concerned.

'What is it?' he asked her.

'You were shouting out in your sleep,' she told him. 'You kept calling for the man called Dogger.'

Eyre stiffly sat up. He rubbed his eyes. Outside their shelter, the rain was still falling in heavy, rustling veils.

'Dogger,' he said; and for some reason the name sounded curiously unfamiliar, like a name in another language, from another age.

Then he looked at Minil, and frowned, and said, 'Do you think you might be having a baby?'

'Why do you ask me that?'

'I don't know. Something I dreamed.'

'Minil said, 'Since we nearly died in the desert, I have had no bleeding. I do not think that I can have babies, not now. Perhaps when this journey is over my bleeding will start again.'

Eyre crawled out from under his *buka*, and began to scrape together a few twigs and branches so that they could start a fire. The rain fell on his bare back, and made him shiver. Minil watched him with infinite sadness and care, as if she were trying to remember every movement he made, so that they would be imprinted on her mind, for ever.

Thirty-Four

They reached the crest of a hill and there below them among the gums and blackboy trees was the township of Albany. It was the first white settlement that Eyre had seen since he had left Adelaide the previous year, and he stood and stared down at it with an indescribable feeling of relief and thankfulness; but also with a surge of something that could almost have been fear. For just a moment, he saw the white people as an Aborigine might have seen them; their neat houses with thatched roofs and white-painted walls; their fences and their streets; their gardens lined with flourishing vegetables. Everything so tidily arranged, and so constricted. He saw carriages and ox-carts moving to and fro through the rutted streets, and beyond, in the curve of water that the Aborigines called Monkbeeluen and which the English called King George's Sound, there were sailing-ships at anchor, and warehouses, and smoke was rising from office chimneys.

'Minil,' said Eyre, and reached across and took her hand.

'Yes,' nodded Minil. 'I know what you are saying to me. You are saying goodbye.'

They began to ride slowly down the muddy track that took them towards the outskirts of town. They said nothing. Their pack-horse walked obediently behind them, as he had walked for nearly a thousand miles. It had stopped raining now, and a watery sun had emerged from the clouds, making the rooftops and puddles glitter brightly.

They passed a garden where a curly-headed Aborigine boy in a white shirt and britches was hoeing vegetables. He stared at them as they passed; and Eyre raised his shapeless kangaroo-skin hat, and said, 'Good morning.' He realised that he and Minil must look two dishevelled scarecrows; he with his bushy black beard and lumpy *buka*; Minil with her tattered scarf wound around her head. The boy dropped his hoe and came to the fence and watched them as they rode further down the street; and then suddenly shrieked out, '*Minil! Minil!*'

Minil reined back her horse. The boy came running after them, his bare feet splattering in the puddles. 'Minil!' he cried. His eyes were bright, and he jumped and danced all around her.

Minil said, 'It's Chucky! It's Chucky! I didn't recognise you! How you've grown up!'

'Minil!' sang Chucky. 'How everybody tells stories of where you went! They say you went with some Wirangu; and then the Wirangu told stories that you left them and went with Mr Walker, the great explorer-man!'

'What?' asked Eyre, in an unsteady voice. 'Who told these stories? How do you know about me? Who said these things?'

Chucky stopped skipping, and touched his curls respectfully. 'Are you Mr Walker, the great explorer-man?'

Minil smiled. 'This is Mr Walker.'

'Minil is my cousin, sir, from New Norcia mission. Many people here in Albany know her, sir. All of her family work at the Old Farm once, with Mrs Bird!'

'But how did you know that she was with me?' Eyre repeated.

'A ship, sir, from Adelaide. Everybody in Adelaide thought you were dead and gone, sir, dead and gone. You were all the talk! Then some Wirangu came to Adelaide,

454

sir, and said that you had gone off to the west with Minil, and with Winja's people. Then there was great excitement! You have been in all the newspaper, sir, my missis told me.'

At that moment, an elderly white man came walking down the street from the house where Chucky had been hoeing. He called, 'Chucky! Chucky! What are you doing, talking to those people? Get back to your gardening at once!'

Chucky piped up, 'But this is my cousin Minil, Mr Pope; and this is Mr Walker, the great explorer-man!'

Mr Pope stepped gingerly across the puddles and up beside Eyre's horse. He frowned at him through his spectacles. '*You* are Mr Eyre Walker?'

'Yes, sir,' said Eyre. He suddenly found that there was a sharp catch in his throat.

'But, you are dead, sir,' said Mr Pope rather bewildered. 'The news came by ship from Adelaide that you had been lost between Woocalla and Fowler's Bay.'

'I am not dead, sir,' said Eyre. 'I am only tired. This girl and I have ridden and walked all the way. I believe it is something over nine hundred miles. We have just arrived.'

He couldn't say any more. He burst into tears, and sat on his horse sobbing with exhaustion and emotion. Mr Pope looked up at him worriedly for a moment, and then took hold of his horse's bridle, and gave him his hand to help him dismount.

'Since you are not dead, Mr Walker, I suppose it is incumbent on me to welcome you to Western Australia,' said Mr Pope. 'Come along, let me help this young girl to dismount, and we will see what we can do for you. I believe Mrs Pope has some fresh mutton pies just out of the oven.'

Eyre was shaking; and so was Minil, as Chucky and Mr Pope helped her to slide off her horse. Eyre said, 'I believe I could do with a glass of beer, if you have any.'

'Beer? Yes. I think we can furnish a beer.'

'Thank God,' said Eyre. And then, to Mr Pope, 'And thank you, too, sir.'

They were taken back to Mrs Pope's kitchen; hot and whitewashed and snug; where Mrs Pope heated up large bucketfuls of water for them to bathe, and Chucky laid the kitchen-table for them and served them with pies and boiled potatoes and beer, although Minil drank milk. They were both too stunned to say very much, and they sat huddled together at the end of the table like refugees from some appalling disaster, and in return the Popes gave them a respectful amount of room, partly out of sympathy, partly because they were so impressed at what Eyre had done, and partly because both he and Minil stunk of rancid pelican grease, and filth, and sodden kangaroo-skin.

After they had eaten, Mrs Pope took Minil to bathe outside in the shed while Mr Pope poured out a basinful of hot water for Eyre on the kitchen flags. Mr Pope drew up a kitchen chair, and lit a pipe; and said, 'As soon as you feel refreshed enough, we ought to take you to see some of our local dignitaries. It would hardly do for me to keep you to myself.'

Eyre turned his back on Mr Pope as he washed. Mr Pope puffed away for a while, and then said, 'Some bad scars you have there, if I'm not being too personal, Mr Walker.'

Eyre looked down at his chest, patterned with the purplish welts of *ngora*, and at his circumcised and sub-incised penis. 'Yes,' he said. 'We had some difficult times in the desert.'

He finished soaping himself, uncomfortably aware that although he had been welcomed back into white society for less than an hour, he had already denied his Aboriginal kinship for the first time.

Later, when he was washed and shaved, and dressed in one of Mr Pope's Saturday suits, which felt impossibly huge and baggy, and which seemed to weigh on his body like a heap of woollen blankets, Eyre was taken to shake hands with the neighbours; and then Mr Pope suggested they visit Albany's town hall, and make themselves known to everybody there. Eyre was tired, but curiously elated, and he agreed.

'Minil should come with me,' he said.

'Well,' said Mrs Pope, fussily tying her bonnet, 'the poor lamb's fast asleep now; and I think it better not to wake her, don't you? And you *are* the explorer, aren't you? The achievement has been yours; and yours alone.'

'I couldn't have done it without Minil,' Eyre told her.

'In that case, she should be proud to have had such an appreciative employer,' smiled Mrs Pope. 'Where are my spectacles, Frederick? Have you seen my spectacles?'

'I wasn't her employer,' said Eyre, although Mrs Pope wasn't really listening to him. 'I was her—'

He looked away. Outside the front door of the house, some of the neighbours had already gathered, and he could hear them chattering loudly; and some of them were whistling and cheering. Mr Pope's neighbours must have spread the news to all the surrounding streets, because the excitement sounded considerable; and there was the sound of running feet on the puddly road, and the rattle and creak of carriages.

'You were her *what* Mr Walker?' Mrs Pope asked brightly, staring at him with her milky-blue eyes.

Eyre said, 'It doesn't matter. I suppose things are rather different in the outback.'

'I should say so,' put in Mr Pope. 'Now, listen to that hullaballoo outside!'

'Come on,' said Eyre. 'We mustn't disappoint them, must we?'

Mr Pope opened the front door, and there was a burst of cheering and clapping; and it looked as if the whole street was packed from end to end with people, tossing up their hats and singing and dancing, and waving Union Jacks. There was even a one-man band there, with accordion and knee-cymbals and a dancing monkey.

When Eyre stepped out into the Pope's front garden, there was a deafening roar of welcome and enthusiasm; and he stood bewildered for a while until Mr Pope raised one of his arms for him, as if he had just won a fisticuffs match; and then the crowd screamed and whistled and cheered again. Two young burly men came in through the white-painted gate, and grinned, 'Come on, Mr Walker, we'll chair you!' and between them they lifted Eyre up on to their shoulders, and carried him right into the middle of the throng, so that the men could grasp his hands and slap at his thighs and the ladies could blow him kisses.

Then, in spite of his shouts of protest, they bore him off down the street, and across the market-place, where more people came running out to see what all the cheering was about.

They took him down to the docks, where stevedores in their brown aprons and peaked caps put down their bales and their grappling-hooks and applauded him as if they were opera-goers at the finale of *Cosi Fan Tutte*. 'He's arrived! He's alive!' That was the cry everywhere. 'He's arrived! Eyre Walker's arrived!' And nobody seemed to care whether he had discovered the inland sea or not; or whether or not it was possible to drive cattle from Adelaide to Albany, or sheep from Albany to Adelaide. All they cared about was Eyre; and his extraordinary journey, and the fact that he had walked and ridden all the way across the treeless plains of Southern Australia to arrive here alive.

He was finally allowed down to the ground outside the steps of the civic hall, where he was greeted by one top-hatted official after another; shaking hundreds of hands; and where even the loudest of speechmakers was unable to make himself heard over the cheering and shouting. From out on King George's Sound there was a dull, pressurised booming; one boom after another; and that was Her Majesty's naval supply ship *Walrus Bay* according Eyre an eleven-gun salute, followed by four ruffles on the drums.

He was showered with flowers; and then taken inside the civic hall for champagne, and more hand-shaking, although the crowd outside refused to go away; and after a while an impromptu silver-band struck up with 'My Lily and My Love' and 'Dragoons'.

The editor of the Albany newspaper came up at last, in a tight-fitting blue coat, and a yellow-checkered waistcoat, with chestnut moustaches perfectly waxed into points.

'Well, Mr Walker, my name's William Dundas, of the *Albany Mail*. What an achievement.'

Eyre felt battered and out of breath, and said, 'You'll excuse me if I sit down.'

'Of course,' said Dundas, and drew him out a chair. Eyre sat down, and a smiling man in a very high collar poured him some more champagne.

'I'm surprised that I seem to have excited so much interest,' said Eyre.

'Well,' said Dundas, taking out a small cigar, 'You're a hero now. A genuine hero, in a country that's rather short of heroes. You mustn't blame us all for making rather much of you.'

'There is no route from Adelaide to Albany suitable for stock,' said Eyre.

'Bad country, hm?'

'The worst. Desert, mallee scrub, mud. No running water for over eight hundred miles.'

'Then how on earth did you survive? What did you drink?'

'I'm beginning to wonder. But, there are springs if you know where to find them. Muddy pools of water that you have to dig for. In extremes, you can dig for frogs.'

'I beg your pardon?'

'I never had to do it; but I was told about it. There are certain frogs that retain water in their bodies. You can dig them up and squeeze them out, if you're really thirsty.'

Dundas reached into his pocket for notepaper, and a pencil. 'Did the Aborigines teach you how to do that?'

'They taught me many things,' said Eyre.

'And what would you say was the most important thing that they taught you?'

Eyre lowered his head. The champagne had already

begun to make him feel drunk; what with the noise and the jostling and the music, and the sudden sense of suffocation he felt, enclosed inside a room after months of living in the open air.

He said, haltingly, 'The most important thing that they taught me was that the white man's way of life is blind, greedy, and completely lacking in spiritual values. They taught me that there is magic in the world, and mystery; if only we can be humble enough to commune with our surroundings, and to respect what God has given us.'

Dundas tapped his pencil against his thumbnail. Then he glanced behind him to make sure that nobody was listening, and leaned forward, and said to Eyre in a cologne-smelling undertone, 'Listen, Mr Walker. You must be very tired after your journey. Perhaps a little light-headed. I think it might be a good idea if I made sure that you got back to wherever it is that you're staying; and that you didn't say very much more about magic or mystery or spiritual values. You're a hero now. If I were you, I'd take full advantage of it; and play it for what it's worth. And if I were you, I'd think twice before I upset people. You won't change them, after all, no matter *what* you discovered in the outback. Tell them how you were taught to squeeze frogs. Tell them how you roasted emus, and how you ate lizards. That's all very fine. Guaranteed to make the gels shudder. Good dinner-party stuff. Fine newspaper copy. But don't try to convert them with all this talk about greed, and blindness, and whatnot. Doesn't go down well.'

Eyre was silent. A fat woman with a coarse English accent and a very purple dress came up and kissed him, without being asked, right on the nose. 'You're a *hero*! she squealed.

Eyre raised his eyes and looked at Dundas with tiredness and resignation. Dundas shrugged, and twiddled at his moustache.

'Yes,' said Eyre. 'I'm a hero.'

When a carriage returned him at last to the Pope's house,

Mrs Pope greeted him on the doorstep with the news that Minil had gone. There was no message; nothing. She had told Chucky that she had gone to see her relatives at Swan River.

Eyre opened the door of the bedroom where Minil had been sleeping that afternoon, and stepped inside. The bed was crumpled, the sheets twisted. He sat down on it, and traced with the palm of his hand the wrinkles that her sleeping had made.

'*Minil*,' he whispered to himself, in the dusk of that room. He looked towards the window; and outside, in the blueness of dusk, he saw a gum-tree dipping and waving in the north-westerly breeze. She had left nothing behind, only these twists and wrinkles on the bed. He sat there for a few minutes, trying to think of her; but somehow he couldn't quite remember what her face looked like, or how she felt, or even what she had said to him, the very last time they had spoken.

He got up at last, and went to the window, and looked out. Mr Pope came into the room, smelling of tobacco, and stood there for a while, and then said, 'Is everything all right? Mrs Pope tells me that the blacky girl's gone.'

'Yes,' said Eyre, without turning around. 'Everything's all right. And, yes,' he said, 'the blacky girl's gone.'

'You'll want some supper, then,' said Mr Pope. 'Chicken casserole do you, with dumplings? And how about a beer? I'm glad of the excuse, to tell you the truth. Mrs Pope doesn't usually allow me a beer, not until Saturday. But, you know, seeing as how it's a special occasion.'

'I suppose it is,' said Eyre. 'Yes, you're very kind. I'll have a beer.'

Thirty-Five

He arrived back in Adelaide three weeks later on the merchant-ship *Primrose;* which was laden with grain and ironware from England. The people of Albany had given him everything he might possibly have needed; from a constant supply of French champagne to shoes and shirts and tailor-made coats. When he had left King George's Sound, more than half the population had turned out to cheer him and wave him goodbye, and sparkling maroons had been fired into the grey July sky. Now he stood in the wind on the *Primrose*'s poop, dressed rather formally in a black tail-coat, with dark grey britches, and a two-inch collar, with a black tie, and a pearl stud which had been presented to him by the Albany Commerce Club.

The *Primrose* leaned against the stiff north-westerly, her timbers creaking like the stays of an elderly woman. Then, across the ruffled waters of the Gulf of St Vincent, he saw the foaming outline of Henley Beach, and the outer harbour; and the masts of all the vessels that were moored there.

As the *Primrose* slowly rounded the point, her sails flapping against the wind, a rocket was fired from the end of the new McLaren wharf; and as soon as she passed the harbour entrance, Eyre saw that the water was clustered with scores and scores of small boats, lighters and bumboats and skiffs, bobbing and dipping, all of them flying bunting and pennants, and crowded from stem to stern with waving and cheering people. There was a sharp crackling noise as Chinese fireworks were let off all along the quayside, and then there was a roar of welcome and approval from the wharf where the *Primrose* would tie up; as hundreds of excited people poured along it from the direction of the Port Road.

'Well, seems as if they're anticipatin' you,' remarked the *Primrose*'s mate, hawking loudly. He himself had never been further ashore anywhere in Australia than Kermode Street in Adelaide for the British Tavern, or the worst alleys off George Street, in Sydney, for the boozers and the cribs, and he understood nothing of what Eyre had achieved. 'They're on one button here,' Eyre had heard him say to his captain, two days out of Albany. 'A fellow like that takes a stroll in the countryside, and they treat him like he's God-Amighty.'

Eyre said, 'You should be proud of your seamanship, to have got us here on the due date. They sent the *Ellen* on ahead of us, to tell them that we were expected to arrive today, and so we have. So take some of these cheers for yourself, master-mate.'

'Oh, bung it,' said the master-mate, irritably; although Eyre could tell that he was quite pleased by the compliment.

The *Primrose* was towed in by rowing-boat, and tied up, and from his place up on the poop, Eyre waved his hat and acknowledged the cheers and shouts from the huge assembly below. He saw Captain Sturt standing at the front, looking severe; and next to him a tall man with silver hair and deep-set eyes who looked important, but whom Eyre was unable to recognise. There was no sign of Christopher, nor of Lathrop Lindsay.

As soon as the gangplank went down, Captain Sturt and the tall man with silver hair were escorted aboard by marines; and up to the deck where Eyre was still waving and smiling. Flowers flew through the air and littered the planks all around Eyre's feet.

'Well, sir,' said Captain Sturt pushing aside some of the blossoms with his shoe. He was wearing a black jacket and a crimson satin waistcoat that was far too tight for him, and although he was grinning he looked particularly displeased; as if he had bitten into an apple and found it unbearably sour.

Eyre carried on waving, and nodding, and smiling. 'Well, yourself, Captain,' he replied.

'It seems as if you have made something of a name for

463

yourself,' said Captain Sturt. 'Allow me to congratulate you.'

'I don't think I really deserve your congratulations, do you?' asked Eyre; and Captain Sturt did not fail to miss the sharp double meaning of what he was saying.

'You have undertaken and completed a great journey of discovery, Mr Walker,' put in the tall man with the silver hair. His voice was deep and rich as plum-pudding, and his chins bulged over his necktie. 'You have crossed a desert that no white explorer has crossed before. That in itself is worthy of praise.'

'I'm sorry,' said Eyre, indicating that he had no idea who this gentleman might be.

'This is Governor George Grey,' said Captain Sturt.

'Then Governor Gawler is no longer with us?'

'He returned to England in May,' explained Governor Grey. 'Let us say that it was simply a matter of having drawn a little too enthusiastically on the London Commissioners. Although, of course, one has to acknowledge that in his short time here he achieved great things.'

Eyre shook hands with Governor Grey; but somehow he and Captain Sturt contrived not to.

'You must be tired,' said Sturt. 'Perhaps you would like to come back to my house and take some luncheon.'

'Yes,' said Eyre, 'I think I'd like that, thank you. But not right away. First of all, I think a procession is called for. That is, if I have your permission, governor.'

'By all means,' nodded Governor Grey. 'It isn't every day that we have such cause for celebration. Today you are Adelaide's most celebrated son, Mr Walker. It is only befitting that we should fête you.'

Eyre went to shake hands with the *Primrose*'s captain, and to wave to the crew, and then he slowly descended the gangplank to the wharf, with both arms raised in acknowledgement of the crowd's tremendous applause.

As he had been in Albany, he was lifted off his feet by enthusiastic young swells, and carried shoulder-high along the wharf, while flowers flew all around him, and fireworks popped off, and so many black top-hats were tossed into the air that the crowd looked for a while like a bubbling, spitting tar-pit.

A carriage was waiting for him outside the port, decked with shrubbery and flowers; and then with seven or eight young men clinging on to the sides, it was driven ceremoniously towards the town centre, followed on either flank by cheering riders and rattling gigs and running children. Eyre turned around and looked behind him, and saw to his amazement and delight that there must have been well over three thousand people following him, hurraying and laughing and waving flags.

At the western end of North Terrace, where the road from Port Adelaide ran at a sharp diagonal into the city, they were met with a fanfare by Captain Wintergreen and his musicians, who had formed themselves into a marching-band, twenty-five strong, especially to celebrate Eyre's arrival. The driver of Eyre's carriage had been told to proceed straight to Government House; and so had Captain Wintergreen; but Eyre shouted to the driver, 'Left, left, over the bridge!' The carriage turned left and rumbled over the bridge, and behind it came Captain Wintergreen and his band, drumming their drums and blowing their trumpets and clashing their cymbals. Behind them, still cheering, still waving their flags, came the first of the riders who had followed them from the wharf; marines and dragoons and cocky young gentlemen in plumed hats. Then the gigs and the broughams and the rest of the carriages, crowded with Adelaide's prettiest girls, in their yellows and pinks and bright blues, spinning their umbrellas and singing like birds. Then the great rush of people on foot: children and farmboys and clerks and shop-assistants and Aborigines, skipping and clapping and chanting.

'Now, make for Waikerie Lodge!' Eyre instructed his driver, and with a nod of his head the fellow turned the carriage along the street towards Lathrop Lindsay's house.

'Why, that's Mr Lindsay's place,' cried one young

Narangy, who was hanging on to Eyre's carriage by the folded-down hood. 'He's going to be as mad as a cut snake if you parade past him with this lot! He's your worstest enemy; allowing for what he's been saying about you, since you've been gone!'

'Well, we shall see about that,' Eyre declared. He leaned forward, tapped the coachman on the shoulder, and told him to draw over to the side of the road, and stop. The driver did as he was bid, and then Eyre stepped down from the carriage, and waited while Captain Wintergreen and his marching-band caught up with them. They were playing 'Sons of Caledonia', one of the most stirring marches they knew, with plenty of drumstick whirling and cymbal-clashing, and their trumpets and bugles were wildly off-key.

Eyre neatly stepped in, right in front of Captain Wintergreen, and led the parade alongside the white fencing which surrounded the lawns of Waikerie Lodge, until he reached the front gate. Then he cried, 'Right—turn!' and held out his right hand, and marched confidently up the path to Lathrop Lindsay's front door.

Every window of the house was flung open; and at every window an astonished face appeared. In the drawing-room window, Lathrop Lindsay himself, in his emerald-green smoking-jacket, his mouth wide open. In the day-room window, Mrs Lindsay, her hair awry, clutching her tatting. Upstairs, in her parlour window, Charlotte, in a sugar-pink afternoon gown.

'Around the house!' Eyre cried to Captain Wintergreen; and with a flourish of bugles the marching-band split right down the middle into two columns, one parading smartly around the left-hand side of the house, and the other parading around the right. Each of these columns was followed by a stream of cheering, dancing, applauding people, some on horseback, one or two on donkeys, but most of them on foot, swarming and swelling into the gardens of Waikerie Lodge, hundred upon hundred of them, until the house was completely besieged with people, none of them knowing why they were there, but all of them festive and happy, and ready for a great celebration.

The marching-band appeared from around the back of the house, and formed up on the front steps, marching on the spot, and playing 'Scotland The Brave'; which in less apoplectic times was Lathrop Lindsay's favourite tune.

'*Mr Walker!*' screamed Lathrop.

Eyre raised his hand to Captain Wintergreen, and the band died away in a few raggedy hoots, toots, and jingles.

'*Mr Walker!*' screamed Lathrop, again. His face was plum-coloured with wrath.

Those nearest to the house heard him screaming, and cried 'Ooooooh!' in response, like a music-hall audience.

'*Mr Walker!*' screamed Lathrop, for the third time.

'Mr Walker!' cried the crowd, in huge amusement. 'Mr Walker! Ooooh! Mr Walker!' And then they burst out cheering and clapping and laughing again, and shouted, 'Mr Walker! Speech from Mr Walker! Let's hear him! Come on now, Mr Walker!'

Eyre climbed up two or three steps, and raised both hands. There was more applause now, and somebody let off a tremendous chain of fire-crackers, that jumped and spat and frightened all the horses.

'Listen!' Eyre shouted. 'Listen!' And at last, still hooting and laughing occasionally, the crowd quietened down. Lathrop stood in his drawing-room window shaking with disbelief and rage, while Mrs Lindsay had clapped both hands over her mouth, as if she were suppressing a high shriek.

'I have travelled as far north to the interior of Australia as a man can go!' Eyre cried. More shouting, more clapping, and some cries of 'bravo! bravo, that man!'

Then Eyre said, 'I have travelled westwards, all the way from the spring called Woocalla to the town of Albany, through desert and scrub, over a thousand miles!'

Now the cheering was so loud that Eyre found it almost impossible to think. His blood was racing and his face was flushed; and even though he had been given nothing to drink, he felt as if he were intoxicated.

'I have travelled all that way,' he shouted, his voice becoming hoarse from the strain, 'I have travelled all that way . . . just to claim the hand of the most beautiful girl in Adelaide, Miss Charlotte Lindsay!'

The crowd screamed their delight and approval. Hats flew up into the air again, even umbrellas and bonnets, and the band rushed into one of those little pieces called a 'hurry', which were usually used to accompany a variety player on to the stage, or off again.

Eyre raised his hands for silence once again. Some of the women in the crowd were openly weeping, and two girls and an elderly grocer had fainted, and had to be laid under the wattle-bushes.

'There is one thing that I must do before I can claim Miss Lindsay's hand, however,' Eyre announced. 'And that is to ask the forgiveness of her father, Mr Lathrop Lindsay; whom I have caused embarrassment and pain, not just once, but several times; and each time worse than the last. I admit to him that there was a time when I was a brash, ill-mannered, and incontinent young man, and I can only ask that he can find it somewhere in that generous heart of his to forgive me.'

Eyre slowly turned towards Lathrop, and held out his hand, as dramatically as Adam holding out his hand towards God on the ceiling of the Sistine Chapel. Lathrop, framed in his window, stared at Eyre in complete horror.

'Forgive him!' cried a wag, in the front of the crowd. But then the cry was taken up again and again, more seriously, until nearly a thousand citizens of Adelaide were standing in Lathrop's garden, trampling his wattles and his orchids, crushing his carefully rolled lawns, roaring 'Forgive him! Forgive him! Forgive him!'

Lathrop disappeared from the window and eventually appeared at the front door. Behind him, halfway down the stairs, Eyre could see Charlotte although her face was hidden in shadow. Until he had conquered Lathrop,

468

however, he didn't dare to look at her. She had meant so much to him for so long that if he were to lose her now, when she was almost within his grasp, he would rather not remember her too sharply.

'Mr Lindsay,' said Eyre, 'I come to you today not as an impertinent young clerk who was too ebullient to mind his manners. I come to you as a man who has crossed a whole continent; and who has been matured and humbled by his experiences. I come to you as a man who has nurtured his love for your daughter through indescribable exploits, through starvation and thirst and terrible loneliness. I come to you as a man who is ready to apologise to you; but also as a man who has gained strength, and courage, and also a lasting reputation.'

At that moment, Captain Sturt forced his way through to the front of the crowd. Lathrop was about to reply to Eyre, but whatever he was going to say, Sturt raised a cautionary and advisory finger to him, and he swallowed the words before he had spoken them, as if they were liver-pills. He stepped heavily forward, and stared at Eyre with the expression of a man who cannot believe the persistence of his personal ill-fortune. There was sweat on his forehead, and his lower lip juddered with all the emotion that Captain Sturt had forbidden him to express.

He knew that he was beaten. The crowd was so enthusiastic about Eyre; Eyre was Adelaide's darling of the day; and if he were to slam the door in Eyre's face and refuse to forgive him, the consequences for his business and social life would be disastrous, at least for the next few months, if not for very much longer. Adelaide took warmly to its heroes; but treated its villains with unrelenting disfavour and scorn.

Captain Sturt was not even a friend of Lathrop's. In fact, he despised him. But Sturt was anxious not to see an important municipal businessman sent to Coventry; and he was also anxious to seek Eyre's favour too. There was much unfinished business between them, Eyre and Captain Sturt; and Captain Sturt was not particularly relishing the idea of settling it especially if Eyre was in an uncompromising mood.

Eyre held out his hand, and Lathrop took it. His grip was like cold moulded suet. 'I accept your apologies,' he said loudly, looking around at the crowd, and attempting a smile. 'Though God alone knows why,' he muttered, under his breath.

And then, loudly again, 'I will also consider giving you permission to marry my daughter Charlotte, if she is so disposed. Obviously, we shall need a little time to consider the matter more seriously, away from this . . . circus.'

The roar that rose from the crowd made the sash-windows rattle in their casements; and two horses threw their riders, leaped over the picket-fence surrounding Lathrop's garden, and bolted down the road. The band played 'Here Comes the Bride' in double-time, and Charlotte ran down the last few steps of the staircase, and came running out on silk slippers with her arms wide, her blonde curls bouncing and be-ribboned, as deliciously pretty and as small and as soft as ever before, and threw herself with a squeal into Eyre's arms, and hugged him tight, and kissed him, and wept and wept.

'I thought you were dead!' she cried, 'Oh, Eyre! My darling! I thought all this time you were dead!'

He held her close to him, feeling her warmth, breathing in her perfume. Then, very slowly, very strongly, he kissed her; until her eyelids trembled and closed, and her little upraised hand started to clench itself involuntarily into a fist.

Behind her, Lathrop snorted in disgust, and loudly blew snuff and phlegm out of his nose with an extra-large handkerchief. Captain Sturt watched with his arms folded and his face quite flinty.

'Thirty-three cheers for Eyre Walker and for Charlotte Lindsay!' cried one of the narangies. 'And thirty-three cheers for Captain Sturt and Mr Lathrop Lindsay!'

The crowd cheered and cheered and cheered again; until, defeated and despondent, and very close to angry tears, Lathrop Lindsay had to turn away and go back inside his house. Eyre stood with Charlotte on the steps, raising his hands again and again, and kissing Charlotte to show the whole of Adelaide how much he loved her.

At last, as the crowd began to disperse, and make their way back towards the river, and to Government House, where George Grey had promised band music and free drinks for everybody, Eyre took Charlotte into the hallway, and held both of her hands.

'I've asked your father,' he said. 'Now I want to ask you.'

There were tears in her eyes, but he wouldn't release her hands so that she could wipe them away.

'Yes,' she whispered. 'I will.'

Thirty-Six

They lunched very late, and neither of them were particularly hungry. They ate a little cold mutton and beetroot salad; and shared a bottle of '37 claret, which had either travelled badly, or been bad to begin with. The afternoon light filtered through the lace curtains as weakly as the light from half-remembered days gone by; and somehow it made Captain Sturt look even older, and tireder.

'George said that he's planning a proper municipal reception for next Thursday,' said Captain Sturt. 'Dancing, tables out on the lawns, even races. I won a three-legged race you know once, when I was in France, with the Army of Occupation. They gave me a goose. Well, that was the prize.'

'You were telling me about Christopher Willis,' Eyre

471

reminded him. Captain Sturt seemed to be ready to discuss almost anything at all, except Eyre's expedition.

Sturt sniffed, and helped himself to more wine. 'Your friend Christopher Willis, yes. From what I gather he acted with considerable fortitude. That's the word. He arrived back here in Adelaide only six days after he had left you out on the salt lake; and he was in very good spirits, though anxious, of course, that you and Mr McConnell should not come to any harm. He set off the very next morning with the boy Weeip and five other blackfellows to leave you those provisions. I gather that he even waited out there for a day, to see if you would appear. But, well, you didn't, and so he came back.'

'Did he tell you anything about Arthur Mortlock?'

'Only that he had become grievously sick, and died.'

'What about Mr Chatto and Mr Rose?'

'Hm?'

'Those two bounty-hunters who came looking for Arthur the day we left.'

Captain Sturt shook his head. 'What about them? They left Adelaide, didn't they? That's the very last that I've heard.'

'Then nobody's been looking for them?' asked Eyre.

'Should they have been?'

'No. But I wondered, that's all. They seemed like very persistent fellows.'

'Persistence is not always a virtue,' said Captain Sturt.

Eyre looked at him over the rim of his wine-glass, and then said, 'I hope you're not trying to suggest that *I* have been unduly persistent.'

'You were persistent enough to travel all the way from the salt lakes to Albany.'

'Yes,' Eyre said, warily.

'An expedition of great heroism. A journey of remarkable courage. An achievement which will no doubt be recognised for generations yet to come.'

Eyre said nothing, but watched Captain Sturt get out of his chair, and walk across to the window with his hands

472

thrust into his trouser pockets, and the tails of his coat cocked back. Sturt frowned out through the curtains at the muddy prospect of North Terrace, and the gum trees which bordered the Torrens River.

'Unfortunately,' he said, 'nothing of what you did was of any practical or commercial use whatsoever. Of course, I dare not say so. Isn't that ironic? I financed an expedition, and sent it off to discover a way through the continent and whatever riches might be there for the taking; and when it failed, with considerable loss of life, and abandonment of irreplaceable equipment, I have to appear to be cheerful about it, and shout 'huzza' along with the rest of the *hoi polloi.*'

Eyre said, 'It was scarcely my fault that the terrain was impassable.'

'You *tell* us that it was impassable,' Captain Sturt retorted. 'That's what you *say*. But terrain that is impassable for one man may well be quite easily negotiable for another.'

'Are you trying to suggest that I didn't do my very utmost to find a way through to the inland sea?' Eyre asked him, sharply. Even as he spoke, he could picture in his mind the horses wallowing and struggling up to their chests in grey, glistening mud.

Sturt pouted, and rocked on his heels. 'I'm only suggesting that my expedition might have been better served by a leader who was less *dogged*, and more astute.'

Eyre leaned forward in his chair, his spine as tense as a whalebone. 'Captain Sturt, just because a discovery is not to your personal liking; just because it doesn't help to line your purse; that doesn't make it any less of a discovery. My companions and I found out that the land due north of here is nothing but miles and miles of treacherous salt lakes; and that the land to the west of here is treeless desert; both completely unsuitable for the driving of cattle. Now at least we know that there is nothing we can do but cling to the coast of this continent, and raise our livestock as best we can, and leave the interior to the lizards and the Aborigines.'

'You didn't even find opals.'

'We were given the name of a site where opals can be found.'

'You were given the name of a site where opals can be found!' parroted Captain Sturt. 'My dear chap, how naive you are! It's astonishing that you weren't killed on the spot, by the first Aborigine you met with a sense of fun. Of course you were given the name of a site where opals can be found! What was it? Bugga Mugga, or Mudgegeerabah? That's eastern Aboriginal for the place of lies.'

He leaned forward and stared right into Eyre's face, his eyes bulging and bloodshot. 'Could you ever *find* this place, if you were to set out to look for it; or if anyone were to be foolish enough to finance you? Of course not! It's a mirage. An illusion, partly caused by the desert heat; partly by exhaustion. But most of all, it is caused by vanity, irrationality, and an immature impulse to make a hero out of yourself and a fool out of me.'

Eyre stared back at Captain Sturt for a moment or two, and then leaned back in his chair again and folded his arms.

'You're being more than unjust, Captain Sturt,' he said, as quietly as he could, although his voice was on the very brink of trembling. 'I personally believe that the discoveries we made were quite considerable, when you think how small our party was, how inexperienced, and how hastily prepared; not to mention the fact that our sponsors sent us off in complete ignorance of the mortal dangers that we would eventually have to face; if and when we achieved our goal.'

Sturt frowned at him. 'Mortal dangers? *What* mortal dangers? What are you trying to imply?'

'You knew about the legend of the *djanga*, the spirit returned from the dead.'

'What?'

'You know what a *djanga* is, surely; you know enough about Aboriginal mythology by now.'

'Well, yes of course I do,' blustered Sturt, 'but—'

'Captain Henry told Joolonga that I was the *djanga*, and Joolonga told you.'

'My dear Eyre—'

'Is there any use in denying it?' Eyre snapped at him. 'Well, *is* there? I know everything about it; why and how. Joolonga told you how long the Aborigines have been looking forward to the appearance of the *djanga*, for more centuries than anyone can count. And he also told you how desperate their prayers have become ever since the white people began to trample over the sacred places, and how they have been hoping against hope that the legend should at last come true. A saviour will come, and give us the magical knowledge, and set us free from the white man! And how callously you traded on that belief, didn't you? and on my life; and the lives of all my companions. Not for glory, though, or patriotism. Not for any greater purpose than to balance the books of South Australia to the satisfaction of the London Commissioners, and to make sure that you yourself did not become a candidate for the green bonnet of bankruptcy.'

Captain Sturt stood with his mouth ajar. His face was the colour of fresh calves'-liver.

Eyre said, in a more controlled voice, 'I have not yet been able to discover whether you knew that Yonguldye would murder us all; or, to be fair, whether Yonguldye was really thinking of murdering us or not. There was a misunderstanding of language; whether to eat a man's brains means literally to eat his brains, or whether it simply means to acquire all the knowledge within him. But when I was out at Yarrakinna, surrounded by hundreds of Aborigine warriors with spears and knives and clubs, I didn't see much wisdom in waiting to find out. Nor did those poor souls who were with me.'

Captain Sturt was silent for a very long time, his hands resting on the cresting-rail of one of his dining-room chairs.

At last, gravely, he said, 'I consider your accusation to be completely fantastic, Eyre, and unreservedly malicious. Why you wish to believe such things of me, I cannot think. All I can tell you is that I know nothing whatsoever of the legends of which you speak; and that certainly I never would have been foolish or irrational enough to send you off on an expedition which I myself financed, knowing that its success depended on nothing more than Aborigine superstition.'

He stared at Eyre and his eyes were chilly and displeased.

'I knew that it was important to you to seek an Aborigine medicine-man in order that the remains of your young black friend should be properly interred. And, yes, I admit that to some extent I used you. But I sought only to harness your spiritual mission to assist my temporal explorations; so that both of us would profit in our different ways. What you have suggested now is that I deliberately offered your life to the Aborigines in return for profit. Well, the notion is beneath contempt. Contemptible! You have hurt me, Eyre, deeply.'

Eyre took a sip of wine and then set his glass back on the table. 'Well,' he said, 'I'm sorry you're hurt. But I have to say that Joolonga was quite specific.'

'Joolonga? You're prepared to take the word of that rogue against mine? Joolonga was irrational; his mind wandered. Drink, *pitjuri*, drugs. He was always trying to pretend that he had magical powers; always threatening to strike people dead and nonsense like that. I'll say that he was a marvellous tracker. One of the best in the whole of South Australia. But up here,' Captain Sturt tapped his forehead, 'Joolonga didn't know whether he was white or black, real or imaginary, coming or going.'

Eyre said, 'Of course he's conveniently dead now, and can't support me.'

'He wouldn't, even if he weren't. The man was a storyteller; a joker; he was probably trying to frighten you, that

476

was all, a novice out in the wilds. It was regrettable to say the least that you took him so seriously.'

'I'll tell you how seriously I took him, Captain Sturt. I killed him.'

Captain Sturt smiled, and slapped Eyre on the shoulder. 'Then serve him right, really, wouldn't you say? Poetic justice.'

'Captain Sturt, Joolonga was a very cultured and intelligent man.'

Captain Sturt blew out his cheeks, and quickly shook his head, 'Opinionated, yes, as most blackies are, but not cultured. They seem bright, you see, because you don't expect any kind of intelligible conversation at all out of a face as primitive and as ugly as that. An orang-utan would only have to say three words and we would say that it was cultured. The same with the blackfellow.'

He reached over and rang the bell on the table. He seemed to have settled down now, and to have forgotten his annoyance at Eyre's accusations. In fact, his little burst of temper seemed as far as he was concerned to have cleared the air altogether, and to have put him into a mood of rather sickly good temper.

His housemaid came in: a Kentish woman no more that five feet tall, with a hooked nose like Judy and a flouncy old-fashioned bonnet. One of her eyes looked towards the window and the other towards the portrait on the adjacent wall of Captain John Hindmarsh, the first governor of South Australia.

'We'll have the pie now, Mrs Billows,' said Captain Sturt. 'The pie, Eyre? It's apple and cinnamon, with cheese pastry. Quite capital.'

Eyre said, 'I don't think so, thank you. I'm rather tired.'

'Ah,' said Sturt. 'A man who is too tired to eat some of Mrs Billows' pie is tired of life itself.'

'To paraphrase Dr Johnson,' Eyre retorted.

'Well, yes,' said Sturt, uncomfortably. 'I, er—I think I'll have mine a little later, thank you, Mrs Billows. Perhaps with some of the cheese and pickles, for supper.'

Mrs Billows allowed her eyes to revolve independently over the entire compass of the room. 'I did 'eat it up, Captin, like as what you required; 'arf a nower in the huvven.'

'Yes, and I'm sure that's very dutiful of you,' said Captain Sturt. 'But I don't think either of us has an appetite just now. Why not ask Tildy to clear up now.'

'Tildy? Tildy 'asn't done a tap since brekfist; nor's likely too niver. Giv 'er the 'eave-'o, I would; 'septing it's not my plice.'

After Mrs Billows had cleared up, very noisily, with a tremendous jangling of cutlery and a clashing of plates, Captain Sturt directed Eyre through a gloomy glazed conservatory, and then out into the unkempt garden, where there was a wooden seat situated under the shade of a stringy-bark gum.

'I vow that you're a good fellow, Eyre,' he said, lighting a small cigar, and blowing smoke upwards into the wind. 'You have your hasty moments, but anyone of your age can be liable to that. Speed's Disease, my father used to call it. He'd catch me running down the corridor, and seize me by the ear, and cry, "What's ailing you, young Charlie? Speed's Disease?" A wonderful man, shed a few tears when he passed over.'

'This all seems so contrary,' said Eyre. 'You think the expedition was a disaster; mainly because of me; and yet here you are telling me how much of a great chap I am.'

'Ah, that's because I have an eye for opportunity. You have to, in business; and even more so in politics. We didn't find the inland sea; no. But you're a hero now, and we must make whatever use of you we can. George Grey suggested that we give you a rather special job.'

'Job?' asked Eyre. 'I was rather supposing that I would go back to the Southern Australian Company.'

'Pfff, a man of your stature, as a shipping clerk? Think of it, you're a hero now. A great gilded hero. And in any case, we don't want you to feel that all of those months of traipsing through the outback went to waste. A man

478

achieves something, and no matter how disappointing it turns out to be in terms of pounds, shillings, and pence; well then, he must be rewarded.'

Eyre looked down at Captain Sturt, who was sitting with his legs crossed, confidently smoking his cigar as if he owned Australia.

'You're buying me off,' he said, in a voice as clear as the afternoon wind.

Captain Sturt licked a stray fragment of leaf back into position. Then he glanced up at Eyre, and gave him a small, confidential smile.

'You're going to be the Protector of Aborigines for the whole of the Murray River district,' he said. 'Important job; suit your new understanding of the blackies. Pay you well, too. Seven hundred pounds the annum, with house. Dignified job enough for you to marry Miss Lindsay in style.'

'You're buying me off,' Eyre repeated. 'You did know about the *djanga* legend, after all.'

'Well, my dear fellow, that's what *you* say. But then you've spent several arduous months with the sun baking your brains and the sand roasting your feet, in the company of savages and other assorted riff-raff. Who's going to take the word of a fellow like you, for all that they admire you?'

'You're buying me off,' Eyre repeated, with even greater sharpness.

Captain Sturt lounged back, and smoked, and smiled at him. 'Yes,' he said. 'But you will never force me to admit it in any court of law; or in front of any inquiry; or within earshot of anybody save yourself. If I were you, my dear fellow, I would enjoy what I had. The name of a hero, and a comfortable job for life. Oh yes, and a pretty wife, too; won at the expense of some considerable chagrin from poor old Lathrop Lindsay.'

Eyre covered his mouth with his hand. He didn't trust himself to answer; and besides, he needed to think. Somewhere along the terrace, in a neighbouring tree, a kookab-

479

urra began to laugh at him. The sun waned behind a cloud, and the garden looked for a moment like a daguerreotype of a day already gone by; colourless, cold, and half-forgotten.

'You say that Midgegooroo survived,' he said.

Captain Sturt nodded, without taking his cigar out of his mouth.

'But, crippled?'

'Won't walk again. But you can thank your friend Christopher Willis for saving his life.'

'Hm,' said Eyre. 'Not that it will be much of a life, will it? A blackfellow, unable to walk? What will a poor soul like that be able to do?'

'Beg,' smiled Captain Sturt. He paused, and knocked a little ash off his cigar. 'But then, you know, we all have to beg at times; in various ways. It's the way that life happens to be.'

Thirty-Seven

He stood outside the house on Hindley Street for almost ten minutes before he climbed the steps to the front verandah and knocked at the door. Below him, already rusted, its wheels entwined with weeds and creepers, his bicycle was propped against the wall. Dogger had promised to look after it for him, but of course Dogger was gone.

He could see her approaching the front door through the frosted glass panes; a dark shadow, with rustling skirts. She opened the door without asking who it was, and stood there, white-faced, black-bonneted, dressed in black satin, with a necklace of jet and ribbons of black velvet.

'Constance,' he said.

'I knew you'd come,' she said, stiffly. 'You'd better step inside.'

He followed her into the parlour. The curtains were half-drawn, and it was musty, and smelled of pot-pourri, and camphor.

'Sit down,' she said, and he did so, holding his hat on his lap. She sat down opposite him, arranging her skirts, and clasping her hands together in a gesture of piety and disapproval.

'When did you receive the news?' he asked her.

She lowered her eyelids. They looked like crescents of white peeled wax. 'A gentleman came from Albany. He said that he'd spoken to you; and that Mr McConnell had been murdered near Woocalla by savages.'

Eyre nodded. There was a very long silence. The clock on the mantelpiece whirred, and then chimed eight.

'You must be very tired,' said Mrs McConnell.

'Yes,' said Eyre. 'I think I am.'

'Then, you may stay here tonight. But tomorrow, I must ask you to go. I would also ask you to take all of your possessions; your pictures; your clothes. I want no trace of you here, nothing.'

'Constance—' he began.

She opened her eyes and stared at him sadly. 'He wasn't very much, Eyre. He was cantankerous and awkward and usually drunk. But he was Dogger, and he was all that I had.'

'I know,' said Eyre.

'He died—quickly?' asked Constance. 'There wasn't any pain?'

Eyre shook his head. 'It was all over in a flash. He only had time to shout one word. He sat in the saddle and lifted up his arms and shouted just one word.'

Constance was waiting. The clock had finished chiming now, and was ticking onwards towards nine o' clock, and the end of another day without Dogger. Eyre said, 'He shouted, Constance! And that was all.'

Constance clutched her arms around herself. In the gloom of the room, her eyes sparkled with tears.

'He called for me? His very last word?'

'Whatever his first word was, when he was born; your name was his last when he died.'

'Oh, God,' wept Constance. She covered her face with her hands. 'Oh, God, he called for me. He called for me, and I wasn't there. I'm his wife and I wasn't there. Oh God forgive me.'

Eyre knelt down on the carpet beside her and took her hand. She shook and shook, and her sobs were so deep that they sounded as if they were tearing her lungs. But at last she raised her head, and took out a black lace handkerchief, and wiped her eyes.

'I haven't cried much,' she said. 'I was dreading you coming back, because I knew then that I would. I knew then that I would have to admit that it's really true, and that he's gone.'

'Constance,' said Eyre. 'Let me fetch you a sherry. Or a brandy perhaps. Come on, something to calm you down.'

'Oh, I'm calm enough,' she sniffed. 'I'm calm, don't worry. Why shouldn't I be calm? There's nothing to get excited about any more, is there? Not even an old dingo-hunter who snores.'

Eyre spent the night in his old room but scarcely slept. He heard Constance walk down the creaky stairs in the small hours of the morning, presumably to make herself a cup of tea. But she didn't disturb him; and when he woke in the morning and went down to the kitchen, he found hot meat porridge waiting for him on the stove, and a note saying that she wouldn't be back until late in the afternoon, and could he please have left the house by then.

He packed the few things that were left in his wardrobe; his carriage clock and his pictures of his mother and father; and these he took across the road to the little notions store run by Mrs Crane and her sister, two ladies who had emigrated to Australia in search of husbands and ended up selling ribbons and needles instead. They agreed to keep his cases in their back room until the evening, and blushed when he kissed them both and promised to tell them about his adventures in the land of Bunda Bunda. Then he went back and retrieved his bicycle from underneath Mrs McConnell's verandah, tugging the weeds out of the wheels; and cycled slowly off towards the racecourse, and Christopher Willis' house.

It was a strange still day; not very hot but humid. As he pedalled out along the racecourse road, between the thick rainy-season bushes and the tall green grass, he heard no jacks nor finches, not even an insect chirruping. He felt as if he had cotton packed in his ears.

Only the monotonous squeak of his bicycle reminded him that he could still hear. That, and his panting. He had forgotten, after months on horseback, how strenuous it was to ride a bicycle.

Christopher was sitting on his verandah drinking tea and reading the Adelaide *Observer*. He was wearing a large floppy calico hat, and from a distance he looked very thin. Eyre dismounted from his bicycle when he was about twenty yards away from the house, and wheeled it the rest of the way over the damp earth.

'What ho, Christopher,' he said, propping the bicycle up against the steps.

'What ho, Eyre,' replied Christopher, without looking up.

Eyre climbed the steps and walked across the boarded verandah to stand right next to him.

'What do the newspapers have to say?' he asked.

Christopher shook the paper and peered towards the editorial column. 'They say that Adelaide is one of the filthiest cities on God's earth. Most people's basements are flooded with filthy water, and that there are open cesspools, dung heaps, and pig's offals lying everywhere.

483

The population are drinking unfiltered water and dying like flies.'

Eyre sat down on the verandah rail. 'Anything else?'

Christopher looked up. Eyre was startled to see how old he seemed to have become, how wrinkled his eyes were, and how washed-out.

'Yes,' said Christopher. 'They say that an erstwhile shipping-clerk of the South Australian Company has returned to the city in triumph. A great hero, after travelling all the way from South Australia to Western Australia, with only an Aborigine girl for company. They don't even mention the Aborigine girl's name.'

Eyre said, 'You didn't come to meet me at the dock.'

'Is there any reason why I should have done?'

'I thought we were friends.'

'Well,' said Christopher, 'we were.'

'Are you jealous?' asked Eyre. 'Are you jealous because I rode all the way to Albany and you didn't? Are you jealous of all this fame; all this public hoo-ha?'

'No,' said Christopher.

'What is it, then?' asked Eyre, softly but insistently.

Christopher said, 'I'm over you, that's all,' He looked up, with a challenging expression on his face.

'Is that a good thing or a bad thing?' Eyre asked him.

'I don't know,' said Christopher. He folded up the paper and laid it down on the table. 'It's just a fact.'

'Does that mean we're not pals any more? Not even pals?'

Christopher shrugged. 'I think I would really have preferred it if you hadn't come.'

'Don't you want to hear what happened?'

Christopher picked the paper up again, and dropped it. 'I can read it all in here, thank you. They say they're going to publish your entire account of the journey. "With Eyre Walker Through The Outback." '

'But I want to hear what happened to you.'

'Nothing happened to me,' said Christopher, off-hand-edly. 'Midgegooroo groaned and shrieked all the way to

Adelaide; but in the end we got here, God knows how, and took him to a doctor. The doctor said it was a miracle that he was still alive, although he would lose the use of both of his legs and one of his arms, and that the experience had probably damaged him mentally; you know, made him into something of an idiot. But otherwise, well, he was fine, and still is. Still breathing, still eating, still excreting.'

'It wasn't my fault, you know,' said Eyre.

'I didn't say that it was. You asked what happened, and I told you.'

'And you?'

'Me? I'm all right. Well, reasonably all right. Not *quite* the same person.'

Eyre walked down to the end of the verandah. Three or four racehorses were prancing across the course on a morning exercise. He heard a man shouting, '*Up, Kelly! Up, Tickera!*'

'You've just got over me, is that what you said?' Eyre asked Christopher.

'I suppose that's the decent way of putting it.'

'What's the indecent way of putting it?'

Christopher looked at Eyre cuttingly, and then looked away.

Eyre said, 'I was very hurt that you didn't come to see me. You know that, don't you?'

'Oh, I don't think you were,' Christopher replied. 'You see, the only person you really care about is you. I'm not blaming you; but it's in your nature. It's the way you are. That's why you're able to survive while everybody else around you dies or collapses or gives in. That's what made it possible for you to cross that desert. Unless you had cared about yourself with such intensity that nothing could possibly have stood in your way, you would still be there now, or at least your bones would be. You have all the makings of a hero, Eyre. I should have believed you when you said that destiny had marked you out for some

485

magnificent and honourable task. It takes perfect self-love. *Un amour-propre parfait.* And I congratulate you.'

Eyre stood where he was, saying nothing.

Christopher watched him, and at last said, 'Would you like some tea? I could get some fresh.'

'Yes,' said Eyre. 'I think I'd like that.'

Christopher clapped his hands smartly, and the door of the cottage opened and out came the boy Weeip. He wore a cream linen sailor-suit, although he still kept a woven headband around his hair for decoration. He looked at Eyre cautiously, and then bowed his head. 'Welcome, Mr Wakasah.'

'Well, well,' said Eyre, 'welcome yourself. I see you've found yourself a comfortable billet with Mr Willis. How are you?'

'You're very well, aren't you, Weeip?' Christopher interrupted.

'Yes, sah, very well. Prays beetroot God.'

'Bring us some fresh tea, would you, Weeip, there's a good chap?' said Christopher.

'And buns, sah?'

'Eyre?' asked Christopher.

'No thank you. No buns for me,' said Eyre. He watched Weeip go back into the house, and then raised an eyebrow at Christopher.

'It's everything you think it is,' said Christopher. 'An innocent young savage who asks no questions and will do anything I require of him.'

'Have you given up Daisy Frockford?'

'Of course not. One must still have lady companions to take to dinners; although I must say that I've been invited to precious few since I've been back. Being a hero may be one thing; all fine and good; but being a hero's helper is of no distinction whatever.'

'You *are* jealous,' Eyre chided him.

'No, I'm not. I've told you I'm not. I just wish that I'd never gone along at all. I wish I'd never set eyes on you; or that damned Joolonga; or Dogger; or Midgegooroo.'

486

'Or Arthur Mortlock?' asked Eyre. 'We mustn't forget about poor old Arthur.'

Christopher made a face to show that he didn't particularly care to talk about Arthur Mortlock. But Eyre said, 'It was an odd thing, you know, about Arthur.'

'What was odd?'

'Well, despite the fact that Joolonga claimed to have killed him with his pointing-bone, he suffered the symptoms of a man who had swallowed a quantity of corrosive sublimate. You know, the vomiting, the diarrhoea.'

'I don't really wish to be reminded,' said Christopher.

'Well, nor do I,' said Eyre. 'But, it was still odd. And the oddest thing was that when I went through my medicine-chest, I discovered that my bottle of corrosive sublimate was empty; although I had used none of it during the journey.'

'In that case,' Christopher retorted, 'it seems to me that the likeliest explanation is that he inadvertently poisoned himself. He would have drunk anything, that man. Methylated spirits, horse liniments. A yoxter like him wouldn't have cared.'

'I can't see anyone drinking corrosive sublimate on purpose,' said Eyre. 'My God, the smell of it alone would have put him off. Apart from the bottle, which was ridged, and clearly marked corrosive poison.'

Christopher drummed his fingers sharply on the table. 'I'm afraid the mentality of people like Arthur Mortlock is a closed book, as far as I'm concerned. And even if you were to open it, you would probably find that it contained nothing but blank pages.'

'You're being very unkind to him,' said Eyre.

'The man was a scoundrel; a ticket-of-leave man, on the run. He could have had all of us arrested and hung.'

'Christopher, why on earth are you so nervous?'

'Nervous?' Christopher demanded. His face was grey and glistening, like an oyster. 'Of course I'm not nervous. Why in the world should I be nervous? I haven't been very well, that's all, since coming back from that expedition. I was down with influenza for two weeks, and the doctor said that I was quite fortunate not to go down with pneumonia.'

'Luckier than Arthur, then,' said Eyre.

Christopher said, 'I have no desire to talk about Arthur. He was a low scoundrel, that's all; and whatever happened to him, and however it happened, he got only what he deserved.'

Eyre considered asking Christopher straight out whether he had poisoned Arthur; but then he thought better of it. After all, back here in Adelaide, it did seem rather improbable that Christopher should have murdered him. What possible motive could he have had? Perhaps Arthur had made homosexual advances to him, and Christopher had poisoned him as a punishment; but Christopher was not ashamed of his inclinations, and had made no secret of them, even to Eyre. Therefore, the motive could not have been blackmail either: a threat by Arthur to reveal that he was a catamite.

Eyre decided to hold his peace; and so when Weeip brought the tea, and poured it out for them, they discussed nothing more than Eyre's journey across the desert, and even this was done awkwardly and with an exaggerated lack of interest on Christopher's part. At last, after half an hour, Eyre stood up and held out his hand.

'I have to get back. The artist from the *Illustrated Post* wants to make a drawing of me.'

Christopher shook his hand, and nodded. 'Being a hero has its chores, no doubt.'

'You won't lose touch altogether, will you?' Eyre asked him.

Christopher said, 'Of course not. But you'll be very busy, won't you?'

'Never too busy to talk to a friend.'

'An erstwhile friend,' Christopher corrected him.

'Well, whatever you like,' said Eyre.

Eyre retrieved his bicycle and began to wheel it away. He

turned once, but Christopher had picked up his newspaper again, and was making a big show of ignoring him. All right, he thought; if that's the way you feel; and he mounted up and prepared to ride off.

At that moment, however, Weeip came running up to him.

'You drop your kerchy, Mr Wakasah.'

'That's not mine,' said Eyre, peering at the crumpled handkerchief.

'No, sah, I know sah. But I have to bring it to speak to you, sah.'

'You want to speak to me?'

Weeip glanced anxiously back towards the verandah, but Christopher was still ostentatiously absorbed in his newspaper.

'Can you come tonight, sah; at seven? Then look in the second window at the back.'

'What? What for?'

Weeip said anxiously, 'You will know then, all about Mr Mortlock, sah. Bless his hole. Please come. Then you see. Mr Willis is good to me, sah; take care of me. Please come. Don't blame him, sah.'

Just then, Christopher looked around to see why Eyre hadn't yet bicycled away; and Weeip crammed the dirty handkerchief into Eyre's hand, and ran back towards the house. Eyre, baffled, waved the handkerchief at Christopher to show why he had been delayed. Christopher gave him a half-hearted wave in return.

Eyre made his way back into Adelaide quite slowly. He was puzzled by Christopher's prickly behaviour, and yet not completely surprised. Upsetting Christopher was not like upsetting a man-friend. It was like distressing a lover. But what could he possibly see through the second window at the back at seven o' clock in the evening, which would explain everything about Arthur Mortlock? Had Christopher really had anything to do with Arthur's death, or not? And even if he had, what could be discovered by creeping back in the evening, and looking through his window?

He was so preoccupied that he allowed the front wheel of his bicycle to get caught in a rut in the road, and he staggered and hopped on one leg and nearly fell off.

Thirty-Eight

There was one more visit to be made; and this visit more than any other made Eyre understand that the purpose of his journey across Australia had been accomplished. For while he had failed to discover the inland sea; and while he had failed to bring back a medicine-man to bury Yanluga; he had been initiated into an Aborigine tribe, and could therefore bury Yanluga himself, according to the proper rituals. And as for the inland sea; well, Captain Sturt himself could go and look for that, if it really existed. The seagulls had been flying north, but then they could have been seeking nothing more than moth larvae, or a swampy patch on the salt-lake where worms could be pecked; and perhaps that was all that Captain Sturt would find.

Eyre talked to Lathrop Lindsay's secretary, at his offices on Morphett Street; and Lathrop Lindsay's secretary talked to Lathrop Lindsay; and Lathrop Lindsay sent back a message saying that there would be no objections of a material nature if Yanluga's body were to be exhumed from its resting-place next to Lathrop Lindsay's favourite horse, and re-buried according to tribal rituals. In fact, a complimentary article would appear in the following day's

Observer, praising Mr Lindsay for his 'humanitarianism and religious liberality'.

Eyre went along that afternoon with four hired Aborigines and several shovels, and in an unexpected drizzle, they dug up Yanluga's coffin from beneath the gum-trees, and laid it on the wet grass, and opened it with a pick. Yanluga lay inside, crouched like a huge spider, half-skeletal, his eyeless face grinning at the Bible which had been interred beside him.

'The Bible,' said Eyre, picking it up. 'And yet all of this poor boy's religion was told by word of mouth, and painted on rocks.'

The hired labourers stood around in their soaking-wet shirts and stared at him uncomprehendingly. They were city Aborigines; black boys who had learned to make a living by scrounging from white people; selling rubbish and clearing out stables. They knew very little about tribal myths, or what had happened during the dreaming. They had already become what Yonguldye had feared all Aborigines would one day become; inferior white men lacking in tribal knowledge, or any of the skills of survival. With them, all the ancient crafts would die away in two or three generations. Some of the languages and myths had already been forgotten, or erased by epidemics of tuberculosis brought ashore by white settlers. A whole way of life was dying, and Eyre knew that the funeral he was giving Yanluga was only a personal gesture that would have no effect on the greater course of history.

The coffin was carried to a sacred place close to the reed beds on the River Torrens, where black-and-white cows grazed, and the gums twisted into the water. The rain had cleared but the soil was still heavy and aromatic and damp as the Aborigines dug Yanluga a grave. After an hour of excavation, Eyre and one of the boys lifted the corpse out of the coffin, and then set it down on a bed of branches at the bottom of the hole, its knees drawn up in a sitting position. The body was so light and brittle, Eyre could hardly believe it had once been human. One of the hands broke off as Eyre was bending it into the ritual position, and the finger bones burst out from the tightened skin like seeds from a pod.

Eyre cried out over the grave, loudly and unembarrassed, the lamentations that were due to a dead warrior. One of the labourers joined in; and for almost twenty minutes they cried and keened together over the corpse that had once been Yanluga. Then they covered the crouched-up body with earth, and brushed his grave with twigs and branches, and lit a fire beside it. The labourers had been paid to keep the fire burning for a week; and Eyre would revisit it from time to time; and say the prayers that would ensure Yanluga's eventual arrival in the land beyond Karta, the isle of the dead, to join Ngurunderi.

'Yanluga,' said Eyre, quietly. Across the river, the cows moved slowly through the long grass. 'Yanluga, you have led me to discover things that I never believed were possible. You have shown me a world that I can still scarcely comprehend. But I promise you that I will always keep faith with you; that my brotherhood with the Aborigine people will never be broken, not until the day I die; and join you beyond the sunset.'

He stood there for over an hour, while the fire smoked and twisted in the early-afternoon wind. This, more than anything else, seemed like the end of the journey. He took off his hat, and closed his eyes, and said the words of the funeral prayer which Winja had taught him, during the days of his *engwura*.

You will live beyond the stars,
You will live in the land of the moons.
Happiness and friendship will always be yours.
And the laughter of those you left behind will always
  rise to you.'

At last, he left the graveside, and walked back along the path which would lead him to Adelaide. The rain began again, suddenly: a scattering of silver droplets on the dark earth track. The coinage of sadness, the currency of repentance, and the specie of tears.

He had booked a room at Coppius' Hotel; and during the early evening he moved his belongings there from Mrs Crane's notions shop. By half-past-six he was both tired and hungry, and thinking of dinner at the Rundle Street Restaurant. But, as he undressed to take a bath, he remembered what Weeip had said, about going out to Christopher's house at seven o' clock.

He was undecided. If he were to dress again, and risk missing his dinner, he could probably get out to the racecourse and back. But the Rundle Street Restaurant closed early; as most restaurants did; and if he came back very late, he would be lucky to get even a bowlful of warmed-up broth.

He looked at himself in the cheval-glass in the corner of his hotel-room. Well, he thought, there's no point in beating about the bushes; do you want dinner or do you want to know who murdered Arthur Mortlock? The thin figure in the long white combination underwear stared back at him seriously. It looked like a figure that could do with dinner. But then he had never taken very much notice of what images in mirrors had to say for themselves.

A chilly wind had got up as he bicycled out towards the racetrack again. It was prematurely dark now; and there were random spots of rain flying in the air. He hoped very much that he wouldn't meet up with a drunken Aborigine, or one of the cosh boys who occasionally attacked evening travellers. His journey had left him nearly two stones lighter than when he had set out, and he was still decidedly weak. Captain Sturt had called him 'all horns and hide', which was how local farmers described a starved yearling.

At last he reached the racecourse, and left his bicycle on the ground, its front wheel still spinning. He could see the lamplight shining through the orange calico blinds of Christopher's house from quite a long way away, silhouetting the branches of the grove of gums in which it was set. The rain clattered harder against the bushes, and something rustled and jumped; a bird or a joey or a dingo pup. Behind the mountains, the sky was oddly light, where the rainclouds had begun to clear, but here it was still dark and still furious, and the rain was sweeping down even more noisily. Wet and hungry, his collar turned up, Eyre made his way around to the back of Christopher's cottage, and trod as stealthily as he could through the unkempt garden, lifting his feet up like a performing pony so that he wouldn't trip up in the weeds.

He reached the side of the house, and leaned against it, breathing hard. More rain poured down, and the guttering at the back began to splatter into the rain-barrel. Eyre took out his watch and peered at it by a thin crack of light which penetrated the cottage's blinds. Two minutes to seven o' clock. He had only just got here in time; although so far he was at a loss to see how he was going to be able to look inside the house, with every single blind drawn. His stomach gurgled, and he was beginning dearly to wish that he had never come. Let Arthur's death remain a mystery, he thought. So much of what had happened in the outback had been without reason or explanation; as if it were a mysterious land with physical laws of its own. How many times had explorers returned baffled from Australia's interior? It was a continent which defied normal interpretation, a land of superstition and inverted logic. Perhaps Arthur had done no more than fall victim to that logic, and a destiny which this upside-down country had been keeping in store for him ever since he was born.

It was seven o' clock. Eyre could hear talking inside the house, and the shuffling of feet on the boarded floors. But another five minutes passed, and still the blinds remained tightly closed. He decided to give Weeip only two or three minutes more, and then leave. The rain had become steady now, steady and cold, and he was shivering.

He was just about to move, however, when the blind closest to him was lifted by an inch, and a pair of dark eyes peeped out into the night. It was Weeip. Eyre waved his hand quickly, and Weeip blinked to show that he had seen him. Then he disappeared from the window and went back into the middle of the room; but left the blind slightly raised.

Eyre was tall, but not quite tall enough to reach the window. He felt around in the long wet grass, and at last 'ound a wooden fruit-crate which had been left beside the rain-barrel. He upended it, and cautiously stepped up, gripping the window-sill so that he didn't overbalance backwards.

The window was partly steamed up, but Eyre could still see clearly into the room. It was a bathroom, very spartan, with a bare floor and a rag rug, and an old-fashioned zinc tub, the kind of bath in which Marat had been assassinated. Beside the bath was a tall enamelled jug, full of freshly steaming water. On the far wall was a crucified Christ, in bronze.

Weeip was kneeling beside the bath, naked. His penis was erect. He had filled the bath with hot water and now he was arranging the soap and the towels. Almost immediately, as Eyre watched, Christopher walked in, wrapped in a striped Indian robe, maroon and green, the kind which travellers were offered for sale whenever their ships docked at Trivandrum or Colombo. He said something to Weeip, touching the boy's shoulder, and then walked across the room and back again. At length he leaned over, testing the water in the tub, and smiled. Weeip stood up, and Christopher reached down with his wet hand and clasped his erection, rubbing it up and down two or three times and then laughing when the boy shivered.

Now Christopher loosened the tie around his waist, still smiling. He was facing Eyre directly, and Eyre flinched, certain that Christopher would notice his eyes looking in at the bathroom window. But Christopher must have had his mind on his youthful lover alone; for he smiled, and then laughed, and moved away out of Eyre's line of sight. Weeip stood up, and followed him, and then reappeared again, tugging at Christopher's sleeve. It was obvious that he was trying to get his master to stand in front of the window.

But what am I supposed to see? Eyre asked himself.
Two catamites bathing each other? Is that all? And what
can this possibly have to do with Arthur Mortlock? But he
could see Weeip glancing towards the window making
sure that he was still there; and frowning; and so he
decided to stay for just a minute or two longer.

Now Weeip suddenly started to dance around, and tease
Christopher, dodging out of reach whenever Christopher
put out a hand. Christopher at last held his wrist, and
stepped back into sight. Weeip quietened down, and
approached his master submissively, and put his arms
around his waist. Christopher kissed the boy's curly head,
and must have said something endearing, for Weeip
nodded.

At last, Weeip managed to draw Christopher around so
that his back was towards the window. Eyre saw Weeip's
hands loosening Christopher's robe, and the tie fall to
the floor. Then Weeip slowly tugged the robe away from
Christopher's shoulders, and drew it down to his waist.

Eyre had been unsettled enough by the sight of Weeip
and Christopher kissing and embracing; but what was now
revealed was a hundred times more horrifying.

He stood in the rain on that lopsided fruit-box, his
mouth open in shock. Then he stepped back, losing his
footing for a moment in the overgrown garden; stumbling;
but recovering himself enough to return the box to where
he had found it; and to make off through the gum-grove
in the same high-stepping way he had come.

He found his bicycle and awkwardly wiped the rain off
the saddle, but he was too dumbfounded to ride it. Instead
he wheeled it back towards Adelaide; as the evening light-
ness at last broke through, and the puddly ruts in the track
turned to quicksilver.

Weeip must adore his master; both adore and respect
him; and do anything to keep him safe. Otherwise he
would never have arranged for Eyre to see what he had
seen tonight. It had been an extraordinary act of loyalty
on Weeip's part; and more than that, a supreme act of

love; although Eyre found acts of love between men to be almost as mysterious as the inland sea. It had been an act of trust in Eyre, too, a trust that had first been forged out in the desert.

It was quite clear to Eyre now that it was Christopher who had killed Arthur Mortlock; and that poor Joolonga had been quite mistaken in thinking that he had done it with his pointing-bone. Joolonga had probably pointed his bone at every one of them, but had convinced himself when Arthur had begun to die that it was Arthur alone who was really guilty; and that it was Arthur alone who was being sacrificed to Ngurunderi.

Eyre also knew that he would do nothing further. He would forget Arthur and as far as possible he would forget Christopher. Christopher had already been punished enough for one lifetime; and it could only have been desperation that had made him take such a risk.

Eyre cursed himself for not having noticed what was going on during the course of the expedition. He had realised that Arthur and Christopher had never got on particularly well; but if only he had begun to understand why.

For when he had looked in at the bathroom window, Eyre had seen that Christopher's bare back was scarred with the criss-cross weals and twisted tissues that identified an ex-convict. Christopher must have been a ticket of-leave man, like Arthur; perhaps they had even been imprisoned together at Macquarie Harbour, and Arthur, after a while, had recognised him. Perhaps Arthur had simply guessed from one or two words in Christopher's vocabulary. In any case, it was likely that Arthur had marked him for a yoxter, like himself. And what had he threatened? Exposure, unless Christopher paid him? Or set him up with a job, perhaps, and a place to stay, and a never-ending supply of rum money? Whatever it had been, Christopher had decided to save himself from the sweated anxiety of interminable blackmail, and the terrifying threat of having to return to prison.

After a while, when the lights of the city came into view, Eyre mounted up on his bicycle and began to pedal. His tyres splashed through the puddles. Knowing for certain that Christopher had killed Arthur, and why, was a huge relief. He began to sing as he rode for the first time since he had got back.

'*All round my hat, I will wear the green willow*
All round my hat, for a twelvemonth and a day . . .'

He was back on Rundle Street in time for a bowl of green-pea soup and a large pork chop, topsidey as they used to say, with an egg on top. He drank a quart of stout, and then went back to Coppius' Hotel for a hot bath and a long sleep.

He was accosted on his way back by several prostitutes; some of them smartly bonneted and pretty. The girls of Hindley Street had become a public embarrassment in Adelaide lately; and several respectable citizens had written to Governor Grey and complained that there were more women of disrepute than the municipality's population could possibly warrant, especially if it had any pretensions to morality at all.

One dark-haired girl linked arms with Eyre and skipped along beside him, nudging him with her breast and smiling and winking most invitingly.

'Give you the best time you've ever had, darling,' she coaxed him. 'Get your gooseberries in such a lather you won't know whether you're here or Sunday.'

On the steps of Coppius' Hotel, Eyre at last managed to disengage himself, and shake his head. 'Not tonight,' he told her, and kissed her on the forehead.

'Give us a deaner, then, for tea,' asked the girl.

Eyre gave her a shilling, and she cocked her bonnet at him and twirled off. He watched her go, and then climbed the steps to the hotel foyer with a smile of memory, rather than amusement.

Thirty-Nine

It was to be the wedding of the year; the most spectacular social event in Adelaide's calendar for 1842. Even Lathrop, who could still be tetchy with Eyre whenever his heart was playing him up, and who had been known to refer to his future son-in-law after two or three brandies at the Commerce Club as a 'penny gentleman', insisted on marquees, and orchestras, and a special white carriage shipped from Van Diemen's Land, where it had once been the property of Lady Jane Franklin.

Eyre had spent most of the six or seven months after his return from Western Australia writing up his memoirs for the *Observer*, who paid him £350 in regular instalments for the privilege. He said nothing of Arthur Mortlock in his story; save that he was 'a trusted family friend from London'; and that he had died 'of a stomach-complaint, brought about by eating bad shellfish'. He did however dramatise their escape from the great corroboree at Yarrakinna, adding a few more skirmishes with the Aborigines for good measure, and including a long and genuinely heartfelt obituary for Dogger McConnell.

'Was there a man more natural and brave, a man whose loyalty to his friends and associates was of such a degree that he saw in danger only delight, that he might serve them more truly, and in death only accomplishment, that he had demonstrated the great nobility of his spirit? The last name upon his lips was that of his beloved wife; and though he has no memorial in the desert, that name will be forever engraved upon the air, even as he spoke it, just as the legends and myths of the first Australians are still spoken by the winds, and by the dust-storms, and by the creatures of the wild.'

When he had written those words, and sat back to sprinkle sand across his manuscript, he thought of Dogger sitting upright in his saddle, transfixed by that terrible death-spear, even as his last words echoed across the plain. *'Brayvo, Hicks!'*

Eyre was given a house on Grenfell Street, overlooking Hindmarsh Square. It was a smart, flat-fronted house of native bluestone, with white-painted shutters, and a small enclosed front garden. His office to begin with was a stuffy little room in the old part of Government House, so positioned that whenever Governor Grey's luncheon was being cooked, most of the smells wafted in through the window, but stubbornly refused to waft out again. There was also a cockatoo which habitually perched on the top of the open sash, and chattered to him irritatingly when he was working, and occasionally flew into the room to speckle his papers with guano.

Eventually, however, Eyre was promised a new house out at Moorundie, near Blanchetown, on the River Murray, where Governor Grey believed he could do the most useful work in helping the Aborigines to cope with the white invasion of their territory.

'We cannot hold back the eventual settlement of all of South Australia,' Grey would say to Eyre, at least once a week, whenever they met for sherry. 'So, rather than preside over the indiscriminate destruction of the Aborigines, we must arrange for their survival—which, in line with the policy of the Colonial Office, means that we must assimilate the blackfellows hook, line, and sinker into the British community. They already have rights as British citizens, rights granted to them generously and without stint. In their turn, they must behave like British citizens.'

Eyre thought to himself: Yonguldye had been right. The magical age of the Aborigines, which had lasted for thousands and thousands of years, was finally over. The great ark of Australia had been boarded, and captured, and towed into the harbour of European commerce.

Almost every weekend, and two or three evenings a week, he would make a call at Waikerie Lodge to pay court to Charlotte. They would have supper; some of Mrs McMurty's leek-and-potato soup; and perhaps mutton cutlets, with carrots and turnips; or sheep's trotters; or mutton collops with cabbage; or boiled sheep's cheek; and everybody knew very well that if they complained about the persistence of lamb on the menu that they would be immediately chastened by Lathrop Lindsay's famous recitation of Thomson's poem about 'the harmless race' whose 'incessant bleatings run around the hills'.

Afterwards, in the parlour, there might be singing; or Lathrop would read from the newspapers any selected titbits which he thought might be amusing and instructive to his wife and family; always concluding with the market prices for sheep. Then Eyre and Charlotte would be allowed a half-an-hour by themselves, although the doorway to the hall would always be left wide open; and quite often Mrs Lindsay would sit sewing in the living-room opposite and smile at them indulgently from time to time.

Charlotte had matured in a year; she was not only prettier but wiser, too, and more independent. She had grown her hair longer, so that it curled into masses and masses of shiny blonde ringlets, which she tied with velvet ribbons. And there was a slight hint of voluptuousness about her which Eyre found pleasantly disturbing, although he did occasionally wonder whether it had anything to do with any experiences she might have had while he was away on his heroic journey.

They went to church together regularly at the Trinity Church at the western end of North Terrace; Eyre in the fashionably tight black morning-suit he had bought with his first payment from the *Observer*; Charlotte in grey watered silk. They were always applauded as they emerged, Eyre for his newly won fame, and Charlotte for her beauty, and both of them for giving Adelaide the gleeful anticipation of the most lavish wedding that the colony had ever seen. It was generally rumoured that Lathrop was spending more than £2,500 on the catering, and that a special order of French champagne was already on its way from Epernay, in France.

Eyre and Charlotte were sitting out on the verandah of Waikerie Lodge in early March, drinking lemon tea and eating Maids of Honour, when the subject of children came up. It was only eleven days now to the wedding, and two men in faded blue overalls were pacing the lawns with one of Lathrop's gardeners to determine where they were going to pitch the largest of the three marquees. The Lindsay's pet kangaroos hopped along beside the wattles; and there was an aromatic smell of eucalyptus in the afternoon air.

Charlotte was dressed prettily in cream lace, with yellow ribbons. The sun shone through the brim of her straw bonnet and illuminated it like a halo. The angel of Adelaide, thought Eyre, and felt most content. He had been putting on weight since his return last year, and he decided that his white waistcoat must have shrunk a little.

'I think five is a good number,' said Charlotte, sipping tea.

'Five what, my darling?' asked Eyre. Then he said, 'That marquee is going to be absolutely enormous; look how far away they've placed that marker.'

'Children, of course,' Charlotte replied.

'Children?' blinked Eyre.

'Yes, five children. Three boys, and two girls. A family of seven.'

'Well,' said Eyre. Then, 'Well, I must say I hadn't really thought about it.'

'But we must. And we *can*, now that you're so successful; and such a hero. And when we're out at Moorundie, or wherever else you're posted, we're going to be glad of the company. Oh Eyre, I can almost see them now! Five, happy shining faces!'

Eyre was silent for a very long time. The day was still bright; the birds still chittered and cackled in the stringybark gums around the house; Charlotte still talked about how she would teach the children to ride, and to play the piano, and what fun it was going to be at Christmas. But a sudden dark feeling had risen up inside him, like a strong cold undercurrent, lifting him up and then dragging him back to the past.

'*You are one of my people now*,' Winja had said, on that grey windy day when they had parted. '*Therefore your son is one of my people; and your son's son.*'

And Eyre had held Winja close to him, and said, '*My son is yours.*'

A pledge, a holy and magical pledge. A promise that could never be broken. *My son is yours.*

He was quiet and withdrawn for the rest of the day. At last, after supper, when Mrs Lindsay was snoozing in her chair in the living-room and the servants were clearing up the dishes, Charlotte asked him what was wrong.

'You're not sickening, are you?'

Eyre shook his head.

'But you're so pale; and you haven't said a word all evening. It wasn't my talk of children, was it? That hasn't put you off? Oh, Eyre, if there's anything worrying you my darling, you must tell me! We must never keep secrets from each other.'

Eyre hesitated for a moment. Then he stood up, and went over to the parlour door, and gently closed it. Charlotte looked at him anxiously in the light from the engraved-glass lamp. A diamond pendant sparkled on the soft curve of her cleavage, and he thought that he had never seen her look so enticing.

'Listen, Charlotte,' he said. He could hear his own voice in his ear, flat and expressionless, as if he were standing on the opposite side of the room. 'When I was travelling across the desert . . . well, certain things happened to me. I haven't written about them in the newspaper, because I wanted to keep them to myself.'

'What things, my darling? What do you mean? Was it something terrible?'

He lowered his eyes. 'Not by the standards by which I was living at the time. In fact, what happened was quite uplifting. Quite spiritual. It gave me the hope and the faith to be able to finish my journey, and to survive. But . . .

well, how can I explain it? Now that I'm back here in white society, certain commitments I made might seem rather surprising. Rather difficult for other people to understand.'

Charlotte said, in a barely audible voice, 'Tell me. Eyre, you must tell me.'

He hesitated, and then he said, 'Well, you remember I told you that I was initiated into an Aboriginal tribe.'

'Yes.'

'It was quite a painful initiation. I mean physically painful. They—scarred me. Scarred my body. It's all part of the ceremony. All part of showing that you're a man, and that you're able to stand suffering without crying out. Also—well, they consider the scars decorative, and beautiful.

Charlotte whispered, 'You have scars?'

'Yes.'

'Why didn't you tell me? Why didn't you tell me before? I would have understood.'

Eyre turned away. 'I was going to tell you. In fact, I was going to *show* you. But somehow I could always think of some excuse why I should wait until later. I thought you wouldn't exactly take to them. I don't know. I just felt that they were something secret, something which I didn't truly understand myself.'

This time, the silence between them was even longer. The ormolu clock on the mantelpiece ticked tiredly, and outside they could hear the clopping of horses as the groom returned them to their stable. Somewhere in the servants' quarters, an Aborigine woman was singing some sweet, monotonous song. At last, though, Charlotte stood up, with a rustle of petticoats, and went to the parlour door, and opened it, and looked out. Then she came back and took Eyre's hand.

'Show me,' she said. 'Mother's still asleep. Show me now. I want to see.'

'Charlotte—' Eyre began, but she pressed the fingers of her right hand against his lips, to silence him.

'Show me,' she insisted.

Quickly, with several sharp tugs, Eyre loosened his collar, stripped off his necktie, and unbuttoned his shirt. Then he opened his underwear, and bared to Charlotte his chest, with its whorls and lines and zigzags of bumpy purplish scars; each one of which had been drawn by his Aborigine kinsmen, and rubbed with ash.

Charlotte stared at them, and then gradually traced them, every one of them, with her fingers. She looked up at Eyre, and her eyes were glistening with tears.

'They're beautiful,' she said. 'They're simply beautiful.'

'You don't *mind* them?' he asked.

'Why should I mind them? They show that the Aborigines think you're a hero; as well as the British. What other man in Adelaide has scars like these, to prove what he's done? I'm proud of them, Eyre; I shall cherish them. And I shall cherish you.'

She kissed his chest four or five times, and then stood up on tiptoe and kissed his lips. 'You should have shown me before, my darling,' she murmured.

Eyre said, 'There's something else.'

'Tell me. Come on, Eyre, you promised to tell me, and so you must.'

'My—' he started. Then he closed his eyes, and blurted out quickly, 'They also circumcised me.'

'Yes?' asked Charlotte, although she blushed a little. 'And is that enough to stop me from loving you? Eyre, don't you understand, I love you; dearly, and passionately; whether you are scarred or whole. I always have done, and I think I always will.'

He took a breath, and said mechanically, 'They circumcised me with a sharp knife made out of a cockle-shell. They also . . . well, I believe the correct term is sub-incision.'

'What does that mean? Eyre, please.'

Eyre knew now that there was nothing for it but to show her. They had attempted to make love before, on that hideous night when Yanluga had died; and there was no question that Charlotte was a full-blooded young woman

505

who expected sex as a vigorous part of her coming marriage. It would also be impossibly unfair of him to expect her to go to the altar without knowing what Winja and Ningina had done to him.

Pray God that her mother doesn't wake up, he thought, and opened his trousers.

Charlotte slowly sat down on the brocade-covered sofa. She stared at his penis so intently that he went red, and began to perspire. I'm embarrassed, he thought; me, who rode naked for hundreds of miles across the plain of Bunda Bunda. Embarrassed, and for some extraordinary reason, humiliated.

But Charlotte reached out with a gentle hand and grasped him, lifting him up so that she could see how deeply the Aborigines had cut into him. The urethra was open all the way from the glans to the testicles; open, and glistening with the lubrication of nervousness and passion.

'Will this . . . does this make it impossible for us to have children?' asked Charlotte, in a trembling voice.

Eyre shook his head. 'No. All the Aborigines have it done; at least, all the Aborigines that I met. It makes no difference, physically; and none of them seem to be lacking in offspring.'

Charlotte stroked him, with exquisite slowness, and he rose in her hand. 'If it makes no difference,' she said, 'then I shall accept it proudly.' She kept on stroking him, still slowly, until his penis reared up like a red sceptre, with a deeply cleft shaft.

'No,' he said, unsteadily. 'No more. We only have eleven more days to wait.' And with extreme difficulty he pushed himself back into his tight evening trousers, and buttoned himself up again. Charlotte touched the thick protrusion on his trouser-leg, and unexpectedly giggled.

'I think it's marvellous,' she said. 'Eyre, it's *marvellous!* I shall be the only lady in the whole of Adelaide to have a baby the Aborigine way! Isn't it exciting! Oh, it excites me! Oh, Eyre! I can't wait eleven days!'

He kissed her on the forehead. She tasted of perfume.

'I'm afraid that we shall have to,' he said. Then he kissed her again, and she lifted her mouth to him, and kissed him in return, her hard white teeth pressing against his lips.

'Now,' he said, 'we come to the most difficult part of all.'

'What?' she asked, her eyes bright, 'Eyre, if it's only as difficult as scars, or a circumcision . . .'

He sat down. He looked at her, and tried to smile. She was so expectant, so alive, so gleeful. How was he going to tell her that he had solemnly promised to give his first-born son away to Winja and Ningina, to be raised as a member of their tribe for ever more?

'It concerns the baby,' he said, his mouth dry.

'But we're going to have *five* babies!'

'Yes,' he agreed. 'Five. But it concerns the first. Well, the first son, at least.'

Why did he have to tell her? Why did he have to give the baby away at all? Who was going to force Eyre Walker, the Protector of Murray River Aborigines, a great white celebrity and a man of influence and income, to give away his first boy-child to a pack of blacks?

Only Eyre knew why; only Winja knew why. The answer lay in the desert, and the scrub and the dry limestone mountains. The answer lay in the integrity of people who have to depend on whatever they can find, and whatever help they can offer each other. Eyre's destiny had become mysteriously interlinked with that of the Aborigines from the first moment he had spoken to Yanluga as a human being deserving of equal respect; instead of thinking of him as an animal or a savage. He realised that there was a terrible primitive justice to what he was going to have to do. He had taken one boy away; and now he would have to give them a boy in return. There was no escaping it. Not if he was going to be able to think of himself as a man of honour; as he had always hoped he would be.

But he looked at Charlotte, sitting next to him; and she

was so excited and aroused and pretty, thrilled with the erotic naughtiness of having touched Eyre's exposed body, and intoxicated by the thought of marrying him in just eleven days' time; and he couldn't say it. How could he explain to her what had happened out there in the desert? How close he had been to death, and despair? How could he tell her about the magnificence of the dreaming; the majesty of Baiame; the thirsty enormity of a land which shimmered with mirages and throbbed with magic?

It was inexplicable; and his duty to Winja and his people was inexplicable. And so he said, hoarsely, 'Our first son, I'd—well, I'd like his second name to be Lathrop.'

And after Charlotte had kissed him in delight, and run across the hall way to tell her mother how marvellous he was, he stood up, and thrust his hands into his pockets, and stared up at the portrait of Lathrop's grandfather Duncan over the fireplace. There was laughter in the house, and the clattering of feet up and down the stairs. But all Eyre could think of was his son, not yet conceived, not yet born, but whose destiny was already entwined with this strange continent as surely and as inextricably as his own had always been.

The parlour door opened wide, and Mrs Lindsay came in, followed by Charlotte, and Lathrop Lindsay himself, and Mrs Lindsay held open her arms for Eyre and said, 'My darling Eyre. What a fine boy you are. You can't possibly imagine how happy you've made us. *Lathrop!* How marvellous! And how generous, too!'

Eyre held her in his arms, and smiled over her shoulder at Charlotte, but it took all of his strength not to cry.

Epilogue

On August 15, 1844, Captain Charles Sturt left Adelaide with an expedition of his own in an attempt to find the inland sea. He was so confident of his success that he carried with him a boat with which he hoped he and his companions would eventually sail from one side of the sea to the other.

Heading eastwards at first to avoid the salt-lakes which had bogged down Eyre, he made camp at Broken Hill, and then headed north. As each day dawned, however, all he could see in front of him was a country of 'salty spinifex and sand ridges, driving for hundreds of miles into the very heart of the interior as if they would never end.'

The daily temperature was higher than 130 degrees in the shade, and nearly 160 degrees in the sun.

At last, 400 miles north of Broken Hill, after crossing a desert of crippling stones, and miles of matted spinifex, Sturt was confronted with what would later be called the Simpson Desert. Ridges of deep-red sand succeeded each other 'like the waves of the sea'. Sturt realised that he could go no further with the resources he had brought with him, and was forced to turn back.

The expedition broke his health and his pride. In 1853, he returned to England, where his journals about his explorations had made him a celebrity, and it was in England that he died, in 1869.

He left many letters before his death. One, which was opened by his executors, was addressed to Mr Eyre Walker. When they read its contents, Captain Sturt's executors decided that it would probably be prudent to destroy it, since its contents, although rather mysterious, might constitute an admission of liability which could cause complications with the distribution of the Sturt estate.

So it was that on a foggy January afternoon in Chancery

Lane, London, twenty-nine years after Eyre had set out from Government House in Adelaide, the last words about the great corroboree at Yarrakinna were burned in an office fireplace; Captain Sturt's firm sloping script gradually being licked and scorched and charred into ashes; the simple words 'Forgive me.'